THE FIRST LADY

Other Works of Fiction by the Author

Annals of the Purple City; Orchid Press, Bangkok 2010
[Crane, Hong Kong & London 1995]

The Malayan Life of Ferdach O'Haney; Monsoon Books,
Singapore, 2009

The Rape of Rye; Martello Books, Rye 2006

Fool's Gold; Silverfish Books, Kuala Lumpur 2004

The Arthuriad of Catumandus; Crane, Hong Kong &
London 1996

THE
FIRST
LADY

Frederick Lees

Orchid Press

Frederick Lees
THE FIRST LADY

First edition, copyright © Orchid Press 2012

ORCHID PRESS
PO Box 1046,
Silom Post Office,
Bangkok 10504, Thailand
www.orchidbooks.com

ISBN: 978-974-524-146-6

FOR MARIE

The First Lady

Madame Griselda Rodriguez Floresco stirs uneasily in her oversize four poster bed. She has slept badly, disturbed by a variety of worries, a clutch of fears. Try as she may to stop thinking, her mind refuses to go blank; the thoughts just retreat a little from centre stage but she knows they are still in the wings, waiting, chattering, whispering until, with a bound, they are back in the spotlight, putting further sleep out of the question.

One of her favourite, though entirely rhetorical, questions, when talking to people who come to see her, is a mournful 'Has it all been worth it?' Then, after a sigh redolent of regret, she describes the idyllic life of the mother of a contented family, spent largely in the country, the ideal of most Carolinos, which she longs for, prays for, dreams of, as soon as her husband has laid down the Presidency. 'Holy Mother, I pray that it may be soon.' Her eyes are upturned, her hand rests on her heart; she is the Mater Dolorosa uttering a prayer. Then her theme becomes the sacrifice she has made opting to be a helpmate rather than a wife sheltering in the shadows. None of the sycophants about her are taken in; neither, for that matter, is the public. But the First Lady cannot admit that the world knows she is lying. Of course her own mind entertains not a shred of doubt. It definitely has been worth it. Even in moments of despair like this, there is one certainty she can fall back on: she would not have things a jot different. And she will fight to preserve what she has won.

Throwing back the sheet she gets up and walks to look at herself in the mirror that extends along one side of the room. The sight displeases her. Like most Carolinas she equates beauty with youth, with teenage youth at that. Even her present flowing garment and the suffused lighting cannot conceal the fact that she is running to fat. This irritates her more than the opposition of underlings to one of her pet schemes could ever do. Underlings can be dealt with in a variety of ways. Fat cannot. Or rather it could only be with self-discipline, by denying herself something she wants. The First Lady always gets what she wants, which makes dieting difficult. Nevertheless she tells herself that she must take energetic steps about her size. Her famed beauty is not only a matter of national pride; she is said to be one of the most glamorous figures on the international scene. 'I believe in beauty', is one of her major themes. 'Man should always live surrounded by beauty. It is his birthright.' With such laudable mantras she sweeps aside criticisms of her extravagance and particularly of her erection of sumptuous buildings in the capital.

All the same the First Lady does not shrink from critical examination of her figure.

Her loveliness has not entirely faded; her skin is silky, her outlines regular though without pronounced features. It would be false to say, what a lovely mouth, what a lovely nose, what lovely eyes; yet everything is just about right on this East Asian moon-faced beauty. Only her firm jaw suggests something different. She admires it for its hint of determination; others see in it the arrogance they hate her for.

The decision to lose weight taken, as it has been on several occasions, she changes into a silk apricot-coloured gown which matches the décor of the room and walks across to the windows, moving from one to another to peer into the palace garden which is, with security in mind, well lit by ornate lamp posts. The garden is beautiful but just now she is not pre-occupied by beauty. Are those little groups of patrolling soldiers alert to their duties? Several attempts have been made, some quite recently, to enter the gardens and once the palace itself. The intruders are often enough harmless petitioners, newsmen or drunks, but she is obsessed by fear that one day a dissident will make a serious attempt on her, or her husband's, life. Theoretically palace security is so tight that only an invisible man could get in, but a principal weakness of the Carolinos is that executive measures, however well designed, soon deteriorate. On many a day presidential orders flow from her husband's office to ensure action on quite routine aspects of administration. Only yesterday he, the Head of State, had actually been obliged to order the disposal of trash from one of the city thoroughfares. The First Lady is sure that without the President—and herself—the country would, in no time at all, fall into chaos.

Her mind set at ease by a patrol that has just emerged from a copse and then filed off towards the ornamental lake, she opens one of the long windows that lets onto a balcony. Her nose puckers at the miasma that commences battle with the air in the room, which is kept at a constant eighteen degrees Celsius. The sun will not rise, fiery and brooding, for a couple of hours yet but the heat of the previous day still lingers, its moist heaviness absorbing like an enormous piece of blotting paper all the emanations of Infanta, a chaotic metropolis of over ten million souls: the dead smells of the fetid Calayag river, the diesel fumes of countless jeepney buses, the foulness of blocked drains or of packed squatter areas with no drains at all. And expansive though the grounds of the DeoGracias Palace are, they cannot completely ward off the distant but endlessly throbbing music, the traffic roar and the sirens of fire engines and police cars speeding to the site of another arson or violent crime.

She closes the window but remains there staring into the night. Now the city looks better, anaesthetised by the cool glass, the lines of its great boulevards hinted at by the glow of their golden street lights, high rise apartments, stylish hotels and offices, all proclaiming order and progress, the chaos banished as surely as she will one day banish it totally from her beloved capital. In the meantime she must remember to have the windows in the guestrooms sealed before the arrival of that supercilious English princess. She will not have her palace the subject of snide remarks around the dining table at Balmoral, especially by the caustic duke.

The thought of that distant Scottish castle disturbs her. She gives up her vigil at the window and sits before a mirror to examine her face untouched by make-up. The site does not dispel her thoughts about the Royals. So much in life depends on appearance. Appearance masks reality, or rather it becomes reality. The reality the Royals create, so lofty, so confident, is the model she has set for herself. Yet was it attainable? A while ago she had decreed that from now on she must be addressed as 'ma'am', only regretting that she could not also decree the curtsey. But it did not seem to work with the Carolinas; they tittered, they smirked, they must be laughing behind her back. They had absorbed too many egalitarian ideas from their former American masters. As she was afraid of looking absurd, 'ma'am', except for her staff, fell by the wayside. All the same she had succeeded in making the television stations provide an appropriately regal background of Handel's music whenever she appeared on screen. Unfortunately they had not followed up her suggestion of the *Water Music* with any of the master's other works, though one pop group had set the themes to a song with hilarious snorts and coughs in place of Handel's kettledrum beats.

Royals could be indifferent to such mockery that ebbed and flowed like the tide for they had one enormous advantage: security of tenure. Not so elected Presidents and their families who come and inevitably go—back to the level from which they came, which in her case was not very high. Of one thing then she is absolutely sure: never again will she play second fiddle to the snobbish Spanish speaking families; those feudal bossmen—the Ocampos, the Quixotes, the Ermitas and the rest who, hardly in secret, despise her origins and even look down on the honourable military background of her husband. After all, what do those aristocratic pretenders amount to themselves? They came to the country as soldiers of fortune centuries ago from a country where many of them had been no better than thieves. She lets out a cry of disdain. "Pah! Aristocrats indeed!" They had grabbed land, established their haciendas and constituted themselves into a proud Spanish nobility. Yet they had submitted to the conquering Americans and toadied to them, forgetting their loyalty to the Spanish Crown, just as later they had toadied to the Japanese, forgetting their loyalty to the so-called Land of the Free. Right up to the time when her husband had occupied the Congress and declared martial law, they had manipulated the bogus United States-style Constitution to their advantage, as if the Carolinos were serfs. But she was of those people; only her height hinted at a touch of Iberian blood. The people knew that and loved her because they wanted to see one of themselves at the top, invested in majesty like a peasant girl in a folk tale. The ambition she has not mentioned, even to her husband, returns to her mind. Her family, the children she has borne to the President of the Republic of the Carolinas, and their children after them, must become a dynasty in this land.

Some thirty kilometres north of Infanta, Father Stephens watched, from the verandah of his modest house, the first touch of dawn silhouetting the mountain range to the east of San Felipe. It was a miraculous sight. First the peaks were edged with a thin line separating the sky from the obscurity below; then in a cleft between two peaks he saw a slight glow that slowly strengthened until quite suddenly a burst of gold appeared and the sun spilled its radiance over the long mountain chain like molten lava. Down and down came the light as the sun ascended, until all the vast plain around San Felipe basked in its warm embrace.

He had once suggested in a sermon that God invaded the unbelieving soul in such a way, starting with a whisper that he was imminent, then appearing in an ecstatic illumination that spread through all one's being, suffusing it with Grace. That was soon after he had arrived in San Felipe. Somehow his eloquence had not got across to the rice farmers, the cane cutters and the small tradesmen sitting before him; the concept of an unbelieving soul was quite alien to them. They believed in anything and everything; the word 'doubt' did not exist for them. In any case they were much more concerned that, as their priest, he should get on with his duties and the customary rituals that guaranteed their safety. And so father Stephens now had the miracle of the risen sun to himself.

His ancient servant, Lourdes, tottered out with his morning glass of tea flavoured with the delicate *Calamansi* lime so beloved by the Carolinos and a slice of sweet bread spread with honey. Having set it down she genuflected before him as though he were the Host, then waited until he had blessed her; a bit unorthodox but it made her happy; indeed without it the quality of her work would suffer all day. And since it was the duty of everyone, so Father Stephens believed, to work for one another's happiness, he observed the ritual each morning without demur. For Lourdes, like the majority of people in the small township of San Felipe, only saw

Father Stephens in a magical role, the village shaman there from time immemorial.

There was, however, one group, and in particular one person, in San Felipe, intent on encouraging a more progressive view of priestly duties: the provincial Catholic Rural Development College under its Principal, Father Oliveros. Housed in a monastic building that dated back to the early years of Spanish rule it lay diametrically on the other side of San Felipe from Father Stephens' house. From where he was sitting he could see the octagonal belfry, divided into five tiers, the only high structure in San Felipe apart from the bell tower of his own church, but that was much lower and had just one thin-sounding bell whereas the old monastery tower had eight, cast in Spain; unfortunately they could not be rung any longer for if they were the belfry might collapse on the college roof. Yet crumbling though the old place was, within its walls Father Oliveros, his small staff and the students were a seething cauldron. No wonder people were talking of revolutionary clergy. Father Stephens shared their vision of a land of prosperous farmers liberated by justice and effective technology and he promised to report any instances of official oppression or corruption in the village that came to his ears to Father Oliveros. Secretly, however, he feared that one day the work of the college might be terminated just as the revolutionaries, who had made the building their headquarters a century ago, during a futile revolt against Spain, had been wiped out.

As he ate his meal, sometimes looking at the lush landscape but ever stopping himself from thinking too much about that college, for it had dangerous implications, Father Stephens recognised that in recent months his notion of where his duties lay had been changing, or maybe been subtly changed. Was it the heat or something about the pace of these people, who at best moved with the deliberation of their little horse-drawn carts with strong wheels and pretty canopies, that had affected him? Whatever the cause, the enthusiasm with which he had quit Australia no longer gripped him. What had become of the serious development proponent, fired by the teachings of ardent priests at the seminary, the young priest who had come here to act as a catalyst for spiritual and technological change? Without lecturing him, the smiling, graceful people of San Felipe had seduced him wordlessly, saying, "Just do what the other parish priests have done here for the past four hundred years. Yes, there may be a time for action but until it comes don't do a thing—and hope it never comes at all."

He had heard people say that the history of the Carolinas consisted of four centuries in a Spanish Convent and five decades in Disneyland, yet beneath those layers he, a mere newcomer, had already sensed the deeper culture, human and close to the earth, that sustained the Carolinos. They laboured on farmsteads hidden in the lush countryside around San Felipe, in huts that, despite decay, seemed ever to look the same. Or they worked in town in mouldering stone houses with walls cracked by earthquakes and woodwork gnarled by time. He was sure that, countless years ahead, these people would still be here, with just another shaman. Why then did a strange fear possess him that the old church of which he was the priest might be the symbol of his life—a baroque façade encrusted with gesticulating saints and sacred symbols dominating the town square, yet inside no more than an echoing barn.

He stood up and stared across the expansive rice fields that were now dry and covered with stubble. The cicadas had started their harsh screeching; they and the heat were getting at him. He longed for the rains when the fields would first be grey and muddy, but once flooded reflect the sky like a thousand mirrors until rice seedlings had made the earth emerald green and finally dappled with the gold of harvest. Further away he could descry less changing fields of sugar cane, tall enough to hide men at work or doing less honourable things amidst growth that rustled and whispered ominously when the wind blew down from the mountains. All at once he noticed a little group of men emerging from a copse, dark clad and moving swiftly. Who were they? What were they up to at this time of the day? What were they carrying? Tools? Guns? Unwilling to know, even to guess, he turned and looked away. That was better; everything before him was still. Across the plain the sites of villages were betrayed by roofs of *nipa* palm peeping above clusters of fruit trees, mango and coconut, passion fruit and sugar apples. If you penetrated them you saw bamboo or timber houses high on stilts, with chickens and pigs below and sometimes vegetables planted among the acacias Yet again he wondered where that little troop he had just sighted was going. He picked up a fan but did not use it and paced restlessly to and fro on the verandah. Well, they might just be cutting cane, he told himself. Then he said aloud, "Stephens, not everything that goes on in this place is your business." "Is that so?" another voice inside his head replied sarcastically.

From the end of the veranda he could see the most wonderful site in the province. There to the west, behind San Felipe, was Mount Sinayi, a perfectly shaped volcanic cone soaring up in isolation above the plain, quiescent just now but, with occasional earth tremors, a fearful reminder of awful forces lurking below. In local legend it was the home of demons, spirits and heroes and also, Father Stephens more than suspected, of bandits and rebels—the sort who appear and disappear out of the sugar cane in the early hours of the day. Dismissing them again he thought it might be a good idea, as the weather was dry, to take a few young people in his old car along the rough trail up there for a picnic. Then his enthusiasm flagged. The mountain was an alien place. He had climbed it once but despite its height the trees that had grown during its tranquillity seemed forever still, as though they lived in fear. He had half sensed a hidden being observing him. No, the picnic was a bad idea.

He went to his bathroom, to which bamboo pipes fed an endless jet of water from a local spring. Some of the villagers had constructed copies of this simple but effective piece of technology which he had designed, so he insisted, to provide a healthier way of bathing than wallowing in canals used for a variety of other purposes. All the same he suspected they had copied it to please rather than out of confidence in what he said. Once again their faces seemed to say there was little point in his clever ideas. Sometimes he felt like standing in the pulpit and saying, "Look. You've no need of me. You've no need for the Latin words you prefer to Spanish. Go back to the spirits you propitiated before the Spanish got here. The old beliefs are stronger than mine. You are nearer to God because you are poor. Never become rich lest you fall from grace." Of course he could never do so. For one thing the people would not know what he was talking about; for another his desire to speak out would be mere self-indulgence. Beside which another reason made him unwilling to upset the apple cart. His slide to unorthodoxy had not been limited to stirrings of intellectual disbelief. Right now he was standing naked in front of a long mirror to make sure he was not losing the athletic build that had known fame on the sports fields of Australia. For lovers, as well as athletes, must take care of their appearance. Father Stephens's seduction by the land and the people of the Carolinas had been as physical as could be.

After arriving in San Felipe he had quickly adapted to the easygoing culture of his parishioners. To work among them was his real reward; nothing else could be asked of them, but before long his innate honesty made him admit, though only to himself, that he was getting ever more obsessed by the sultry beauty of some of San Felipe's fit young men, especially as his searching glances were often reciprocated. The problem weighed heavily on him. In the Australian seminary he had kept temptation under lock and key; there had been so many forms of companionship and intellectual excitement that self-control was no burden. But here where he was not so cerebrally active and stimulating friends were few, and above all, in this warm, sensual Eden where soft lipped youth seemed to have sex on the brain, it was not so easy. For months he tried hard to be chaste but in the end, in this very bathroom, he was quite unable to resist the lustful grappling of his golden skinned altar boy Salvador, who, like everyone here, was near to God and therefore, with Pelagian certainty, knew what they were doing to be innocent. Salvador had easily read his wanton eyes. And why shouldn't they be lovers? With love the quality of his work had improved; he was sure many of his parishioners knew exactly why. Yet the guile with which a stripling had artfully manoeuvred his fall still amused him. Now, the badly leaking bamboo pipe, the help Salvador gave to repair it and afterwards their need to cool off together under the rejuvenated shower were all too obvious. Circumstance was ever the mother of opportunity. His former reluctance to make love must have been solely conditioned by a vocation in which such acts were forbidden. But the floodgates once opened could not be closed. Whatever his brain said, in his heart he could no longer admit, any more than Salvador, that sin was involved in their mutual pleasure. Indeed for a while he hardly knew why he went on making confession to Father Oliveros:

"What sins my son?"

"Sins of the flesh, Father."

"Of the usual kind?"

"Yes Father."

"With Salvador?"

"Yes Father."

"And with anyone else?"

"No Father."

Sometimes Father Oliveros asked for more information: was there penetration? How many times? Anal? Oral? To all of which Father Stephens replied openly but soon in explicit detail for it diverted him to observe his Confessor finding his sins so interesting, though however explicit his confession the same light penance would follow. He thought sometimes of experimenting to see what sort of penance he would get if he said, 'And with Beda and Luiz and Ricco and half a dozen others'. He was sure there would be a marked increase in the severity of the verdict. Father Oliveros seemed more concerned with his constancy than his purity and the fact must be faced that Salvador was Father Oliveros' nephew. Father Stephens suspected that if the Church could devise a form of marriage for himself and Salvador, Father Oliveros would perform the ceremony and give his blessing. What the capricious youth might think of marital fidelity was less clear. As for old Lourdes, one afternoon when a thunderous downpour was muffling all human sound she had entered the bedroom where he and the ever amorous Salvador were in *flagrante delicto*, delightedly lost to the world. The wayward boy had not even let them pause nor had Lourdes bothered to clear off, but just continued with her dusting, murmuring, "Ah young men, young men." Certainly the people of San Felipe were very near to God.

Zeny Vizcarra, one of the First Lady's personal maids, which also meant being one of her 'eyes' about the Palace, was breathless as she entered the bedroom where her mistress, seated at an opulent dressing table, was attended by four beauticians engaged in her coiffure and trimming and polishing her nails. The toilette of the First Lady was exhaustive but she never regarded it as time wasted;

on the contrary it gave her time to relax and think and it provided her with pleasure especially when accompanied by a session of massage which, in the Carolines, was an activity classed among the finer arts. Unfortunately the worried expression on Zeny's face, visible to her in the mirror, said at once that her pleasure was in jeopardy. "Leave," she commanded abruptly and her attendants disappeared in a trice. "Well?" she asked. "What is it? Is she alright?" Zeny's special duty at present was to keep a close watch within the Palace on the activities of Conchita, the President's eldest daughter. Others had this duty outside. And so the reason for her anxiety was apparent with her first words.

"She slipped out during the night ma'am. She came back twenty minutes ago."

"Why didn't you tell me at once?" The firmness of the First Lady's jaw was now a barometer of menace before which the diminutive Zeny shrank yet smaller.

"I didn't see her go out ma'am. Someone told me she'd gone to her room so I went to bed. I thought it would be..."

"You didn't see! You were told! You thought? Holy Mother of God! You're paid to watch, not sleep."

"I was very tired ma'am. I'm very sorry." Zeny's voice was hardly audible. The First Lady quietly echoed the words of the terrified creature now kneeling beside her. "Tired. Very sorry." Her wrath seemingly dissipated, her voice quite patient, she asked sweetly, "Well Zeny, what have you found out? Where did she go? Did you contact Captain Manzano?"

"Yes ma'am but none of his guards saw her leave. At least not in an official car."

The First Lady sighed profoundly. What was wrong with these people? Why couldn't the girl see that if Conchita wanted to slip out, she would not call for an official car. She'd be up to some ruse. And ruses need accomplices. Which meant that Conchita must have allies in the Palace. Allies who were not one hundred percent faithful to the President and his wife. And if servants could be treacherous in matters like this, they could be treacherous in other ways. If it was so easy to get out maybe anyone could get in. Her head had begun to throb; she put her hand to her throat. Everything was in doubt. Everything was in flux. Had it all been worth it? What was she doing in this Palace designed for a Spanish Viceroy? She turned in her seat and eyed Zeny coldly.

"Don't tell me. Manzano's guards only saw the usual delivery vehicles leaving and entering the grounds. They checked all the passes and everything was in order—entirely in order I'm sure." Her voice was unpleasantly sarcastic now. "That's how my daughter went and returned isn't it Zeny? In some delivery van."

"Yes. I suppose so ma'am. No ma'am. Well, not exactly ma'am. Ma'am, she came home in a taxi."

"A taxi!" The words burst forth like a guided missile. "In a taxi!" The First Lady picked up a bottle of expensive perfume and smashed it down on the dressing table where it burst open. The gorgeous fragrance of one of Chanel's rarer perfumes spread abroad. This was an act of public defiance. A challenge. Such a challenge had to be taken up—without delay. "Send for her. Go and get her. D'you hear?"

"Ma'am, she gave instructions to her maid that she was not to be disturbed until lunch time."

"Summon her, bring her," The First Lady screamed. "She's been to see that man. Get her here. Tell the guards to break the door down. Now. Now."

Zeny was glad to receive an order that gave her a chance to escape. Alone the First Lady leaned forward head cupped in her hands and sobbed in misery but not for too long. Furiously she rang her antique Javanese bell, a gift from President Suharto, to recall her minions. Her toilette had to be properly completed; her image was of national importance.

President Antonio Floresco was vacationing at his favourite retreat, high in the mountains at the northern end of the Cordillera over which Father Stephens had watched the sun rise. Fort Roosevelt was the last official building that the United States Government had, with a burst of grandeur, undertaken before the Carolines had been occupied by the Japanese. As the summer residence of the Governor it had been provided with the amenities and luxury appropriate to the representative of an imperial power. Unhappily this had, in the first instance, turned out to be General

Hiroyuki Kurihara, whose name in the Carolino vocabulary was synonymous with brutality. The golf course, which lay in a tree-girt bowl below the classical façade of the house, was often, during Kurihara's tenure, the scene of live target practice and more imaginative tortures. For it had been his sport to witness American prisoners of war, and later ever increasing numbers of Carolinos who had run foul of the Nipponese, shot, burned, bayoneted, exposed to hand grenade explosions and other horrors then left to die without a *coup de grace*. Kurihara's own nemesis, so the official Carolino account reads, was the result of an heroic action towards the end of the occupation, taken by a future President. Against all odds Lieutenant Antonio Floresco, an idealistic young man, always top in his grades, commissioned in the United States Reserve only a few weeks before Pearl Harbour, led a party of guerrillas furtively through the golf course until they reached the graceful Ionic pillars of the portico, rushed the guards, and swept up the staircase to Kurihara's bedroom. There they cornered him and bit by bit sliced him up with his own samurai sword on the beautiful black and white squared marble floor. His disgusting unwarrior-like squeals had been heard by other Japanese soldiers but none came to help him as it was naturally assumed that he must be indulging, probably for the last time, in one of his more esoteric pleasures. Certainly Kurihara had been done in nastily by Carolino guerrillas but there were some who denied that anyone with the name Floresco had been in the attacking party. For the present however, a struggle of a different kind had brought the no-longer-young putative hero to Fort Roosevelt: his forthcoming visit to Europe, where he hoped to restore something of his régime's flagging image by speaking up for the economic interests of the Third World.

Floresco's relations with the Americans, on the other hand, were in no need of repair; his contributions to the Republican election coffers ensured that, as long as James P. Souris was in the White House, whatever little irritants might arise between the Carolinas and the USA, all would be well. Nor was the friendship between his own wife and the astute Minnie Souris to be discounted. But dwarfing all else was the fact that even though his country was no longer host to the gigantic US air bases needed during the Cold

War, enough military co-operation vital to American dominance of the Pacific remained for him to be sure that if the chips were ever down, President Souris would see him through.

At nine thirty in the morning, when his physical exercises and a low calorie breakfast had made him feel that many more than his present sixty two years lay ahead, he drove himself in a sporty little MG higher up the mountain to a hunting lodge to meet a delegation from Schuster, Schuster and Bligh, an internationally renowned public relations company. Both Schusters, Hymen and Solly, were there, as well as Max Bligh, the brains of the team, since the contract with the President was the biggest they had ever won.

"Now gentlemen," said Floresco when the preliminary chitchat was done, "I want our dealings to be transparent. By the way do drop the Your Excellency bit when we talk in private. Call me A.F. or Tony if you want. That's what my wife calls me—when she wants something." Laughter ensued while everyone helped himself to the rather early morning drinks set before them. It must have been the only important Carolino meeting that day without a host of smiling waiters milling around to serve people.

Max Bligh, younger though balding, and more carefully groomed than his partners, replied in precise tones with an accent that was neither decidedly American nor exactly English, the sort of voice that in acting circles used to be termed mid-Atlantic. "Yes. Your Ex—sorry A.F. That's exactly how we see things. Unless we are all open with each other, we could make mistakes. Our reputation is at stake. We can't afford failure."

Floresco nodded appreciatively. "Good. We've all read the programme of the visit. Then I suggest we don't concern ourselves with its detail. The staff has made a good job of it. Just now I want to concentrate on the difficulties my government is facing. Your job is to help me surmount them—where Europe is concerned. Now I think you know our history. It's set out in Paper Five." There was a shuffling of papers and voices said, "Five, oh yes, five, very clear, fascinating stuff," until Floresco cut them short with, "So you know that not long ago my love of this country obliged me to suspend…"

"Abolish," interrupted Max Bligh, not quite *sotto voce*.

For an instant the President fell silent. "Well yes, as you want truth, abolish," he replied, shooting a surprised glance at Bligh.

He had grown unused to interruptions and corrections were by now almost unimaginable. More robustly he continued in 'man of destiny' tones. "I abolished the Constitution foisted on us by the American imperialists because it was inappropriate to our people."

Max Bligh held up a pencil, pointed it like an unsatisfied teacher in the President's direction and narrowed his eyes. "One observation and one question A.F.: the Americans did not draw up the 1935 Constitution, though it had to have Congressional approval. According to Paper Five it was devised by a committee of Carolino constitutional lawyers and politicians, including your national hero—sorry, the late President Cuervo, which brings me to my question: could you explain what you mean by inappropriate?"

Floresco felt himself cooling further towards his persistent interlocutor yet warming to the dialogue—after all this is what he must be ready for when he faced those impertinent TV interviewers in Europe, especially on the BBC. "By inappropriate, Mr Bligh, I mean that Carolino history has been different from the American. Our social organisation is different from yours. We were, underneath we still are, a rural, no a village people. You must have read that when we have a problem we like to arrive at a consensus, rather than a duality. And we like that consensus once reached to be carried out by the village headman, firmly. If anyone fights against the decision he gets out or he's finished. That's why an American style constitution isn't appropriate here. As to that constitutional committee, sure, it was composed of our people but all from our rich landed families, US educated guys, or shall we say brainwashed balls carriers. So-called democrats who still think the sun shines out of the great American asshole. In any case, any other sort of constitution would never have got congressional approval. You must know that."

There was silence. The vulgar words betokened anger. How safe was the contract? In more respectful tones Max Bligh said, "We do hear what you say sir, but a village and a country are two different beasts. The sanctions open to a village headman and a national government are quantitatively different. You can't run a country like a village. A western style constitution only formalises on a national scale what goes on in minuscule in a village but in a way that limits the potential for oppression open to those in authority."

This time the silence was profound. In his convoluted way Bligh had identified the malady that had given rise to censorship, arbitrary arrest, secret trials, no trials at all, the universal fear of unjust death, the cancer that proliferated at the heart of the President's New Social Order. The four men grew conscious of external sounds— distant music, a few shouts, children's laughter, the shrill cry of a bird, until somewhere outside a clock chimed as though to signal the next round.

Hymen Schuster, the senior partner in the firm, coughed politely and leaned forward. His manner exuded confidentiality, conspiracy even. The President felt he was a man with whom he could do business. Perhaps it was his soft grey eyes under thick grey eyebrows or his mouth, generous and sensual, that had drawn Floresco to him when they were chatting before the meeting. "Tony. Your Excellency," he began as though deliberately telling his host, 'Yes, a man you may be but for good or ill you are a President, a man who should merit respect.' "We do, I believe, understand your situation. You are a fine leader who has done much for his country, you have begun its process of modernisation, you have started to draw it into the global economy but, maybe because of sinister forces beyond your control, your régime has acquired a certain reputation, an unfortunate reputation, for undue severity in its treatment of opponents. I must say that some of the evidence against your police and military is, well, pretty damning. What's more, your government has acquired another reputation—for graft. Again, from what I've learned there may be some truth in the allegations. Now my team is not here to judge. We are here to do a job. But our work can only be effective if we face up to realities. Only then can we make suggestions, produce arguments, justifications if necessary, to produce what you want. We are like physicians making a diagnosis."

The President felt as if he'd just been diagnosed with Alzheimer's Disease. Before long he'd be rolling his shit into little balls and eating it. Maybe it would be better to entrust the job to his own PR people. Then he thought of his Social Enlightenment Office with its American hard sell, its bland denials of reality, its inefficiency. That worked in the Carolines but not in the West. No doubt about it, he needed this firm. Very well then, let them hear how persuasive he could be. Staring, it seemed, far away he began quite gently, "Gentlemen, for many years my father worked long hours in various government departments in Infanta; that's why my brothers and I got a good education. But his was a poor Infanta family. My mother's people were better off. She came from the northern province and her village once held happy memories for me. As children we sometimes went there to stay with her family, but not after she died." His voice became wistful. "We all loved that village; it was not so far from the sea, in a fertile valley where streams tumble down from the hills over falls and into lakes. How wonderful it was for children like us to laugh and play in such a lovely place. There was always enough to eat, rice, fruit, meat and wonderful fish. Of course some people were poor but no one went hungry because people helped each other. We knew everyone there, not the very rich but always the very poor."

So affectionately did the President describe this little paradise that any listener might have imagined that the waves, the streams and the laughter were still audible to him, but he went on so long that his voice grew a bit hoarse. "Oh forgive me," he said, "I talk too much. Let me lead you on to the end of my story. A few years ago I went back to that village just after it had been 'liberated' by the Communists for two days, just two days. Would you like to know what happened in those two days of freedom to families who refused to give money and supplies to the Reds? To the self-styled Freedom Fighters? Floresco's voice broke, his eyes moistened. "They were tied to trees with wire and disembowelled, not quickly but in sight of one another, boys, girls, mothers, fathers, the very old, whole families. People my brothers and I knew." He paused but not in silence. The hard-boiled trio heard his sobs and saw his shoulders shaking. They sat motionless until he resumed calmly, "So when the bastards that had done it were tracked down, how do you think my soldiers behaved?" His jaw jutted Mussolini like, his voice abruptly sharpened. "Well, like good soldiers they just obeyed orders. My orders. And my orders were that every manjack of them must become more terrible to the Reds than I had been to General Kurihara, deaf to cries for mercy and glad to mix their laughter with the screams of the Reds. My soldiers enjoyed it. They exulted in it. Should I be blamed for that, gentlemen?"

"Terrible, terrible," breathed Hymen Schuster as he made a rather priestly gesture with both hands over his balloon of brandy. "Mr President, I think you have really told us how we should proceed in the matter of so-called human rights. We shall begin by posing an important question: are human rights applicable to an individual or a group whose actions deny them to others? A philosophical question to which we shall formulate a measured reply, a negative one of course. The lust for revenge—not only among the *hoi polloi*—will run in our favour."

Floresco dabbed his eyes with his handkerchief. It would not have surprised him if Hymen Schuster's analytical voice had said, 'Cut. That's it. Now let's shoot it again.' as though he were an actor and his tears not genuine. How could he sway others if he had not convinced these men? They were entirely cold; they were manipulators. They would produce a scenario for the Reds if a contract were at stake. But before his gloom could deepen Max Bligh spoke up cheerily, "Right A.F. I don't think we'll have much of a problem over human rights. We just wanted to make sure you could come up with something really good. And you did. After all, revenge is part of the human situation; it always will be. No, what may give us a real problem is the honesty of your administration. Here I'd say that if you can show that you are working to uplift the toiling masses (there was something derisive in the way he pronounced the last two words) your position is secure." He added seriously, "In reality as well as in a PR sense I'd say."

The querulous New York Jewish voice of Solly Schuster now deflected the President's attention. "Yes. That's the difficult issue. Criticism of your economic and social policies is widespread, not just by the left; a lot of it comes from Catholics the world over, using reports from missionaries—priests and nuns, working among your own people, though not from the hierarchy of course. Mr President, the problem you face is right here. The spotlight is on domestic issues." Solly hesitated before taking an unexpected but risky plunge, "And on the source of your personal wealth."

Too rapidly the President started to spout his government's line, sounding suspiciously defensive: the National Assembly had recently passed anti-corruption legislation; more control was being exercised over officials; not a few corrupt executives and one Minister had been sacked. However they must realise that in a poor country like this graft was seen by many if not most people as a justifiable means of increasing their earnings. Eventually rising prosperity would make it unnecessary.

Useless to go on. Cynical faces told him that this was not what they were waiting for. The meeting looked set to founder on his own failure to be as frank as Max Bligh had requested. Screw them, he thought. How did they think he was going to pay their fat fee? Yet the discussion had come near to a subject he wanted kept secret, eternally secret—his money, the money that had made his *coup d'état* possible. It was not from graft or corruption but from a small part of the vast treasure seized during the War from all over East Asia by an imperial looting agency directed by Prince Chichibu, the Emperor's brother. The immense spoils had been concealed in the Carolines, in the Philippines and in Japan itself, with the object in due course of financing a revanche of Japanese imperialism. Floresco thanked God that the torture he and his brothers had inflicted on three of Prince Chichibu's aides and his driver had enabled him to unearth a huge cache of gold, hidden in a cave providentially near his mother's village. The four victims had been deposed of in its deepest recesses. His find was nothing to what the White House had finally squirreled away but that was not his business. Though he had no legal right to the find, it had made him richer than any of the feudal Carolino families and with it he had laid the foundation of his power. Yet now his position was unassailable his ambition to do his best for the people constantly nagged him, arguing that the rapacity of his supporters mirrored his great theft? No, that criticism was surely untenable. The strong always made money out of government. What were the rich establishments in democratic countries but enlarged cliques of the powerful? Nevertheless in those countries the rich at least knew their limitations; here the oligarchic families lording it in Infanta and on their haciendas had wanted to give nothing away. Therefore had the Carolinos, especially its poor, welcomed his overthrow of a false democracy, nor had he ever rejected the notion that his own strongmen should profit from the oligarchs' downfall. The questions were: to what extent and for how long?

His misgivings refused to go away. Had his partisans become worse than the oligarchs who had at least maintained the democratic form? Was it possible that he and his wife had let their friends go too far? He knew the Achilles' Heel of his people. To the Carolinos the family was all-important. Neither he nor his wife had transcended that. Despite her glamour Griselda Floresco was, like him, a peasant. That was the basis of their strength, but also their weakness. Like many Carolinos his wife could not help favouring her family and her hangers-on, but as the years went by her generosity had ballooned. Maybe she thought it made her universally beloved, but it might be the cancer to destroy him. In a village it wouldn't matter but as First Lady of an entire state she was at the centre of a widespread web of patronage, in which parasites were easily enmeshed in corruption. Sternly he admonished himself for not disciplining his followers. He must exercise greater control, especially over the First Lady, her relatives and her toadies. But he should also watch out for these three sharp men, who might well be United States agents as well as PR experts. There must be no more questions from them about his money or his wife.

"Gentlemen," he said, with the disarming candour he had perfected. "I am a simple man, I assure you. Not simple in the intellectual sense but where my habits and needs are concerned. Wealth means little to me. What most gives me pleasure is my family, my books and sport. And of course, I must say my wife, but she's a very independent being, so if you want to know anything about her, you must contact the DeoGracias, which she has made into such a splendid showcase for the country. As for me, splendour and prestige are as the wind which comes and goes and is silent." The far-away look which official photographers were told to record whenever possible again entered his eyes and, to the disconcertion of the Schusters but not of Bligh, he broke into Latin, *"Cur valle permutem Sabina divitias operosiores?* Why would I change my Sabine dale for the greater burden of wealth? No, gentlemen, I am only here for the Carolines, to help my poor country, which I have always loved, until I can hand over to better men. Let the whole world know that. I have nothing to hide."

Three pairs of eyes were united in admiration. Before them truly stood a liar of genius. Hymen Schuster brought his hands together almost, it seemed, in a gesture of applause. "I think you have provided us, A.F., with the line that needs to be followed. If I may speak as a professional, our task has been greatly assisted by your obvious sincerity and your capacity to express yourself so movingly. We promise to do you proud, Excellency."

The courtesies over the President, ever the simple man, revved up his MG very loudly and roared off. As their hired limousine swept the PR experts down the serpentine road, escorted by wasp-waisted police outriders on huge motor bikes, Solly sneered, "What was that Latin stuff? Poetry? The nasty little shit is well read."

"Max Bligh replied casually, "Yes, but no poet, just an emperor with the usual Roman vices. Oh, it was the first poem in the third book of Horace's *Odes*. I never mentioned that I'd read Classics in my CV to you. I thought it might put you off. Well guys, the hypnosis is over. Let's hope we can make another silk purse if we are lucky enough to get anywhere near the First Lady.

Salvador Alvarez was very fond of his pigs—or rather his and Father Stephens' pigs. He had given them all names and found that they quickly responded when he shouted Amy, Clara, Rita or Pete. He also observed that they could be very jealous of each other—and vicious. In short they had a lot in common with human beings, including himself. So he thought it rather stupid when Father Stephens told him that he was like St Francis with his adored beasts. Father Stephens clearly knew little about animals and Salvador often doubted whether he knew much about human beings either. If only he knew what some people who came to church were like when his back was turned. If only he knew what cruelty went on in their houses. He was just too good for them. Salvador had come to the conclusion that one of his own duties was to shield Father Stephens from the nastiness that lay all around.

Today the pigs received less than his usual attention. When Clara seemed reluctant to eat, instead of coaxing her—which Clara liked as it made clear to the other denizens of the sty that she stood higher in Salvador's affections than the rest—he smacked her with a rattan, which quickly put an end to her nonsense. For Salvador was preoccupied with the problem of how to tell Father Stephens that he wanted to get married, in fact that he had to get married because he had made Rosalinda Cortez, the daughter of a local car mechanic, pregnant. For better or for worse Salvador had done his utmost to convince Father Stephens that their affair was the only love interest in his life. This was not difficult, for, like most youths in San Felipe, he was practised at appearing passionate and giving his body generously. But Father Stephens was not like them; he was as good a lover but his passion was serious. Salvador was unsure which way the cat would jump. If the priest took the news badly the people of San Felipe might feel the effects and those in the know might blame their errant altar boy. On the other hand those cynical about clerical morals, and they were not a few, might guess that as things had gone swimmingly with Salvador any one of the handsome boys in the town could satisfy the Priest's needs. They might even find a substitute, though Salvador was sure that none among the potential candidates could surpass him in good looks. It was this honest vanity that had led to his problem.

His features were fine and regular, his smile suggested an inner radiance that drew people easily to him. His body was strongly built and lithe as a gazelle, and though only twenty he looked not a day older than sixteen. But his bronzed skin, clear as a child's, his eyes dreamy under long lashes, his inviting lips, often slightly parted and not surmounted by a hint of down, sometimes made him a delectable but vulnerable target for the machismo of other boys. As a result, incensed by their remarks about himself and their parish priest, especially when they called him the Father's bum boy whereas in fact the two lovers enjoyed pleasing each other every which way, he decided to win the lovely Rosalinda Cortez, who was regarded by his peers as the most desirable catch in San Felipe. However, it so turned out that Rosalinda's craving, once aroused for Salvador, stayed no less on the boil than that of Father Stephens, with the result that her surrender and her pregnancy occurred sooner than anyone had thought possible.

To Salvador's surprise neither Senor nor Senora Cortez had exploded with anger. They did insist however that the marriage should take place as soon as possible. The Cortez's were good judges of character. Salvador's prospects might not be so great but he had been a good student and Father Stephens would surely use his influence to get him some sort of job before long. A better-heeled mate might have been found for such a lovely girl but better heeled might not mean of better character. The Cortez themselves were reasonably secure and they kept a good table, for a car mechanic's services were ever in demand. The truth was that they loved their daughter and felt it was time she had a strong man to provide them with grandchildren. Salvador was clearly capable of this, for one of them was already on its way. Senor Cortez was unusual in that he never attended church and sometimes liked to draw Rosalinda and her new fiancé into talk about communism, for which he professed a secret sympathy. He also scoffed at Salvador for still being an altar boy, not realising the duty was a good excuse for a continuing association with the priest rather than an expression of religiosity.

What really worried Salvador about Father Stephens was not how he might react to the news of his marriage—being inevitable it must be lived with—but how he and the pregnant Rosalinda would be treated in Church at a marriage ceremony performed by the man discreetly known to be his lover. In the close society of San Felipe, where face mattered a lot, Salvador knew that the scandal had already caused some sniggering; only a ripple so far but he did not want it to mount into a wave of ribald laughter on his wedding day. The Carolinos were an easy-going lot but they never said no to a good laugh.

In the mid afternoon Father Stephens, like the rest of San Felipe, was accustomed to take a siesta. Despite the heat it was his favourite time for hotter action with Salvador, a sacred time he maintained when all else was at peace and near to heaven. When they were in bed together, whether before or after love making, Salvador always enjoyed the security of the Priest's close embrace. Today would be no different; the encircling arms were already comforting him and starting to stray, when without opening his eyes, Father Stephens sniffed and said, "Clara, Clara, what a lovely little pig you are."

Salvador giggled. "Sorry. I should have taken a bath. Do I stink?"

"Yes, with the porcine odour of sanctity but I'll put up with it for St Francis' sake."

"I'm sorry I woke you. I really wanted you to have a good rest."

"Liar. Something poking into me is saying what you really want. Anyway I wasn't asleep. I was thinking of you. I often think about you."

"Well that's a real lie. I saw a mosquito on your prick and you never hit it."

"Then I must have been dreaming of you."

"Sinfully I'm sure. But you love sin, don't you Father? Hah! Priests shouldn't dream of boys." Having said this Salvador continued to rub himself tantalisingly against his lover.

"Why not? God sends the dreams. He knows what He's doing. But how do you know my dream was sinful? It was quite innocent. In it I saw you going to church. There was a great crowd there, all in their best clothes and cheering."

Salvador fell still. "Go on Father," he said apprehensively.

"Yes, and then followed the bride, a beautiful girl in a little carriage with a pretty canopy, drawn by a white horse. Oh, now I remember; I was at the Altar"

The Botticelli angel with bewilderingly wild hair drew in his breath. Father Stephens had surprised him yet again. Just as he had surprised him during that first afternoon of love under the shower, for when he'd been aroused the gentle priest had turned into an untamed thing. He'd said that it was his first time yet he'd made love like a drunken whore. You thought he knew nothing but it turned out he knew everything. The question seemed hopeless but the boy had to ask,"How do you know so much about me Father?"

Father Stephens took his hand away from the twist of black curls he had been playing with; indeed he drew away from the boy's body completely before answering him very deliberately. "In my mind's eye I can see you anywhere on earth, Salvador. Sometimes when we are far apart we are most together; in such moments you are nearer to me than I am to myself. If you ask, how can I be in your heart when I am cut off from you, I must tell you that such is the miracle of love. To begin with it was not so; for a little while it was no more than willful lust for your beauty that made me need you, but when to have pleasure with you had grown into my sole ambition, I knew I adored you. Then the snags cropped up. I entered a dark forest of confusion; I was attacked by awful doubts. I feared that I was going to drift for ever and ever down an everlasting Nile of grief but at last, quite suddenly, I awoke to find myself sailing over a shoreless sea under the unconquered sun. And yet my adoration contains its own tyranny. Do you get me, my sweet mouthed tormentor?"

"Father Stephens, what a hard sermon! Couldn't you just say that you love me in a peculiar Australian way whilst I love you like a straightforward Carolino? But I don't think there's any difference really. The only word I don't get is tormentor? A strange word to call the innocent boy you seduced so wickedly, when he was doing his best to fix your leaky old pipe. Tormentor is the wrong word for a lover."

"Not so, you little twister. It's spot on. A holy prophet is constantly tormented by separation from his Saviour; a lover by separation from his beloved, and this lost priest by separation from his Salvador. We all long to be reunited with the source of our being. That's why you liked to fuck around with so many hot guys in town before you met me. Love knows no difference between a church and a wine bar. Longing, Salvador, longing. The torment of longing is the strongest evidence for faith and for love."

Salvador looked amused, then seemingly puzzled. He asked slyly, "So? If I marry a certain lovely girl, will your little friend Father Oliveros say that I must be tormented by no one but her—and by no-one else?"

The question was significant and Father Stephens saw that it needed more than a contrite answer. Whatever he replied as a priest would merit a judgment not on his self-willed love but on his obedience. A flickering candle could be a moth's calamity. He stared up at the ceiling fan and let its slow rotations continue for a while before saying, "He might indeed, Salvador. But I don't always obey little Father Oliveros as you call him, so why should you, if you don't want to. You are as free as I am." They were both silent again until he added in no more than whisper, as if wanting no one, and particularly not God, to hear, "Many a road has two tracks. Married or not, whichever track you take, you can always turn and come back when you need me. I can embrace the torment of separation because through you I have understood a mystery. Salvador, you showed me where my joy lay hidden. You are my rod, the dowsing rod of my life."

Of a sudden they grasped each other roughly, as if this was the last time they might be together. Their sweat mingled, their lips met, their tongues searched and probed greedily, their hands explored, yet encountered nothing unfamiliar, their bodies rose in desire. Yet after, when their rapturous conflict was over, Salvador stayed awake, still worrying. It was easier to accept Father Stephens' rabbiting on about his joy and his rod, which obviously just meant screwing together, than to understand why the Cortez family was so relaxed over the marriage. Did they know something going on in San Felipe that even Father Stephens had not discovered; a secret thing which, had he known it, he would certainly have revealed in this sacred time when no secrets were allowed to divide them? Could the price to be paid for the beautiful Rosalinda Cortez be as hidden as that?

Zeny Vizcarra tried in vain to get through to Conchita but the receiver was off the hook. She tapped lightly on the door but all was silent. Then she knocked ever more fiercely, so that the noise attracted some curious footmen loitering along the corridor. The door opened so suddenly that her fist almost hit Conchita in the face, which made the President's daughter give a loud laugh just like her father's. "Zeny you silly girl, just tell her I'm not coming. If she wants to speak to me it will have to be tonight." Zeny was left standing and frightened. The servants exchanged grins at her discomfiture, for the First Lady's 'eyes' were not popular among the Palace staff.

Before long the news of Conchita's defiance percolated from the flunkeys to the clerical staff, the guards and the gardeners and thence by swift degrees to tradesmen and to busybodies who made it their duty to know what was afoot in the Palace. But Conchita didn't care a fig for any of them as she lay down, eyes closed, thinking of the night she had spent with a friend, no older than herself and now her lover, Julio Abulencia. Her mind was made up. There was no point in being a President's daughter if the price to be paid was imprisonment. Not long ago she had been in Oxford at Lady Margaret Hall, as her parents wanted her to speak British English rather than American and to see how properly educated Britons did things. The college had mild regulations which, compared to her present situation, meant almost total freedom. There had been parties in Mayfair and Chelsea, weekends at country houses and visits to discos, all of which she remembered with pleasure. But because her father feared that she might be kidnapped by someone among his many enemies he had asked the Foreign Office for protection by security guards. None of them were like the goons around the DeoGracias; the Foreign Office knew how to arrange things discreetly for important foreign guests, particularly from countries where there was British investment.

She had not returned to Infanta as an uncritical Anglophile but she had learned to see the world in a distinctly un-Carolino light, as a result of mixing with all sorts of educated but often cynical people, who had succeeded in putting many of her cherished beliefs to flight. It had been a two-edged process of disillusion. Even right wing Britons, though not proposing her father's downfall, always spoke on the assumption that the Carolines was a right wing dictatorship where freedom was ruthlessly suppressed. Before she had learned better she would try to tell them of her father's genuine ambitions for enlightened reform, of his New Social Order and of the young now benefiting from his educational and health programs. Those who listened tended to be dismissive and inclined to categorise with phrases like, ' Oh, Populism,' or 'Just like Peronism', and should she describe the National Youth Movement she might get a chilling, 'Ah yes, modelled on Nazi Strength Through Joy'. They could also be witheringly condescending. A banker told her, "We don't blame your old man, Conchita dear. I'd do the same in his place. But what else can be done in these Third World countries? At least he's made your country safe for investment—provided one coughs up the right back-handers." One conservative M.P. explained that her country's real tragedy was that the British had not held on to it after the Napoleonic wars. "Then you would have avoided Spain and the USA. The Inquisition and Coca Cola. Could anything have been worse?"

Conchita learned to hide her resentment, but it is not possible to spend impressionable years in another country without picking up some of its values, especially those of ones contemporaries. But she had never behaved like some LMH women she knew who thought nothing of slipping out at night to sleep with boyfriends, a few of them of them real weirdos. Nor had she been seduced by any of the polite young men called upon to escort her to parties. She knew they were generally briefed by the Foreign Office that she was a special and risky package. But mentally she was no longer prepared to take things for granted, so that as soon as she had set foot again in the Carolines she found herself questioning anything and everything, like the blasé young English woman who now, schizophrenically, existed inside her.

Julio Abulencia had boarded the same plane as herself on the way back to Infanta. He had been to Dublin at a student conference, so he said vaguely, when, seated by chance or design across the aisle from her, they had struck up a light-hearted conversation. Soon after the Carolino official sent to chaperone her had fallen asleep she gave up her seat next him and took the vacant one by the window next to Julio. It was rather forward of her but how better to kill the long time flying all the way to the Pacific. Julio was a good listener which suited Conchita, who rattled on, making it pretty clear that she knew little about the harsher realities of life in her own country and nothing about the decline in her family's popularity. Julio was intrigued by her ignorance, for he knew who she was. He was attracted by her vivacity but observed that her looks were nothing out of the ordinary, though improved by expensive clothes, French he did not have to guess, for his student days, now completed, had been spent at the Sorbonne. While doing most of the talking, she was making sharp observations about him, mostly related to his strong features and his friendly manner, often helped by a winning smile. These seemed to accord with the romantic notions about Carolino men she had picked up from her mother, who loved to boast about her many fine suitors, of whom the President had been the finest and most attentive. Conchita could believe in the second quality but had doubts over the first, her father being distinctly short. When Julio got up to visit some French guy in business class, a friend from his Paris days he told her, she was surprised by his stature, for most Carolinos were of medium height; she also noticed a sudden depressed look pass over his face as though something unpleasant had come to mind. She wondered why. Most Carolinos, including herself, whatever their inner feelings, tried to hide their troubles and look cheerful. His voice, she observed later, when he was telling her about the fun of Dublin at night time, had a soft velvety quality where most Carolinos affected an American nasal twang—unless of course they belonged to the Spanish speaking élite, to which the name Abulencia proved that Julio did. By the time the plane was circling over Infanta and she knew everything good about Ireland, she had decided that this was going to be the first of many encounters with him.

Reality only broke in after the 'fasten your seat belts' announcement when her chaperone called in a voice that sounded more like an order, "Senorita Conchita, return to your seat." Julio swiftly pulled back his legs for her to pass, showing that he too had heard the order and must obey. Then, just a moment after the plane had touched down on Floresco Airport and everyone was experiencing relief—for one never knew where the Carolines Airline was concerned—the chaperone put his head close to hers and whispered. "Be careful, Senorita. The Abulencias are out."

That she had arrived in a country that seemed changed to her was apparent once off the plane. She was ushered rapidly into the President's lounge, while ordinary mortals wended their way past the uncertain requirements of the country's customs officials. Julio, rapt in conversation with his French friend, gave her the merest nod, not even accompanied by a smile, as he disappeared into the crowd.

The First Lady put her daughter's bewildered look, as she met her, down to fatigue and said in her usual effusive way, "Darling you'll be alright after a good night's rest. Listen, Conchita, I'm going to see that you have everything you need." Such however was not to be the case.

Now, half a year later, her affair with Julio was under enemy pressure. After running the gauntlet of strangely interrupted mobile calls, conversations with him from public phone boxes, secret meetings, aborted trysts, unsatisfactory arrangements, final realisation that the Abulencias, not excluding Julio, hated, and were hated by, her father's régime and terrible rows with her mother, Conchita was engaged in her own liberation struggle.

The loud thump on the floor outside her salon door was like the start of a drama on the French stage, or so Conchita thought, when both portals swung open and the First Lady made her entrance. "So," she proclaimed like an actress, "the mountain must come to Mohammed. But it doesn't matter to me in the least." Conchita could see that it did matter very much to her mother, who resembled not so much a mountain as a volcano in full spate. She stood there in a fiery red national dress with puffed up shoulders that looked like erupting flames and placed her hands firmly on her internationally renowned hips. The gesture was intended to convey determination as well as outrage, but to Conchita her mother suddenly bore resemblance to the more vulgar type of English stage barmaid. She got to her feet, as that way she felt less vulnerable when the tirade began. "My daughter, Senorita Conchita Floresco, there is one thing that is all-important in our national life; the family and loyalty to the family. In this family we are all loyal to your father, His Excellency Antonio Norberto Floresco, President of the Republic. I am loyal, my dear mother and sick father are loyal, and the President's mother is loyal; indeed though she is entitled to obedience as his respected mother, she would never oppose him. Your younger sisters are loyal and even your brother, who is only eleven, understands the meaning of the word loyalty. But you, though merely twenty, have chosen not to be loyal. In fact you have chosen to consort with a family that is opposed to your father, a family that not only opposes him for its own selfish reasons but gives money to the terrorists who would destroy him, to the communists." The last word was uttered in a sort of growl, which suggested that the provenance of the communists was hell itself.

"Now hear this." Despite her fear a little titter hovered inside Conchita's mouth for she could not help thinking of American movies in which that very phrase was often used before the issue of dire commands like the one she now heard. "From now onwards you will never, I repeat never, see that rotten Julio Abulencia again, nor any member of his family of degenerates. If you do there will be dire consequences—for him especially. Do you understand what I am saying?" The misfortune to be was that Conchita did understand the First Lady's words, but not completely.

Outside the confessional Father Oliveros was reluctant to speak to Father Stephens about personal matters, so his visits to the Priest's house were invariably related to his own work in the Rural Development Training College. Father Stephens on the other hand now wanted to talk about his own problem, for he was increasingly doubtful about his vocation. "I am not a sensual man," he began, not entirely truthfully, as they sat together on the verandah enjoying a bottle of red wine, "But..."

"We are all sensual men," cut in Father Oliveros with a smile.

"Well, not an excessively sensual man," Father Stephens snapped back sharply, wondering exactly what his words had implied. "Forgive me, Father; I was brusque. I mean that I am an affectionate man. I can give my love to God and I am conscious of God's love for me. But human affection, that's a different thing. It's complicated; it disturbs me. I can't manage it. I'm in a quandary. Maybe I'm not sufficiently self contained to be a priest."

"And if you were not a priest what would you be? I can't see you not being a priest. You have won the affection of the poor here because of your work. The people you have helped in San Felipe need you. You have generously given them earthly affection, so why shouldn't you fulfill your own desire for the crescent moon, to put it poetically?"

"Crescent moon?" Father Stephens was surprised to hear such an expression from a normally stern churchman.

"That's the sort of love you want to talk about isn't it? Because you're in a bit of a mess aren't you? Spiritually I mean. Just now you sounded on edge. But you're not the only priest this has happened to, you know. If you're afraid to speak freely then how little you know the Church."

The time for reticence was over. The truth gushed out. "Then I'll tell you Father how little you know me. I never confessed the whole truth to you, only prurient details describing my lust. But it's more than lust. The truth is that I am a drunkard; madly drunk with love for a boy. I would rather give up my vocation than give up Salvador. Yes, you are right. For me he is the crescent moon, beauty incarnate, a rare jewel though maybe you can't see it. Even the mole on his cheek rouses fire in my heart. I sound extravagant, don't I? You see how far I have fallen. My present hell is that I might lose

31

him altogether if I stay here. Shall I jump ship and ask him to come with me to Sydney? He would do that, I'm sure."

Oliveros poured himself another glass of wine, sipped it appreciatively and smiled at his non-penitent quizzically. "For love of you or to get to Australia? To Browns vineyard maybe. This is a subtle wine; you certainly know your Ozzie vintages. No, Father Stephens, first let me say 'no' to that stupid question and second let's agree that we are not going to talk metaphysical nonsense about love or chastity or the sanctity of human sperm. Your duty, but not mine, is to find a pragmatic way out of your quandary. Yes, I certainly do know the sensual side of your story. You told it to me in such detail that now I summon up the lechery of Salvador to mind when I... well you know what celibates do to keep sane. But your love seems extravagant to me. Is it love or obsession? I sensed the latter during your confessions, which were enjoyably pornographic and obviously calculated to corrupt me a bit. But Father Stephens, whatever your intent, even before you came here my beliefs had withered beneath the harsh realities of this place. I no longer accept the teachings of our Church. Its theology is a sham, its hallowed beliefs fairy tales. Now I do my best to help my students see the stupidity of its dogma and to sabotage the so-called great theologians. For instance, last night in the College the students and I had a good laugh reading St Augustine's chapter on whether we will retain our sexual characteristics after the Day of Judgment. The discussion was hilarious. No rational being would consider such rubbish in this day and age except as a joke. But your problem is no joke and I comprehend it completely; how can a completely normal desire survive when condemned by antique laws lacking any scientific basis? I could tell you exactly how our Cardinal would counsel you but I won't because I no longer trust him either."

Oliveros, his eyes closed, took two sips of wine slowly. Father Stephens looked at the astute little priest incredulously, but soon the crafty eyes opened and the homily resumed, "My dear Stephens, I wish you could see as clearly as I do that we are on earth, and in this little town, for no providential reason. As far as I can see it's no more than an accident, not even a practical joke, so we can't hope for divine guidance. But it's also a cold fact that we are working among the poor and the oppressed. Now I've realised for a long time that we can't expect any support in our job from the hierarchy because they know little about the poor, and certainly care less. Ergo, it's left to us. So just concentrate on the plight of the people, your flock of workers and peasants, and do what you can do for them. Work out a plan to help them in their struggle and teach them about their rights. If you are strong on rights, your own included, you can help them to organise. But don't count me in as your confessor any more. That was a charade. There's no need for confession because there's no such goal as salvation. My dear young man, the most you can ever hope for is the warmth of success, and if you're lucky more time with Salvador. But watch out; he's tougher than you and he'll do what he must."

The unexpected Oliveros anti-confessional required some getting used to. It terminated in a way that was disturbingly Delphic. Father Stephens' surprise must have shown in his face, for his erstwhile confessor said, "What I tell my students, and I'm telling it now to you, is this: none of us has the right to let personal problems take precedence over the titanic struggle of the masses. I'm talking of issues like this." Father Oliveros took some papers out of his case, put on his glasses and began to read aloud. "'We the workers on the San Lorenzo Sugar Corporation Estate in the Parish of San Felipe humbly ask that our basic wage be increased by five cents an hour. We beg this because we are no longer able to buy the food and clothing necessary for our lives and the health of our children. Some of us cannot manage at all. Everything has gone up in price. We know that this has also caused problems for Management. That is why we are only asking for a small increase, just enough to keep us going.' It's signed by sixty two people—all from your Parish." Father Oliveros' tone seemed to imply that the matter must be the Parish priest's responsibility. "Well, what do you think about it?"

Father Stephens thought a number of things about it, but he must be careful how to reply. Oliveros had clearly turned his back on his faith. What other forms of authority was he ready to defy? Public information, or social guidance as it was called, was regularly distributed to churches. This had recently included a presidential decree that all wages were to be frozen in view of the deteriorating economic situation. Aware of this Father Stephens picked up the petition and read it for any turn of phrase the authorities might consider subversive, before saying, "Short of the people crawling on their knees they could not have put it more innocuously."

"Which won't prevent the police from seeing something dangerous in it," replied Oliveros, staring hard at Father Stephens. "You know that we're getting near to breaking point don't you? No, to the point of no return. The poor really don't have enough to go round." He emptied the rest of the wine into his glass and gulped it down. "I can't stand the sight of the wretchedness, the sickness, and the despair all around us and I can't stand the thought of that lot," he gestured up the valley towards the hacienda of the Bersamina family, "up there still living in luxury. They know how to avoid taxation but they see nothing wrong in paying their workers a pittance."

"We could both go to see Manuel Bersamina and put the people's case to him." For the moment Father Stephens could think of no better course of action, even though his predecessor in the Parish had tried it twice before and been firmly rebuffed, the second time quite roughly.

To Father Oliveros the suggestion was not worthy of comment. He got up and stamped about gesticulating like a revivalist preacher. "We could teach the people to open up land on the mountain sides. I know it's poor but with terracing crops could be grown. We could organise the young people to do something useful in the villages, maybe to build a club or a health clinic; the Red Cross could help in that. Jesus, we must do something, anything. We've got to give them hope Stephens, not hope for the next world. If we don't, more and more of them will join the other side and who can blame them?"

Father Stephens wished that Oliveros would stop ranting; it was unsettling and got neither of them anywhere. Why boil water if it all went up in steam? The people worked hard all the hours God made cutting cane for almost nothing but they wouldn't see any point in squeezing a bit more out of their bodies in cosmetic tasks when some slight financial adjustments in the sugar industry could provide the relief they needed. In reality the people would be better off if they never had to cut cane at all. With its volcanic soil and abundant rainfall the Parish could produce enough rice, fruit and vegetables to sustain a reasonable life for all. But the fertile plain extending up to the barren mountain sides all belonged to the

Bersamina family, which was unlikely to hand over land it had held for three hundred years. No wonder the communist slogan, 'Land to the people' sounded so sweet in the peasants' ears. It sounded sweet in his own ears, very sweet and most reasonable. He tried to put a brake on his rising anger but all at once surprised Oliveros by shouting, "If I can stray so far from the teachings of the Church in private morality, why can't I stray as violently where public morals are concerned?"

The two priests were silent. Unanswered question hovered in the air, for each was wondering where the other stood, how far was he prepared to go. But neither asked a question nor felt ready to explain himself. Had a point of no return really been reached and was this conversation its very epicentre before the quake and the violence? To break the silence Father Stephens opened a second bottle and suggested that a few more glasses would help them think more calmly, to which Father Oliveros replied by putting his papers back into his case. Resignedly he said, "Maybe we should go and fawn on Bersamina's estate manager. But maybe not. Why humiliate ourselves for nothing?"

They walked together though the poorest part of the town talking inconsequentially about College students and the behavior of some parishioners, sedulously avoiding anything more serious. But, near the bus stop, Oliveros looked Father Stephens straight in the eye and said, "How lucky you are to possess your jewel. A single night's debauch with him and I'd worship any god he chose for me, except the insane Trinity. If he was in the College they'd fight over him." All at once he looked startled, seemingly taken aback by his own admission. Was he now lost in a medley of his own skepticism, of his hidden lust, of the workers' struggle or of the lot, who could tell. When he came to, he said mournfully, "Yes, I can see it all very clearly. There will be fighting everywhere, over everything."

On the way home Father Stephens called on a number of sick people to comfort them and their families and to hear confessions. Yes, the wretchedness was increasing. There had never been so many sick children in this part of town since his arrival. Could he mention that to Manuel Bersamina? It was an irrefutable fact and not evidence of communism. On the verandah he noticed that Oliveros' case was still on the chair where he had been sitting. Unlike him to forget; perhaps he had drunk too much. He put the case in a drawer and got on with some Parish accounts that were not in a bad way, since the Bersaminas had maintained their traditional grant. What a pity they could not be as generous to their workers. The petition still worried him, however, though less than the pressure from Father Oliveros that he should take part in the struggle of the masses. Masses! A word with different connotations for Catholics and communists. As an Australian he should not get involved in matters outside his Parish duties. But what was afoot in the Parish? He remembered Salvador's words that he did not know what was going on among the people. However he did know that money could do something for them. Opening the Statement of Accounts he wondered if he might transfer savings in the Fabric Fund to the Relief Fund, but, having read on that such money was solely for the former purpose, he gave up and decided to take another look at the petition and its list of signatories. Father Oliveros would not mind his case being opened. It was not locked and invited inspection.

Under the petition was a book that hardly surprised him, Oliveros being an economist; *Observations on Capitalism* by V.I. Lenin, published by the Foreign Languages Press in Beijing. But another volume alarmed him; it was entitled, "Wage structures in the Caroline Sugar Industry, an exposé." The book was banned, first because it was by one of the President's most violent political opponents, Paul Santos, now in exile in France, and second because it contained a scathing indictment of the way in which wealthy American and Carolino interests made huge profits out of an impoverished labour force kept in harsh subjection. The book contained lurid photographs of burned villages, scattered corpses and people mutilated by security guards in the wake of a strike over working conditions no more than a year ago. More dangerous yet were some pamphlets by the Communist Liberation Movement. One was subversive indeed; *Evidence that Antonio Floresco was a Japanese Collaborator*, and another even more so; *How to defeat the Floresco Military Thugs*. He decided to hide them all away. As he did so a new doubt flared up: could Oliveros have left his case in the chair deliberately, to recruit or involve him, or worse still to influence Salvador? The ever-curious boy might pick up a pamphlet and then, horror of horrors, be reported for possessing it by some vagabond who envied him. How dreadful to lose his idol through a false accusation, yet things like that happened a lot in the Carolinas. Before he put the petition in his pocket—he would need it if he called on Bersamina—he ran his eyes over its list of signatories; surely some of them were workers' leaders, but how many might be communists? He could not say. Yes, he lived in ignorance of the struggle going on around him, in disturbing ignorance. Today, in the early light of dawn, Salvador had awakened him with sensual caresses and intimate kisses whispering, "Wake up, wicked Priest. You never care what's going on in your Parish once I've made you hot for my prick do you?" But where was his wanton seducer now? Why isn't he home in the safety of my arms? Where is the music that makes me one with him? All was in doubt; everything in life was precarious, his quandary was deeper than ever. He reached for the untouched bottle of wine, poured himself a full glass and started to drink, too quickly for sure. By the time he was pouring a third glass a sharp wind was blowing down from the mountains, scattering papers and leaves around the veranda. Sadly he sat alone, measuring out the wine, and thinking of mad lovers who can only measure the wind.

The massive wrought iron gates of the DeoGracias Palace swung open, and guards sprang to attention as a convoy of white helmeted police motorcyclists, five Land Rovers bearing soldiers in battle dress, a radio patrol car and then the First Lady's long silvery limousine surmounted by her personal standard, swept out, followed by more police vehicles. A helicopter hovered noisily overhead, keeping the progress under surveillance and ready to contact the police on the ground should there be trouble.

In the cool dark interior of the vehicle the First Lady, from behind her shades, looked out at a world that seemed both physically and metaphorically dark. Ahead lay an exhausting schedule of public appearances—a speech at a United Nations Seminar on Beauty in the Human Environment, a subject she had made her forte; lunch at the City Hall for the Directors of the First Lady's Women's Development Movement; a visit to one of the universities and then, after a return to the DeoGracias for a couple of hours' rest, dinner with the new Russian Ambassador, Valery Resanov, a man she could not abide. It exasperated her, given the goodwill she had shown during a visit to Moscow, that the Russians should send a man who had treated her with a minimum of courtesy, addressing her only in French which he knew she did not speak well. Her favourite Russian contacts had always been with former KGB officers, worldly sophisticates who, though clearly cultivating her for political reasons, sometimes provided her with tip-offs that she found useful on the world stage.

Although she had given orders that Conchita's activities should be watched carefully she did not trust the Palace security officers to do the job properly. Her daughter was smart and would not find it difficult to outwit that pack of dimwits again. She picked up the phone and asked to speak to Senorita Floresco. The operator replied that the number was engaged. "Cut in," the First Lady ordered. "Don't you know who I am?" The next instant she heard her daughter's voice in mid sentence saying, "Just tea and a prawn sand... hello, can you hear me?"

"Operator, can you put me through to my daughter?" Conchita heard her mother saying mellifluously without being taken in by the attempt at dissimulation. She remained silent until the operator said apologetically, "You're already through ma'am."

"Oh, am I? Is that you Conchita sweetest?" The First Lady's voice fluttered through the ether light as a dove. "I'm so sorry we had that little contretemps. I didn't mean to shout at my darling. It's only because I love you, dear, and want the very best for you. I only live for the happiness of my children. You know that don't you dear?"

Conchita replied in tones equally dulcet, "Of course mummy. I shouldn't have locked the door. Sorry. Really mummy I am sorry."

The First Lady breathed an inward sigh of relief. An apology! And they were talking decently to each other. "What are you doing today my darling?"

"I don't know yet mummy. Not much, I should think. I'm terribly tired after last..." Even as she spoke Conchita knew her mother would conjure up the name Julio Abelencia. Awful mistake; in an attempt to distract further probes she said, "I think I'll get on with my correspondence. So many people to write to in Oxford. I owe so many letters."

"Yes dear. Do that," the First Lady replied coolly and all went silent. Conchita held the phone to her ear a bit longer then put it down despondently, after which she switched to the Government controlled TV channel on which an enthusiastic woman commentator was describing the scene at the National Conference Centre. "And in a few minutes no less than the First Lady will be arriving to address..." Conchita switched off the sound and just watched. 'No less than' preceded her mother's name so regularly from the lips of oily-mouthed TV announcers that it was beginning to sound like an honorific. Perhaps if her mother were around long enough it would acquire the same dignity as, 'Her Royal Highness'. She stood up and addressed herself in the mirror. "Ladies and Gentlemen. No less than Conchita Floresco, the biggest fool on record for returning herself to prison."

Yet prisoners, she reflected, have to find ways of bearing their imprisonment if they can't escape it. How could she deal with a warden of a woman who had turned so implacably against her, not out of misgivings over the character of the man she loved but solely on account of his political affiliations, which, true enough were hostile to her father's system of government. Surely there must be a way of gaining her parents' consent, or at least tolerance. There must be a weak spot in their armour and since it was her mother who was proving so difficult, best to probe her foibles.

She had made no plans to slip out of the DeoGracias Palace knowing that over the next few days she would be spied on until, in the usual Carolinas way, guards would relax, orders would be forgotten, and exit would be easy. In the meantime what better to do than study how her mother operated in public for she was behaving in curious ways quite different from Conchita's remembrance of her in those pre-Oxford days in Infanta. She had seen her mother's program for today in the press and knew it would be reported and televised *ad nauseam*. She could do her research easily like a couch potato by following her mother on the box. The food she had ordered had been brought in, so she curled up in one of the palace's huge gilded armchairs to eat and observe in comfort.

On the TV the silvery limousine was gliding up the curved ramp of the Conference Centre, a severe concrete cube flanked by translucent pools, well tended shrubs and abstract sculptures. All at once fountains spurted up from the waters; a bit late, thought Conchita. In the portico, which was very wide but sufficiently low for people to comment on the building's human scale, functionaries applauded the First Lady as she emerged wearing an emerald green national dress to receive a bouquet from a little girl. A close up of her heavily made up, unsmiling face told Conchita that her mother's fury, though abating, had not entirely gone.

The cameras now spotlighted Madame Floresco moving into the foyer, which rose the full height of the prestigious Centre, which had been constructed, so she maintained, under her guidance but in fact at her insistence, regardless of cost. Opulent crimson and gold furnishings and on high a galaxy of glittering chandeliers gave the impression of grandeur, for the huge enclosed space was intended to awe. In its vastness human beings looked like Lilliputians, as they surged after the First Lady up the stairs leading to the Conference Hall. Either side of her 'No Less Than-ness' were the expensively dressed matrons of Infanta society wearing the smiles people put on in the presence of power, hoping that the divinity will at least notice their presence. However the First Lady walked on, impervious to greetings or the presence of a soul. Her mind was still filled with the problem of her errant daughter, who at that moment was chuckling at the antics of the Centre's reception committee jockeying for position. "Just like *Alice in Wonderland*," Conchita said aloud. "Oh my ears and whiskers what will her No Less Than-ness say?"

Salutations and introductions preceded the address of the First Lady whose features had burst into a set smile. Conchita turned up the volume to hear her speech delivered in an inflated, melodramatic way, accompanied by gestures of the sort sometimes used by schoolgirls reciting poetry. It was not a speech that a reasonable person could listen to seriously for its content but more a doctrine enunciated for the ears of the faithful Carolino people. It asserted, thrice though in different ways, that like herself the Carolinos were natural believers in beauty. With hands clasped together as in prayer she added that her own belief in beauty as a higher reality was only surpassed by her fervent belief in the truth of our Lord and Saviour, Jesus Christ. Now lying on the carpet, for the armchair was not so comfortable after all, Conchita wondered whether her mother had ever read Plato. Unlikely, but all that stuff about beauty as a higher reality and truth made her think of philosophy tutorials in Oxford, so very long ago it seemed, though only half a year away. It sounded very Platonic but could not be so. Certainly her mother evinced no philosophic calm with her lips curling angrily and her voice braying, "Of course I know that some people, especially foreigners, have attacked me because of my craving for beautiful objects and buildings like this fine Centre." With a disparaging laugh, in which some of the audience saw fit to join, she then expressed contempt for those who assailed her for her choice of dresses, shoes, jewellery and elaborate coiffure. "Unhappily those critics are bitter people with no aesthetic sense; people who do not understand, no are jealous of, the Carolino peoples' desire for beauty. I want the world to know that possessions do not matter to me in the least, but if I modestly succeed in expressing beauty, it is not out of vanity or desire to spend money but because I long to appear as the personification of my people. Delegates, it is my destiny to represent not merely what the people believe but what at heart they actually are—the children of beauty. In my person the Carolinos have found their true expression, as in them I have found love. The world must understand that everything acquired by me belongs to the people of this country. I want that wealth to make them fertile in mind and body so that they may blossom with many cultural flowers."

At this stage of the address Handel's *Water Music* was softly fed into the auditorium, providing a majestic background to the First Lady's concluding words that commended the Carolino way of life to all the countries in the United Nations and promised to make modest funds available for people from other countries to study her country—and of course the New Social Order of her heroic husband President Antonio Floresco.

As she watched and listened with disbelief Conchita's eyes filled with tears. She could not remember her mother talking such rot before. How had it come about? Despite her resentment, indeed her fear, in a deeper zone of her mind where there was no rational thought her love for this fearsome woman remained, though metamorphosed into something akin to pity. But before she could examine her inner conflict further, from somewhere in her entourage the First Lady had summoned a handsome young

41

pianist in evening dress, though it was only morning, to join her on the stage at the long Steinway piano against which she leaned languorously like a night club artiste. The pianist began with a series of sweeping arpeggios that everyone recognised as the opening to a Carolino love song which a much younger Griselda, née Honteveros, had sung publicly to woo her future husband when she was the national beauty queen and he an ambitious Army Officer. At once there was applause into which Madame Floresco's soprano voice soared with all the panache of a superannuated diva whose no longer precise tones wobbled horribly whenever it was needful to sustain a note.

"*O Toni, te deseo y solamente usted.*" Twice she repeated the refrain and each time the picked audience of bureaucrats and businessmen and their smart wives clapped and cheered." The TV cameras homed in on her head, thrown back dramatically and her eyes shut tight by a surfeit of emotion. 'My God,' thought Conchita, 'she believes that they really adore her.'

Long ago, or so it felt to Conchita, the Floresco family atmosphere had been one of warmth and real love. Her mother had been the centre of serene content, which, in memory at least, was seldom broken. Her father had done his duty, first in the Army and later in the National Assembly but he had always found time for his family, even as a Senator. In those days her mother had indeed been a dominating personality—how could a national beauty queen in the Carolines be otherwise—but then the happiness of her family had been her objective whereas now happiness was entirely bound up with the political position her husband had won and for which both of them must fight to maintain.

Yet even in those happier days, Conchita recalled, her mother had the capacity to ignore things that displeased her and to exaggerate trivial matters in her own favour; her own gifts to people would be overvalued, the gifts of others to herself denigrated. But hurtful though they were, those faults were small change compared to her mother's inability to admit the awfulness of the conditions in which so many of their countrymen lived. If the poverty of a squatter area were mentioned she would say that people could always work their way up and out as she had. True it was that her immediate family was not rich but her mother had been the concubine of a rich man of the Spanish noblesse. Even though their home on his hacienda was not inside his great mansion but in a pleasant garden house with a corrugated iron roof, internally it had every comfort. Yet in the First Lady's recollections, or maybe imagination, her early life was not pleasant at all; she would describe how she used to suffer from sleeplessness when tropical rain thundered down on that metal roof, often making her head ache terribly. Despite which Conchita never believed that her mother had much to complain about, though she never dared say so. On the contrary her mother had the good luck to be born with great beauty which was why Antonio Floresco, imbued with the Iberian machismo of most Carolinos for distinction as a conqueror of female loveliness, had married her. Yet even her present eminence could never make her disregard the sound of rain on a metal roof, for it reminded her with every noisy drop that once she had not lived in the great mansion with a mother who was its legal mistress.

Within the hour Conchita watched the silvery limousine proceeding to a less salubrious but still respectable part of Infanta, taking her mother to the old Spanish Casa Consistorial, the City Hall where her Women's Development Movement had its quarters. Another TV crew was on hand to greet her and record her every word. This time she spoke without pomposity but moved among the Directors and staff intimately with a concerned expression on her face so that they got the impression that their activities were really valued on high. When replying to questions from two elderly women with very lined faces, farmers' wives perhaps, who unlike the lady Directors were severely dressed, she leaned forward graciously to emphasise the rights of the poor to certain basic standards of life. They listened to her with bemused expressions. Conchita wondered whether they, like her, were wondering how the First Lady could talk as if they were ignorant fools? Everyone, except the First Lady it seemed, knew that conditions had so deteriorated in many parts of Infanta that the most basic requirements for a decent life no longer existed. Did she know the truth? Or had she just erased truth from her mind? How long had it been since she visited one of the squatter areas or an overcrowded tenement? When she left the DeoGracias she sped down broad boulevards cleared of traffic. Well bordered with trees and bushes, the horrors behind them were passed too quickly even to be glimpsed by the First Lady in her silvery, insulated chariot of darkness.

As the TV began a reprise of her mother's extravagant speech in the Conference Centre, Conchita switched off the sound again but that was not the end of the obscenity her mother was projecting. Dangling from her ears and around her neck diamonds of great value flashed in the lights that played on her. Couldn't the woman see that while the ostentation of wealth was just about acceptable, if on occasion vulgar, in a comfortable society, in a poor country it showed deplorable taste, and worse still could be politically disastrous. She switched off the set, shut her eyes and was once more in the lovely gardens of LMH near the River Cherwell, in a time of great happiness that was always there to refresh her. After all, wasn't the motto of the College, '*Souvent me Souviens*'? But 'often I remember' had another meaning for her now. Inevitably she was finding solace in thoughts of her love for Julio, conscious that in its glow the world had begun to look different again. Though she was twenty and quite attractive in the way of her countrywomen, she had never considered herself a beauty like her mother. Beauty was an unattainable quality way beyond her, undesirable because it brought both love and pain. Yet her first experience of physical love had been gentle, whether on account of the skill or the reticence of Julio she could not say. It had all happened as naturally as the slow opening of a flower without any declarations of passion, but as it unfolded quite unexpectedly she had realised with complete certainty that she needed Julio as her companion for life. The English part of her brain told her that he was Mr Darcy rather than Heathcliff but this accorded with her notion of love.

A sympathetic voice that now arose from this love began to insist that her mother was overtired, and overworked; that the pressures of state were too great for a woman who, though clever, lacked the education to make balanced judgments. If only she could have gone to Oxford, Conchita thought, though quickly disabusing herself of the idea for she could not see her flamboyant mother flourishing among the cultivated academics of Lady Margaret Hall. She then considered that maybe her mother was cut off from human affection, from the sort of love she now had. Yes, that could be it. Her parents were not together enough these days. She could not believe that if the two of them could spend a quiet evening together with her and Julio, they would find anything objectionable about him. A fantasy developed. There would be a new relationship. She and Julio would travel about the country and report to her parents how things actually were, in place of the rubbish fed to them by sycophantic officials. In time even her mother would understand the reasons for her disobedience. Conchita thereupon decided to plan her moves with her compliant lover.

Her system of contacting Julio was simple enough and never broken by the eavesdroppers of the Palace. A phone call was made to a well-known couturier, Artur D'Orsay, actually Hamish Bernstein from Sydney, requesting a fitting on a date when Julio would be called to the Infanta Hotel. There the boutique D'Orsay and other shops of quality were situated in an extremely luxurious establishment much frequented by the country's former Japanese and American imperial masters. The date she fixed was in two days' time, when the First Lady had another heavy schedule. Tonight and tomorrow she would see to it that both of them had time together in the Palace, where she vowed to be submissive and mild. Then, remembering her promised correspondence, she wrote seven short letters to friends in England and France, leaving the envelopes unsealed so that her mother could read them if she chose. An eighth, much longer, letter was sealed to be posted from outside the Palace when the opportunity arose. It was to her closest friend at Oxford, a glum faced but brilliant girl who had suffered not cruelty but indifference from her eternally busy aristocratic parents. Conchita found it easy to unburden herself to Brenda Thatcher, whose emotional comforter she had been for almost three years. The letter typed on her computer read:

Dear Brenners,

Should have written to you donkey's years ago. I'm sorry. Be sure I've not forgotten you. But knowing you, you've probably been thinking I'm a rat. Anyway what's with you? Have you got a job in the City as you threatened or are you just loafing about at home waiting for your stinking parents to turn up? I hope neither. Why don't you come here for a while? My mother, of whom more anon, says she'd love to meet you. Nor arf she would too. I'll take you all over the place and show you how we NATIVES live.

I expect a long letter from you V.V. soon, especially about people we both HATED; the moronic Charlene Windsock, the long limbed snob Peony Cameroon and that ghastly self-centred prude Georgia Browne. Please make me happy by telling me the last named was gang banged by syphilitic sex maniacs in Brixton.

But enough of this badinage; I have things to tell you about me. First, it's really happened. Just a few weeks ago and, as they say in the women's mags, I'm the happiest girl in the world. But seriously. His name is Julio Abulencia and naturally he's tall, dark and handsome. At least I think so. But it's not his looks that matter. He's interested in the things I like, though he's much better informed. Mainly though I suppose it's because he treats me as a rational human being, rather as you did. He also gives me a sense of perspective. What I mean is that without making me feel that I don't matter, he stops me from thinking that my own problems are all important. I guess it would be good to be married to him but in this country that would mean fifteen children before you could say Jack Nicolson, and that I'm not ready for.

I can hear you saying, then get married you silly bitch and always wear a Dutch Cap or words to that effect. But it ain't so easy. You know what my mother is like and she's become much more so. My father never wanted to take up permanent residence in this palace which is so over decorated with Lewis Cans reprods you wouldn't believe it. I feel out of place without a crinoline and a birdcage on my head. Truly Brenners, it's really vulgar but I wouldn't admit it to anyone but you. Also if you came here I wouldn't like you THINKING things and not saying them to my face.

My mother wanted to live here and the place has gone to her head. The pomp is ludicrous, like the kingly guards Nixon tried to put around the White House. I guess that if you Brits had been here it would at least have been a bit dignified—and STUFFY to boot. But it's no laughing matter; it's for real. My mother sees herself as a monarch which makes me, God knows what—a sort of Princess Royal without the nags. Unhappily too, and now I've come to it, Julio's family is anti-Floresco, by which I mean really hostile to my father's régime. With my mother it's something else too. The Abulencias are an old family of the sort my mother hates because she's convinced that they look down on her.

The rest of the letter was in Conchita's longhand as Brenda became the person to whom she exposed her inner feelings.

The fact is that I don't want to live here any more Brenners. I'll do my best to get things right with my mother but I don't think it will be possible. She's become a thing of steel. With dad, I just don't know. He was/is? such a kind man really and he'd be the perfect dad if he had not become a national leader, no Brenners, a dictator. A process of deification is going on. He's never photographed in the old natural way. Everywhere you see pictures of him with a weird faraway look in his eyes like a visionary glimpsing a marvelous remote future for our people, who presumably will then all think like him—or my mother. Oh God! Maybe he's only wearing a mask but people can become what the mask represents. If only I could get through to him on his own. The trouble is that as he gets older my mother gets stronger. She's ten years younger than him and I'm afraid that when he goes, she won't.

I feel trapped, Brenners. Completely trapped. Why did they send me to have your sort of education without the consequent freedom it brings—but in your case only if you decide to use it. Come out and help me if you can. I'm not happy and to tell you the truth I'm a bit frightened of what might happen

Your Loving Friend
Conchita.

She addressed the envelope, "The Horrible Brenda Thatcher", continuing an old joke, but tore it up to write on another, "Lady Brenda Thatcher, The Coach House, Landridge Gardens, London."

Towards the end of the afternoon she heard the roar of motorbikes and knew that her mother's cortège was returning. Having secreted Brenda's letter in a safe place she went down the stairs to the Puerta Cochera to greet her mother with the friendliest smile she could muster.

The bus jolted down the laterite mountain track, then snaked through sparse grassland on a road that gradually mutated from cobbled surface to tarmacadam, from very narrow to indeterminately wide. At length it joined a concrete feeder road traversing the farmland around Infanta until it debouched onto the super highway. Father Oliveros, thin faced and scraggy, was glad that the motion of the bus had become less bumpy for now he was able more comfortably to observe the endless undisciplined traffic streaming to and from the capital. The sight made him wonder whether he might have got it all wrong about conditions in the country. Many people were prospering; some must be doing very well. How else could here be so many cars, some of them expensive new models, and lorries laden with goods. But he had only to think of the poor of San Felipe and of Infanta to know that prosperity was an inconstant tide lapping around a vulnerable shore.

These days economics fascinated him more than theology. But the more he read of it the more he was baffled. It was supposed to be a science. So, given specific facts, the inductive method, the great achievement of the West, should produce identical conclusions. But the variety of conflicting conclusions reached by economists proved otherwise. Was there some factor that was never taken into account—a factor in the area of human personality that defied quantification? Might it even be the factor he was supposed to deal with as a priest? A factor he had overlooked?

Nothing was clear to him any more. Father Stephens had problems but they were of his own making or rather his weakness. Apart from agonising over whether to fuck with Salvador, always it seemed with an answer that resulted in his pleasure, he could get on with his parish duties. Of course young Stephens was well aware of the wrong doings of the poor but maybe they seemed on a par with his own lapses, easily confessed and easily shriven. However, people cannot confess the sickness, abuse and hunger underlying their sins in the expectation of a remedy as easy as absolution. Nor did they have the luck to be like Stephens, able to return to the well-heeled suburbs of Sydney where no doubt there were problems but none like those that gripped the poor in the Carolinas.

Who, Oliveros demanded, am I to judge if the poor sometimes lie, steal and fight to survive? What if some of them even kill the officials and bankers who oppress them? After all violence had often been condoned by the Church. Popes had gone to war, crusades betrayed the Cross and heretics were burned, all because the Church thought it expedient. Christianity was not a religion of non-violence. Christ had whipped usurers in the Temple. Unpleasantly violent for a small moneychanger with a family to provide for. He had also said 'Render unto Caesar the things that are Caesar's' but when Caesar took too much, what should people do? The problems of modern society were more complex than those of remote Caesar and a small town prophet. Economics did not seem to have the answers at all.

He longed for help. Instead of just leaving his brief case hoping it might be opened, he should have spoken to Stephens months ago. An Australian could look at the Carolinas situation, even at a revolutionary priest's problems, sympathetically yet dispassionately. Oliveros longed to return to San Felipe but then he recognised that the advice he had given about a trivial affair with an altar boy was of a different order to what he might be told about his own involvement with the communists. Salvador was of no interest to the state; the communists were. And so he let the stops slip by one by one until the bus reached the outskirts of Infanta.

Here again perplexity. He saw workshops, warehouses and crowded yards where monster trucks bore huge containers. All were providing jobs for people. What did it matter if the companies belonged to the rich or the state? Wealth would trickle down, as the government economists confidently predicted. If someone didn't think his share was fair, seize on every chance and rise to the top. "Set your eyes on California," the President had told them. "If we all work hard, we shall be as rich."

The bus was crawling along. Father Oliveros glanced ahead: a road block; police were ordering people out of cars for a body search, opening vehicles to look inside. There were few people on the bus, mostly men but also an old woman with two little children, one of them coughing and spluttering. Oliveros, whose ineffectual appearance was heightened by his wire rimmed spectacles, sank further into his corner seat. He had started to tremble, for under his cassock was a bundle of communist literature whose possession could mean long imprisonment or worse. The bus halted with a jerk and a sergeant came aboard shouting, "Everybody off." The men obeyed but the woman complained that one of the children was not well. The sergeant was on the point of repeating his order when he saw the Father bending a reproachful and rather saintly look on him. "Alright you can stay on," said the sergeant. "And you too, Father." Oliveros controlled his trembling but said "Thank you my son. God bless you." The other passengers returned quickly enough, grinning with relief, and the bus went on. Soon they were entering the built-up suburbs, until they turned onto Panares Boulevard. This ran adjacent to the sea, skirting the city centre, and commemorated in its extent the career of a noble writer and revolutionary patriot, Abelardo Panares, whose career, like the boulevard itself came, to an abrupt end in the Park of the People, where he was garroted by a Spanish executioner in 1903.

Would Panares, Oliveros wondered, as the bus drove rapidly along the boulevard, still believe that his almost single-handed efforts to endow the people with a national consciousness, a literature and appreciation of their own culture, had been worth it if he could see what bordered the route bearing his name? Facing the sea were several high rise hotels, some architecturally distinguished and all expensive, but flanking them were many more two storied love motels with up and over gates that allowed men wanting sex upstairs to drive in unnoticed, smart night clubs, sleazy strip joints, gay bars, discos blaring out western pop music and, for the most part nestling near the hotels like chicks around a hen, a variety of baths, Nordic saunas, Turkish hamams, Japanese onzen, staffed with well trained young girls and boys ready to do the customers' bidding. Not for nothing was Infanta called the sex capital of Asia. Along this road it was as though the Carolinos had set themselves the task of absorbing everything tacky in the American way of life—and succeeded triumphantly. Oliveros groaned so loudly that the old woman actually asked him if he was feeling well. He shook his head derisively not at her but at the music he heard, the pleasures he saw offered, and the aspiration of his countrymen to become smart in a culture devoid of meaning. The young were being maimed because a short life of glitter seemed preferable to drudgery on the land or the underemployed squalor of the city.

He turned away from the prospect of degradation and looked towards the west and the endless sea. The sun was setting in fiery confusion. The clouds were bloodstained, their red glow obscuring the horizon and staining the waves with a huge expanse of gore. 'Something is happening to me' was all Oliveros could think. I am cold and trembling yet my heart is burning. He gripped the seat on which he was sitting tightly, as in his mind's eye he saw Christ driving the usurers from the Temple. Their punishment was insufficient. How could Christ be so lenient? He, Oliveros, longed for a steel whip, a machine gun, a cache of hand grenades to purify Infanta and the Carolinas, to wipe out the American, Japanese, European and Arab tourists who swarmed along the boulevard of the national hero, battening on the flesh of his beautiful brothers and sisters. He longed to obliterate the pimps, the traffickers in flesh and drugs, but above all the rich Carolinos who owned these places in an orgy of slaughter. He would silence the moronic pop music, extinguish the neon lights, shatter the high hotels and cast everything into a furnace more terrible than the setting sun.

He was faint; his eyes were brimming with tears. He murmured, "Oh Christ forgive me. I should not judge like this. Thy will be—

No," he yelled and everyone on the bus turned towards him in alarm. "Are you alright Father?" asked the old woman with two children who were cowering against her. He mopped his face with his handkerchief and replied, "Yes. Yes. Thank you. I just remembered. I've forgotten something." He jumped up. They were approaching the bus stop he wanted, near a church where he knew someone was waiting for him. The bus halted. He turned round at the door and said to the passengers before he got off, "Bless you, my children. Forgive me. Bless you all." A minute later he had disappeared into the street throng.

The Church of the Apostles was large and gloomy. Only a few people were in it, kneeling in the half darkness of the side chapels where flickering candles made gentle pools of light. Father Oliveros went into one of them and sat in a pew from which he had a view of the nave. Not a man to be seen. He looked up at the Madonna over the altar. Her face was remarkably like the First Lady, even to that disdainful jaw. But devotions were not on his mind. Again his eyes searched the nave. Still no one he was looking for. His mind went back to Father Stephens. If he had opened the case and seen the literature what would he be thinking? What might he do? Oliveros felt uneasy. No. Stephens might admonish him, tell him he was acting unwisely but he would never report him to the authorities. Then he remembered seeing two communist suspects, only young peasants, in the San Felipe Police yard, just left in the sun as an example, beaten up, hog tied and still screaming with pain. He could not take it. Supposing Stephens was not everything he seemed. The Party had ordered: trust no one. The US had agents everywhere. Maybe Stephens had been infiltrated by the CIA to report on what was going on. Then, disoriented though Oliveros was, the idea seemed preposterous. Stephens loved his parishioners. His intemperate desire for Salvador expressed that love. In that moment Oliveros felt the very image of Salvador redressing his panic.

A shallow cough broke the silence. A tall white man, almost bald with sharp features was ambling up the nave toward the High Altar. From time to time he stared up at the pillars, the windows and the ceiling, though in the dim light little could be discerned. Maybe he was an amateur of church architecture. Such tourists often came to historic Infanta. Caution was important. The man's eyes swept over him and up to two angels kneeling either side of a sarcophagus. Then the man continued his walk, softly tapping his right leg with the magazine he was holding. That was the signal.

Oliveros got up slowly and walked along the aisle to stop before a low table covered with sacred literature. Picking up a pamphlet he saw a picture of a man and a woman gazing lovingly at each other below the even more rapturous face of the Virgin Mary. Between them was a sign entitled, 'The Sanctity of Catholic Marriage'. Several happy children, presumably their offspring, were pointing up at the words. The unknown visitor joined him, bent down and drew a black parcel from under the table. Holding it out he nodded at Father Oliveros who looked at him inquisitively. "I came in earlier," the man said softly. "Take it and go. I'll leave later." The Father took the parcel but at the same time thrust a small envelope into the man's hand before he walked out.

Max Bligh watched the priest make his way slowly from the church. The money and other contents would be safe with such a man, a contemptible little thing no one would dream of searching. But despite his confidence that all had gone well, Bligh lingered for a while in the church, still ostensibly the tourist. His training had been meticulous so he followed the rules and left nothing to chance. Before going out he knelt for a while before a side altar and opened the envelope. Inside he found the address, presumably where the priest was staying, of Radio Ecclesia House, which he knew to be the only media station not controlled by the régime's information department. How indiscreet of the priest to reveal his Infanta address when his contact had no need of it.

Since arriving in the country Bligh had become convinced that the push must be made soon. His encounters with the President had convinced him that the whole rotten edifice was in a state of crisis. Even the Government's own propaganda betrayed nervousness instead of the strident confidence that it needed. At the heart of the malaise was the President's advanced age. He might appear healthy but there were ominous symptoms, of which all his Ministers were aware. Only his prestige kept the system ticking over for the time being. But the time being had almost run out.

Everything told Max Bligh that at this stage he must be cool. But his commitment was too deep and long standing for that to be easy. His driving force was hatred for the system in his own country, a hatred nurtured at Harvard, somewhat cautiously as an Intern at the White House, and then in certain radical circles California where he had worked for an influential left wing film director. Hatred made him strive, hatred filled him with joy, hatred gave him zest when he moved in the company of the rich, the powerful and the corrupt, whose destruction he encompassed. Odd, he told himself, as he used his Ciceronian Latin to read the Church Latin on the funerary monuments around him, that his hatred should be in tenuous alliance with this religion, and maybe dangerous. Religion was supposed to be the opium of the masses and hence the ally of the system he detested. But here and in South America part of it, imbued with liberation theology, was becoming an agent of social change among the masses and it was to that part of the Church that he had committed himself most uneasily. When two motivations worked together for the same ends, each had to be careful not to play into the other's hands and so lose its own soul. His mind turned to the priest he had just met. No, there was little to be feared there. Priests could be made use of easily enough; the ones who had become revolutionaries must really be a muddle-headed lot. Five minutes had passed and the church was quiet. He lit a candle in the deserted chapel of some obviously not very popular Saint and said, "There you are old chap. You've got as much right to a bit of light as the others." Then he left the Church for a meeting with a member of the Abulencia family.

Conchita stepped out of her cream Mercedes to be greeted obsequiously by the Manager of the Infanta Hotel. Passers-by paused to stare at the President's daughter who was familiar from official portraits of a happy presidential family but otherwise scarcely known. Unaccompanied, she passed quickly through the great atrium but gave not a glance at its Iberian splendor, for she was anxious to get to the boutique where Julio Abulencia must be waiting. Artur D'Orsay, ever considerate of the needs of his more distinguished clientele, ushered them both into a private room reached by sliding back a deep glass-fronted section of the wall wherein a few of his more sumptuous dresses were exhibited. Conchita, who today displayed a radiance that made her almost beautiful, was quickly in her lover's arms and fell with him in amorous delight on the large four poster bed termed by D'Orsay his 'lit des victoires dégagées', since on it he would 'unconcernedly' promote the careers of the seemingly endless number of pretty girls all aspiring to be the top model of Infanta.

When their repeated pleasure was finally over, for neither of them wanted their brief encounters to be brief in the least, the almost frigid coldness of the air-conditioned room obliged them to snuggle together beneath an embroidered woollen coverlet. Julio still murmured words of endearment in Conchita's ear for he was an adept at expressing his passion in sentimental phrases that made Conchita wonder whether love such as theirs could ever have happened before or was likely to happen again. She felt herself basking in love and wanting this minuscule particle of time to expand to infinity, but soon the depressing reality of their situation intruded in full force into her content. After a deep sigh she said, "My mother has been told about us, Julio."

In fact the young man already knew one way or another, whether from spies or gossip he could hardly tell, so he observed dryly, "A difficult situation to live with—for both of you. Quarrels and accusations I suppose, with neither of you giving in. She's in one of her famous rages, isn't she? Can you cope with her?"

"To answer both questions, yes and again, yes." She spoke the words quite curtly as though answering a police enquiry.

His reply seemed just as cold "And I guess she's forbidden you to see me. We shouldn't be here really, should we?"

"Are you very frightened of her, Julio? Most people seem to be. Are you one of them? Are you saying I should obey her?" A spasm of fear passed through her. He seemed so indifferent after his passionate lovemaking that she remembered the jibe that the reputed charm of the Carolinos rested principally on the practised ease with which they could make love at the drop of a hat.

"How dare you ask such a thing? "Julio seized her, rather harshly she thought, but that must only be an expression of his passion. He gave her an admonitory kiss. "All the same, we have to think seriously about our position. Did she say anything about me—other than that I'm a degenerate member of the family Abulencia?"

Conchita wondered whether to tell of her mother's threat against him. She had tried to banish it from her mind but love and fear brought it back sharply. Apprehensively she turned towards him and felt his strong nakedness against her body. Drawing him as close as could be she blurted out, "She wouldn't dare to have anything done to you," thereby revealing the gist of some unknown peril.

He put his arm around her and reciprocated the tight embrace before lying back calmly, as if prepared for the worst on her account, then said, as if he were asking for nothing out of the way, "Will you marry me Connie?"

Conchita was silent, sat up and looked searchingly into Julio's eyes, allegedly the windows of the soul, but saw nothing to help her out, so she said, "If that's what you really want. Jesus, you didn't half spring it on me. Are you sure it's what you want, what with our families—Montague and Capulet and all that jazz? Well yes, I suppose so. I suppose it would make me happy." Then suddenly like a cloud burst they began to laugh aloud and cry; at least Conchita's tears flowed. The proposal and her acceptance had been so unromantic as to be funny. They held each other but only briefly, as being hilarious made kissing and hugging difficult.

"I suppose so. Suppose Conchita? An uncertain word. It sounds like a hesitating way of saying yes, or maybe, or possibly no. Shakespeare should have used it in Romeo and Juliet. 'O think'st thou we shall ever meet again? *I suppose so!* And all these woes shall serve as discourses in our time to come'. In which case I don't think there would have been a tragic ending, because everyone would have been calmly working out their moves very conditionally."

"Which might have been sensible, Julio. They could have talked it over with their folks, made a good deal over the dowry, got married and had six children. But stop showing off with quotations. It's just as serious here. Getting married is what people in love are expected to do, and to procreate like rabbits. But it doesn't make any difference to me really. I'd be just as happy living with you, only you, in New York or Moscow, married or unmarried but in Infanta it's not so easy."

"Madame U No Hu would never let the President's daughter and an Abulencia just live in sin together and we both know it. I'd be a hit and run target for a bullet each time I went out."

"Then we must get married, Julio," Conchita stated firmly, putting aside any notions of not behaving in accordance with the customs of the Carolinas. "There'll be trouble of course, but we'll just have to bear it. There's nothing they could do about it in the end, once we'd had a church wedding with the Bishop—the Cardinal too if you want, I'm sure. Everything would settle down, especially once I had a child."

Julio began to potter about the room lent them by Arthur D'Orsay, an experienced lecher if ever there was. It was more like a prostitute's boudoir than a man's bedroom, claustrophobic with flamboyant ceramics and pinkish mirrors that flattered wasting flesh, alright for making love since when in action one did not look at the wallpaper, but unsettling for Julio in his current situation. He could quite imagine the First Lady bursting in and denouncing him for leading her daughter astray and undermining the President's New Social Order. Yet he must stay calm. After all what, in his mind, the President's wife had just accused him of, was exactly what he had always intended to seduce, to marry and by degrees worm his way into the first family, with the aim of gaining influence and—then what? Fate probably had nothing spectacular in store for him. No, the problem facing him was more immediate than any unachievable ambition. In the process of seduction he had unexpectedly been seduced. How had it happened?

Conchita's features were pleasant rather than beautiful; but her body was lusciously curved and aroused him inordinately. It stirred him; he needed it; it was here on earth to satisfy him. He could no longer withdraw—even if it were wise to do so. Absurd and unexpected it might be, but he had fallen in love and now the happiness Conchita had brought him was counterbalanced by the misery of his deceit.

Moodily he saw that his plan could never have worked. The hatred of his family for the régime was too great. Once his father had admired Antonio Floresco, believing the President had to take emergency powers to clear up the country's crime and corruption. Initially crime had decreased but not the corruption; indeed official corruption had spawned a protected form of state criminality in which the police and the rich allied to milk the poor of their land and their rights and keep them in poverty at the bottom of the social ladder. Eduardo Abulencia had, before his death, finally concluded that the President's assumption of absolute power was a treasonable act for which impeachment was the remedy. Julio knew that his family, like his father, had reached a state of mind in which they would support any measures necessary to rid the country of the Floresco régime. It would take more than a family match to heal such a rift.

Reflected in a mirror he saw Conchita eyeing him carefully. What would she say if she knew he had been manipulating her for his own ends? Would it be best to confess everything to her with emphasis on the fact that he did love her or rather that what she was had made him love her? Yet how could she forgive him? A schemer once could be a schemer again. It was his nature. He must erase the weakness in his personality in secret, hoping Conchita never glimpsed the truth. He turned to face her. She must have seen his doleful expression. He hoped that her inexperienced eyes would not descry his guilt and shame but only the look of deep concern on her account.

"Sit with me," Conchita said. "Tell me what's going on in that handsome head of yours. I can't help unless you tell me. Perhaps you want to end this wonderful thing we have together. I'll understand if you do." He stood still and just stared at her, wishing that everything could be simple as it was between so many people he knew. Or as it seemed to be simple. Competing notions were pestering his mind. Had he been in the game for power or love or just sexual fun? What did he know of power and the way people acted when they were obsessed by desire for power? He admitted to wanting the good life; he was ready to intrigue and struggle to get it. But there were limitations to what he would do. To get to the top you had to be completely ruthless, as Conchita's parents must be. Though he had always felt that he could not be like them because the Abulencias were a civilised and cultured family, like a callow fool he had sailed into the choppy waters of their contentious life without considering the consequences. Now by a series of almost unnoticeable steps he had created bonds between himself and this impressionable young woman such that each felt a need for the other's existence to be alive. That simple fact was going to bring them into conflict with the head of state and his formidable wife, though such being the power, even the arrogance, of love that he was determined to stand up to them and to salvage what he could for a modicum of happiness. He joined Conchita, who had taken to lolling on the great bed. Softly he enfolded her in his arms. "What do you think we should do then," he asked, "where your mother is concerned? And what about the Pres—I mean your father? You told me that he really loves you; that he's always ready to listen to what you say."

Conchita turned and stroked his face like a sympathetic elder sister and noted the way the little curls of his sideburns gradually mutated into soft down upon his cheeks. She closed her eyes and drew in her breath at the sight of such unadulterated beauty. "I'm every bit as determined as my mother," she said, "but I don't have her power, do I?" She kissed him and then adopted a confident air as though she really knew what was best, "The first thing is not to panic," she said, though something akin to panic was wriggling in her brain.

"And the second thing is?"

"To meet my parents in an ordinary sort of way; to win them over; to see if we have anything in common. If they see us happy together they might accept us easily, or rather my mother might accept us more easily. I have a feeling that she's said nothing about us to my father."

"You sound hopeful. Maybe your mother thinks he'll be on our side. Alright then, when are you going to arrange it?" Julio looked at her admiringly thinking she certainly has a bit of her mother's vigour.

Conchita told him she would work something out. The conversation had not really helped her to clear her mind. Talking about things did not always make problems easier. Quite to the contrary, this problem now seemed more difficult. She had expected Julio to act with confidence but he had mooned about the room without giving her the lead she wanted, but which she had been obliged to take. Recalling her mother's veiled threat against him she suddenly felt that she did not know her mother at all. A mother's demeanour was always expected to be loving. But suppose the mien was merely a masque. What might lie behind a masque when ambition was frustrated? She remembered the TV shots of her mother at that United Nations seminar. What force must lie behind the dreadful spectacle the First Lady presented. She seemed impervious to all adverse domestic comment and dismissed as fabrications criticism of herself in the foreign press. Worst of all, she could unblushingly deny the drab economic facts of life under which so many of the people laboured. Was the Floresco régime so weak that it required constant repression to stop the pot from boiling over? If that were the case the First Lady could obviously convince herself that anything she did to control her daughter's life would be justifiable, even the removal of Julio. The more Conchita thought about her lover's position the more she was gripped by the icy hand of fear.

Julio had closed his eyes, his head was resting peacefully on her breast. She knew that, though he was older than her, he was more vulnerable. Of course he must have sought her out because she was the President's daughter. But how else could she have found a lover so easily? Most young men were turned off by the very thought of the DeoGracias Palace and all it stood for. She was like one of those daughters of the immensely rich who know that their money, rather than themselves, will always be the main ingredient and the main flaw in their lives. Yet even if that were so, whether his motivation was ambition or love, greed or desire, did not seem to be at issue. All that mattered was that she had him here at this moment, a beautiful flower that she could never have discovered on her own. The fear of losing him made her tense and tearful again; Julio at once recognised the change in her mood and knew that her tears were no longer joyful. His mood quickly reflected hers. It was as though their meeting had lost its magic, but neither of them could explain why it should be so. Perhaps they each recognised in one another's sadness the possibility of tragedy to come. They clung to each other desperately. "Make love to me, Julio. Make love to me again," Conchita whispered.

After their sad parting with its promises to meet again soon, she left the Infanta Hotel by a side entrance. The libidinous but kind Artur D'Orsay looked woebegone as he escorted her from the boutique, as though he sensed that all had not gone well. In the car her driver Laminato, smart in every way, and probably told to spy, asked where her new dresses were. Had she asked Senor D' Orsay to deliver them to the DeoGracias directly perhaps?

"Dresses? Dresses?" she questioned absentmindedly before remembering her alleged reason for coming here. "Er, no Laminato, I didn't like them. Much too showy. No I didn't take to them at all."

Laminato smiled at her sweetly in the mirror revealing perfect teeth and designing eyes. "Perhaps you should think of changing your dressmaker, Senorita Conchita. There are other experienced dressmakers in Infanta. Senor D'Orsay isn't the only man who knows how to satisfy the tastes of beautiful women."

She saw the impertinent look in Laminato's eyes. No, it was not her imagination. "Drive home," she ordered imperiously in a voice that sounded remarkably like the First Lady.

The First Lady glanced from time to time at the President, who was scanning foreign newspapers opposite her. They were alone together for the first time in several weeks and she was worried about his appearance. His face was a bit puffy, which made his small eyes smaller than usual, but he still walked straight and ate well. She was sure he was just showing the strain of office. Also public appearances took their toll; they might look easy but, as she knew, one could never relax on stage.

The First Lady did not look her usual sophisticated self. Her long hair fell down her back. She hadn't bothered to have herself made up heavily and she was dressed not in one of her form flattering dresses but in a long silk dressing gown. Lounging with her bare feet up on her chaise lounge she glanced occasionally at a copy of Vogue which lay on her lap, after which she closed her eyes apparently in profound thought.

Was this the moment to seize the opportunity and speak to Antonio about Conchita or should she let the evening pass in peace as they had agreed. But it was not like her to let someone else relax when she was not at ease. Sooner or latter she would betray her feelings, maybe with a look, a gesture, which her husband would at once take as a signal that all was not well.

A chuckle from the President made her glance at him. He was in good spirits; once he had rested he would look as healthy as ever and put paid to the rumours about his health constantly spread about by his opponents. Madame Floresco picked up Vogue again and concentrated on an article about the Queen of Thailand, who, she noted with satisfaction, appeared in a colour photograph wearing a broach given to her, so the blurb said, by the First Lady of the Carolines as a symbol of the amity between their two countries. But other pictures of the Thai Royals in different majestic settings in their Palace inevitably made her feel envious of their traditional status.

When Griselda declared that beauty was all-important to her, she was being genuine. When she saw a concert pianist pitting her entire virtuosity against a full orchestra with the audience fascinated by her facial expressions or bodily gestures that suggested the inner spirit motivating her performance, she longed to be such a cynosure of eyes herself. That was true prestige. In fact the country had benefited from her unfulfilled longing. A fine Cultural Centre and some theatres had been built, orchestras and a national ballet established and promising young performers sent to New York to Moscow, to any centre of artistic excellence where they could be trained properly. All these prestigious activities were acceptable to the President as they glorified his régime, kept the First Lady out of other more delicate political activities, and built up in her mind the image of herself as the patron of everything that was, or should be, good in the nation's life. The public was also given a hint of her inner image when the National Art Centre of the Carolines was designated the Diwanaraja Centre. Ordinary people knew that Diwanaraja had been the goddess of art and dancing before the Spaniards had arrived and had the temerity to impose Catholicism on their land. As she looked once more at the pictures of the Thai King and Queen, despite her Catholicism Madame Floresco could not help thinking how convenient it was to be a monarch who was semi-divine. It must be possible to have many domestic evenings together without worrying about threats outside the Palace walls.

The President put his newspaper down and took off his glasses. "Why can't they do eye transplants?" he said. "I read for a bit then the words go blurred."

"You read too much," the First Lady said, directing a concerned frown at her husband. "But you won't listen to me, you obstinate creature."

"I like reading. Why should I give up my principal pleasure?"

"You don't have to read all those rags. You have secretaries who can prepare summaries of the things that matter."

"How wrong you are. Secretaries only look for political items, economic items, boring items I know all about. It's the human reports that tell me what's really going on in life, the odd things, the unexpected things, and the mysterious things. I think they reveal an underlying pattern in existence."

"Well then, Antonio, why don't you get some of the secretaries to read anything you want aloud. Or sing them for you. Their voices might bring all sorts of mysterious tales to life. I think you really are a peasant at heart, a believer in magic and potions. Just tell me what human-interest stories have you found tonight?" Madame Floresco's voice was full of mockery, though she knew that she was more a believer in the spirit world than he was. "And what did they reveal about God's creation?"

The President picked up a copy of the Straits Times. "Well now would you believe this: Wednesday 2nd of July, Ipoh. Mr Wong Ah Fat suffered a grievous loss when he went to relieve himself in a mining pool yesterday. A turtle bit off his private parts when he was squatting in the water. Although Wong Ah Fat tried to catch the turtle it got clean away. Mr Wong is now in hospital in a state of shock. It's so ridiculous. It couldn't happen, but it's true." He held out the page for the First Lady to see, roaring with laughter as he did so.

"I don't want to see it. It's not so funny. I'm very sorry for Wong Ah Fat."

"Well, so am I. In fact I feel like telling the Minster of Finance to donate something to compensate poor Mr Wong for his loss. It could be put down to capital depreciation." The President's mirth redoubled.

Madame Floresco smiled at her husband. Though she knew that the turtle testicle story often appeared in Far Eastern newspapers when copy was short, she did not disillusion him but joined in his mirth. She loved to see him with his face lit up and to hear the sound of his laughter echoing round the room. She saw him once more, as the randy little man, a peasant despite his military rank, muscular and over-endowed for his size, whom she had married because she couldn't imagine being in love with anyone else, so, at least in her memory, uncompromising had her passion for him been. Briefly the thought of Conchita and her lover clouded her mind; if Julio Abulencia was as greedy for love as Antonio, Conchita would never give him up. How well the First Lady knew that love could be a wrecker of many a subtle scheme. She went over to her husband and knelt on the floor leaning over his lap and pushing the newspapers in a heap on the floor. He looked down at her and ran his fingers through her long lustrous hair. "Are you alright, honey?" he asked. "Is everything going fine?"

She took his hand and kissed it—several times, before returning to her chaise lounge. How lucky she had been in life. She might have been just another army officer's wife or the wife of a businessman (she could not envisage anything lower), but here she was living in a palace once occupied by Spanish grandees, married to a Head of State who was on familiar terms with the most powerful people in the world. And yet, despite the grandeur, they were alone in this room as close together as in the first days of their marriage. What was more she had something that was a rarity for most Caroline women, a husband who had remained faithful to her—well more or less. What he had just said to her about reading was true. He was at heart an intellectual, a scholar. Even if he had never become President he would have been a renowned professor, a philosopher. She heard him speak her name and smiled lovingly at him. "Thank you," he said, quite simply not about anything in particular but about everything. She believed that his thoughts were the mirror image of her own.

Since the evening looked as if it was going to be everything they, or at least the President, had expected, the First Lady decided that it was better to let sleeping lovers lie for a while and confined herself to wishing that the whole nation could see her now, a serene woman whose existence was based on love, in a setting of tranquil beauty. Unfortunately, just after ten o'clock, when they were thinking of going to bed, there was a knock at the door and a footman told them that there was an urgent message from Captain Manzano. Senora Floresco's face fell. There was no doubt what it would be, for the Captain had been given explicit instructions that if any reports came in about Conchita and Julio Abulencia, she was to be informed at once whatever the hour.

It was a misfortune that Manzano had been told to report in person and not on the phone, which the First Lady never trusted to be secure. Useless to leave the room; that would arose Antonio's curiosity. If the story must be out, best for it to come from the Colonel Considering Manzano was an intelligence officer, he did not behave very intelligently. Instead of giving his news straightaway, after which Mme Floresco could have dismissed him and sorted things out with her husband, he stood there gawking before saying, with a couple of facial twitches, "Ma'am, Mr President, about Senorita Conchita."

Immediately the President sat up and said, "What about her? There hasn't been an accident has there?" He remembered his daughter telling him that she sometimes drove herself across town to a concert or to see friends. Controlled for his family or not, he never trusted the traffic police in Infanta and still less the traffic.

"No, no. Nothing like that sir," replied Manzano turning towards the President even though he was supposed to be speaking to the First Lady. "I have to report that she met Julio Abulencia this afternoon in the boutique of Senor D'Orsay."

"Well?" the President demanded but only got a puzzled stare in reply. "Well. Where's the urgency. I thought she'd been blown up or something. The way you've come here at this time of night."

"You may go Captain," the First Lady said firmly.

The tactless Captain was mumbling something about the Senorita being there for over three hours, when "Go," the First Lady thundered which made him beetle off very quickly.

The President looked at his wife curiously. "What was that all about? So she goes about with young Abulencia. Everyone knows that. Why should it have to be reported to you, to me, to anyone?"

It was the First Lady's turn to look baffled. She sneered, "Julio Abulencia," then repeated the name "Abulencia" very loudly. "Doesn't that worry you? A boy from a family that's one hundred percent against us. You actually knew? And you didn't care?"

The President's face took on a wry expression. He said, "Of course old Abulencia is an enemy, alright. But he's no fool. And he's a gentleman of the old sort. He wouldn't use a trivial report of our children going out together to embarrass me. Anyway who else would care? Conchita's bound to meet a few boys before she settles down and marries. You did I seem to remember. Why shouldn't she have the same rights?"

Senora Floresco arose from her chaise lounge, walked around and sat on it again, heavily. She did not look very graceful. Her face had taken on the sort of pout that signalled the advent of a bad temper. Then she addressed him as though he were an idiot child. "They are in love, Antonio. In love. L-O-V-E."

The President found this somewhat amusing. At the same time he did respect his wife's judgment. He was not entirely unconcerned about his daughter for he admitted that he had not spoken to her much over the past few weeks. Perhaps there was some other reason for concern that his wife had not mentioned. He joined her uncomfortably on her chaise lounge. "Young people easily imagine they're in love when it's just infatuation or a bit of fun—maybe to make others jealous. Come on Griselda; remember how you behaved when you were young. We don't need to take it seriously."

"It is serious. It isn't just dating like a couple of adolescents. It's an affair, Antonio; they're sleeping together. I hope they're taking care. I don't want her to tell us one morning over breakfast that we're going to be grandparents."

It was that notion that shook the President out of his complacency. It was not the thought of his daughter marrying an Abulencia that bothered him. It was the thought of her marrying at all—just yet. He had been promising himself for some time that he would spend more time with her. Perhaps take her with him when he went abroad on an official visit. Her involvement with Abulencia could scupper that idea. Yet he was not angry with her. He had seen too much, especially of suffering, during the war to expect people to do as their parents told them. He rarely did. Young people making love was a way of coping with stress as well as of achieving transitory happiness in a nasty world. It wasn't just a product of these more permissive times. It was a sort of constant. He wondered why his wife had ever agreed to send their daughter to a place like England, where, he was told, social controls had evaporated, if she had been so concerned over such matters?

His wife had taken to walking dramatically about the room, her face tense, her dressing gown sweeping after her like a long cloak and swishing when she abruptly changed direction. It made him think of his favourite actress, Bette Davis, in *The Little Foxes*. He closed his eyes and felt that one half of the room had vanished. They were on stage and a thousand eyes were on them in the darkness. Without doubt Griselda was about to break into a great speech. Would he have the right lines to answer her? It almost happened as he imagined.

"What is the point of us living here—in this great palace?" She gestured about her imperiously. "Do you think we are ordinary people? What is the point of all your work, your ambitions for the country and its people, if your achievements fall into the hands of your enemies? I want to know, Antonio." The question was rhetorical but all the same she waited for an answer. "I am a simple woman but I can recognise greatness just as I can recognise beauty. The two are the same in many ways. I now live in the shadow of your greatness and I would have it in no other way. You and I will not last forever but your work will live on if there is a family bearing your name, with the desire to ensure your greatness will survive. That is why I want our children to marry well and by that I don't just mean into rich families. I intend them to marry people of intelligence, who understand what you have achieved and so will devote themselves to preserving your legacy. If we were peasants or Chinese shopkeepers I wouldn't care who they married provided they were happy. But we are not ordinary people any more. It is you, Antonio, who has made us not ordinary. And so the responsibility for our future rests on your shoulders. Now understand this: I shall protect your legacy if you are too tired to do it yourself."

She fell silent, her speech ending with a strange little gasp. Her face reddened, for she had uttered the thought of which they were both aware and yet had kept secret; that the President was ageing, was ailing and, with the best doctors and will in the world, was unlikely to last much longer, whilst she, his wife, had ambitions beyond those inherent in the President's temporal existence. However the words were dressed up in terms of legacy and achievements, they could not disguise the reality of human mortality.

He got up and walked about quite aimlessly until he caught sight of himself in a long gold framed mirror, of the kind his wife used for a final check that she was perfection before she launched herself in the public eye. Certainly he looked small, older, less full of zest than his wife did and he sympathised with her position. Indeed he really agreed with everything she had said, which did not prevent him from feeling a surge of destructive anger welling up in his brain. Every great man understood what Louis XV had meant by 'après moi le déluge'. It was not a prediction; it was a hope. It meant I don't care a damn. I don't care if the deluge is long, terrible and as destructive as hell because the worse it is the more people will remember me, regret my absence, think of me with nostalgia and wish me alive once more. He imagined the envy the dead might feel for the living, though in truth he had long shed belief in the afterlife. Yet as he looked at his wife he was filled with the most extraordinary pity, a pity he had never felt even for the innocent victims he had expunged from the state. This woman really did love him. He knew she would cast herself into the flames for him if it were necessary. If by some magic they could exchange their ages she would give him her surplus years. Why shouldn't she have ambitions of her own and why shouldn't she forward them as much as she could whilst he still lived. "Come," he said, "Let's sit together on that big settee where there's room for both of us. Let's just talk about you and me and the old days. I'm glad you've said what you think."

The First Lady was suddenly transformed from being the grand melodramatic figure of a few minutes earlier into his dear Griselda Floresco. Underneath the growing fleshiness of her years he could still discern the radiant beauty, Miss Carolina, he had wooed and won, though without much difficulty, half a lifetime ago. She wept a little, crying despondently that she wanted their life together to go on and on forever. She was distraught by her own revelation and it required all the powers of persuasion the President could muster to calm her down. But her love for him, her ambition and her determination to have her own way, were so fused together that her feelings could only be assuaged by some sort of surrender on his part. "Don't worry," he said. "When I go you won't be pushed out in the cold. Our family will still be here in this Palace. Yes, I have been making plans but we must walk carefully."

"And Conchita?" she asked, not forgetting the immediate object of her concern.

"I will speak to her. No, we will speak to her. But remember, she is your daughter as well as mine. She's bound to be determined. We must act diplomatically."

They went to bed and made love together for the first time in many weeks. The President soon fell asleep but the First Lady lay awake thinking not of Conchita but of the remarkable life she had lived with this tired man who lay so still beside her that he seemed as though dead. But her life was far from over. This evening, she was sure, the period of her ascendancy had begun.

Father Stevens woke with a start and shivered. It was very cold. He looked at his watch and saw it was after midnight. His dreams were still vivid, but if he did not think about them they would quickly fall into oblivion, never to be recovered. Why was the mind so cagey about what it had dreamt? And why, despite that, was there always a little window left open just for a moment, when you woke up and the brain's defences were down? Yes, it was the dream he always had when he was particularly worried. Or to be precise the same setting for the dream. He had been back in the Seminary of St John the Divine, first built well outside Sydney but now quite engulfed by expensive houses whose materialistic, nay hedonistic owners seemed like a besieging army around a place devoted to simplicity.

He had never been happy at the Seminary. At a time when most Australian boys were, outside their studies, occupied in sports and more intimate physical pleasures, he and his classmates had been wrestling with the demands made on them by a celibate Catholic routine, the existential problems of which were far from clarified by the tortured behavior of some of their priestly instructors. His dream had been about one of those uptight men, Father O'Malley, who had committed suicide.

He sat up and cupped his face in his hands. After so many years his grief was still raw, especially in the loneliness of a silent night. Unlike himself, Father O'Malley had been born with a complete conviction of sin as an absolute force. He was a real Catholic, which Father Stephens was not. "My God, why did I say it, why did I say it?" he asked aloud, closing his eyes, desiring to be back in that dream again. But now his brain was no longer host to a dream, but burning with the memory of dreadful reality.

He would never have entered the Seminary at all had it not been for his parents. He had not been born with a spiritual nature that responded to the call of the Church, but he had been imbued by his father with a feeling of intense responsibility to the will of his parents who had reared him for the priesthood almost from the moment when the doctor who delivered him had announced his sex, a responsibility that had stopped him from walking away from St John the Divine before it was too late. How could he have imagined that Father O'Malley, who gave such brilliant lectures on biology, who made little jokes about Mendel being the first to subject the struggle between God and the Devil to quantitative analysis, could really have believed that to sleep with a prostitute was a dreadful sin? He remembered that balmy afternoon when he and O'Malley had been lying in the grassy quad joking and talking and he had pooh-poohed his teacher's doubts over whether either of them, susceptible to lust as they were, was a fit person to be a priest with something as facetious as Wilde's 'the only way to get rid of temptation is to give into it'. Never had he imagined that O'Malley would do precisely that in a King's Cross brothel, a drug ridden place, on the very day it was subjected to a well publicised raid by the Sydney vice squad. It was no good telling himself that Father O'Malley would in any case have committed suicide sooner or later because of his irreconcilable inner conflicts. He was sure it was his own superficial advice, light as the hypothetical butterfly's wings, that had chaotically precipitated his friend's tragedy. Just now he had yet again had the dream of that happy afternoon, but despite its prescient awareness of O'Malley's death, he had awakened laughing unaccountably as at a joke. How foolish to take a road when no one knew where it led. Now another priest had confided in him, if in an indirect way. He was afraid of giving advice to Father Oliveros in case something as awful as O'Malley's death resulted from an unsound phrase slipping from his tongue.

Bed was no place to be alone with thoughts like these. He wished Salvador was with him, even asleep so he might lie close to those tempting lips and inhale the soft breath of the boy who had enslaved him. But Salvador had said that tonight he had to go to the house of his future parents-in-law for a family celebration. Not wanting to indulge in thoughts either miserable or lustful but in either case unfruitful, Father Stephens threw a blanket over his shoulders and went onto the verandah to enjoy a pipe of Balkan Sobranie, the only physical link he retained with his father, who had given him his last tin of the precious brand when he left home—a sure sign of paternal devotion. He filled his pipe at the end of the verandah, for there he could enjoy the far off lights of Infanta glittering so profligately that they threw a glow on the clouds that drifted above the fabled capital, though not over San Felipe where the sky was clear. When he had filled the pipe he realised that he had forgotten his matches, but as he went to get them his eyes made out in the starlight something sinuous moving slowly across the field that lay below. He stared hard. It was a group of men moving single file. There was no need to stare any more. He had guessed already. The men were carrying rifles and since their clothes were not military uniforms, but dark or peasant black, they must be guerrillas of the Communist Liberation Movement.

Later Father Stephens reflected that, if the matches had been in his hand, he would not have walked along the verandah and seen the guerrillas and the whole course of events that followed might never have taken place, though this merely reinforced his view that divine intent or purpose were chimeras invented by theologians. Events in life resulted from little accidents that could divert the flow of things willy–nilly, this way or that. But at this particular moment he could only admit that, whether he willed it or not, his knowledge involved him in a specific situation. Even to fail to report what he had seen to the police would imply that he accepted the justice of the guerrillas' cause. He would thus for the first time align himself automatically with the likes of Oliveros.

Again he reflected that this thought was a lie. He had already faced the identical problem in his imagination. When his parishioners were talking he often picked up words and sentences which he pretended not to understand. But no genius was needed to guess what was meant by 'The jungle people' or 'The people inside' or just the word 'They', said with a certain emphasis. Some time ago he had decided that, if he heard or saw anything like this, he would do nothing, which implied a vague sort of commitment.

Now, however, the event was taking place right before his eyes. The snake had continued its wary progress until it vanished into the secrecy of some trees. He was a party to its disappearance but his secret knowledge would not be the secrecy of the confessional, where he was an intermediary listening and granting absolution on behalf of the Deity. In this case the act had, as it were, been committed by him. Did that imply some sort of moral guilt? If he remained silent what further steps might he take for Oliveros, who would then, in an unaccustomed way, become his confessor again?

Hopelessly unsure of what to do next, he started to devise some sort of balanced neutrality in which, as parish priest, he would do his best to preserve polite relations with the police and others in authority whilst giving to his parishioners a general impression of sympathy for those struggling for social justice, without referring explicitly to the 'jungle people'. It would be difficult, if not impossible. But his mental wrestling was brought to a full stop by the voice of Salvador calling him urgently from somewhere in the darkness. "Father Stephens, Frank, it's me, Salvador. I see you are awake?" The next minute Salvador had climbed onto the verandah. His appearance gave his lover a greater shock than the file of guerrillas had done. Salvador, usually so trim and clean, was roughly dressed, his face grim and blackened and he carried an armelite rifle.

"You! A guerrilla. You Salvador. I don't believe it."

Salvador looked solidly at Stephens who for the first time saw the boy as someone other than his epitome of innocent sensuality, his golden skinned Ganymede with whom he had made love and loved in every way possible. This unknown person was bereft of magic. The usually serene face was rock hard and if beautiful suggested cruelty, even extreme cruelty. For the first time Father Stephens saw Salvador as a commonplace man. It seemed impossible that he could ever address him as a lover.

Yet unexpectedly that was how Salvador addressed him. "Frank, dearest Frank," he said sweetly. "Francis, you've got to help me. I wouldn't have come here at all but when I saw you looking at us, I decided to take the risk. Please help me, dearest Frank."

"Help you? But you're a.... Do you realise what you're asking me to do?"

"I do. I do, Frank. Listen. One of our men. He's not from San Felipe. He's from the jungle. He's injured. There's no danger for you. We just want a place for him to hide. He's outside, under the trees. When the police make house searches they never search our house. I promise that my friends down there will keep away from our house too. There'll be no risk."

Father Stephens took a sliver of comfort from the words 'our house', as if it was tacitly underwriting an ongoing warranty for a product: the boy is in full working order and fit for purpose. But for how long, Stephens wondered. He said harshly. "Yes, I saw them alright. They should move more carefully and keep out of sight."

Salvador quickly interpreted the priest's words in terms of guerrilla training and so of his lover's approval. "You're right. We're not properly trained yet. Most of us are San Felipe boys like me. We only operate when we're told that there's something for us to do." Salvador's lack of training was apparent from his blabbing.

"And what precisely was to be done tonight, Salvador? Do tell me."

The guerrilla became the altar boy again, his head falling coyly to one side and wearing a devout expression like an angel in an icon. "Just training, Father. Nothing to worry about. A waste of time really. I don't want to involve you."

The *non sequitors* made Father Stephens suspicious, but one never got much from a Carolino by exerting pressure. Mildly he asked, "Yes, I know that but tell me, what if I say 'no'?"

Salvador looked for an instant as though he could not make up his mind. Should he play hard, or compliant. A look of bewilderment spread over his face. Tears appeared in his eyes. "But I thought we were—I thought that you loved me."

For the first time Francis Stephens regretted the unguarded words he had used several times during the ecstasy of holding this perfect creature in his arms. To what foolishness had those lips impelled his own tongue. "I'd do anything for you, Salvador. If you're in any kind of trouble, anything at all, just come to me. You can rely on me." His total obsession had made him sign an open cheque and now Salvador was entering the figures. There was no exit clause. It had to be honoured. "You can bring him in," he said curtly.

"I'll stay with you when I've hidden my gun," Salvador said, mauling Stephens' hand.

"I don't want a reward, Salvador."

Salvador gave a reproachful look and said, "It won't be as a reward. It never is," and disappeared over the verandah into the darkness.

Waiting for whoever it was to be brought into the house, Stephens thought up some coverage for the Australian press. 'Sydney Priest turns revolutionary. Father Francis Stephens, son of Mr and Mrs Kevin Stephens of Cambeltown, arrested last week for joining the Caroline Communist Party and assisting its military wing'. But before he could go on to imagine a press interview with his incredulous pre-Vatican II parents, four men, two of whom he recognised as locals, carried a fifth into the house. Salvador hovered at the doorway onto the verandah, his gun at the ready. Stephens saw that the other two bearers wore bottle green battle dress, as did the injured man whose leg was bandaged. He ordered them to carry the man into the room he used for diocesan visitors, in fact on one occasion for Cardinal Peccata himself, and told them to lay him on the bed. "What's wrong with his leg?" he then asked.

"A bullet wound. In his thigh." The reply came from one of the men in battle dress. Stephens realised that this was his first exchange with one of the jungle people. The man went on coolly, "He's alright now. The bullet's out."

"Who took it out?"

The man chuckled nervously. "I did, Father. Who else?"

"Are you a doctor?

"No, but I'm smart with a knife. But he didn't like the pain. Give him some aspirin and change the dressing."

Without more ado the guerrillas made off, leaving the priest with his patient. He moved closer and looked into the man's face. He was about thirty, thin bearded and tough looking. His eyes were closed and he was groaning continuously. It was not clear whether he was fully conscious or not. Father Stephens leant over him and was aware of the stench of his body. He knew that medical attention was needed, but that would mean taking some one else into his confidence. The only doctor near to San Felipe was Dr Philip Chan, a friend of the rich Bersaminas, the affluent in general, and the police; certainly no man of the people. It was said he had once smashed to the ground a bottle of medicine a poor woman could not pay for, rather than let it go for the few pesos she offered. The only thing to do was to change the bandaging and clean up the wound himself. Fortunately he could do this properly, for a country priest was given some medical training and a supply of basic medicines. He removed the man's clothes, which were foul with blood, shit and vomit, attended to the wound and then covered him with two blankets to keep him warm. The filthy battle dress he put in a plastic bag and hid it away from the house where Lourdes would not find it. Then, after considering the depth of the wound in the man's thigh, he gave him a penicillin injection, hoping it would prevent infection. As the hypodermic needle entered his flesh the man burbled incoherently. The work done, Stephens poured himself a stiff whisky and waited at the patient's side.

He knew why he was now in a better frame of mind. By nature he was an optimist who believed in taking action to improve the world, and during the last hour he had improved it. The wounded man was now clean and comfortable; he had stopped groaning and no longer looked a hopeless case. Father Stephens believed in his heart of hearts—that is in the place in which belief is not susceptible to coherent expression because there is no need for it— that if everyone in the world could clear up the mess in his own vicinity, the problems besetting mankind would quickly diminish. His viewpoint was more positive than Voltaire's resigned advice that a man should just cultivate his garden. It was an assertion of what Stephens believed to be the essential teaching of his faith, love of ones neighbour. No theological treating of good and evil, no need to be saved from original sin by human sacrifice and resurrection, no need for fairy tales about virgin birth and miracles could hold a candle to acceptance by men of their duty to their neighbours. Such unquestioning love was the best answer to mankind's problems.

Gradually he convinced himself that his position was not so dangerous. Surely, if his actions were found out, the government must realise that to succour the wounded was his paramount duty as a priest. He also took satisfaction in the thought that the guerrillas knew that his heart was with the people; otherwise they would never have sought him out in the middle of the night, but maybe he forgot Salvador's special role in this process. He reinforced his optimism by drinking quite a few pegs of whiskey and even thought of giving one to the wounded man, who, however, was now sleeping like an innocent and could be left to recover. Some time before sunrise Salvador came back, transformed from guerrilla fighter into his true self, the reservoir of his love overflowing with unusual torrents of lascivious caresses and kisses, after which Father Stephens felt that his own cup of joy was truly running over. But when he awoke and saw the sun high in the heavens the euphoria was gone and reality began to press on him once more.

Reality took the form of Lourdes, who bustled into his bedroom with tea and fruit but with nothing for Salvador. She did not stop to receive her morning blessing and Stephens knew at once that something was seriously amiss. For the last few days she had been staying overnight with a sick relative in San Felipe, which meant that she had to walk through town to get to work. On the way she was stopped and questioned by soldiers and searched like others walking along the road. She was not told why, which had angered her, but the townsfolk told her that something really bad had happened on the Bersamina hacienda. If she'd not had trouble enough, when she arrived at the priest's house she heard someone being sick in the bathroom and discovered the wounded man. Her face remained expressionless but her eyes showed her employer that she was busy making connections. What an idiot I am, thought Stephens, not to have probed Salvador for facts, but he knew full well why he had not done so. Reality could be so unpleasant that it was better left on the back burner. As usual he had preferred to let the edges remain blurred to obviate the need to commit himself further. Back in the bedroom Salvador tried to pull him down to play again but unconvincingly, for the wily boy knew that what was wanted of him urgently was not love but information.

Father Stephens did not push him away but held him close and said, "You've involved me in all this. I promised to give shelter to that man. Now let me know what you've let me in for."

Salvador must have been doing some hard thinking, for he said in a straightforward way, somewhat untypical of a Carolino, "Last night we carried out an ambush near the Bersamina mansion. We knew that Senorita Bersamina was at home but not her husband. We killed a member of her family, the estate manager who had co-operated closely with the police. He'd cut the wages of some farmers who'd opposed his treatment of the labourers. He accused them of being liberation fighters. He enjoyed watching the police torture them in gaol. Two died because of him. And there have been other victims. He was a murderer."

Father Stephens recalled that he and Oliveros had been thinking of approaching the Bersamina estate manager on behalf of the workers. It was water under the bridge now. He asked weakly, "So you—your people murdered him?"

"No we didn't. We had a meeting—no, a trial—without him. We sentenced him to death." Salvador drew Stephens down to him so that their faces were only inches apart. "Government courts condemn men to death like that. Government goons kill farmers and workers. Why shouldn't they fight back?"

"Did you kill him? I mean you personally." But before he received an answer Stephens tried to pull away from Salvador who took to gripping him tightly. "No, no. I can't be in your arms and talk like this about murder. It's..."

"It's what Frank? Wrong? Sinful? Shameful? What Frank? Is it wrong for you and me to fuck together? No. We're not ashamed of it because it's good. Is it wrong for me to kill a monster? No. I'm not ashamed of it because it's good. Why can't we talk about both things in one another's arms? Both are true and good. It's just how things are. But perhaps you're afraid of other men's truths, Father Stephens."

"You did kill him then," Stephens murmured giving up the effort to free himself from Salvador's hold.

"What difference does it make? I fired like the others. It might have been my bullet. We ambushed him in his car. It burst into flames. We saw him roasting and heard him screaming like a fiend and we laughed. If you had been there you would have joined in."

Father Stephens ignored Salvador's assertion fearfully. Might it be true? He asked, "And that wounded man. Was he there? How, why was he shot? If you were the ones with the guns?"

"Don't worry Frank. We don't shoot people on our side. Our comrade was hit by soldiers days ago in the hills. The jungle people looked after him but they haven't got medical supplies. So they brought him to us."

Now they both lay on their backs staring up at the fan rotating indifferently like a remote galaxy under the mould-speckled ceiling. Father Stephens felt that he had entered a new dispensation in which the abnormal must be discussed as a matter of course. Very flatly, he said, "It wasn't a good time to carry out an ambush—with a wounded man on your hands. Why didn't you wait?"

Salvador turned on this side and again looked intently into Father Stephens' eyes. "We couldn't. We had information that the bastard was on his way from Infanta. We had to take action quickly. You can't think of personal convenience in war."

"In war," Father Stephens repeated more to himself than to Salvador, who had clearly faced up to all the realities about him. A war was going on and he, the parish priest had refused to see it because people came to church, sent their children to school, paid taxes and treated him with respect. Outwardly everything was normal but where did the people's loyalty lie? Stories about his grandmother's family in Ireland in the old days stirred in his mind. It had been just as it was here. Many priests must have found themselves in his position. But surely their role in the confessional was arrogant, asking people what they had done and why. In dangerous times men were impelled to act as they did by the circumstances raging around them. Who was he to grant absolution to others? To escape from the dilemma he said, "What about Lourdes? She's seen your comrade."

"None of the people round here will say a word." Salvador paused. "It's more than they dare."

Father Stephens went to see the guerrilla, who was now conscious and looked at him distrustfully, refusing to reply even to a question on how he felt. Salvador came in and said that the priest was to be trusted, though this did not help the man to say a word, and Lourdes brought some food, making it clear that, guerrilla or not, he was going to do as she said and eat. Salvador then went off to feed his pigs and Father Stephens began to feel superfluous hanging around at home.

But hanging around did not suit his nature. When he wasn't doing something useful negative thoughts assailed him. This time Salvador's words about the people's fears struck home. Both sides cowed the people. Ireland came back again: tarring and feathering, beatings, knee capping and murder. The communists looked better to him just now because they were opposed to the tyrannical government, but what would they be like if they had full control of the people? He was not in the same position as his parishioners. Was the Church right to send an expatriate priest here where he floated above the people like a ministering angel without participating in their terrors.

He decided to walk to San Felipe on his usual rounds. It might look suspicious if he did not, assuming anyone was in the least interested in what he did at present. He had hardly set foot out of the house when, for the second time in twenty four hours, he saw something unusual: Father Oliveros who never came to San Felipe other than by bus, was walking across the field but doing his best to keep to the shelter of the trees. Stephens returned to the house to await his arrival.

Father Oliveros was hot and sweaty; so sweaty that his glasses kept on slipping down his nose, making him look more bewildered and pathetic than usual. Stephens could not believe he was a person the guerrillas could trust to keep secrets. But once again he had the feeling of being superfluous when Salvador turned up and, addressing only Oliveros, said, "We struck camp. You looked for us over there, eh? Well, Enrico is here—in the guestroom. He'll tell you what to do." Father Stephens felt he had at least the right to go to the room with Oliveros, who was greeted by the said Enrico, evidently someone of importance, with, "Have you got it?"

Father Oliveros held up a leather bag he was carrying. "It's all here. Quite safe. God, I'm glad I found you." He turned to Stephens and said, "I was sure you must be with us."

Enrico had no time for small talk or expressions of gratitude. "Ill be off as soon as I can. But it's too hot around here to carry that stuff with me. I'll leave it here." He frowned at Stephens and said, "You must have a safe place for it?"

Now was the time to show a bit of independence, so Father Stephens said, "Only if I'm told what it is. The safe is Church property." At once he thought how daft. He could have said 'No'. But it was too late. Enrico sneered, or so it seemed to Stephens. "You needn't worry. It's nothing explosive. Just money. No one would think it unusual to find money in a Church safe."

Father Stephens still wanted to play for time. Whether the others liked it or not he asked Oliveros directly, "Did you know there's been an ambush on the Bersamina hacienda?"

Father Oliveros looked not at Enrico but at Salvador and asked, "Ramon Bersamina?"

"Yes," said Salvador. "We got him at last."

Father Oliveros crossed himself and said, "Thank God for that. God rest his soul wherever it is." The news disturbed him not a jot.

Salvador, sensing that Stephens had grown resistant to Enrico, put on his appealing voice and said, "Even Father Oliveros would be searched today. He can't take the bag with him. You must help him, Frank. Just look after the money for a few days."

The pressure was all around him but Father Stephens still wanted some way of justifying what he was about to do. He asked, "What's the money for?"

"To help the people, to help the sick and the poor," Salvador said firmly at the same time gesturing to Oliveros that he should hand the bag over to Stephens.

"To help the people," said Father Stephens, weakly pushing to the back of his mind what form that help might take. "Alright then. Just for a few days."

As he saw Oliveros off, this time on the road to the bus stop, Father Stephens gave him the case he had left on his last visit. "I did take a look at some of your pamphlets, Father."

Father Oliveros smiled with gratitude. "What a way of trying to win you over. You must think me a fool. I felt in my heart that you were already with us though. In fact I was sure of it. We must pray to God for help in these troubled times. They," he gestured toward the guest room, "mightn't think prayer matters. But it does. Pray to God for strength, Father Stephens."

Father Stephens looked down at the little trusting man, doubting whether God would think any more of their prayers than the communists. "Yes. I certainly shall. Go in peace, Father Oliveros."

The Abulencias were rich, but not wealthy in comparison with the great Caroline aristocratic families that all but owned the country. Rather it was characterised by talent, nurtured by a tradition of scholarship reflected in a fine library, a remarkable collection of musical instruments and even, though little used now, an observatory on the roof of a spacious old villa on the outskirts of Infanta. Over the past two centuries the family had produced a number of writers, mainly on academic subjects, and an astronomer who had achieved immortality by having the asteroid he had discovered named after him. However, having never produced a man of genius, the star of the Abulencia family remained for the present below the horizon. Despite this, with its claim to be as old as the year of the Spanish conquest and forming an essential part of the Caroline heritage, it had a sense of destiny, though its genius perhaps lay in waiting until the nation had need of it.

Naturally the Abulencias thought little of the parvenus who occupied the DeoGracias. Indeed they had respected no one who had occupied the Palace since the departure of the last Spanish Viceroy. Not unnaturally the members of the family espoused all causes hostile to the President and his First Lady. They represented themselves as one of the country's hopes when democracy was restored and made a point of never attending any of the great national occasions graced by the Florescos. On the other hand they extended their patronage to any cultural activity which did not have the backing of government. Unfortunately, as the First Lady, the grand patron of culture, gradually extended her patronage in all directions, that of the Abulencias was gradually reduced to events

81

of a less popular nature—chamber concerts in uncomfortable halls and exhibitions of art by uncompromising artists. The sad truth was that, despite their pretensions, the Abulencias were starting to feel that their star had somehow or other disappeared from its orbit. And so, almost out of desperation, the head of the family, Cesar Abulencia, had started to ride his favourite hobbyhorse, that of revolution, which few in history have ever mounted with certainty of success.

Cesar Abulencias was in fact the very epitome of everything that had earlier led to the collapse of the American style Caroline democracy. He would intrigue, plot, split political hairs, and analyse every legal nuance in the hope of gaining advantage, as much financial as political. The last trait was typical of the Caroline rich, for under the American aegis the old families had quickly been converted to the divinity of the United States Dollar. However, since Cesar identified himself ostentatiously with the antique grandees of Spain who affected to despise mere wealth, he often failed to get the most out of the graft that riddled Caroline public life. The scions of other families who knew how the country really ticked thought that Cesar was a highly sensitive fool but continued to treat him with respect, just in case his reputation for honesty turned out to be a winner in the long run.

Max Bligh's first meeting with Cesar—they had met as it were by accident in a museum—had been cut short. Bligh always had the feeling that he was being followed, a suspicion that afflicts many an agent and is invariably wrong. They arranged their second meeting to take place in a botanical garden on the outskirts of Infanta. Both men approached it at different times and from different directions, so that Max Bligh felt reasonably certain that no one was observing as he walked in to the orchid garden.

He would have preferred a cooler rendezvous. The day was very hot and humid with not a trace of a breeze. He was sweating and uncomfortable. Generous entertainment since his arrival had increased his waistline and his belly pressed uncompromisingly against his belt. It was with a touch of envy that he saw Cesar drifting toward him wearing a light grey suit, a silvery tie, correspondence shoes and a white straw hat, stopping just now to peer with an excess of interest at a rare orchid, his ivory topped cane poised in mid air as though the ecstasy of the moment had made further motion impossible.

What had riled Max a little was that, though Cesar was in his fifties, from afar he looked like a slim youth. On the other hand he remembered with a smidgen of malice that close up Cesar's face was lined like the surface of a desiccated planet and his skin was the colour of old parchment. Max felt sure that however high the temperature soared not a hint of moisture would appear on Cesar even in his armpits. There was something of the famed pride of the Abulencias about him and he looked decidedly an intellectual. A soft, cultured voice addressed him in New England tones, "Behind the hedge, Mr Bligh, there is a marble bench in a little arbour, quite cool in this heat. The view is charming. Will you join me there? I understand that you want to know something of my opinions." Max nodded and complied.

In fact Max Bligh's superiors knew as much about the situation in the Carolines as it was possible to know: the corruption, the unemployment, the harshness of the security forces, the people losing faith in the state and turning to the liberation fighters, and so on and so on. Bligh and others like him were deployed to suck up vast amounts of material of this kind, as vacuum cleaners suck up useless rubbish, which most of it was.

How tedious all Cesar's information was—to begin with. How big companies donated money to the First Lady for her pet projects to retain her patronage. How infrastructure contracts were given to construction firms that supported the régime, how the Florescos had put millions into Swiss and US banks, how the gold found by the President had been brilliantly invested in hedge funds to accrue an enormous fortune and how torture was used more and more to deal with the terrorists. Everyone knew this, but Max Bligh said, 'yes' and 'really' and 'is that so' and even raised his eyebrows in surprise in the hope that something more significant would fall from Cesar's lips.

At length he said, "Senor Abulencia, I know the liberation movement is growing in the provinces. But it can't set up a rival government—even to control some of the islands or the Muslim provinces. I'd like to know what the traditional, the liberal, parties are doing. To me they look powerless; their leaders in exile in the US are excellent orators but that's about all. They ooze confidence but I don't see it reflected in their followers here. It's impossible for me to suss out some Caroline organisations—they're tight as clams—and as for the big families, they are a mystery. Maybe plans are being made by somebody, somewhere. I'm at a dead end. Isn't anyone among them thinking of running for office against the President. After all, you still have elections of a sort."

"I'm glad you've come to the point—at last," said Cesar as though it had been Bligh who had been rabbiting on about nothing new or useful. He leaned forward confidentially and lowered his voice, though there was no one around who might hear him. "The issue is not replacing the President. As long as he's alive he'll be President— no doubt about it. The issue is the succession. Things will only come to a head when Antonio Floresco goes to his maker—whoever that may be." He ran the tip of his finger along his upper lip as though testing its willingness to reveal something else—something not quite seemly. "Of course, things could be brought to a head if the President's departure were to be, how shall we say, accelerated."

Max Bligh was lost for words. Was Cesar merely speculating or hinting that something significant was being planned? Or was he putting out a feeler for assistance? If the latter, no go. Who could guess which side would profit, which side would go under, if some ill-considered plot were afoot? The questions racing round Bligh's head made him feel unpleasantly unsure. However it was not necessary to prompt Cesar Abulencia to continue. He loved the sound of his own wisdom. "What we need to prepare, Mr Bligh, is a grand coalition of all the elements that love freedom— the liberals, the church, the left wing. Oh, I'm not terrified of communism. In the Carolines it would take a form consistent with our way of life. But, Mr Bligh, I did observe just now that for a moment you were, well, tongue-tied. You were thinking that it might not be to everyone's advantage if the President were to leave the stage too quickly. Allow me to dissent. The First Lady is strengthening her power base. If she were to take over we would have a Floresco régime lasting beyond even your lifetime. Like you she's far from old and she has children. There could be, God help us, a Floresco dynasty. Now I'll warn you about that woman: she may not be an intellectual, she may not be particularly intelligent, but she has cunning—the cunning of a peasant." Bligh noticed that Cesar's tone was far from contemptuous when he spoke the word. "So she understands what peasants respond to. She's busy creating a populist movement to undermine our liberal traditions and confound the left. Have you noticed how old cults and new religions spring up so easily here? No, probably not. You don't know us well enough for that. Then let me tell you, Mr Bligh, that simple people, and I mean at least half of our people, regard the First Lady as a sort of divinity, a goddess. Believe it or not I am telling you the truth."

Max Bligh was still in a quandary. Vain Cesar might be, but at the same time he seemed shrewd—but was he dependable? His motivation seemed to be pride rather than principle. At the same Bligh reckoned that Cesar Abulencia would fit his present purpose. "Senor Abulencia," he said. "I'm sure you realise that I didn't ask to see you just to discuss the political situation, though I must say I find your *tour d'horizon* extremely interesting," He gave Cesar a searching, indeed a sincere, look, like someone savouring the unfamiliar presence of greatness. "Indeed illuminating. If it were possible I'd like to listen to you much longer but we have to be careful over our meetings. People are sometimes followed." Cesar nodded his head sagely to suggest both his awareness and his discretion. "However, Senor, my real reason for wanting to talk with you is to find how we can assist one another, or to be frank how you might be able to help me. It so happens that there is a way open to us at present."

Cesar had been wondering why he had been invited to this meeting with a strange American, so he returned the searching look that had been cast on him without letting his curiosity show, though he did so in a kindly way, as if he was dealing with a pleasant but dim student. Max Bligh then explained that the firm for which he was working was responsible for the public relations work involved in the President's forthcoming visit to Europe. "You see Senor, the President is anxious to combat the hostile opinion he's been getting in the world press. You are well aware of the sort of criticism that is made of his government; unfortunately much of it well grounded. In fact the First Lady has doubts on the wisdom of accompanying him as she too has been the butt of unkind ridicule in the European media. So to sum up I'd not describe our objective as being to combat hostile opinion so much as to neutralise it." Bligh let his last words hang in the air to intrigue Cesar the more, "To neutralise it by another exercise in public relations."

Cesar had to ask, "Neutralise? A peculiar word for a PR exercise?"

"Let me clarify," said Bligh. "There's a freelance television producer in Hong Kong, Hilary Arbuthnot, who has made a reputation for himself producing documentaries about countries in South East Asia. You know the sort of thing—ethnic customs, traditional ceremonies, culture and history all set against smashing scenery and full of pretty people. Now my firm has put up the money—very discreetly of course—for him to make a film on the Caroline Spanish inheritance—architecture, music, dancing, you name it. Arbuthnot is all set for the commission. He's a perfectionist who should have gone much further in the hall of fame, they say. The Information Ministry knows his work so there won't be problems about an entry permit. What he produces must be ready for the President's visit to Europe. I know the television networks there are anxious for background material on the Carolines so we anticipate a substantial audience."

Cesar's face at once showed his interest but, contemptuous of the commonalty that lacked his sort of erudition, he affected to despise television, even to the point of banishing the single set in his house to a special room. Despite which there was nothing he would really have liked more than to appear on it. "As a matter of fact," he said, "I have met Arbuthnot. Interesting man. He once came to my house—I think for a play reading. Do you think you could use him? He seemed to be an independent sort of man who'd want to do things his way. But a man of principal I'd say."

"Exactly so. A man of principal. He's getting on in age of course. A real old fashioned left winger. No, I don't think there'll be any problem in enlisting him to do a job which will cast a searching light on the Carolines and, obliquely of course, an even more searching light on its leaders."

"And my own role in all this?" enquired Cesar, somewhat peremptorily for he was by now unsure where Bligh's loyalties lay; to his alleged PR firm, to the CID, or to something more sinister? These days one could never tell. But did he pay for what he got?

"Oh a very important one. The film will need a key personality—a Carolino of course but a Carolino of stature. I'm convinced you have the charisma that's needed. I want you to ensure that the film presents a balanced and coherent view of what's going on in the Carolines, but particularly in the provinces away from Infanta. I believe that you and Arbuthnot have the temperament to work together. I sincerely hope you will join us in the project." Bligh added somewhat apologetically that there would naturally be a generous fee for such services but his words were cut short by a decorous nod from Cesar, indicative both of his assent and of the fact that, when acting for his country, money would be a matter of no account or might it not turn out of no object? Bligh was not sure which.

Harmony and mutual interest established, agreement in principal was soon reached and the sincerity of both parties suggested by a long handshake. Each gave a courteous bow as Max Bligh went off, leaving Cesar alone on the cool marble bench with his head brimming with illimitable visions of his future. Could this chance provide the stepping stones to his becoming the great alternative to the President. Of course he would be manipulated, but by whom exactly? He still could not make out where Bligh stood. But two could play at whatever game it was. He closed his eyes and saw himself projected into millions of households, the honest scholar speaking more in sorrow than in anger of his country's heritage, his words interjected into, and intermingling with, a script that led the viewer from one architectural jewel of the Carolines to another. Each lovely building would provide an opportunity for his pithy comments. He would be regretful over the shortcomings of the President and shake his head sadly and perhaps amusingly over the extravagance of the First Lady. As though he found it impossible to believe, he would now and then drop snippets of information on the iniquities of the Police and introduce despairing clerics telling of the suffering of their flocks. But he would also hint that there were good men quietly working to alleviate poverty and to restore freedom, not violently but tempered by justice that would even recognise the early achievements of the President. At this stage he might speak admiringly of the buildings and highways created by Antonio Floresco, so adumbrating him with Adolf and Benito for those who had not yet got the point. The world would be left with a picture of the Carolines as a cultural gem within which he, Cesar Abulencia, stood high, a man of virtue like Quinctius Cincinnatus of old, who was ready to save the republic when called upon.

The sweetness of his vision was broken by the voice of a park keeper telling him that the gardens were closing. Yes, he should be seen in the serenity of a garden, leaning on his stick beneath a canopy of trees, perhaps with a ruined fane nearby, the philosopher amidst nature tamed. Approaching the gate he was jostled by a troop of children and other visitors and if he had not held on to his hat and stick he might have lost them in the uncouth mêlée.

Julio Abulencia was attracted by the offer. He looked at the embossed emblem of the Carolines above the words, 'Ministry of Foreign Affairs and Trade' and at the signature of the Foreign Minister, Catalino Guzman himself. No, it was not a hoax but a genuine and decently paid offer of a post in the trade section of the embassy in Washington DC. One paragraph took his eye. 'In view of your proven academic record and your success in marketing the products of your family's firm, it is considered that your contribution to the work of the embassy would be useful at a time when we are trying to increase our export earnings.'

That was nonsense of course. The old fashioned methods of Uncle Cesar had led to a decline in exports of the once renowned Abulencia textiles, nor had Julio been able to improve sales when he went abroad. The Florescos were clearly using one of their more refined ways of getting rid of someone who was an embarrassment. But for a young man who had not made his mark in the world a diplomat's income with its perks was attractive and the prospect of working in the United States alluring. For a foolish moment he thought that the job had been offered so he could marry Conchita and take her off to Washington, where she could play a useful role for her country. But of course that was nonsense. Conchita would be groomed for a higher destiny. Momentarily tempted, he thought of telling her, 'They'll never let us marry. We'll have no peace from them and you won't be happy. Forget me. You'll be alright in the end and better off for certain.' Most young men would have said that.

But Julio was not like most young men. He was an Abulencia, imbued with all the family pride and some might say its stupidity. The thought of Conchita's captivity, like a princess in a king's castle, heightened the aura of romance which his love affair already possessed. Conchita was no great beauty but his memory of her fierce passion when she gave herself to him made him long for her when he was in all sorts of places, at the theatre, the races or at a crowded cocktail party, anywhere he was she was too, arousing the self-willed part of his body that was never entirely indifferent to desire. It was not impossible that the seed of his unchecked sentimentality had been sown in his childhood by his dead mother, whose room he remembered cluttered with portraits and mementoes of the handsome but never to be forgotten father he had seen only intermittently. It was only at a later and less impressionable age that he learned that his mother had had many handsome lovers and that his own paternity was in doubt. However, whatever the rival influences of heredity and environment, Julio knew that he was too much in love with Conchita to be tempted by the Minister's offer.

He told her so when he saw her in Dulcinea, the little Spanish cake shop where they sometimes met, hidden away in the fashionable shopping quarter of Madogi. Away from the public eye in one of the little alcoves in which each table was set, he produced the Ministry letter with some pride, as though his rejection of it was absolute proof of his adoration.

Conchita however was not impressed. "Take it," she said. "Take the job Julio. They'll never forgive you if we don't give each other up."

He was taken aback. "But I thought you were going to arrange for us to have a heart to heart talk with your parents. I thought you could win over your father at least. That's what you seemed to be telling me."

"I could persuade him if he were the only parent I have."

Julio was silent wondering perhaps whether it might after all be better to accept the Ministry's offer. Perhaps Conchita was getting over him. He said, "You are really certain that your mother won't be persuaded then?"

"I've told you. She'd stop at nothing to prevent us marrying. That's why I asked both of my parents to do this for you. To protect you Julio." She gestured towards the letter that lay next to a platter of Dulcinea's delicious chocolate torres.

Julio's voice rose so full of incredulity that the waiters darted glances at him. "You? You are responsible for this? You want me to go, to leave you—perhaps for ever?"

Tears welled in Conchita's eyes. Impetuously she grasped Julio's hands across the table sending one of the chocolate torres flying. "How can you say that? Of course I don't. But since I've come back I've seen what the government can do to people who don't play ball. An offer is made first. At least they like to look humane. My mother was delighted when I made the suggestion—really to forestall her. She thinks she's beaten us already."

"And has she?"

Conchita was silent. She dried her eyes and helped the waiter who had come to clear up the mess. She even said what a waste of a beautiful cake. Julio could see that she was strained and knew she had acted out of love for him. This made him defiant. What could the damned Florescos do to him? His resolve not to accept the offer strengthened. More than honour, love was at stake. At the same time he was realistic enough to suggest to Conchita that they should confront her parents directly. She promised to fix a meeting if humanly possible. Then she would make it clear that any damage done to Julio would be damage to herself. Dare they risk that if the matter became public?

As they left Dulcinea an unpleasant incident took place. A lurking photographer took several shots of them together and two harpies, reporters from an Infanta gossip magazine, bore down at them yelling staccato questions:

"Is it true that you're to be married?"

"What do your families think of your affair?"

"Mr Abulencia have you met your future in-laws?".

"Is it true that the First Lady is mad with you?"

In no time a crowd had gathered to watch the action. Conchita was frightened and cried, "Go away please. We've nothing to say." Julio lost his control and shoved one of the women reporters who were jostling them far too roughly, so that she stumbled back, legs flailing into the storm drain, just in time for the photographer to record the incident. Julio got Conchita to her car which sped off and then went to the parking lot followed by the mob, which had grown aggressive. As he was about to drive off the woman reporter he had humiliated put her head to the window and bellowed, "You're going to regret this, Mr Thick Dick."

The journey home, made tedious by traffic jams along the crowded streets, gave Julio plenty of time to reflect on his awkward situation. What a fool he had been to turn down the chance of freedom Conchita had offered to him. Why hadn't he said yes and softened it by insisting that once in the States he would somehow or other find another job—perhaps with some of the Carolinos who were in exile from the Floresco régime—so that Conchita could join him in a new life there. But no, it was not possible. Once separated their trust in each other would be at risk, love would wither and it would be the end of their life together. Of course the whole of Infanta must be talking about their affair—that is, the affluent set which had the time and leisure to think such things mattered. Yet he and Conchita had kidded themselves that their amateur efforts at secrecy had been successful. Within a day or so all sorts of nonsense would be published about their inevitably torrid love affair. They would be trailed. Even tea in Dulcinea would be a thing of the past, as more importantly would their hot trysts in Artur D'Orsay's hidden boudoir. The more Julio thought about the last deprivation the more certain it appeared that a beautiful chapter in his life was at an end. However, he justified his failure to endure the unendurable by telling himself that his suffering was necessary to protect Conchita. As soon as he got home he replied to the Honourable Catalino Guzman saying that he had given careful thought to the offer so kindly made to him and that he would be honoured to accept it. He added that he looked forward to giving his best services to the Catalines.

He read through his reply for errors but the only one lay in its betrayal of Conchita, of his family and of himself. All the same he did not tear it up for he knew enough of his own nature to admit that his inability to decide might easily make him change his mind again—and yet again, so that only God in heaven knew what his last decision would be.

Normally Julio did not talk to Cesar about his personal affairs, because Cesar was fond of saying that though he was the head of an ancient family, the Abulencias were men of any age in one important respect: "We are free men who make our own choice. That is the fundamental strength of the Abulencias." In reality Julio suspected that the real reason for Cesar's detachment was that he found other people's problems tedious and distractive from the cultivation of his own personality. Indeed Cesar had not shown even a modicum of interest in the sad decline of Julio's mother, but all that lay in the past now with her suicide. However, since his affair with Conchita was no merely personal affair but one that might affect the political future of the Abulencias, Julio knew he must explain the situation to his uncle.

He was certain that Cesar would not have heard anything about the affair. He was not an approachable person—even his relations with his wife were now distant—so it was unlikely that any acquaintance would have put him in the picture. His spare time was largely spent in doing research into Caroline history, at least those parts of it in which there was an Abulencia involvement. This activity was carried out in the fine house library. Here the furniture was heavy and antique, the floor of large alternating pieces of red, purple and white marble and the high ceiling rich with coffers of white moulded plaster. It was a noble room intended as a home for elevated thoughts. Nevertheless, white lace curtains looped against the three tall windows opening onto a patio luxurious with rare plants, hinted at a different, more frivolous, ideal. Cesar smiled at Julio over a table at which he was sitting with a large open volume before him. "Ah Julio, look at these prints. They've just arrived from Madrid; views of house interiors of Infanta, printed between 1745 and 49." He turned the volume to point at a piece of furniture shown in one of the prints. I'm sure it's that very desk over there. It came from my mother's house in San Fernando. Julio peered at the print but did not think the detail was adequate to form a judgment, but he said, "Yes. I agree. It's the very one. How interesting, Uncle Cesar."

Cesar beamed at him "Now the room in the print is in the Viceregal small palace, not of course the DeoGracias. Let's see the date—1747. Ah yes, the Viceroy at the time was Count Almaviva.

But I'm sure you know there was a family connection between the Almavivas and us. That must have been how my mother's family acquired the desk." Julio again agreed, while thinking that if this represented the quality of Cesar's research, his conclusions might not amount to much.

When they had settled in two gargantuan chairs which had not been designed with Carolinos in mind, Cesar said, "How nice to see you. You don't often want to spend your time talking with an old man like me. But I do understand, Julio."

Julio pretended to protest, "Old man indeed. You're too fond of posing. But I admit you do it very well."

"You must know all my secrets then, Julio. Which gives you an advantage because I know none of yours."

"But Uncle, I thought you always made it a point of honour never to enquire into family members' secrets."

"But that doesn't mean that I don't mind hearing them if they are given freely." Cesar chuckled. "No, I'm lying. I'm not keen on knowing other people's secrets if by that they mean their affairs, which are invariably boring to those not participating. After all affairs are pretty much the same everywhere—one bit of flesh going into another. We don't get excited over the ways people blow their noses yet noses are as necessary as pricks. You might compare it to putting a plug in a socket; it's only worth it if the lights go on. So many plugs these days seem to fuse easily."

Julio smiled and responded to his uncle's *jeu d'esprit* with, "We might see it differently if we blew one another's noses."

"I have a feeling you are going to tell me whose nose you've been blowing, dear Julio."

"Perhaps. But first uncle I'm going to ask you a question. One of concern to the family."

Cesar spread his hands like a man waiting to catch a ball. "How flattering. You make me feel that I still exist. Out with it then."

Julio smiled no more and stared straight at his uncle before he said heavily, "As head of the Abulencia family, how would you take it if I were to accept a position with this government?"

Cesar clasped his hands and cracked his knuckles. Then he said, "It seems to me that maybe you have been won over already if you dignify the thing that runs this country as a government. However, since you have asked me a straight question I shall give you a straight reply. No, I wouldn't like it at all. In fact I would dislike it very much indeed."

Julio smiled benignly at his uncle, lent forward and patted him on his knee, an action which seemed to surprise Cesar, who was no longer used to affectionate gestures either from men or, so it was said, from woman. Then he rose and walked about the room, touching the antique furniture, glancing through the window at the beautiful plants, allthe time followed by Cesar's shrewd eyes. How odd his uncle was, and this house and himself; he had not escaped the pattern. What did it matter if he took the Ministry job or not? Vain indeed to invest the matter with such importance in this room that had no more life than those in Cesar's volume of prints.

A twinge of curiosity now made Cesar ask, "What sort of job were you speaking about anyway? I can't imagine those fascist Florescos letting an Abulencia have any sort of responsibility. So I guess your question was academic."

By way of answer Julio produced the letter from Catalino Guzman and placed it over a typical Caroline drawing room circa 1745. Cesar read it and said with some surprise, "From Catalino. Well he's the one man among them I still have some respect for. He knows what they are like but he concentrates on foreign affairs because he believes he can still serve the country in that way." Cesar paused, perused the letter again and asked, "And in Washington too? I think you should give me an explanation."

The story of Conchita and Julio filled Cesar with misgivings. On the one hand he regretted that the Florescos had become unacceptable tyrants, for an alliance with the Presidential family was not to be despised; on the other to attach Conchita to the opposition would be a coup. Yet Cesar had a nose for danger. The First Lady's threat might extend to himself before long. This again was two edged. Persecution could be a useful ingredient in the quest for power. It also struck him that he had become aware of Julio's information in nice time; it could be made use of in the television coverage that Max Bligh had offered him. He came to a snap decision. "Don't accept the offer and go on seeing Conchita. The girl loves you and she will understand your motive. You can show the world what sort of people Conchita's parents are. Matters of principle are involved. You must act in the tradition of our family. One day you will be its head."

Julio knew his uncle too well to place much credence on his judgment. But, though his own mind was in a dilemma, he really wanted to take the risk and so he decided to accept Cesar's advice. Yet conscious of the wrong decisions that had often been made by his family in the past he sensed that his decision might be disastrous. But that in itself made him excited. Now all he could do was to wait and see if Conchita could fix up a meeting with the President and his Lady.

He did not have to wait long. Early next morning when he was still in bed, Conchita phoned him. "My father says I can bring you to the Palace this evening—at seven. If you've any other plans, cancel them. He's off to the provinces tomorrow. There won't be another chance for ages."

"And Senora Floresco?"

"I haven't spoken to her. I didn't see her. But she'll be there. My father promised me. He thinks we should all meet. That's a good sign, Julio."

Conchita put the phone down and sank back in her chair, doing her best to relax. She tried to take comfort from her father's words, which as ever were spoken to her gently, lovingly even. No, he had no objection to the Abulencia family but he did not think that its present head was a very clever man. "No wonder Cesar sticks to the Spanish culture. He's a sort of Don Quixote himself. Tilting at windmills, that's him. The weakness of that family is that it never comes to terms with reality." Then he had ended by saying that it was only fair that he and his wife should explain what they thought of a match, "I'm not the tyrant people say I am," he said proudly. "And I'm no tyrant where my own children are concerned." Conchita realised that the interview would turn out to be a final judgment. Then she and Julio would have to decide whether to accept it or whether it was possible not to do so.

The meeting was to take place in the President's study, a simple room lined with bookcases that stretched up to the ceiling. As a child she had loved to play up and down the steps that could be pushed from one bookcase to another to give access to the higher shelves. Comfortable settees in dark leather ensured that no one could tower over anyone else and the atmosphere was academic rather than political, redolent of reason even though reason had not always prevailed there. Conchita met Julio, who was dressed in a dark blue suit with a most restrained tie, at a side door of the Palace and took him straight to the study. There she expected to find her father reading. A little latter, as was her wont the First Lady would no doubt join them.

Such was not the case. The President was not there but the First Lady was there looking out of one of the windows with her back to the room. She said, "Antonio..." as she turned in response to the sound of the door and ended somewhat icily, "Oh it's you." Conchita started to introduce Julio who gave a slight bow and extended his hand, but the grande dame gestured airily and said, "I have met Mr Abulencia," though in fact neither of them had ever clapped eyes on the other in person. Nor did she suggest that they should sit but returned to the window in silence that Conchita knew boded ill and was intended to indicate displeasure. Conchita took Julio's arm but nodding to her he stepped away and stood almost like a soldier on guard, looking straight in front of him. Conchita realised that this would not make the President, a stickler for politeness, feel pleased with his wife. And so she followed suit. They stood for an embarrassing minute or so until the President came in at which point the First Lady became all movement. "Do sit down," she gushed with a gracious smile. "Antonio, this is Julio Abulencias. I don't think either of us has met him before."

It was all done so quickly that the President had no chance to see the couple's awkward situation. But the First Lady's behavior had told them, 'You see; you can't play the President better than I can. I'll run rings round you.'

The President apologised for being late, not however because of some matter of state; he actually said, "I was on the loo as they call it in England. Why is it called a loo, Conchita?" With a laugh she said that she hadn't a clue while the First Lady went to a sideboard on which there was an array of bottles and poured out drinks, in three cases on the basis of her knowledge of their tastes but Julio found himself with a large vodka."

"Cesar, your uncle Cesar, how is he these days?" the President asked genially following it up with, "My most honourable enemy; I respect him greatly."

Julio said that his uncle was well and untruthfully extended his best wishes. He went on, "Mr President, I can truthfully say that though my uncle does not see eye to eye with you on some matters he does have great respect for you as a statesman and as a great Carolino, and that respect includes your gracious lady." He bowed to the First Lady as well as the comfortable settee allowed.

"It makes me glad to hear that," said the President. "And that's how things should be among people who believe in democracy." Julio winced mentally at this. Did this man actually believe that his system was democratic? Yes, the old devil probably did. Nevertheless he said that there was one thing on which his uncle and the President must surely agree and that was the fundamental superiority of the democratic process.

This set the President off. "You know Julio, you know Conchita, I'd like to be a truly constitutional president. I'd like a chamber with a president's party and a president's loyal opposition. Not this rigid American system we have here. It's not subtle enough for the Carolinos. Yes, the democratic process is superior to all others but to make it work properly something like the Westminster model is needed. It's flexible, subtle, enduring and strong." The President gave a sharp laugh and added. "Like we Carolinos are accused of being in bed, eh Julio?"

Conchita and Julio both thought this might be a rather earthy lead into their affair, but abruptly the First Lady asked. "Julio, did you ever meet the head of the Westminster system when you were in England?"

Cautiously Julio said that he had not, but added, "Well as a matter of fact I did once attend a garden party at Buck House. Our ambassador in London was unwell and he asked me to accompany his wife. So you can say that I was once in her presence."

"Good heavens. I can't imagine Her Majesty calling her home Buck House. Some wit might change the initial letter." The First Lady gave a tinkling laugh but no one joined in her mirth.

"It's just a joke," said Julio. "I believe the Queen has a sense of humour—unlike some eminent persons in the world." The mistake caused Conchita's warning hand to press Julio's arm.

But it was too late. The First Lady's humour had given way to a grim stare. "Elizabeth the Second. Seconds never have the power of firsts, do they?" The First Lady's voice did not rise but became unpleasantly sharp as she said. "Of course in the DeoGracias I am Griselda the First."

The President chortled. "Of course you are, my darling," he said. "Who could ever doubt it. You know," he turned seriously towards Julio and Conchita, "my marriage has given me such strength. I know I can always count on Griselda for complete support. But I wonder how I would manage without her. When people are contemplating marriage they should examine each other's characters sincerely. Failure to do so can lead to a life of sorrow. One must be sure one is taking the right step. Now as you know, in our country everyone, male and female, can choose freely." He then went on to eulogise the Caroline system of government, its freedom of expression, the impartiality of its justice system, the equitable distribution of taxation. He even explained how the security services were struggling like heroes to maintain the people's freedom. So persuasive were his arguments that Julio began to doubt whether he had been seeing things correctly before this encounter with so wise a man. Had he, Cesar and all the Abulencias been wrong about Antonio Floresco who had just revealed his liberal soul? Then unexpectedly the President said, with a puzzled expression, "You know I would be much happier about an alliance between the Floresco and the Abulencia family, if people like Cesar could see the reality of the Caroline situation as I have done my best to explain it to you. But all is not lost. Perhaps you, Julio, could act as a bridge between my régime and your noble family. Please inform Cesar of my progressive views and persuade him to stop his wild personal criticisms, which cause me great sadness."

The First Lady could see very clearly what was afoot in Julio's mind. She had been at this show before and knew how easily the President's persuasion and hope of personal advancement could make people capitulate. If Julio now agreed to follow the advice he had just been given the President would quickly see an advantage in allowing his daughter to become an Abulencia in name as she already seemed to be in spirit. The First Lady was angry but dared not speak yet. Antonio defended her against all criticism, but sometimes he enjoyed giving her a dressing down in front of others. It wasn't going to happen this time. Let her bide her time.

Conchita broke the President's spell. She had heard to her father's words and feared that Julio would succumb to get both her and Washington. Yet the moment he did so she would lose faith in him. But once he had accepted her father's version of the world it might be difficult to refuse him. She might even find herself becoming the ally of her mother. She would not let Julio be ruined by these people. She preferred to give him his entire freedom. Quite simply she said, "Father how do you expect people not to make wild criticisms if you never allow them to tell you the simple truth, the complete truth, not your own version of it? The truth is that your régime is corrupt and disgusting."

As obedient to Conchita's manipulation as any puppet, the First Lady stood up. She stood there proudly, her head in its bouffant hair slightly thrown back so that her eyes seem to be staring down on every one there like an angry gorgan. "Ah, you see, Mr President, you see how your enemies have corrupted your eldest daughter."

For a moment the President did not see anything. He looked like a man snapped out of deep hypnosis, which indeed he was. It was possible to contradict some detail of his policy, even to disagree on less important facts, but it was not permitted to conflict with him on the grand illusion of the essential justice and freedom of his régime. Without heeding the First Lady's wrath he wanted only to make sure that he had heard aright. He stood trembling slightly and asked Conchita to repeat what she had said. This she did loudly and distinctly.

The Griselda Antonio alliance at once went into full swing. On his side this meant total silence, his look of anger mutating into one of satisfaction as his enraged wife gave her emotions full sway. Conchita was a pitiable wretch and a traitor but one not entirely responsible for her actions. The real traitors were political enemies, of whom Julio was a contemptible tool. Behind him stood the Abulencia family and behind that the atheistic communists and a hotchpotch of perverted liberals. Never, never, never would Conchita and Julio be allowed to marry. Never must Julio darken the DeoGracias Palace again. If the First Lady had her way the Abulencias would be thrown out of the country, lock, stock and barrel and consider themselves lucky that nothing worse had happened to them. For that they should be grateful to her father's goodness of heart. "See," she demanded of Conchita, "how you have upset your father. Your father who has put his entire being into ensuring the happiness of his people. As for you," she snarled at Julio. "Get out now. Now, before it is too late."

The President nodded his head as though to give assent to his wife's judgment. Julio bowed to him and took Conchita's hand to lead her from the room. But for a short time she pulled away from him, stood her ground and turned towards her mother, saying in tones full of contempt, "Thank you, mother, for doing what I expected." Then she looked at her father and said, "Thank you father. You will always be dear to me." The lovers then left together.

As he stood before the altar with Rosalinda, far from being embarrassed by Father Stephens officiating at his wedding, Salvador was happy, for he felt that his married life was peculiarly blessed by the priest's support for the revolutionary cause. Father Stephens on the other hand had deep misgivings. Whilst he sympathised with Oliveros and the liberation priests, he saw that they could be jumping from the frying pan into the fire by espousing communism. Precise philosophical definitions did not mean much to Carolinos and Stephens himself thought that those definitions, like those of theology, might be so much mental onanism, but surely Oliveros must see that Communism had a view of life and morality different from Catholicism and that it was making use of people like him for its own ends. But it came as a shock when Oliveros told him that he had been a full member of the party for over a year. This he learned when they were walking through San Felipe, where the mood was sombre following the assassination on the Bersamina hacienda. For a while Stephens was silent until he burst out, "You can't be. It's impossible to be a priest and a communist at the same time."

"Then I have done the impossible, Frank, for I am both."

"You understand that Marxism is atheistic."

"So I am told. But philosophy doesn't appeal to me. I doubt if it has any real meaning. I'm only interested in actions. If I had to construct a philosophy it would be based on action. But I'd base it on the words 'by a tree's fruit shall you judge it'. Academic notions, idealism, communism, atheism, leave me cold. People who invent them generally live in comfort. They know little of life as it is."

"Men who make 'isms' see life though prisms," said Stephens with a chuckle and Oliveros said he must remember that for his students. "So what do you think the communists' attitude to the Church would be if they seized power?" Stephens asked, curious how Oliveros might reconcile contrary actions.

Oliveros decided to be facetious. "Good Catholics often flagellate themselves at religious festivals here. And what is the result—their faith is strengthened. So it will be for the Church when the reds take over. We shall suffer but we shall emerge stronger. Then I'll renounce the party. I might even become a martyr. In the meantime I'll stay in it because the most important thing for me is the achievement of social justice. The inequalities that exist are destroying the soul of our country."

"And you think that communism will establish social justice?"

"Things will be better than they are now. Of that I am sure, Father Stephens."

Father Stephens could not confute that. It was useless to argue that it would be better for the Church to take an independent line apart from the revolutionaries. The President himself had pressed for that and opened a dialogue about it with Church leaders. All that took place were a few meetings in Infanta. In the countryside the depredations of the security forces continued, corruption went unchecked and poverty deepened. Some Catholics and other concerned men actually went to Infanta to petition the President and tell him what was going on but, soon after receiving a promise that their petitions would be looked at, a statement would emerge from Police Headquarters alleging that the petitioners were known communist sympathisers trying to embarrass the government. Because of this Cardinal Peccata, head of the Catholic Church in the Carolines, had decided to break off political dialogue with the DeoGracias Palace.

At the gateway into San Felipe the police asked to see their identify cards but looked at them hardly at all for clerical garb gave them a sort of immunity from the restrictions placed on ordinary folk. Few people were about, for the local military commander had imposed a curfew that would continue until facts were coughed up by the people to help him find the assassins. Since Manuel Bersamina, the most powerful member of his family, was the Minister for Defence, the curfew was no short-term threat. It could go on and on; if he could not show that the Government had control over the part of the country where his family was all-powerful, nowhere in the Carolines could be considered safe.

They walked down the main street. All the windows and doors were closed on police orders. Inside each little house the heat would be intense and the depression overwhelming. The people earned little enough from cutting cane. Now their meagre wages would be down to nothing. They heard voices calling their names softly, "Father Stephens, Father Oliveros." They replied, "Bless you. Bless you my child," to each hidden greeting.

Father Oliveros began muttering under his breath. He stared at the ground and occasionally kicked at a stone, and once at a can that clattered noisily across the street. The words spat out from his mouth were neither charitable nor forgiving. "They'll pay for this. We'll get the bastards one day." Father Stephens hushed him. He had noticed two officers staring at them as they advanced down the street.

"Father Stephens, Father Oliveros?" asked one of the officers and the priests assented. "Most unfortunate all this," he went on politely. "How can the government carry out its development plans if people support the communists?"

Oliveros asked harshly, "What development plans, officer? On the moon perhaps?"

The officer smiled, "I understand your concern, Father. Many of us in the Army feel that not enough is being done to improve the people's lives. But as far as I can see development planning seems to be more difficult than fighting a war or running a church."

Stephens observed in as thoughtful a way as he could, "Are you sure that the people of San Felipe are involved? Suppose they have no information to give the police. They can't just invent it. I'm sure that all the people of San Felipe condemn the murder. I must confess, sir, that I have some doubts about your tactics."

The officer eyed him critically and Stephens felt like a sinner under the scrutiny of a worldly wise priest. "Father, you are an

Australian so you can't be expected to know all there is to know about our people. They..."

Stephens interrupted him. "They are hard working, good people who only want to bring up their children properly and to be good Christians. And I love them, one and all. I doubt if any of them is a communist."

The officer replied "I don't doubt most of what you say, Father, but I can't agree that none of them is a communist."

The second officer, whose face wore an angry scowl, broke in. "That's what we want to talk to you about, both of you."

"Talk to us?" asked Stephens with genuine surprise; the moment he opened his mouth he had thought, 'if everyone has kept their mouth shut how can I be a suspect?' Then he was gripped by fear. If someone had blabbed wasn't it possible that his house was at this moment being searched and the wounded guerrilla could be caught.

The polite officer gestured at the surly guy, who at once stood back. "Yes, I'd say that most of the people here are not communists. In fact there are a few men and woman who are very loyal and like to help us. That's why we opened the anonymous post box. You'd be surprised at the bits of information we receive. Come Fathers, let's walk to the Police Station."

Stephens thought of asking, 'Am I under arrest then?' but that might suggest a guilty mind. He felt that he could, if necessary, explain away the presence of the wounded man in his house as a priest's bounden duty. But he was not sure about his fellow, less cautious, priest. Was a tighter net being drawn around him?

They turned a corner to go to the Police Station and went past the large Cortez house where Salvador was living with his bride's parents. Stephens was trembling for he remembered that Salvador had been out the night of the murder with the guerrillas. Suddenly he heard a girl's voice, it must be Rosalinda's, crying out desperately. "Father Stephens, help him, help him." Other voices told her to be silent. Salvador had been arrested, that was for sure. For an instant Stephens turned around. The people must be watching him from behind the shuttered windows. He and Father Oliveros both muttered a blessing on the other, held their heads high and walked to the Station. There the manner of the polite officer changed. He advanced to the centre of the room saluted a senior officer very smartly and shouted like a soldier in an American movie, "Sir. We have brought the two priests as instructed." He then did an about turn and stood beside Father Stephens, who said aloud but really to himself, "So we are under arrest?"

"Not exactly so," said the senior officer, a jovial man who must have had ears like a fox. "But we would appreciate it if you would help in our enquiries. Please follow me." The priests were led off to separate rooms without having a moment to exchange a farewell word. Father Stephens found himself in a windowless cell furnished with a long narrow table and two chairs either side. The senior officer took his place facing Father Stephens, who just then noticed straps hanging from the table, obviously to restrain anyone lying on it. They wouldn't dare, he told himself. I'm a priest and an Australian citizen but others might not be so fortunate.

"We don't suspect you of anything serious," the senior officer began, "but you must realise that the people here can be very cunning. Some of them might try to inveigle you into activities which you mightn't realise are illegal."

Stephens, losing his control, replied in an angry Australian voice, "Cut the cackle, cobber. Why have you arrested the boy Salvador?"

The officer raised his eyebrows, his eyes twinkled with something or other, maybe amusement and he said, "Oh you are an Australian then. I wasn't sure before. Your accent didn't fit. I assume you mean your boy Salvador Alvarez."

"Yes my boy Salvador, my boy. I want to see him now."

The officer smiled; he became geniality itself. "Certainly, Father. So you shall. You have that right as his comforter, I mean his spiritual comforter. He put his hand beneath the table, a bell rang and a guard appeared. The officer ordered, "Bring prisoner S. Alvarez here"

After a delay during which neither man spoke a word, the door opened and Salvador appeared, sagging between two gaolers.

Father Stephens rose in fury. "What has happened to him? What have you been doing to him?"

The question was superfluous. Salvador had been tortured. His tear-stained face was swollen; his left eye was hardly visible; his almost naked torso was welted and bruised; his shorts were bloody. Stephens turned on the officer. "How dare you. I am an Australian citizen. The world shall know of this."

"And of your lust for him? What will the Church think of a priest who seduces innocent boys?"

"I don't care a damn. I am unimportant, but this atrocity," he pointed at Salvador, "is very important." He tried to go to the boy but his progress was barred. He heard Salvador whimper, "I'm sorry, Father. I told them everything."

"Good," said the officer warmly. "I'm glad you heard it from Salvador's own mouth. The other prisoners confirmed his evidence. We know all about Oliveros. We know which San Felipe boys were with the guerrillas when Ramon Bersamina was roasted in his car. We know about the wounded man in your house. He's being picked up at this moment." The officer paused. "Yes Father, go to your pretty boy. Hold him against your body. That's what you love above all else, isn't it? Not your holy vows as a priest. But your obsession is helpful to me. It will make you come to the right decision."

Father Stephens went over to Salvador and gently stroked the boy's hair. "What decision?" he asked quietly.

"Well now, shall I put it like this? This brave boy Salvador stood up to questioning as long as any man could. Much longer; he's a real Carolino. He tried to protect you, Father. He loves you. So don't you think you have an obligation to protect him now?"

"How can I protect him now? It's too late. You know he was with the others."

"True, but we have no evidence that his were the bullets that felled Ramon Bersamina or that he threw the brand that set the car on fire. In the absence of evidence we could drop all charges. Perhaps just a fine for striking an officer."

"You could do that?" Father Stephens said weakly, for the sight of Salvador and the contact his hand was making with his wounded body were affecting him strangely. His body and his mind were wracked with dread of unknown torment. His judgment was shattered. He wasn't ashamed of surrendering. His will was dead except for the will to love and be loved again. He was in hell until Salvador was free.

"We can do almost anything—if people cooperate, Father." The officer's voice was seductive, quite concealing the contempt he must be feeling for this weakling priest.

"What do you want of me? Tell me what. In return for Salvador's freedom."

"Good, very good. Let's agree that you and Salvador were tricked into doing what you did. Just like people were tricked into heresy in past times. We know how it happened—to help the wounded was your Christian duty, wasn't it? Many people have been tricked into doing bad things for good reasons. Your penance, forgive me if I me call it that, is simple. Speak to the people, to your own parishioners, not once, not twice, but consistently, teaching them what Communism really is. Cooperate with us in a 'hearts and minds' operation. I'm sure Salvador will support you and you will have him as much as Rosalinda allows. Oh don't worry, she'll soon find other interests. Then, Father, it will be just like old times again."

"And Father Oliveros?"

The officer shrugged his shoulders. "That's beyond my power. I believe the President himself is determined to have public trials of treacherous churchmen, no matter how high. The world must know how the so-called liberation priests of the Carolines have been betraying the people."

Stephens slumped into the chair, holding Salvador by his waist. The boy had become grim faced; there were no tears now but Stephens dared not guess at his thoughts. In the darkness of his mind he pleaded for compassion. Do not condemn me; hadn't they been confronted with ruthless power impossible to oppose? Surely even Father Oliveros would have told them to surrender. Somehow or other he must tell Oliveros to compromise. He drew Salvador close to him and asked, "Can I take him with me?"

"Sure Father. But let's get him cleaned up. We don't want him looking like that in public do we? So I assume you are going to cooperate?"

Father Stephens nodded his head. Guards took the prisoner off to thrust him under a cold shower much stronger than the one in Father Stephens' house—but Salvador saw fresh blood still smearing the tiles—leaving the priest to wallow in the knowledge of his own cowardice. The officer must have read his thoughts, for he said, "Father Stephens, I know this is distressing to you but heroics are for idiots. You have done the right thing."

"Have I?" said Stephens, "I pray that I have." Then, anxious about the fate of Father Oliveros, he asked if he might see him. The reply was short and definite. "No. You may not. It's no longer necessary."

"The curfew. If the government..." Stephens corrected himself swiftly, "I mean if we are to win the people's hearts and minds, you must let them go back to work. Lift the curfew soon."

"But Father, see how we are already thinking alike; we have lifted it—even as you were agreeing to cooperate with us."

The President's visit to Europe was only a few weeks off but the untimely arrest of an unimportant priest, Father Oliveros, was having an effect on his travel plans, for when he reached Italy, the last country on his itinerary, he was to be received by the Holy Father. The Oliveros question was in fact causing something of a rift between the President and the powerful Minister for Defence, Manuel Bersamina, who, as he sat before the Presidential desk, was showing every sign of being obdurate.

Bersamina was slightly built, even for a Carolino, but he had presence. The President sometimes wondered how such an insignificant man was invariably able to impose his will on meetings large and small, public and private. It was said that the only person stronger than him was his wife. But Bersamina did have certain physical advantages. He was handsome, though not in the smooth boyish way of Caroline filmstars; his lined face suggested experience and character and was seemingly intellectual. Then there was his voice, which was deep and resonant, capable of penetrating any babble of opinions going on around him, so obliging people to listen to his views which were always cogent and authoritative. Above all he actually did what he said he was going to do whereas the activities of other ministers often withered away, overtaken by more recent decisions which in turn resulted in corruption or sank like a rotten ship in the murky waters of Caroline indifference. The

107

President had once hurled a heavy onyx ash tray at the complacent round face of Senor Wong Hung Tau, Minister for Labour, who had just announced a drive on the abuses of child labour, regardless of the fact that he himself tolerated the worst offending factories, his own, in the country. The President would never have thrown anything at Bersamina's face, even on the television screen, for this man was to be reckoned with and perhaps held the key to what might happen in the Carolines once the President had gone.

"Couldn't the arrest of the priest have been deferred until I return?" the President complained. "It's very inconvenient. You've even announced the date of his trial."

"I could hardly have asked the communists to defer the murder of my nephew, Mr President," replied Bersamina with a touch of irony. "In any case the trial of a priest and his accomplices, young men he converted to Marxism, is a public matter now. It can't be hushed up. The Western press has ways of finding things out. We can't duck out of things as we used to when we had martial law. And the Church is watching."

The President did not reply. The Church was becoming more than a thorn in his flesh, a dagger more like. Rome would not take lightly to one of its clerics being tried by the secular power when the offence was not criminal, for no one had alleged that Oliveros had been directly responsible for Ramon Bersamina's death. The priest's involvement was circumstantial and there was also the matter of his clerical freedom to act in the light of his conscience. Why had Manuel's ministry been so zealous? The round up of suspects should have excluded the priest and his harsh interrogation. Had Manuel countenanced the measures deliberately, hoping that foreign observers and pressmen would flock like hawks to watch the régime's discomfiture?

"Senor President," said Bersamina casting a sympathetic look at his leader. "I recognise your dilemma. But it may not be such a problem after all. I know you want to create a good impression in Europe, but in my opinion an excellent way of presenting you most favourably in the public eye would be to divert the attention now being given to this domestic issue to what you will do and say in Europe. Listen to me; you can make it clear that we are an independent nation and that no external power, temporal or spiritual, can interfere in our politics. Independence is best safeguarded by attack—especially where the Church is concerned. In the Western secular democracies you can be portrayed as a modernizing, progressive force in Asia. The arrest of the priest can be represented as part of our long-term struggle for national freedom, an epic struggle against Spanish, Papal, Japanese and US imperialism which you continue to lead. My friend Antonio, the attention you get in Europe will be maximised to the full."

The President sat back to chew the matter over. Manuel was a callous man who believed in giving a free hand to the soldiers and police when he thought it necessary, and truth was never high on his agenda. But Manuel was twenty years his junior. On the protected Bersamina hacienda he had not reached manhood until well after the war and had never seen how cruel men could be given half a chance. Did he just turn a blind eye now to reports of atrocities by his security forces or did he perhaps enjoy them vicariously? In his heart the President knew the plight of the Caroline peasant, dependent for everything on the patronage of the rich, tilling the land for a pittance yet still hardly owning a papaya tree to call his own; he knew the subservient position of peasant women who could not even call their body their own if the feudal lord wanted to play with it. And he knew how terribly the peasants suffered when military operations were mounted around them. In his lifetime he had seen how obstinately the Caroline peasants had fought against the Japs when their families were in danger of death and outrage. They were a brave people because they had to be. Nor could he forget Conchita's words at the end of that unhappy interview—that he had not allowed people the freedom to criticise. He looked Bersamina in the eye and asked, "Manuel, can you say that this priest Oliveros is wrong when he maintains that it is us and our methods that are driving people into the arms of the communists? Can you say that our army, our police, our civil officials never ill-treat people? If I am asked that question in Europe, how shall I reply?"

"Well, Senor President, I won't reply as you ask because you know the answers as well as I do. Let's face facts; life is a shit sandwich; it looks good outside but the taste is vile. All you should say in public is that Caroline troops, like all troops, occasionally behave badly, but you must always maintain that such behavior is against your Government's policy and army regulations." Since Bersamina did not like to discuss moral issues, which invariably gave rise to indecision, he continued in a firm precise voice, "Antonio, you know as well as I do that in some provinces there are two governments in power—ours and the communists— or in some places one of the same two and a Muslim group. In every province the peasants have one aim in common—to get on with their own lives in peace. Naturally they support whichever government gives them most security. Your government, and all the forces opposing us, have one weapon in common, military force. So like it or not we are involved in a balance of terror. Whoever questions his will to use terror when there is no other way will lose out. So you must not weaken; neither of us can weaken. We must brazen it out, Senor President, or else we end up as cat food." Bersamina rose to his feet, leant across the desk and grasped the President's hand. "Tony. My friend, my leader, you cannot weaken. Cast all doubt from your mind and depend on me. I am your oldest supporter."

"Let's continue our talk more comfortably," said the President anxious to escape from Bersamina's hold and leading him to the long settee that he sometimes used for a nap when alone in the office. There they took corner positions after helping themselves liberally to whiskey and choosing one of the superlative cigars which Fidel Castro had given to the President, who, once settled, was ready to overflow with reminiscences. "Ah Castro, it was difficult to get a word in edgeways when he was here, but Griselda could do it. You know Manuel, I was once in—well, almost in—the Communist Party. I thought it was the quickest route to becoming the national leader. But I could never stand the dependence on foreign communist parties, the Russian, the Chinese, the Cubans all manipulating what they imagined were dim Carolino comrades for their own ends." After some derisive exchanges about their wives' expensive tastes in jewellery and shoes they helped themselves to more Scotch and later even more, while the President told stories about the personal quirks of Brezhnev, Mitterand and other world leaders he had met. Best of all were those about Yeltsin in his cups, which hardly surprised but greatly amused Bersamina, who was getting quite drunk himself by the time he heard the President saying, "What I could never stand about the communists were the long hours I had to spend discussing tedious aspects of their damned philosophy, their Dialectical Materialism; it's completely alien to our hot peasant sensuality. Honestly Manuel, it was worse than studying theology. Yeltsin told me he felt the same; maybe that's why he chucked it out so easily. Oh Boris, he could have made his home happily among the Carolinos. Anyway, you can see why it made me so happy to join up later with fellow army officers, patriotic Carolinos with no foreign axes to grind, who could see that our so-called democracy would soon land us in the shit. So I never became a Castro, an Uncle Ho or, grateful thanks to the Blessed Virgin, a Pol Pot."

"No, but you became very rich," said Bersamina at which both of them laughed loudly, as if this truth was the greatest joke on record. "What about Prince Chichibu's crock of gold? It must have appreciated enormously in value. No, don't look worried; I don't want to play 'you show me yours and I'll show you mine.' And you also get eight percent on the value of all merchandise passing through the Port of Infanta; that was a clever deal for you and the First Lady."

"Five percent would have been too small," said the President in mock seriousness.

"And ten percent would have been indecent," replied Bersamina laughing uproariously as he curled his small body into his corner of the settee.

"But eight percent is just right. The First Lady and I are entitled to it considering what we've done for the country. Yes, I've earned it but I regret that I never got the economy booming like Japan or Malaysia," the President said ruefully. "Perhaps I'm too ignorant about economics or more probably I came up against the rich Seigneurs like you Bersaminas who took everything of real value, I mean the land, centuries ago and won't give up a thing. But Manuel, despite the stranglehold you big guys have, I did my best to make the economy work. We spent millions on infrastructure and Griselda and I invested some of our own money in businesses, hoping there'd be a flow down of wealth to the poor. But recession has made it difficult to compete with the prices of other Asian countries. Our exports have fallen and it's clear that you rich sods have decided that the losses are not to be at your expense."

For some reason, the whiskey most probably, Bersamina suddenly found that he just did not care what he was about to say. "But you Florescos have taken a goodly share of the cake all the same, though I agree that you and Griselda deserve it. However, despite what you say about feudal families like mine, you've never done much about land reform, have you? But that's not so odd. I guess we are partners in crime after all—rich partners!" For a while he and the President were silent, drinking and gazing at each other with blank faces. Their mutual honesty had become embarrassing and their good humour peculiarly ominous, for neither could make out the other's motives.

The President became mournful and replied, "Yes, that's true. We've got it made. You know that pop song *We Are the World*; well, my family likes to sing 'we've got the world'. But can we hold on to it, Manuel? If the economy is failing and insurrection grows, it's inevitable that we won't be able to hold the countryside for long, even with terror. And if the countryside goes, Infanta will follow and all its rich bourgeois will be scattered to the wind."

Ever the calculator, Bersamina replied, "Well, with people like us, Senor President, there will always be the United Sates as our last retreat. Neither of us is going to starve. And I feel sure that one of us will always be somewhere on top—to help the other of course."

Hearing those words, tipsy though he was, Antonio Floresco was certain that this man intended to succeed him. The First Lady could scheme as she might, but she could never rival Manuel Bersamina when it came to weighing up the odds. More than anyone it was Bersamina who had prevented the emergence of a moderate opposition. An alternative leader to the President, or to Bersamina, might well be favoured by the United States but if all moderate opinion had been driven underground or into the arms of the communists the United States would have to support whichever of them remained as head of state. In this matter how skilfully they had both played the Americans. Even though the Caroline constitution banned all atomic weapons from its territory, under Bersamina's influence the President had allowed the construction of deep missile silos hidden away in the mountains for potential

American use. As long as the United States felt threatened in the Pacific there was nothing to fear. It could not quit the Carolines completely. A feeling of confidence took hold of him again. The Pope can go to the Devil; perhaps he is the Devil. Then he looked at Bersamina pouring himself another whiskey. What did this man know of love of country? Wealth, family and power were Manuel's gods. He, President Antonio Floresco, was different; he still loved his country. But he was only a man and now he felt tired and anxious to be on his own. It was time to decide how he would act when he saw the Holy Father. "Very well Manuel, let's call it a day. But first I'll tell you that I shall follow your advice and be the son of the Church in matters spiritual. But I'll be absolutely firm over our right to try anyone, especially priests, who act subversively. That's what you really want, isn't it, Senor Atheistic Bersamina?"

"I do indeed, especially priests. But you can always show yourself accommodating over the things that really get up the Pope's nose—birth control, abortion, divorce, but keep your mouth shut on things the church pretends not to enjoy, like fucking choirboys. Keeping Rome happy will cost us nothing."

The President thought that Bersamina's crude refusal to show even a residual respect for the Church was dangerous but he confined himself to observing, "A rising population is costing us a great deal. It should be controlled, Manuel."

"With birth control? Condoms? Hopeless! Let it go. Don't try to crack down on the only ecstasy left to the poor. Carolinos won't make love in a raincoat. The cock is their real God. No Antonio, anything you say about that to these stupid peasants is useless. I remember my wife once joking that even rabbits couldn't breed as fast as Carolinos. They'll go on reproducing until there's no room left to move, even on the mountains. But we'll be dead by then and our families can be miles away. So best to give Rome all the support it wants on trivia. It will have to pay one day."

The President found himself heartily disliking Bersamina. To him the Carolinos were just 'these stupid peasants', so much vermin. What was more he knew that Bersamina's grand Spanish-speaking wife regarded himself and Griselda not much higher. All at once the Minister, through his whiskey bleared eyes, had seen the President's dangerously angry frown and began to gush out a eulogy about the way Antonio had cleared up the mess in the country after declaring martial law and how the Bersamina family would never forget that achievement. He only paused in his flow of words to say very gravely, "But Antonio, my wife and I have one great criticism of you. Yes, look at me like that if you wish, but I must say it: Antonio Floresco you are too humane. A ruler must be as hard as granite." Then he smiled sadly as it were to himself before ending with, "Despite that there's no one living in the Carolines who could achieve even half of what you have accomplished."

The President's mind hovered incumbent on the fleecy air, uncertain where to land. He had for so long succumbed to the danger of having men around him who sang too sweetly. Yes, he was flattered but he remained suspicious. In a surge of what looked like good feeling he said, "There's just one thing I've got to ask of you Manuel. I want you to come with me to Europe. It's not too late to make the necessary arrangements. I need your shrewdness. If you have no objection I shall inform the Cabinet when it meets."

The full Cabinet of the Caroline government was quite unlike the cabinets of most countries that aim at privacy and desirably the smallest possible size. Infanta was home to a large number of Ministries, several with overlapping functions, each with its minister and generally an assistant minister, all of whom, attended by their officials, trooped into the cabinet room, a beautiful Chamber in the DeoGracias where the Spanish Viceroy had once held court and on whose chair of state Antonio Floresco presided today in place of the Prime Minister. As Cabinet sessions were often taped for television, the coming and going of technicians and cameramen together with the constant services of waiters keeping the flower-decorated tables supplied with refreshments gave rise to a noisy assembly of people, the majority of whom had no contribution to make to the proceedings.

The reality was that, though run of the mill matters were discussed at tedious length in the room, under the Chairmanship of the Prime Minister, the Cabinet was only cursorily informed of major decisions. These were taken by the President himself in secret conclave with a few trusted cronies, one of whom was Manuel Bersamina and another the First Lady, who bore the title Minister of Culture and Humanity in Development. This title apparently entitled her to speak on any subject under the sun and as long as she saw fit. But there was another man of influence, a man of different calibre from the usual go-getting Caroline politicians, the Prime Minister Bienvenido Loyola. The strictures that the President applied to all his Ministers except Bersamina could not be levied at the Prime Minister. Loyola was not one of the long time supporters of the Florescos. He was there for no other reason than his talent. A distinguished economist, an intellectual and a man of total integrity, he had been asked by the President to give up his Chair at Harvard to instill some planning into the country's chaotic economic life and to provide an impression of trustworthiness to satisfy the Carolines' creditors, particularly the International Monetary Fund and the World Bank. Other ministers might jockey for power against one another but around Loyola there was an aura of calm and respect which was physically evident in the Cabinet room.

Such was not the case in regard to Bersamina. Ministers might fear him but their fear was not translated into much respect. There were those who supported him because he controlled the security forces and there was those who intrigued against him mainly for personal reasons. Few actually liked him. By the time he had taken his seat in the Cabinet room he was internally in a state of fury. The more he thought about it the more he was convinced that the President was afraid to leave him in the country when the visit to Europe went ahead. Had the invitation to accompany him been thought up by the President himself or had the First Lady worked on her husband to ease herself into the position of being available as his legal successor, in the event of his illness or worse when abroad? Despite these concerns he made a point of chatting fulsomely with his neighbours, cracking coarse jokes and telling them he had just received a piece of pleasant news that they might hear about soon enough.

The first item for the Cabinet to consider, indeed the only substantive matter for the morning, was discussion of what was described in the agenda paper as the First Lady's 'most important contribution to the life of the nation'. This was the President's reason for attending the session. In pursuit of her desire to put the Carolines on the map culturally she had erected, regardless of expense, a huge Opera House magnificently situated on the sea front of Infanta. It was not unfitting that the building should resemble a brutalised version of a Roman temple, as its completion would be something of an apotheosis of the Florescos. The money for the building had largely been provided by the First Lady's Caroline National Construction Company, supported of course by donations from domestic and foreign firms anxious to keep in Senora Floresco's good books. Unhappily the scale of the building had made demands beyond their resources or their willingness to pay and it was now apparent that the Opera was likely to be the last of the First Lady's architectural achievements, unless some great improvement occurred in the economy. Nevertheless large unbudgeted sums of government money had already been sequestered by the President's office from the National Bank to complete the project in a manner appropriate to the First Lady's view of her role in the world of art, music and drama. This provision had become especially urgent, as early in the following year an international festival of opera had already been scheduled, at which renowned artists from all over the world would appear. Senor Teodoro Yamsuan, the notoriously corrupt Minister for Public Works, proudly announced that before the Cabinet was asked to give its formal approval for the additional financial requirement the First Lady would give her overview of the objectives and purpose of the great work which he sincerely hoped would eternally commemorate the Floresco's name—if the first family graciously so consented.

The First Lady inclined her head graciously towards the members of the Cabinet and launched into a lecture on the role of art in society. Those who had the nerve to take their eyes off her curvaceous figure clad in a shimmering richly embroidered pink national dress, noted that the President had closed his eyes and sunk back within the confines of his huge vice-regal chair as soon as she was on her feet. He thoroughly enjoyed it when she inflicted her monologues on his courtiers, generally obliging them to suffer in silence the sort of drivel a schoolgirl might put in an essay. "In past times we find that primitive people always found a place for music and art in their lives," she proclaimed roundly. "Even today

116

within our beautiful country we find our remote tribes celebrating significant events, birth, marriages and deaths, in festivals which are characterised by song and different forms of drama. Nor have these celebrations been forgotten in our towns and cities, and since we became Christians important events in the Church calendar have been dramatised in plays and processions at which ordinary people can show their simple faith." On and on her voice went, resonating up to the painted ceiling whence plump-bottomed putti and Spanish royalty might have given her their attention, had their eyes not been riveted in ecstatic contemplation of a distant sunburst, presumably God the Father, illuminating with His Holy Spirit the resurrected Saviour and a soaring Blessed Virgin. As she continued, Bersamina scratched his ear so he could slyly glance at his watch while Loyola's small mouth became so tightly pursed that it resembled a full stop, which was what most people present would have liked to apply to the First Lady's stream of words. But worse was to come. A blackboard, brought from the children's nursery, had been placed beside the First Lady's chair and before long she was demonstrating with pictures her theory of the place of art in Caroline society. First she drew a hat. "That represents the Caroline people," she said, as a piece of chalk broke in her hand. "Oh, I'm not a very good artist am I?" At this a number of sycophants laughed loudly while everyone tried at least to smile. Bersamina looked as though the lines on his face might break into fissures, while Loyola closed his eyes and took to yoga-like calm breathing. "Now the Caroline people plus work plus art," said the First Lady, pausing to draw a plus sign followed by a spade, another plus sign and a G clef symbol, "together equal progress." The last word she represented with a rocket. "Right?" she asked with a joyful smile and now everyone laughed most genuinely for the elevation of her missile had a distinct resemblance to a rampant penis. Bersamina muttered something vulgar to his neighbour but converted the sound to a polite bout of coughing. This did not deter her and she explained the symbolic meaning of her drawing a second time.

At last the First Lady concluded by expressing her regret, in a chiding way, over the negative attitude of some Ministers towards her project. "Please, my friends, please develop a positive attitude towards the Opera House," she cried passionately, opening her arms to the whole company. Then her voice fell, she knitted her brows and her peroration, softly spoken, ended with, "In life, fellow Carolinos, if you have the right attitude, you can do anything. That is the secret of my own success in life."

Of course there was loud applause and banging of desks for her speech, the President joining in enthusiastically even though he had a gnawing pain in his lower back. After a while, out of the desultory chatter slithered a non-agenda yet increasingly heated discussion about the commissioning of a new Opera by a Caroline composer, a protégé of the First Lady, to celebrate the inauguration of the Opera House ,until, almost apologetically, the Clerk of the Cabinet asked for assent to the request for additional financial resources. As though it was a foregone conclusion there was a bored chorus of 'ayes' in the course of which, somewhat tentatively, Bersamina raised the pencil with which he had been doodling and said, "Your Excellency, I believe Senor Loyola has something to say."

The President gave his nod. "Senor Loyola?" expecting a few words of general approval for the motion. The merits of rival composers ceased to be at issue and everyone began to shuffle their papers in anticipation of the next agenda item. But the noise shuffled to a gradual but profound halt when Loyola rose, took the roving microphone from an usher and said quite simply, "Senor President, I regret there are no budgeted funds from which I can make an appropriation to the CNCC and under the circumstances I am unable to accede to this request."

The President was flustered. Decisions of the inner group were never questioned. "Well, there must be some other vote, contingencies of some sort or other. What about the Ministry for Culture estimates?

"Like the Ministry for Public Works estimates, already overspent," responded Loyola dryly.

The President frowned. Things like this did not happen at Cabinet meetings and were inconceivable where requests from the First Lady were concerned. If Loyola had said something critical of Griselda the President would have sprung to her defence, but all Loyola had uttered was a simple statement of an irrefutable fact. Before the President could decide what to do Loyola had taken the microphone again saying, "Perhaps under the circumstances I might be permitted to speak further on this matter." to which the President with inner misgivings said, "Of course Senor Prime Minister."

Bersamina's expression had changed not one iota, but the mask that had concealed anger a short while ago was now but a fig leaf to cover his pleasure. The meeting had come to life—for him and for everyone else. The First Lady's face too gave not a hint of her feelings, but everyone in the room could imagine the rage that must be stirring under that bouffant hairdo. Loyola pursed his lips for a moment, raised his hands as it were in an attitude of prayer, and leaned his head to one side—the perfect picture of a professor about to give a lecture on nothing more remarkable than, say, the mating habits of the conger eel. "Your Excellency," he began. "Fellow Ministers, as you know less than a month ago I was in Washington at the headquarters of the International Monetary Fund negotiating a further tranche to cover our budget deficit. I have already submitted to all of you in writing a cogent account of those not very pleasant negotiations. I only succeeded because I gave a number of undertakings, in particular those concerning the ring-fencing of our ministerial estimates of expenditure. I made it clear to you that the IMF would only provide funds if my undertakings were underwritten by all heads of Ministries, including of course the Office of the President. In other words none of you was excluded. There can be no more of the inefficient financial management we have seen in this instance." Loyola then held up a Ministry of Finance briefcase and said, "The signed assurances already given by all honourable members concerned are here, in a dossier." There ensued a pregnant silence during which the proverbial pin might have been heard to drop had the floor not been covered by thick and very expensive red carpet. Loyola had said enough.

It was enough too for Bersamina that Loyola's words had been spoken. For once criticism of the First Lady had been voiced, explicitly yet without the naming of names, in this sycophantic chamber. The tip of an iceberg had been descried, suggesting that in the depths all sorts of uncurbed movements were surging around. For the moment however Bersamina knew that Antonio Floresco must be got off the hook, so he caught the President's eye and got his permission to speak.

"Your Excellency." He paused to give an ingratiating smile in the direction of the First Lady, who was sitting bolt upright. "This morning has been one of those occasions that has been truly inspiring. The First Lady has reminded us that as a government we are working fundamentally as a team for the intellectual and artistic advance of this country. We need to be reminded of that fact amidst the more tedious duties of administration. The First Lady has set our eyes on the horizon but Senor Loyola has warned us that on the long road towards it there will be stony patches. But I don't think there is the least conflict between the wisdom of the two parties who are so valuable in our deliberations. Were I a communist, Your Excellency, I would say that we are involved in a dialectical process. We have to balance the aspirations of our people with the requirements of the IMF to produce a happy synthesis. No one has suggested that we should exceed our overall estimates. All that is needed is the service of a few dedicated people to examine where and how savings can be effected in government Ministries to enable the First Lady's most laudable project to proceed and to succeed." He gave a self-depreciating smile and a boyish chuckle. "Now I am always ordering my police and military to lose their big bellies. To begin with I'll convene my logistics team to see if we can trim some fat from the Ministry for Defence estimates; then I could look at the estimates of other Ministries. We must all find enough money to meet the bill for the Opera."

On that harmonious note Bersamina sat down and the President expressed to the Defence Minister his appreciation for something which, of course, he had known all along could be done. The meeting then closed and the President left at a snail's pace, with the First Lady like a royal consort on his arm radiating her smiles on everyone except the recalcitrant Minister for Finance. Bersamina however kept close to Loyola as they left the Cabinet room and put his arm on his shoulder as they ambled along. "You were very bold," he said. "I'd like a few people like you in the Ministry for Defence. She'll be after your head, Senor."

Loyola stared owl-like at Bersamina. "Yours more likely," he said. "After all I didn't patronise her or drop a hint that she was administratively incompetent. And I didn't give people the idea that I was ready to subject other Ministries to the inquisition of my logistic team—as though I was the head of State."

"But I must thank you for giving me the opportunity to do so. A casual observer might even think we were acting in collusion, Senor Loyola."

Loyola darted a telling glance at the crafty Minister for Defence; he had got the message all right but he replied with a world-weary air. "The truth is, Manuel, that political life doesn't hold any attraction for me. Elizabeth and I were much happier at Harvard. I miss the stimulus of brilliant students. Here…" He shrugged his shoulders.

"So your sally was really an opening gambit to the retirement of our best ever Minister for Finance?" Bersamina asked cautiously

"It could be, but I prefer to think of it as a statement of my position. Floresco brought me here to try to make sense out of our country's economy. He wanted me to improve it and I thought I could do so. Just remember, after the war the Carolines had a reasonable infrastructure, a functioning economy and a largely English educated people. It took me some time to find out how deeply the country had plunged into the mire. Rebellions, martial law, stupid education policies, the debt trap, and a population increase run wild have ruined it all. Worst of all our country is cursed by an entity that can't be found in any textbook on economics— the Florescos. So much disappears into their maw. They are like a black hole in physics. They suck in matter but never spew anything out—well not in the Carolines. Perhaps what they take passes through a worm hole into another dimension—composed of Swiss Banks." Loyola laughed but at the same time he faltered in his steps. Bersamina took his arm and steadied him. "You know Bersamina, I love this country. I could do something about it even now but it would mean everyone, not just the Florescos but the rich seigneurs like you listening to me and changing. If I am not listened to, disaster lies ahead and I don't want to be around when chaos erupts and the blood is flowing."

Bersamina was impressed by the confident way in which Loyola had spoken. Yet though confident too in his own security network the prediction of widespread mayhem and death from this brilliant academic was disturbing. As they made their way to the car porte

he said quickly. "I for one have absolute trust in you, Senor Loyola. We must follow your advice. And I think we must be prepared to support one another—for the country's sake."

His Eminence Cardinal Lorenzo Peccata did not want his journey to the Ministry for Defence to remain a secret. In fact his staff had made it known through a number of channels that his eminence would arrive at four in the afternoon at the functional building from which Bersamina controlled the security forces of the Carolines. Many Carolinos, being respectful of priests, but especially of one so elevated as a Cardinal were always happy to receive an ecclesiastical blessing and so just outside the thick metal gates of the Ministry's forecourt a little group of people, mostly women and elderly at that, clapped and cheered the Cardinal as the electronically operated gates swung open to let his car in.

It was easy enough to get into the Ministry, but would Manuel Bersamina receive him? An official had phoned to say that the Minister was aware of the Cardinal's intended visit to the Ministry without saying whether the Minister would be present, still less available for a meeting. The Cardinal knew that the family Bersamina was Catholic and paid lip service to the Church, and continued its donations to churches, schools and charities built up over the centuries, but he was also certain that Bersamina's belief in the tenets of the Church was minimal. The sight of the little crowd outside the gates was reassuring. Successful or not it indicated that the whole Catholic population of the country would know of his journey. If he was not received press headlines like 'Cardinal humiliated by Minister for Defence' would appear in the newspapers on the following day. He did not think that Bersamina would risk such an outcome.

An officer, a colonel the Cardinal guessed, for he was not well acquainted with military ranks and badges, conducted him deferentially to a well appointed waiting room but disappeared after asking the visitor if he would like a refreshment, which was politely refused. Nothing had been said on who would receive him. It was unusual for a person of his eminence to be kept waiting at all, except by His Holiness of course, so the Cardinal picked up a glossy magazine that contained a laudatory account of the 'modern Caroline Army'. Opposite the preface was a photograph of an unsmiling Senor Manuel Bersamina. The Cardinal studied the runneled face before him; intelligent—certainly, careworn—definitely, humane—the Cardinal could not guess.

He did however know that there were certain facts about Bersamina on which guessing would be superfluous; of these most important was his unpopularity. In many provinces, especially those where counter-insurgency operations were underway, he was detested by peasants, workers and middle class bourgeois, many of whom had suffered from the rapacity and cruelty of the soldiers and police. In consequence they largely took on board the communist line that he ran the huge military machine as though it was his own, for the defence of himself and his class, even though it was paid for out of national tax revenue. If true it was larceny on a grand scale but of a kind commonplace in dictatorships. At a personal level Bersamina was reputed to be honest, though in reality his wealth obviated any need for corruption; few Carolinos were unaware of the extent of his land holdings and the immense wealth his family had made out of sugar and copra.

The Cardinal thumbed through the magazine. Pictures of healthy young men with grinning faces, impressive military vehicles from France, weaponry from Russia and surveillance equipment from the world over made him apprehensive. He reflected that underpinning this expensive hardware lay Bersamina's reputation for efficiency, a characteristic few other Ministers could be accused of, though an ingredient of it was the speed with which, owing to the President's declining health, Bersamina was now allowed to fill top military and police posts with well trained men personally loyal to his cause. All in all the Cardinal recognised that Bersamina, truly a potential successor to the President, was to be treated with caution, but more importantly with respect. Quite surely he admitted to himself that his submissive visit to Bersamina might be worthwhile in the long run even though its immediate cause was the case of the lowly priest Oliveros.

Bersamina had still been wrestling with Loyola's prescription for austerity if the economy was to be saved, when an aide told him of the Cardinal's arrival. He knew at once it was on account of that priest in San Felipe. He had just stood up to the President on the matter and he did not feel like an argument with the Cardinal, which he would surely lose under a salvo of Augustinian logic. "Why didn't you say I would not be in office today?" he asked the aide.

"Somehow or other he found out when you were returning. His car arrived here just a few minutes before yours. He knows you are here for sure."

Confrontation with the Church being at issue, this was an occasion when Bersamina wanted to make sure that he had the President's backing. But for once the aide could only get through to a DeoGracias assistant secretary, who said that Senor Floresco was not to be disturbed on medical orders. This meant he was attached to his kidney machine; it was the only time when it was not possible to contact him. Even on the golf course he was accessible in case of emergency. Bersamina observed his social secretary, diminutive Mina Ocampo, an ardent Catholic, monitoring him from the corner of the room. Could she have leaked news of his movements? Well then, the whole population knew about the visit. He was trapped. The Cardinal must be seen. He smiled at little Mina and said as if he meant it, "Oh Mina, please tell my aide that I shall be honoured to receive His Eminence. No, not here Mina. In my reception room."

The door opened; the aide announced, "His Eminence Cardinal Peccata," and withdrew. The imposing figure of the Prince of the Church, Nuncio of the Holy See to the Government of the Carolines, Archbishop of Infanta, wearing clerical garb and a red skullcap, swept in. Bersamina bowed and gestured the priest to sit down. He then took a chair facing him, smiled and said it was an unexpected pleasure to receive the head of the Caroline Church in his office.

The Cardinal nodded his head and raised his hand in a gesture that might in other circumstances have been taken as an incomplete benediction. Then, without more ado he plunged into matters that were really agitating him. "Senor Bersamina, I cannot really understand what this government is doing. We are essentially a Catholic nation. For centuries the Church has played an important role in our life. Past Governments, especially the American, always co-operated closely with the Church. Yes, the Japanese were difficult—they certainly interned priests who were enemy nationals—but even so they recognised the Church's position in society. But now, when the people are facing all sorts of economic problems, when disruptive social evils are at large, your Ministry seems intent on creating a dangerous crisis between Church and State." This tirade, loudly spoken, caused Bersamina to open his eyes in genuine surprise. Was the Cardinal really a diplomat? A mountain was surely being made out of a molehill by this seemingly angry man, who had taken to wringing his hands together in a way that suggested real agony of spirit. Nor had he finished. "Senor Minister, I am sure you are well aware of my reason for coming here: the arrest and mistreatment of a priest in San Felipe, a certain Father Oliveros, a misguided man no doubt, but a priest under my jurisdiction. Whether he has done right or wrong is of far less importance than the broader question of relations between Church and State—and your reasons for souring that relationship."

But he is a diplomat, and a crafty one at that, Bersamina told himself. Why should he speak so aggressively if he does not want to cause embarrassment? So, nodding his head sagely as if he concurred with much that had just been said, he said, "Your Eminence, I think that you know that I and my family have always been faithful followers of the Church, both in faith and in support for its needs. That tradition will continue as long as I live and I am sure after I have departed. But I know that you, as a man of great experience, will be aware that when disputes arise between people or institutions blame does not always lie on one side. Please accept the fact that if a matter of Church doctrine were at issue, I would follow your judgment to the letter. But this is an issue of criminal law. No one in the Carolines, neither you nor myself, is above that law. I know you would not dispute that. But it could be you are seeing a crisis where none exists." Bersamina paused and looked like a penitent son of the Church as he enquired, "Advise me, Father, how you think this matter might have been handled. I do not claim omniscience. If there is a better way of dealing with Father Oliveros' offences, I would certainly be prepared to follow it."

"Of course no one is above the law," said the Cardinal. But I think you are only speaking theoretically. In reality I and my priests are only too aware of many crimes—crimes Senor Bersamina—

that are committed by the servants of the State, in particular by military and police personnel for whom you are responsible; I suppose I could say criminally responsible. No, I don't want to discuss the relationship between Church and State. That was settled centuries ago. But I want to pose a question. How do you expect the Church, in particular its parish priests and sisters who work among the people, to support you when they see so many of their parishioners living in fear and poverty? Do you expect clerics like Oliveros, whose families are peasants, to remain silent when they see the government following courses of action which grind people down into abject misery? Where does the guilt lie, Senor? In the puny protests of Oliveros or in the repression of yourself and your minions?"

Bersamina could not easily reply; the Cardinal's facts were undeniable but his censorious argument discounted the realities of civil war. He bowed his head a little as though acknowledging such a stern admonition, which gesture netted the Cardinal, who continued in a milder voice like a priest lifting the curtain of repentance to reveal salvation. "But there is another way. Show yourself willing to listen to the arguments of the Church and make reforms. As for Oliveros, leave me to deal with him in the Church's way. He is in need of instruction. I believe we can lead him back to the light."

"It would be making an exception to the operation of the law but for expediency's sake perhaps..." Bersamina hesitated as though giving the suggestion careful consideration.

"Precisely, precisely for expediency's sake," the Cardinal cut in quickly.

"Ah, so it is permissible for the sake of expediency for the law to be ignored from time to time?"

The Cardinal was irritated by Bersamina's casuistry. "If you intend to indulge in clever argument for its own sake we're not going to get far."

"I assure you that is far from my intent, your Eminence. Nor do I want to anger you. But I have to point out my difficulties. The situation is more complicated than you have painted it. Do you think I like cruelty? I do not. I hate it. I have seen too much of it. But it is sometimes expedient to be harsh in war. Let me tell you why.

The communists put immense pressure on the people to give them support. They punish people who do not provide them with food or money. Their penalties for refusal are cruel, as you must know. But if the penalties we impose for co-operation with the communists are severe the people have an excuse for refusing to support them. We know from experience that this is so. The people can say, look if we help you the government is going to take away even what we have. The communists do not wish to lose the people's allegiance. After all it is their proud claim that they and the people are one."

"Senor Bersamina, again you are begging the question. I don't oppose your measures provided you apply them legally, even under martial law, but you must apply them with humanity. I am talking now about police and soldiers who steal property from the peasants. I am talking about military detachments who torture on grounds of mere suspicion or because they want people to hand over what little money they have. I am talking about men who rape women in front of their families. I don't believe you are ignorant of such things."

"I do know of them, Father, and I have ordered my officers to take severe action against offenders."

The Cardinal drew himself up in his chair and stared hard at the Minister. "Do you really believe what you say? Tell the officers to take severe measures? It's often the officers who are the worst perpetrators! A little of what you say may be true but overall what you are telling me, Senor, is a lie, a monstrous lie. Your security forces have more than a small complement of bad hats and thugs."

How, Bersamina wondered, did this man believe that it was possible to keep up the morale of the forces, who were fighting in dangerous conditions, if they were to be perpetually chivvied and punished for behaving as ordinary human beings when under stress? How did he think it was possible to curb his men's violence when the so-called liberation fighters roasted, maimed and beheaded the soldiers they captured? All the same the Cardinal had made a valid point and one to which he must reply openly and to the advantage of his Ministry.

He said, "Your Eminence, I give you my promise: I will do all in my power to enforce discipline. Military Law provides for the severe punishment of men who commit the abuses you have talked of. You can tell the world that I have made this promise. But in return I ask you not to oppose my bringing Father Oliveros to trial. Surely the discussion the trial will give rise to will help the Church to clarify its own position on communism, perhaps even on liberation theology. But first I must tell you that we do have absolute proof of the Priest's guilt. But if and when a court finds him guilty I shall ask the President to exercise clemency on condition that the Church sends Oliveros to some place—a seminary perhaps—where he can receive instruction. The Caroline people must learn that support for the communists will never be tolerated—even if it comes from priests."

The Cardinal asked Bersamina to repeat his proposals. He then made a note of them, actually in Latin, in his pocket book. As he slowly wrote the translated words, under Bersamina's fascinated eye, he reflected with some satisfaction that even if had not been able to stop Oliveros' trial he had received a concession on its outcome and a valuable promise on military discipline from the Minister. Equally significant was the fact that he had opened a personal dialogue with a very important member of government, maybe the successor. Almost as a way of sealing their co-operation he said, "Senor, you said that you have absolute proof of Oliveros' guilt. May I be given a sight of it."

"Father, it so happens that everything concerning security in San Felipe is here," said Bersamina as he went to a shelf to take a dossier from a box file. "You are welcome to examine any of these documents—not just those on Father Oliveros. You have every right to see them."

The Cardinal suggested that it might be more convenient if he were to look at so many papers in another room, but Bersamina said in the friendliest of ways. "Oh no, Father. Stay where you are. I have to go to my office to phone my wife. Please feel at home here. I shall see that refreshments are brought to you while you are reading. Good afternoon Father and let us hope that the interesting and frank conversation we have had will be the first of many."

The Cardinal made a little hand gesture suggesting affability, if not benediction, as Bersamina left and settled himself in a more comfortable chair, the dossier before him. He thumbed through the documents which pleased him by their clarity and good organisation. Those concerning Father Oliveros were flagged and so he soon learned about the priest's extensive contacts with the communist guerrillas and indeed the help he had given them by way of supplies of food and provision of hiding places in his college during their operations. Some documents were photocopies, the originals, it was noted, being in the hands of the Public Prosecutor. There were also photographs showing Oliveros with liberation fighters, some possibly his students, for they looked so young and vulnerable. The Cardinal quickly recognised that Bersamina did indeed have all the proof needed for a successful trial and so, after making a few notes, this time in Spanish, in his pocketbook he sat back to enjoy an excellent claret, cheese and biscuits and a bowl of fruit that had arrived. As he continued to flick through the file he noted the names of a number of people he knew, though not well, but a short report on a person with a non-Caroline name drew his special attention, that of Father Francis Stephens, the personable Franciscan parish priest with whom he had stayed two or three times. On one of those occasions he had been pleased to serve in the San Felipe baroque church the Tridentine High Mass in whose Latin he gloried. The account seemed no more than an indication of how easily a priest's sympathy could be aroused by the plight of the poor among whom he worked. Nothing more than friendship with Oliveros was suggested; certainly no collusion with him in aiding the guerrillas. Nevertheless on the last page the Cardinal read how Father Stephens had been manoeuvred into helping the police in their search for a wounded guerrilla by arresting and pressurising his altar boy. 'Why an altar boy?' the Cardinal asked himself momentarily as he took another sip of the seductive claret, yet his sensitive antennae were already alert to what would follow in the next paragraph. The report did not say that the priest and the altar boy had sex together, which sort of lapse the Cardinal had often encountered, but that Father Stephens was obsessively enamoured of the boy who apparently reciprocated his affection, which was a matter of common knowledge in San Felipe. The Cardinal, who had an eye for beautiful things as well as for gracious living, then recalled that, as he incensed the altar in San Felipe with *Ab illo benedicaris in cuius honore, Amen*, he had given the censer to an altar boy with a face of angelic beauty. Later in the priest's house he had smiled at the boy, this time serving wine at the dinner table.

The report disturbed him, not because of Father Stephens' lapse but because it was an open secret, indeed hardly a secret, in San Felipe. Such lapses had been, were and no doubt would always be commonplace among celibate clerics, but the Church in its wisdom kept them under wraps. But now it seemed everything must be made public. Perhaps the Carolines would soon go the way of California—free love, sodomitical weddings, women priests, maybe the sanctity of birth control in place of the sanctity of marriage. In the past when priests sinned they confessed their sins and received absolution, but today, at the drop of a hat, some of them were prepared to justify sin by saying that it was an outdated construct. He felt grateful to Bersamina for the information he had discovered. Their co-operation was already working, yet how to deal with Father Stephens?

As his thoughts dwelt on the iniquity of the age, he gazed around the room in which he was sitting. It gave him some comfort. All the furniture belonged to a more dignified time. The pictures on the walls were of old Caroline towns together with some severely dressed worthies of past centuries. Everything accorded with his own tastes, Tridentine rather than of a new order. At the end of the room was a large black wooden cross unadorned by a crucified figure. The room could have been the study of a bishop and was similar in feeling to his own office. He reflected that Bersamina, in the midst of many an agonising decision, must look up and see that symbol of salvation. It was not just there as an ornament. It was there because it was surely needed. He was glad that he had accepted the Minister's offer of collaboration. Could this man, so different in spirit from the President and the First Lady, a man who rode above the vulgarity of the crowd, be the hope of the country's salvation, a true aristocrat who could enforce strict morality on the licentious Carolinos whether they liked it or not?

The door opened and Bersamina returned, although not expected by the Cardinal who at once rose and went towards him with extended hand. "Senor, I am truly grateful that you were able to see me. Our talk has been worthwhile." He became reflective. "God's ways are strange. Something prompted me to come here almost on the spur of the moment. How mysterious is the Providence that brings us together."

When he was on his own again Bersamina put the Cardinal in a section of his mind that contained the figures of a number of potential allies. He also felt a little flattered that God's Providence might be working for him. After all, it had been suggested by His Eminence and if anyone really knew about such things, a Cardinal should.

Max Bligh had completed his work on the President's forthcoming visit to Europe. He had stayed longer than his partners Hymen and Solly Schuster so as to make technical arrangements with the Department of Information and to keep the President briefed in person on the arrangements being made for television interviews with commentators and journalists in Europe. He had also amassed coverage of material showing all aspects of life in the Carolines, much of it flattering. He was also encouraging Cesar Abulencia to summarise his views on the political and economic situation of the country. These, if satisfactorily edited, could be used to undermine the Floresco régime. But telling pictures even with sardonic commentary by Cesar would not be enough. Something more concrete was needed, something with punch.

That something was provided to him before long by the Infanta Gazette, which accompanied the large breakfast delivered promptly to his hotel room each morning. He had just finished his mango juice and cereal and was pausing over coffee before demolishing the smoked bacon, pork sausages and three fried eggs, sunny side up, to glance at the front page. There in the centre was a photo of a familiar face, a priest called Oliveros, a place called San Felipe, unfamiliar names to Max but the priest was undoubtedly the person to whom he had passed money for the guerrillas in the old church. His immediate reaction was one of fear, but then he felt sure that he could not have been compromised. No one had seen the exchange and Oliveros had no idea who had given him the money. It was also probable that the priest had got rid of the money before his arrest. All the same Bligh was so shaken that he ate not a sausage, none of the bacon and left two of the eggs untouched. He felt glad that he would soon be back stateside.

When he had his next meeting with Cesar that afternoon, for anonymity's sake in a crowded cinema foyer deluged by pop music, he sensed at once that the dapper little man had something to tell him. Cesar bought a ticket and after a little delay, Max did likewise. The auditorium was full, the audience mainly of young and largely jobless males keen to see the latest star packed product of the Caroline film industry. Cesar had as usual found a seat on the back row of the rear stalls, a zone of constant movement on account of male on male pick-ups, where Max joined him. The sound track was very loud but failed to offset the noise flowing in through the foyer doors that were opening and closing like fans. Against the cacophony, the burble of conversation from the audience commenting unceasingly on the action of the film and the sound of popcorn packets being opened and crinkled, banished from the minds of Max and Cesar any fear that what they said might be overheard.

"We may have found an interesting ally, "Cesar hissed, just at the moment when a lovely Caroline heroine was screaming loudly but vainly for help before an oncoming Japanese rapist. She yelled that she was pregnant but the attacker was ruthless, his lust indicated by staring eyes, sloppy lips and jerky hand movements in the vicinity of his fly, which, as the zip descended, were lost off screen.

Max was all ears; the noise made him so. The woman was backing against a wall, even though just beside her was an open street door though which she could easily have made her getaway. "A bit louder please," he whispered angrily at Cesar.

"In the DeoGracias," Cesar went on in a 'believe it or not' voice. "You'll never believe it." Not having had the chance as yet, Max remained silent which was more than the woman on the screen. Her flawless face visible over the rapist's pulsating back was emitting animal sounds, interspersed with Mother of God imprecations, proving that penetration was underway.

"The Devil's daughter—Conchita." At Cesar's words Bligh turned incredulously to look at his informant who was preening himself with satisfaction. Grunts and a deep-throated "Yaah" of pleasure were coming from the rapist. Some of the men in the audience clapped and hooted.

As the rapist fled leaving his victim distraught, the woman's handsome young Caroline husband, a current screen heartthrob, arrived and took to berating his wife for giving in. The on-screen neighbours and the in-house audience clapped approvingly and jeered. Amidst such uproar it was easy for Cesar to unfold quite breathlessly the story of Julio and Conchita, above all their decision, especially the unhappy girl's, to fight against the First Lady. As the film more sympathetically now was showing the woman weeping but still a Caroline glamour-puss, Cesar concluded his dramatic news with, "Conchita hates the régime as much as I do. I tell you, Max, we can make something of this."

Max could not decide whether the information was useful or not. It might be no more than Infanta title-tattle without substance. He could not judge its worth. Nor just now could he fathom why this excitable young audience was again showing its approval as the wronged husband returned to give his still beautiful wife not compassion but a basketfull of hysterical abuse for shaming him, his mother, his father, his land, his religion and his entire family. Her tears evoked no pity from anyone.

"Well," asked Cesar. "What should we make of it?"

"Depends on what you care about I suppose," Max replied coolly without thinking of anything off screen. "How you were brought up."

"What d'you mean? How you were brought up? I don't think your hearing is much good." Cesar squirmed irritably in his seat. "I hate this bloody place."

"At least this bloody place is safe, Cesar. Sorry, I mean we must both be careful how we proceed. That's all."

"Careful! We don't need to be careful in this case. Max, can't you see? We could make use of the President's daughter." Cesar's voice had become much too loud.

"Yes, careful. And I mean now. Keep your voice down. I'm only saying you can't be sure what people will do when they are in an emotional bind. Just look at that guy on the screen." The outraged husband was now in a massage saloon with two nymphets, the three of them each wearing nothing but a ludicrously transparent thong. The guy was moaning and quivering with pleasure as four hands teased and tantalised every inch of his voluptuous body while the anticipated delights of oral sex were suggested as the girls exchanged boiled sweets decidedly phallic in shape, between their mouths which finally spawned them one by one between his slobbering lips. This went on for some time and stimulated the audience considerably, to judge by various shouts and lewd remarks. But just as one girl was using her teeth to pull off the boy's thong and the other's mouth was moving towards its content the scene changed. To the strains of a triumphant male voice choir a swift montage showed joyful farmers, a rich landscape and a Japanese soldier being slowly garrotted by laughing peasants—the footage lingered over ghastly close ups of his agonised face—until in abrupt contrast there was a crowd of kindly women and the audience finally beheld, now to the sound of angelic voices, the raped woman giving birth to twins which her reunited husband, now fashionably clad, held up joyfully to savour their soft skin with his well taught lips. The music exploded with trumpets; the couple kissed passionately; the audience applauded enthusiastically, and Max said, "You see Cesar, no one can tell what will come of lust."

The lights rose from almost obscurity to a dull glow. A lot of movement took place as people bought ice creams and more popcorn and in the case of some youths sitting on the back row generally readjusted their clothes. There also a bit of seat changing took place, as guys tried to make out with a new companion to play around with during the major attraction, which turned out to be yet another showing of Cleopatra. Max decided that he could not take Elizabeth Taylor's acting, still less her tinny voice, again and suggested to Cesar that they should risk having a bite together in the cinema's Chicken Nugget House. Cesar said something about from the frying pan into the fire but agreed, though neither of them had more than a coffee when they got there.

The place was awash with parents and noisy children stuffing chicken bits into their greedy mouths. No one was interested in anything else so Max felt free to ask a few questions urgently. Could Cesar tell him anything about a place called San Felipe? Was it safe? Did he have there any contacts who might be useful when making a documentary. The name of the town caused Cesar to launch into a tirade against the Bersaminas with a lot of hearsay about underpaid workers, disaffection, police atrocities and support for the guerrillas. But off hand he could think of no one in such a place who might be useful. In fact Cesar was by now irritated with Max Bligh, whom he thought stupid not to recognise the potential of the opportunity put before his nose. It was only when leaving and Max said unexpectedly, "Cesar, keep me informed about this Conchita business," that he relaxed sufficiently to say, "I'll see what I can find out about San Felipe for you, Senor Bligh."

Senor Bligh watched Cesar walk down the road where a black Mercedes was waiting to take him off. Their attempts at secrecy were surely superfluous. There were observers everywhere who could quickly report their meeting to the Security—if they thought it worthwhile. He himself was persona grata with the régime but he felt sure that Cesar must be regarded as—well, almost a nonentity. But as a nonentity he was typical of the self-satisfied bourgeois élite that could never be revolutionary with any seriousness. If the Abulencias wanted to be rid of the Florescos it would not be to improve the lot of the people but just another round in the Caroline game of political musical chairs. Squalid though the cinema had just been, Max felt that he had learned more about the Carolines from the violent film than from Cesar's diatribe about the Bersaminas. Was the country a likely place for a revolution at all? Guerrillas were up in the hills, so they said, and there was no reason not to believe it. But wasn't it likely that the spur to their action was just a demand for land? This so-called war against communism was just another facet of a peasants' revolt, not a call for radical change. These people were stuck in a morass of ancient values. All that mattered to them was the family, the preservation of their traditions and, he could not help thinking, the quite extraordinary preoccupation of the menfolk with a possessive form of sex. The film had said it all. The people were fundamentally conservative and their thought patterns remained at a decidedly pre-scientific stage. But behind these fascinating Caroline realities lay the power of America, its geopolitical concern with those secret bases and underpinning it all the corrupting influence of American money. It had seduced these pleasure-loving people with the dream of becoming Asian Uncle Sams. It sickened him to see how the Carolinos aped American styles whenever they could, the music, the fashions, the Hollywood-style jokes and gimmicks. For every Carolino who became a revolutionary, a thousand would sell their souls to achieve the American way of life, most desirably on a one way ticket across the Pacific.

As he sauntered through the fashionable street of Mahdogi, its gleaming shops, smart boutiques, fine restaurants and super supermarkets confirmed him in his view of the total hopelessness of his revolutionary cause. A feeling of revulsion grew in him for the attractive smiling people milling around, until the fashion conscious girls made up to kill and the slim, just as winsome, boys became in his mind the material for a grotesque experiment in changing humanity, something on a Cambodian scale that would wipe the grins off their faces and entomb for ever their stylishness, their Catholicism, their romantic sentimentality, and their dangerous proliferation. All the features that these people manifested should be wiped clean and a new start made. Then he had his doubts; was it their immemorial culture, or was it just how they were brought up, that had made them what they were? Or was there something genetic that would always turn them into beautiful, sensual lotus-eaters as soon as unbearable pressures were removed?

He caught sight of himself in a long mirror inside a shoe shop. He had put on weight, his stomach was protruding, and in comparison with the Carolinos passing by he was an unkempt giant. How did he look to these svelte people, most of them apparently little more than twenty years old? Was he secretly laughed at or merely tolerated because he was a large Caucasian with too much money. He longed for his family, much as Gulliver longed to be home from Lilliput. He wanted to be back with his faithful wife and two studious children in Europe where neither they nor his neighbours had the slightest idea of the secret, Janus-headed life that lay behind his ostensible profession as a PR man. He felt even more isolated at present because the Schusters had gone to Europe. Without their constant companionship his mind had moved into a negative state that was dangerous to his complex work. More from a need for psychological relief than out of desire, he called a taxi to take him away from Mahdogi to a raunchy part of Infanta and the expensive Cater-For-All-Tastes sauna he had once visited with Hymen Schuster, who had a penchant for plump girls. But once prone on a disturbingly green marble table top he was not able to function at all, even after a long bubble bath in which he was fondled subaqueously by a couple of jolly masseuses. Why didn't he tremble with excitement and groan like that boy in the film? Why didn't the skill of those clever fingers transport him to paradise? He was nothing but a piece of cold cod on a slab. One of the girls gently suggested that perhaps he needed a boy; if so she'd call her brother Mario, by all consent a true artist in giving pleasure to man or woman, but he made the excuse that he'd overdone it the night before and wanted only a massage to recover. When leaving he felt humiliated, but Mario's sister took his hand and gave him a genuine smile "You're a very kind man," she told him. "I can tell." How she might tell he could not guess but her sympathetic words helped him for a while. If the people at the top in the Carolines were self-seeking shits truly he could, as a fervent Marxist, believe that there was more than a streak of human compassion in its earth-bound poor.

The next morning Cesar Abulencia sent a note by hand to the Infanta Hotel informing Max Bligh that in San Felipe there was a certain Father Stephens who, he had learned from a parish priest, could tell him a lot about the town. Quick to sniff things out, Cesar had connected Max Bligh's inquiry about the town with the name of the priest who, so the papers said, had been arrested there. But how could a PR man working on the President's foreign tour be concerned with such a matter? To show his concern Cesar also warned Bligh that, as the San Felipe area was likely awash with military and police, he should be careful what he said and did.

Max was not perturbed by this advice. He had already informed the President's private office that he was off to San Filipe with Hilary Arbuthnot, the freelance photographer, to photograph ancient buildings, especially churches and old houses. The visit gave rise to no comment but it was decided that the vehicle to be put at Bligh's disposal should not be a car from the presidential car pool but a more utilitarian job from the Defence Ministry, as operations were proceeding in the area of San Felipe. When they left the hotel Bligh was disconcerted to see a camouflaged jeep with a uniformed driver, a soldier who saluted him smartly, said his name was Luis, and promised he would take them anywhere they wanted in the San Felipe area which he knew well. He added that instructions had come down from Senor Bersamina himself that they must feel free to visit his hacienda and photograph anything that took their eye. When the driver went off for a short while Bligh whispered in Hilary's ear, "For Christ's sake don't talk politics. Luis probably has big ears." Hilary nodded as he always did when people seemed to be addressing him but in fact his hearing was so bad that he did not hear a word that was said. He gave a warm smile to Luis and sat beside him while Max took the rear seat with most of Hilary's photographic equipment.

His inability to hear had unfortunately made Hilary very loquacious, mainly about his encounters with the various politicians he had once interviewed or photographed, not necessarily singly, and of whom he now heartily disapproved. In his youth he had been a committed member of the British Labour Party despite which his bête noir was Tony Blair. He also hated George Bush and in his youth had taken against Margaret Thatcher, Lee Kuan Yew and a host of others. When rambling on about these people he insisted on talking of Tony, George, Maggie and Harry as proof that such familiarity gave him the right to hold them in contempt. Looking over his shoulder to address Max Bligh as the jeep sped on through Infanta, he said, "Oh yes, Maggie and Harry are chips off the same block—intolerant know-alls who don't understand how ordinary people like you and me live. As for Tony, a class traitor if ever there was. How could a man with a modicum of scientific knowledge flirt with Rome? At least George never pretended to scientific knowledge; his head is just stuck with glue between the pages of the Old Testament. Why is it that such people come to rule our lives, Max?"

Max replied, though it probably went unheard, "Because they want power more than ordinary people like you and me. Or rather they concentrate on getting it more than we do." Max never thought of himself as an ordinary person so he did not try to enter the friendly chatter that quickly developed between Hilary and the courteous Luis, who somehow or other seemed adept at communicating with the elder man. What he did hear made him feel that though Mr

Arbuthnot was at least twenty years his senior, their actual ages should be reversed. The countryside that Max thought parched and drab, to Hilary was alive with subtle and vibrant colour. The young men whose faces seemed to Bligh as featureless as unworked putty, in Hilary's eyes suggested the vitality of a reborn country. The slim women Bligh saw as shrimps to Hilary possessed a marvellous poise and beauty that put European women to shame The squatter huts which were clear evidence of exploitation Hilary affected to find picturesque, though he never wanted to stop and enter them.

At length they reached the Bersamina hacienda and were driven straight to the sprawling house, which might have been in Castile. It was a rare privilege to be there, for upper class Carolinos were an exclusive set that rarely permitted access to their inner sanctums. Yet the severe featured Senora Bersamina was actually on hand to greet them, offered them refreshments and after a few gracious words disappeared, on her duties so she averred. Hilary's enthusiasm became boundless as he went hither and thither photographing antique furniture, pictures and architectural details. Luis knew his place and stayed in the jeep but Max Bligh sat on a terrace with a cool drink brought to him by a servant and gazed over a beautiful garden set within a rectangle of gleaming white walls in one of which an arch gave onto a statue-lined swimming pool. Outside the domestic elegance he had already glimpsed stables for polo horses, workshops and garages and houses for retainers, and further away hectares of well cultivated land. As he stared at this serene manifestation of wealth and power, hatred made him feel young again.

They set out for San Felipe, some fifteen kilometres from Bersamina's residence. To begin with there were lush meadows with sleek cattle and plantations of pineapple, mangoes and a variety of fruit, all well tended with the benefits of scientific agriculture and occasionally a well built house, but as they got near to San Felipe there was a marked change. Now they saw small plots and a countryside characterised by sugar cane and wooden houses with attap or corrugated iron roofs. At intervals broad spreading trees were scattered in clumps and bananas and papaya were often adjacent to the dwellings. Small boys rode on the backs of buffaloes but overloaded motorbike carts and bicycles crowded the narrow road which passed through San Felipe on its was down from the higher land to an immense plain. There, they all knew, lay a great mosaic of rice fields just now mostly emerald green with many small settlements and a rural population whose poverty had, over the past century, been the cause of many peasant revolts.

Max could see that even here there had once been prosperous farms for there were still a few attractive stone houses all looking very decrepit and obviously occupied by several families. Their gardens had run wild and were used for pig and poultry rearing. But in San Felipe the huge baroque church and its tiered campanile still stood in good order, though the tower had developed a slight tilt that suggested it would ultimately crash unless money was found to restore it. Luis stopped the car before its imposing façade which Hilary at once started to photograph.

"Hilary," Max ordered distinctly, "You must find the priest since you are going to make a record of his church—and I hope of him." Always ready for another personality to interview, Hilary asked Luis to drive around town and ask for the Father wherever he could. Once on their own he really did hear Max telling him very loudly. "A lot of clerics sympathise with the rebels and it may be the case with this priest. If you can get him alone try to record his opinions. It would be interesting to find out what's really going on around here." Before long the jeep returned at speed in a cloud of dust with Father Stephens who, in view of his present position as police suspect and collaborator, was not too happy to be summoned by a military driver in a jeep, but he could hardly refuse to come along.

The priest soon found himself subject to a number of questions, not of the police variety but about the history and the culture of his parish. Once he realised that Hilary was hard of hearing Stephens answered him in the very loud voice he often used when giving a sermon, and gave a run down of the days when the first missionaries appeared and built a little wooden church, of which the present building was the third successor. He did not, however, give the usual Catholic version of the conversion to Christianity. The Malay tribes, he explained, who lived here in the sixteenth century had their own developed system of traditional law, a written language and a society as sophisticated as the Spanish which sought to replace it. For the first time the Carolinos, as they were now to be called in honour of the Holy Roman Emperor Charles V, learned from the Spanish Friars how fortunate they were, for though they were living in sin and that life was inevitably a vale of tears, they could attain an eternal joy once they accepted Jesus Christ as their Saviour. Stephens made no bones about what the vale of tears had meant for them. Cruelty enforced by superior Spanish weapons and fear of punishment in the afterlife made conversion swift. The Spanish conquerors with the Friars at the forefront soon carved out vast areas of land on which the people became virtual serfs at the mercy of their new masters, especially the clerics whose concern for their souls was not inhibited by their vows of celibacy. Initially surprised that a priest should give such an honest account of a shameful story, Max soon left him at it with Hilary in the church and took to mooching about a ruinous building nearby. At its centre was a desolate garden that looked sad and ominous, but the cloisters were cool and a good place to enjoy a cigarette. Even though the building must once have been a monastery, Max felt at home there. Its present state resembled his own despondent views on the uselessness of all human effort. Yet he could not help reflecting that the monastic life might be a good one. How pleasant it would be to live in a community, preferably of people vowed to silence, carrying out a fixed daily routine, performing tasks of moderate usefulness like growing cabbages or illuminating books or useless but pleasant ones like singing and perhaps praying, though he could not see himself doing the latter with any constancy.

A discreet cough made him look around. It was Luis, wearing not the usual serene Caroline smile but one that was unusually depressed. "This isn't a good place to stay," he whispered. "Come away, Senor. There could be snakes in this garden. It's so overgrown."

"Snakes? Rubbish. Come on Luis; tell me what's really wrong with the place?" Bligh asked curiously. "It's cool and quiet. I like it."

Luis affected to shiver. "It's cold because of…"

"I suppose you're going to tell me it's haunted," Bligh said with a sneer for he was contemptuous of superstition. "In any case you know that ghosts only come out at night."

Luis began to leave. "Stay if you want to, Senor Bligh," he said.

141

"Stop. Tell me why it's haunted—if that's it."

"I will—outside."

Out of curiosity Bligh followed Luis from the ruin towards the campanile, from the top of which Father Stephens was audible though not visible. "They'll be up there for ages because the priest can point out all sorts of places for your friend to see—and photograph." said Luis. "But he can't show what's in that garden." Luis' voice fell again and he continued rapidly, without any introduction to his story. "They had to dig the hole deep and wide. Then they were forced down in groups, five at a time. They obeyed. They lay down. They were machine gunned. When it was over other prisoners shovelled soil over them but people say you could still hear cries and moans coming from the ground." His voice was now almost inaudible. "Sometimes they can still be heard. One day I thought I—no, I never want to go in there again."

Bligh asked respectfully, "When did this happen Luis? In Spanish times?"

Luis looked at Bligh pityingly, as though at an ignoramus. "Just after the war, Senor. The Japs had surrendered. The Caroline police had been working for them but now they had to take orders from the Americans. There were many guerrillas in the area; men who had been fighting the Japs. The new Caroline government didn't like them. Neither did the Americans. About a hundred guerrillas came to San Felipe—really on their way back home. They wanted food for the night and shelter." He gestured towards the monastery. "Well, that's where they got their shelter."

"How do you know about it?" Bligh asked reluctant to accept another atrocity story without proof.

"My father lived through it all. He saw it happen." Luis fell silent as though he regretted his words but when he next spoke his voice was high and arrogant, "But they deserved it, didn't they? They were communists, weren't they?"

It was that raised tone of voice that troubled Max Bligh. How had Luis' father lived to tell the tale? He said no more than, "So your father was a witness to it all, Luis?", got no response and asked no further questions.

After that Luis avoided Bligh and asked Hilary to sit beside him again as they drove to Father Stephens' house for some refreshments.

As soon as they were seated on the verandah Bligh discovered that he must have left his briefcase at the hacienda. Luis said he would go back for it straightaway, at which point Hilary said, "I say Max, Luis' father lives nearby. He's a retired soldier. Do you mind if he has half an hour to visit him on the way back?"

Max repied, "Not at all," wondering more dubiously now what role Luis' father might have played in the massacre.

Once settled down with cold beers and some glutinous cakes produced by Lourdes, Hilary soon began to talk of the iniquities of the wider political world, again with Blair and Bush, the two bastards as he called them, as his main targets. This prompted Father Stephens to enquire what work his visitor was doing now and Hilary replied that he and Bligh were preparing a glamorised picture of the Carolines for the European media, as a background to the President's visit. "You know, an up to date version of those old Fitzpatrick travelogues. And as the sun sinks slowly in the west over the exotic, erotic Carolines, we drink our beer and eat our—"

"Very sweet local cakes," said Father Stephens.

"Oh they're quite nice really," Hilary replied taking another bite at a banana cake. "Once used to them, you find you've grown quite fond of them. Like everything else in the Carolines."

"I don't think I could ever grow fond of the Carolines," said Bligh looking at the priest challengingly. "But as a matter of fact— even though I'm not a Catholic—"

"Hardly a Christian," interrupted Hilary.

"I admire people like you," said Max seriously. "Cutting yourself off and living all alone up here."

"With some eighty thousand parishioners," laughed Father Stephens.

"That's what I mean by all alone I guess," said Bligh. "I don't take to these people at all—especially the men. They are too polite, too smiling but really as hard as granite. And real money grabbers too. Every time one of them looks at me I can see the peseta sign in his eyeballs."

"You are judging them by Infanta." Stephens sprang to the defence of his beloved Carolinos. "If you were poor and living in a slum you might be the same."

"And the superstition." went on Bligh discounting the notion that he could ever be poor. "Even in the science faculties the students pray to saints for examination success. It'll be an age before these people can think rationally. Oh, sorry for disparaging your saints."

"Not at all, I'm with you entirely," replied Stephens. "But what excuse do we have in the West for still being superstitious when we claim to have been thinking scientifically for over three hundred years. In the Vatican they have an astronomer who is studying the big bang, quantum physics and the like. And he is a Jesuit. I wonder how he makes the connection between science and the Virgin Birth, Mr Bligh. Perhaps he'd say there are some things not susceptible to reason or being a Jesuit he'd devise a logical link between the two."

"Not possible, Father," replied Max. "Even Jesuits have to make a leap of faith. There is no logical bridge to walk across. But I'll be crude: maybe that astronomer has got a nice job in Rome, excellent equipment and doesn't want to upset the great Catholic apple cart. I'd understand that. If you have a job you do what the paymaster orders. It's a refined way of lying. But I think you are an honest man, Father. If you heard cries for help from under the earth in the cloister garden would you find a way of explaining them or pretend they were not there? If you can't make a connection, make a break, Father Stephens."

It was though he had touched a raw nerve. Stephens frowned. "You've heard of it? It was a terrible crime. A real war crime. But victors are never brought to book, are they? Later people asked the priest—one of my predecessors—to have the grave opened and the bodies properly interred, but the government refused permission. In the end even the church said let them rest there. Not even a small memorial. No wonder people think they can hear their grief and are afraid to go there."

As Hilary was told the terrible story that Luis had let slip out to Bligh, Father Stephens began to lose his reservations over his visitors. They seemed civilised people who were only doing a PR job for the government. But though he listened in silence, Bligh's awful words revived his anger about the massacre. He had told them that people feared to go to the lost garden but there was one Carolino who was never afraid to go there. Sometimes Salvador led him by night to that place of death, where they lay on the earth and made love. "It's a way of making my comrades come to life," the boy insisted. "When they hear us coming I know they feel life stirring in their dead bones and I can hear them laughing. When we play with each other, though they are martyrs, they join in and forget to be sad." Stephens could not say that Salvador's private belief was less valid than the teachings of the church. His self-made faith was one of conviction and acted out with love. He could not talk about this secret ritual to the two visitors but as they had come to San Felipe to do research for a film why should he not give his own unvarnished views on the place, which would be different from those in government handouts. He told them of his intention and asked Max Bligh to switch on the recorder that Luis had brought in from the jeep.

There was a time, he began, when the area around San Felipe was fairly prosperous, back in the nineteenth century. Society was feudal, aristocratic Spanish families had long replaced the Friars, but the secular owners felt a sense of responsibility for the land and the people with whom they could identify. Aristocrats and peasants alike believed in church doctrines and ancient superstitions equally. The rich had no more protection against endemic diseases than the poor. Look at the parish records and you can see that mortality struck all classes equally; well almost equally, for the rich were better fed. Yet there were all sorts of mutual obligations. The poor man had to bring his weapon if his overlord was in danger but the rich landowner had to help the poor man when he got married or had children. Undoubtedly there was cruelty and life was extremely hard but society was more unified than they might think.

As he spoke Max Bligh maintained his personal reservations but made sure the sound equipment was functioning properly while Hilary Arbuthnot moved purposefully about, filming Father Stephens who looked benign in his Franciscan garb and spoke gravely in beautifully modulated tones from which all traces of the Antipodes had fallen away. Hilary thought he even sounded high Anglican rather than Roman but this would go down well in Europe, whilst its slow pace would facilitate dubbing.

Stephens' next tranche accorded more with Max's view of history. There had been some efforts at land redistribution, both by President Floresco and by presidents preceding him. However, though many peasants received land titles they were not helped with grants of capital or equipment needed to work their fields. Their poverty deepened and a gradual estrangement from the rich had developed. Now the peasants fitted in more securely with the Marxist categories with which Max was acquainted. He began to feel that he was grasping, which was a way of saying intellectually controlling, what had gone on in the area.

Whereas Bligh saw matters in abstract terms, Hilary was affected by the tragic anecdotes of poverty with which Stephens larded his story, so that at one point Bligh saw tears in Hilary's eyes as he listened to the stories of the of the peasants' sufferings. But the priest also insisted that, during the occupation, the peasants had helped the guerrillas to fight the Japanese, though without believing in communism. Unhappily their plight had worsened after the war under the American style constitution controlled by rich families who, over the years, grew richer and richer. Finally these families had become like a race apart from the ordinary people, whose voting power it was easy to sway with bribes and vain promises. Though American and European capital had come in, the power of the rich rested securely on their ownership of land and their control of the primary commodities, sugar, copra and coffee and their manipulation of money in the banking houses of Infanta.

Whilst some technical adjustments were being made to the equipment Bligh said that he thought Stephens analysis was skewed. "You talk as though there are only rich and poor but in Infanta and the other big towns one is struck by growing numbers of middle class people consuming imported luxuries and Caroline goods." As soon as they resumed filming, Father Stephens admitted that the new affluence and the construction of infrastructure were the main achievements of the Floresco régime. But he emphasised that he had been talking of the rural areas where the majority of the population lived. Nevertheless the growth of the bourgeois class, which had escaped the poverty trap, was the main reason for Floresco's survival. The bourgeois liked the régime for the discipline it maintained over the country. They were now in sufficient numbers to keep the régime going indefinitely. Only if they ever became disaffected would the Florescos' fall.

With mounting anger, Stephens gave his opinion of the Florescos' cunning moves. In addition to the middle class rich they had created a class of dependent Carolinos—police, soldiers, security guards, municipal workers and so on—people with lowly jobs that were not well paid but all the same permanent. Such people were ardent supporters of the government. "You must have seen in Infanta how there are thousands of street workers wearing pink tee-shirts."

"Oh yes. The PAB; the Peoples' Action Brigades," said Hilary.

"Did you know there are almost twenty thousand of them in Infanta alone. All paid from the First Lady's office. She watches over their interests and gives them bonuses from time to time—especially when she wants a great crowd for a demonstration. If need be they would be her big asset in a revolution. The PAB leaders get first priority when land titles are dished out and priority in housing allocation. All this mass of people feels indebted to the President and the First Lady whose patronage is enormous. Even if the President died tonight I believe the support the First Lady has created on the streets and in the poor areas of towns would carry her though to the presidency." Father Stephens looked from one member of his small audience to the other, paused, took a bottle of whiskey from a sideboard, pored himself a large draught and took a deep gulp. His visitors said they would stick to beer. "Mr Bligh. Mr Arbuthnot, I think I've said enough on camera and on the recorder. Could you switch both machines off and we can talk more comfortably." There was no argument about it. Both men complied and Luis was asked to take the equipment to the jeep and then to wait somewhere for them.

As they settled down again, Bligh asked, "Are you telling me it's that easy to control the masses?" The concept clearly did not accord with his view of revolutionary struggle.

"People are mainly interested in where their next meal is coming from. If you're a good boy you get your chance in life. If you're naughty some way will be found of kicking you up your arse," said Hilary, thereby showing that his feet were more firmly on the ground than those of astute Mr Bligh.

"But the Church, it's outside the system. It can still speak out," Bligh complained.

Father Stephens finished off his drink. He looked almost patronising as he turned on Max Bligh, "It can and it does—sometimes. I'd like to think the Cardinal does his best. He's been here. I like him but his influence is limited. Some priests are so sickened that they have made common cause with the communists. You've heard of Liberation Theology, I guess. Very Latin American. Well we were once under the Viceroyalty of Mexico, under the dead hand of Spain, so it figures. But the government will hardly listen to church men. Western style liberals were swept aside by Floresco and now, at all levels of the public service, corruption is rampant. Why should officials fight corruption when they live by it themselves? But Bersamina's police are both efficient and corrupt and they watch even parish priests like hawks. And occasionally they pounce."

Sympathetically Bligh let out "You must be talking about Father Oliver."

"Father Oliveros, Mr Bligh."

"Sorry. That's the name. I read of him in the papers. But after all, Father Stephens," Max Bligh said with the air of a man wanting to be scrupulously just, "He did more than make common cause with the communists; he joined the Party but I guess that liberation theology allows for that. Yet as Caroline law stands, the Government has to take action against him."

Stephens looked at the ceiling and repeated Bligh's words. "As the law stands. The problem is that the law doesn't stand at all in this country. Do you know the one wise thing I ever heard from President Floresco? He said, 'This country has forty thousand lawyers and we'll never get anywhere until they are all shot'."

Hilary chortled and said, "Very true, very true but that could be said about most countries. Lawyers should be burned off the body politic as we do leeches in the jungle."

Everyone laughed, but Father Stephens said suddenly, "No Mr Bligh, I was not talking of my good friend Oliveros. I was talking about myself." He then told of his accidental involvement with the guerrillas, the arrest and torture of Salvador and the pressure put on him to collaborate before the boy was released. Though he did not mention his relationship with Salvador, the warmth with which he reiterated, "a lovely boy, a lovely boy," stirred a little suspicion in the minds of Bligh and Arbuthnot, for what else did a priest do when he was on his own in the back of beyond. Nor did he mention the fact that once he was free and went home he quickly found out that, though the police had arrested the wounded guerrilla, they had not discovered the package Oliveros had brought from Infanta. Above all he did not say that he had opened the package, found the money someone must have given to Oliveros in Infanta and finally that, with Salvador's help, he himself had passed it on to the communists.

It was now the brilliant Bligh who made a slip, for it had struck him that Father Stephens might be in it more deeply with Oliveros than he had let on and might therefore know what had happened to the money he had passed over in the church. "Did he give you anything before he was arrested, Father Stephens? Anything incriminating?"

"Yes he did, Mr Bligh."

"Well what happened to it, Father? Did the police find it when they searched this house?" Bligh felt that if he had hair it would be standing on end.

"Yes of course. They took all Oliveros' things." Despite the whiskey Stephens was now as wary as a fox, or should he say a rat.

"Oh my God, a hundred thousand dollars, "groaned Bligh, but only half aloud. Though to judge by the way Hilary's eyebrows had shot up, he had heard the words as clearly as Father Stephens, who said, "A hundred thousand dollars? No I never saw anything like that. Are you sure, Mr Bligh?

"But you said the police took all Oliveros' things." Bligh expostulated.

"They did, they did. Communist literature and some shots of an archaeological site near Mao Tse-tung's birthplace in China."

Further conversation seemed to have been killed off at the mention of the Chinese leader, but it was a vague fog of mistrust that made them feel there was nothing more to be said. Soon they heard Luis starting up the engine and clothes and bags were packed away. Hilary, ever ready to do the right thing, discretely passed a cheque to Father Stephens to spend as he chose for the Parish. Bligh still felt worried over his slip about the money, but said with absolute sincerity that he looked forward to being back in the States very soon. He still could not make out Father Stephens, who in turn remained unsure whether the two visitors intended no more than to ask his help in making their film. Max Bligh's behavior left him nonplussed; with a man like him it was like playing a part in the Chinese play, in which two blind men have to fight but neither knows where the other has got to. Lourdes brought in a big basket of fruit for the Father to give his guests to eat on the road.

When they drove off Stephens felt light-hearted to see the back of them. Then he took a shower and lay down, though not to sleep. A feeling of satisfaction was stirring deep inside him; he may have been a fool to drink too much and talk too freely but he had not said a word that the government did not know already and not a thing had he let out about the money, which could even now be in use to destroy the men who had arrested Oliveros, and tortured Salvador. It was not a Christian attitude but the thought, far from filling him with sorrow, gave rise to a glow of pleasure. He was embarked on a course that might really help the humble and the meek. Perhaps it had started at college when a theology teacher taught the class about Pelagius, a Briton who held that man's nature was fundamentally good, that neither man nor woman was born in sin. Though still a boy he thought the heresy self evidently true, though perhaps even then he had sensed that it made the idea of Christ's sacrifice superfluous. No, his belief in Pelagius' common sense had even earlier roots. As a boy he and some friends had been caught masturbating in the school showers after rugby. Even as a lad he had thought it ridiculous that some tortured old priest should tell them that they would become lechers and fornicators doomed to dire punishment in the next world if they indulged in such beastliness. Most of the boys had indeed listened seriously to what they were told but it did not stop the wanking sessions from continuing with greater glee, because they all knew they were sinning, which was fun. The marvel was that he had ever got through those years of training and taken holy orders, concealing from his superiors what he could not accept and persuading himself that what really mattered was the priest's Christ-like role among his flock, as teacher and harbinger of comfort. But the trajectory of his disbelief was strengthening. Just recently he had taken public action against the precepts of the church by encouraging the visits of the family planning association to the surrounding villages. He could not accept that it was God's will that so many children should starve and suffer from disease and sickness or be sold into prostitution because of the ignorance of their parents and the insane doctrine of the church, which seemed to hold that a bodily fluid like semen had some magical significance. Finally, to clear his mental deck he had abandoned all the doctrines derived from ancient cults: the virgin birth, the sad myths of sacrifice and resurrection, the messianic gobbledegook, and belief in life everlasting, when a dolt could see that once the brain is dead the mind can function no more. As to there being a divine purpose in human life, how could intelligent people, he wondered, swallow such a notion when anyone who could read or even had a television set could nowadays learn how the universe had come into being and would probably end. Beyond that, what mystery sustained the entirety of things no one knew or might ever know, but Stephens felt certain it was not revealed by the Christian fairy tale. His decision to abandon every bit of nonsense cluttering his mind meant that he was approaching a time of change, but he was totally unafraid for he perceived that what lay ahead could only be the fulfilment of the liberation already working in him.

He had just dozed off when Salvador arrived and woke him with words of love. He saw close to him no longer the soft skinned boy he had first wanted with a kind of madness, but a young man strong in body and ruthless in purpose, the face of a lover who knew the bitterness of life and its sorrow but also, by the same token, a lover who cherished the fire that burned in both of them more profoundly than in their early years of passion.

At length Salvador said, "Francis, I know you're supposed to be responsible for my behavior—to the police I mean. I don't want to get you into trouble but I can't stay in San Felipe any more. I have to fight. I must go into the jungle."

"It seems that you have already made up your mind, Salvador."

"Yes, but I have to hear you say that I am free to go. If I went without hearing those words, I wouldn't feel right."

"What about your wife? What about Rosalinda and her parents?"

"Her parents support the communists; they've worked for the Party since the war. They know what I am like. Senor Cortez always said I was a natural rebel who got whatever he wanted. It's true, Frank. Remember how I took you. That's why they had to accept me once I'd fucked Rosalinda. She's coming with me into the jungle."

"To fight! Little Rosalinda?"

"Rosalinda is like me. She takes what she wants. I'll never keep her for myself but she's good while it lasts. It's not like you and me, Frank. Oh, you don't know women at all. Francis, especially Caroline women."

"I do. I do. I've seen them working in the fields. I've seen them working everywhere. Yes, I do know them. I hear them every day." Stephens passed his hand over his forehead. "Of course you are free, Salvador." Then the tears poured freely from his eyes. "I am going to miss you so much, Salvador. I can't find words to tell you how much."

Salvador looked into Francis's eyes as though through them he might glimpse his lover's soul. "And me?" he said. "How do you think I feel? You mean more to me than I have ever said. You'll never be apart from me." Then he tried to look cheerful and swore that they would often see each other.

Of course they made love, not once nor only twice, for as paradise was what they sought little time was wasted in sleep. Their love was no longer a sensual playtime but acceptance of a mystery in which they would live for the rest of their lives. Together they whispered a secret mantra, "We are one, we are one," when they were joined, for the act was the symbol of all they meant to each other. When he awoke early in the morning, Stephens saw the reddest of suns rising over the houses and he knew he was not free but born into a new commitment. He kissed the sleeping head beside him, touched the twisted curl that fell over his brow and Salvador awoke. For a while they lay looking at each other, knowing they were not poor souls made bankrupt by the morning after. They were still rich with love.

"It's time now," said Salvador. "Will you help me to get my things together?"

When Salvador was ready, he kissed Lourdes, who was weeping when she left them. Stephens gave him money from the safe, in value the same as Hilary's cheque. "Take this. It will be useful to you and Rosalinda."

"The guerrillas will want it."

"Good, let them have it. They need money for the struggle."

"It's too much."

"I'm glad of it, Salvador."

"Will you bless me, Father Stephens?"

Stephens hesitated and then said, "I can't bless people any more. But wasn't last night greater than any blessing, Salvador?"

Salvador hugged him and then picked up his bag. They went to the gate together but after taking a few steps Salvador turned and said, "Much greater than any blessing, Francis."

Stephens returned to his house. He knew that he and Salvador had tumbled together like fish into the ocean of love and that there would never be a hook to haul them out.

As the First Lady left her magnificent new Opera House she turned and looked up at its soaring façade bathed in golden light, as beautiful, she thought, as the Parthenon but happily not in ruins. Her eyes caught the sculpture in the entablature; there at its centre was Bathaluman, the ancient Caroline goddess of beauty, her face unmistakably the face of the First Lady, but the drapery that fell around her half naked body Greek enough to make her also Pallas Athene. Appropriately enough, for tonight had witnessed the apotheosis of the First Lady, or something like it.

All the luminaries of Caroline society had been there: the members of government, the Diplomatic Corps, the Military Brass, the heads of the rich families that controlled trade and industry all with their ornately apparelled wives. In addition there had been a clutch of international cultural celebrities—writers, artists, musicians and patrons of the intellectual world in half a dozen countries, as well as several slightly passé Hollywood stars, some the personal favourites of the First Lady. A few of the celebrities had come at their own expense but the favourites were guests of Griselda. This distinguished throng, reinforced by a packed audience that could pay enormous prices for the non-official seats, cheered the new opera written by a Caroline composer, constantly described as the First Lady's protégé. Whenever this was said she would shake her head in modest denial. Yet after the final curtain, fulsome speeches had been made glorifying her role as the patroness supreme, she herself, quite reluctantly it seemed, had been obliged to come on stage to respond. Her theme as usual was the need for beauty in life, a need which had to be fulfilled more than ever in these times of economic stress, when amidst their hardships ordinary people wanted to see a vision of what life could really be like, that vision of hope which dwelt like a flame in her heart.

She had moved with poise and infinite condescension for she was in a good mood; even towards those people of the upper crust who hated her she had been gracious, often surprising them with a kind word, taking care never to look bored or to allow her inner feelings to show even briefly in her features. No one must accuse her of arrogance tonight. The President, always beside her though a step or so behind, had invariably followed her words with a little *bon mot* of his own without ever suggesting his primacy. Tonight he asserted to one and all, was the First Lady's night and he was not going to steal any of her limelight. Her triumph was indeed so complete that it even brought a hint of sadness to her mind. Nothing could ever surpass this evening, however long she reigned over the Carolines and its capital.

With the presidential pair as they drove off were their three children, their young sons, Popong and Ricky, enjoying the excitement of it all, and Conchita, serene yet glad to be taking part in her mother's happiness. Unlike her brothers she did not enjoy public appearances of this sort but since her return from England her parents had taken care to see that all their children should appear with them on state occasions, as it were to emphasise Caroline family values. Over the past few weeks, however, Griselda had intensified her efforts to see that Conchita should be seen in public, either with both or one of her parents, and occasionally quite on her own.

Carolinos crowds did not go in for loud applause. The best one could hope for was for some clapping, friendly waves and radiant smiles. But as Carolinos often sported radiant smiles it was not so easy to judge what was going on in their heads. The First Lady knew that their interest centred on the razzmatazz, the music, the clothes and all the displays of wealth they would like to own themselves.

"Wave to the people," she commanded. "Wave like this." She gave a little demonstration. "And sometimes look as if someone has caught your attention and point towards them with a grin. That's what Bill Clinton does."

The President smiled at Conchita and she laughed back, sharing a bit of pleasure with her father at her mother's expense for he had begun to do exactly what Griselda had suggested, making gracious little gestures in front of his chest and occasionally singling someone out, even turning his head towards them with a smile. This did in fact evoke a few shouts of greeting, but not many. Conchita followed suite. It was true how people loved to be singled out. To the ordinary people lining the boulevard, looking at the long limousine with its occupants radiant in a pinkish light, a united family of gods was passing by.

"You see," said Griselda to her children as the crowd thinned and the car picked up speed. "You really belong to them. That's why you must always do your best to make them feel that you love them."

"But I don't love them," said Popong, who was only seven. "I only love you and daddy—and Conchita. And Hirohito but I wish he wouldn't bark at night."

"What about me?" asked Ricky who was twelve. "And Hirohito shouldn't be in our room at night."

"He should too," Popong said firmly. "And I only love you when you're being nice to me and Hirohito."

Ricky reverted to his mother's admonishment. "Mummy, Popong and I don't belong to all those people. Only to everyone in this car— except the driver." He was silent for awhile, giving a few waves at the odd knots of people staring at the passing limousine and once pulling bacon quickly at a fat bystander. "How do you know they love us, mummy? Maybe they don't like us at all, especially seeing us in this big car."

Griselda smiled at the boys and said, "You'll understand what I mean when you're older." Conchita thought regretfully that they would indeed. Maybe Ricky was beginning to catch on already.

Later in the evening Conchita joined her parents for dinner. This was the sort of occasion the President loved—to be alone with the two women who meant most to him—and he was in good spirits, his humour centering on the behavior of various people who had attended the opening of the Opera House. "Did you see that idiot Menchior? He knows I'm getting rid of him soon. He was around me like a young girl in love, trying to catch my eye. He nearly fainted with joy when I gave him a smile. Funny isn't it but the more people feel they're not wanted, the more they stick their necks out in alarm like panicking geese. The clever ones stay in the background. I always look out for them. They are the most dangerous. And did you see Fajardo's wife? My God, what a dress! It made her look like a wedding cake."

Conchita smiled thinly, whereas her mother roared with laughter. Her father's humour often struck her as being unkind rather than funny. How could Senora Fajardo help her figure? With a husband who maintained a kind of harem in a luxurious condominium in Mahdogi, the poor woman's main comfort must be in food. "Are you getting rid of Fajardo too?" she asked.

"You bet I am," replied the President. "He's no longer an asset. The private lives of many of my ministers are pretty raw but they keep them under wraps. Fajardo's ménage is a public liability."

"Poor Senora Fajardo," said Conchita thinking of the private woes that must have lain beneath the dressy appearance of many a women in the foyer that night. "Poor thing, she was probably doing her best to bring credit to her husband."

"And she landed him in the red," said Griselda with a giggle at her own wit.

Conchita rounded on her angrily. "Don't you feel sorry for her at all? Don't you ever feel sorry for anyone?"

"Conchita," the President chided. "What's wrong with you? We were only having a bit of fun. Of course Griselda is sorry for the poor woman. Fancy being married to Fajardo. I remember the wedding. It was terrible. Everyone was embarrassed. She never wanted to marry him and he certainly wanted nothing of her. Only the four parents were pleased and they wanted the match for business reasons—mean minded buggers. The whole of Infanta was sorry for her from the very outset." He raised his hand to his mouth and blew a little kiss at Griselda. "Not like our wedding was it Grissie? We were in love."

156

"Yes, your wedding must have been beautiful. *Amor vincit omnia*—love conquers everything, doesn't it, daddy?" said Conchita pointedly.

The First Lady saw the dangerous drift of the conversation and changed the subject to her protégé's new opera. "Didn't you think the death scene in the last act was beautiful?" she asked. "I'm so glad that Ludmilla Lunacharsky agreed to sing the part."

"Agreed?" scoffed Conchita. "She'd probably been phoned by Vladimir the Impaler himself and told that she'd lose her job at the Bolshoi if she didn't sing." She managed to restrain herself from adding 'the hackneyed drivel'.

"They don't do that sort of thing any more," said the President crossly. "You know as well as I do that the Russians are free now—certainly to make money, to judge by Madame Lunacharsky's fee."

"Ah, and all the while I was thinking Russia was still like the Carolines, when all the time it's free. The Russians must have been so clever to make such a change, don't you think so mummy?" Observing her parents' expressions Conchita fell silent. Yet how she longed to bring up the question of herself and Julio, which had not been spoken about since the night of his visit. For the situation remained unresolved. On her mother's side the order not to see Julio had never been repeated; on her side it had been disregarded, though she had no doubt that her mother would have been kept in the picture about the continued trysts at the Infanta hotel, though latterly at the house of Cesar Abulencia. In this there was nothing so unusual. The First Lady often flew into tempers and issued orders which people initially obeyed but later ignored. The procedure had its uses for Griselda herself frequently regretted her impetuosity, but found it more in keeping with her dignity merely to forget what she had said rather than to admit a mistake. Conchita was living in the hope that this would be the case where she and Julio were concerned. She suspected that her father was of the same mind because one day, when she had told him very shyly that she had been talking to Cesar Abulencia, which occurrence was most likely to have taken place in company with Julio, he had just smiled and said, "Oh Cesar, what a foolish man he is; but charming if he wants—like all the Abulencias, eh Conchita?" Yet the uncertainty of his eventual support was nerve racking which accounted, she admitted to herself, for her sharp manner when she was, as now, alone with her parents.

They all rose from the table; Griselda said a blessing and crossed herself as did the President, but when crossing herself Conchita looked at her father and got the impression that he was staring at nothing and there was a strained expression on his face. She had not noticed it when they were all seated a minute ago. His eyes closed and all at once he gave a strange throaty sound—a sudden indrawing of breath which again suggested pain. Conchita caught her mother's eye and motioned towards her father. "Are you alright, daddy?" she asked. He opened his eyes and nodded his head before saying, "Yes darling, it's been a long day. I've been on display for too long I guess." Griselda made him sit next to her and put her hand on the back of his neck, stroking him gently and saying he was just tired. Conchita also sat beside him. He repeated the words he had just spoken as if they implied something more than mere tiredness. "Yes," he repeated quietly, "I've been on display too long."

Conchita recalled her mother's instructions about waving to the people. Whatever Griselda wanted it was not for her at all. When she looked at her father, now at the summit of his power but also so tired, she could hardly believe that the life he now had was what he wanted. He was trapped in office as much as any prisoner. The trappings of power; a peculiar expression she thought, with more than one meaning. "Mummy, I think daddy had better go to bed now. Maybe we should call for the doctor." The words were hardly out of her mouth when the President came to life.

"Not that quack. Not Doctor da Silva. I'm all right. Just a bit tired."

Conchita looked closely into her mother's face. In this little worried group how different she was. The haughtiness, maybe a sign of inner tension, was gone. There was even a touch of tenderness. This was the mother of her childhood, which she remembered with gratitude. Instinctively she put her arms around her mother's neck saying, "Oh mummy, mummy, I do love you so."

"Of course you do darling. I never doubted it. Now, let's all go to bed. Come Antonio. Lean on me, my dear."

Conchita kissed her parents and said, "It was a wonderful evening. Thank you both for taking me with you." Then she left the room.

Antonio showed no sign of getting up. He no longer tried to smile as he had done when Conchita was with him. "That was quite a pain," he said "And I can feel it still. Perhaps you should call for da Silva. I'll be all right. I just need a shot of something." He sat back with his eyes closed whilst Griselda was on the phone. She knew there was little she could do while they were waiting. This had happened before and it probably would, as he had said, be all right. But one day, no one knew when, it would not be so at all. She sat comforting him with her arms and her lips, wondering what she would do if he were really ill, if it were the end. She felt vulnerable and weak. How much of her strength, how much of her authority was in reality his. If he was no longer with her, would she suddenly find that within herself no resources were left to exercise control. Or when he was gone would she find that the anxiety to obey her that at present was brimming over in everyone around her had evaporated into thin air. She became aware that she was sweating and was startled when Doctor da Silva asked, "Do you feel ill ma'am? Let me take your temperature."

"No, no. I'm fine I was just so worried sitting here waiting for you to come."

"We came as quickly as possible, ma'am," da Silva said. "And I have brought my assistant, Doctor Aguilar."

Griselda turned to look at her husband releasing him a little from her embrace. He seemed to be asleep, "Antonio dear. You must wake up. Doctor da Silva is here." The President did not respond. The First Lady shook him gently but he still did not wake up. She made way for the doctor who pulled back the President's eyelids and then took his pulse. "He's unconscious," he said sharply. "We must get him to the medical centre at once."

Griselda stood up. Her heart was beating rapidly. A mass of doubts and fears within her whirled about quite out of hand, yet outwardly none of her misgivings showed. She looked calmly at the two doctors and the attendants who had been summoned and ordered very slowly and distinctly. "No news of this is to be breathed to anyone. No one must know. I will follow you shortly."

The attendants carried the President into his bedroom and then beyond that into a specially equipped room jokingly called by the presidential couple the medical centre. Griselda then went to her own bedroom and all alone took off her evening gown and the jewellery which had so recently flashed brilliantly for all the world to see. When she had changed she sat down, poured out a brandy and drank it straight down. She saw very clearly that if the President died all sorts of ambitious forces would start to rear their heads. There could be confusion and the whole edifice that her husband had built could come crashing down. That question which sometimes reared itself up in her brain returned: 'Was it all worth it? Was this the life she wanted?' And then, like the return of a tsunami after the tide has been sucked out into the distant ocean, the answer rolled back in full force: yes, yes, yes, she did want it and she was going to hold on to her position against all odds. In that moment of turmoil she thought again of the future. Her two boys were too young to be ready to assume the mantle of a dynasty, but Conchita was young and intelligent with all the stubbornness of her mother. In her lay the future of the Florescos. She must be the heir eventually, but not an heir affianced to a hostile family like the Abulencias. Strangely enough and yet not so strangely perhaps, because it was a quotation not absent from her mind at moments of danger, came the words of Lady Macbeth in the play which Griselda had studied at school and had loved on the stage in London. 'If it were done when 'tis done, then 'twere well it were done quickly.'

For some time Conchita's behavior had obliged her to consider every eventuality and to formulate a plan for action when the hour struck. She feared that it had struck now. Every detail of her plan had been considered in secret consultation with a few devoted supporters in the Army. Before she went to see Antonio in the medical centre she phoned a trusted accomplice at a Military Unit. There was an immediate reply in response to the code word she had given. Her most trusted lieutenant was prepared.

Captain Manzano had known Griselda since their childhood. As little children they had for a few years played together but when they were older he had learned his place as the son of a worker, whereas she lived, if not in the great family mansion, securely in her mother's home, a substantial villa appropriate for a favoured mistress. The course of their lives had taken different routes, Griselda upwards to a good school, college and sophisticated society whilst little Nikki Manzano went to a village school, and then a Catholic boys school which specialised in preparing well favoured lads—and he was very well favoured—for the military college, where he graduated *cum laude*. Yet his loyalty was never fully given to his profession. He had never forgotten pretty Griselda and from a safe distance he worshipped her—the more so as she advanced in influence.

His love, if one could call it that, was not unreciprocated. Griselda, through her political friends, had always managed to trace Manzano's career and as her contacts grew she had contrived to secure promotions for him, which eventually brought him to the Infanta Headquarters of the military establishment. At last, quite miraculously it might seem, he found himself a captain in a crack military unit assigned for special security duties in cases of emergency. To his joy one evening he was called to the DeoGracias and into the presence of the First Lady as she had now become. She had actually, if briefly, embraced him. She knew he was now married and had children but love was not on the agenda, for both of them were too circumspect to have risked such a path. A series of confabulations between them on such security matters as the protection of the DeoGracias led to a rapprochement between them, which became as warm as their childhood affection for one another. All this had been done with great secrecy but the outcome was that Manzano knew what she needed of him and most willingly became her man of liege, if not of limb. These special duties gave him a formal post in the security office at the DeoGracias.

The plan they concocted was simple, and daring but completely outrageous; Julio Abulencia was to be kidnapped and would disappear from view. It would in due course be given out that the perpetrators of the outrage were the so-called liberation fighters, who were endeavouring to get at the President through his only daughter. It would later be revealed that the Communist Party itself was demanding a ransom from Cesar Abulencia, so casting him broadly speaking in the camp of the Florescos. On his ransomed release, ways would be found of discrediting Julio, but a job of some sort would be found for him, probably in a private Caroline company abroad. Conchita, it was confidently assumed, would, with her parents' support, in due course move on emotionally and the threat to the dynasty would have vanished. Had they been more percipient of human nature Griselda and Manzano might have guessed that this farrago would turn out to be more honoured in the breach than the observance.

The First Lady had an immediate watch and wait part to play. Doctor da Silva's report had reassured, even surprised, her for she had got it into her head that the President's end was nigh. But in what was left of the night he recovered consciousness, slept well and in the morning was enjoying coffee and toast when she returned to his bedside. Immediately she summoned Conchita and the two of them sat with Antonio caressing him, chatting happily about the new Opera and receiving his assurances that he was back on track.

"Now Conchita, darling," said Griselda. "I think you should carry on with your life as usual. I will always be here with your father. If anything goes wrong, which God forbid, you'll be the first to know. Please just go off and have a good time. Don't you agree, Toni?"

"Of course. Of course," replied the President in a burst of affability "Go and see your boyfriend and while you're at it give that silly ass Cesar my love." Having said this he chortled so much that a piece of toast almost got stuck in his throat.

His statement was for Conchita both wonderful and amazing. Surely it meant that her father at least no longer opposed her love for Julio. But what about her mother? It was difficult to believe that for both parents all was well. Yet it seemed to be. With no hesitation Griselda joined in the fun. "Love to Cesar? Well I never knew you and he were like that. See how careful you have to be with men; one never knows what they are up to. Conchita dear, don't look so surprised. Go and have a lovely evening with Julio. Go to that new restaurant in Mahdogi—the Alcazar I think it's called. Now kiss daddy and mummy and off you go."

The First Lady's next message to Captain Manzano was received with not a little relish. He did not like the relationship between Conchita and an aristocrat who, being an Abulencia, he saw as a traitor to the régime. In his view Julio should be humbled and Conchita made to toe Griselda's line. It was not necessary for Manzano to be told that the lovers' next assignation was imminent, certainly during the next three days and possibly at the Alcazar; his network of informers, widespread over Infanta's restaurants and hotels to which he gave protection in return for a substantial pourboire or the right to unpaid entertainment, quickly informed him of the meeting's precise date and place—not the Alcazar, which Julio thought pretentiously Beverley Hills, but in a small French bistro, the Piaf, where the cuisine was superb, the lights low and the music appropriate to the establishment's name.

Because of his loyalty to the First Lady, Captain Manzano was anxious that neither her name nor indeed his should be involved in the affair. Others must do the discreditable work. However, neither Manzano nor the First Lady were totally disconnected from some of the less creditable members of society. The First Lady had for some time been building up her influence among the masses, not excluding a few criminal elements. They thought of her as something like a saint protecting the poor of Infanta and flocked to join her People's Action Brigades organised by one of her clever young protégés, Rich Rarang, a popular singer but a cleverer persuader of young people. Manzano, on the other hand, had influence over certain quasi-independent military units—most people referred to them as bandits for that was what they were—which often used the People's Action Brigades as recruiting pools. The leader of one of these units was a fanatically anti-communist former army captain named Oscar Diasanta, a man whose cruelty was so excessive that even the Caroline Army could not tolerate him. His private army, composed of sadistic murderers and thieves like himself, constantly carried out violent action against the communists and any peasants who supported them. The communist guerrillas could be cruel when they chose, but Diasanta enjoyed exceeding in cruelty any atrocity of which the communists were accused. Because of their recruiting links with the People's Action Brigades it was not unusual for Diasanta's men to slip in and out of Infanta at will. A group that made a regular habit of this, experts in urban blackmail, kidnapping and torture, were the Holy Thugs to whom Manzano over-confidently entrusted the seizure of Julio.

The plan went off without a hitch. Conchita and Julio had enjoyed their meal at the Piaf where the food and the wine were excellent, but they had taken greater pleasure in one another's mere presence. During Piaf's *Hymne à l'amour* their eyes reflected each other's happiness, their hands touched lightly and conducted a tremor of desire between them, and when from time to time they stole a kiss there could be no doubting their passion for one another. Conchita enthused over her father's approval and her mother's good humoured acquiescence of their affair and persuaded Julio to join in her optimism. Of her mother she even said, in contradiction to many things she had told him before, "She isn't so bad really. You know she would fight tooth and nail for him. I think she would die for him. She loves him just as much as we love each other, Julio. Do you know I think I'd die for you if it was necessary—though I hope I won't be put to the test," she concluded with a laugh.

Julio had heard too much about the deviousness of the Florescos to banish his misgivings entirely, but he did his best. Conchita must know them better than he did. Turning the conversations a degree he asked her mischievously what she thought of the new Opera House, since she knew he disapproved of lavish expenditure on prestigious buildings. But she was ready with an answer, "Didn't you see how many people turned up, even from abroad? It will be an economic success. Long term there'll be a big return on the investment." But lest he should think she had lost all her critical faculties she added, "I did think the opera was a bad choice. Too derivative. Rather like over-cooked Pucini, especially when Madame Lunacharsky was kicking the bucket."

"Yes, it's obvious," said Julio in the patronising voice he sometimes used to be one up on people in argument. "That's because the composer wasn't at ease with himself. We shouldn't be thinking in these Western forms. Opera is alien to us. Yes, a lot of Carolinos will go to the place, but they'll all be bourgeois. I can't see the Opera packed with peasants. Why can't we do things based on traditional forms."

"Because, dearest Julio, as well you know, our tradition is a mixture of European and Asian whether we like it or not. You should know with your Spanish blood. I can't see you in a loin cloth worshipping spirits and doing a stick dance—though I admit you'd look rather dishy if you did."

"I didn't say we should go to extremes. I know our roots are from two cultures but it seems to me that when two sets of roots get mixed up they tend to wither. The peasants have a single root, a strong root, and that's why they are tightly bound to the earth and close to nature."

"Now you're starting to sound just like those Russian landowners in Dostoyevsky, talking romantically about the strong earthy serfs without having a real connection with them—apart from possessing their bodies." For a moment Conchita was silent; then she added. "You know, Julio, Griselda is the President's wife but she hasn't forgotten how to make the connection—at least the poor seem to think so."

"I know why as clearly as Griselda knows why; she is the peasant's fairy tale come true. Cinderella who marries the prince. Just what the poor dream about whether they're girls or boys." Julio and Conchita were both smiling at each other when he spoke these acknowledged truths, but he had to add a rider. "The question is, how did Cinderella behave when she'd been married to the prince for fifteen years? Maybe she started to behave like her ugly sisters."

"Julio my dearest, I know what you really think of Griselda. See it from my point of view. She's my mother. I love her. But I see her as something of a tragic figure. She's a bit pathetic, wanting to be at the centre of everything. If she, if the two of them, gave it all up we could be such a happy family. All the other Caroline Presidents have given up office in the end. Why not the Florescos?"

Julio felt he had been unfair to pressurise Conchita in the smallest degree, and he turned the conversation to intimate matters and jokes which made them both serene and happy , as much as was possible in their situation. Both of them were sad when the bill had been paid and Julio said he'd see her off home. She promised to come and see him tomorrow at Cesar's house and the three of them would talk about everything under the sun except the Carolines. He replied with three such people such an exclusion was impossible, and that in any case Cesar would not be there as he was tied up with some people making a film about the Carolines. They kissed in the doorway of the Piaf and he took her to her car. The driver was asleep and took some time to pull himself together, so she sat beside him and shook him. She watched Julio walking ahead to his own car. He waved back before opening the door.

As he did so three men ran out from a doorway and seized him. He started to struggle with them violently. No, no it was not happening. The windscreen had become a television set. She was watching a gangster film. A large car had driven up; thugs in black wearing stockings over their heads were jumping out, punching Julio, threatening him with guns. A blow to the head felled him and the men bundled him up and thrust him into the boot of the car, which started up as the men jumped inside ready to make off. It was all over in a minute.

Conchita's driver saw the danger at once. To stop her leaving he held her arm tightly until the violence stopped, but once the thugs had gone they both got out shouting vainly after the retreating vehicle. Conchita ran back to the Piaf shouting, "Call the Police, call the Police." Voices around her were shouting, 'The President's daughter—Julio Abulencia—gunmen—kidnapped—kidnapped' and one voice said, 'murdered'. Then everyone fell silent and Monsieur Ercole, the manager of the Piaf, could be heard telling the Police what had happened. He spoke loudly and clearly and in a romantic French accent, but Conchita knew it was too late.

Griselda loved to hear the French language; she believed that it represented intellectual civilisation and material culture at a level infinitely higher than that of Spain, of England and very definitely of the USA. Her enthusiasm was not the result of studying Voltaire or Sartre, or the observations of the Encyclopaedists or even watching, with only the slightest understanding, the plays at the Comédie Francaise which she had indeed been obliged to witness, but because of her devotion to Parisian *haute couture*, Parisian artists and Parisian cosmetics and perfumes. Her bedroom was full of the luxury products of France and her closets were overflowing with the expensive creations, not to mention the accessories, jewellery, handbags, hats and so forth, of Chanel, Dior, Balenciaga, Ceruti and, for her shoes, of Jean Paul Gaultier. In Paris. which she managed to visit at least once a year, always staying at her favourite hotel, Le Meurice on the Rue de Rivoli, she loved to admire the collections of up-and-coming couturiers, gazing in rapture as though she was experiencing a kind of epiphany, at the passing pageant on the catwalk of haughty, anaemic beauties sneering or posing indifferently before the overblown purveyors of women's fashions. Then having watched she would buy, buy, buy even though the clothes did not always suit her. They were never disposed of but always added to her fabled collection of garments in the DeoGracias. She easily justified the enormous sums expended by maintaining that her collection, destined for a gallery, would inflate in value as the years went by and, the world of fashion being what it is, who was to say that her prediction might be wrong?

She maintained that she would never speak to a Frenchman in French unless she could speak the language perfectly, which meant almost never for she had no time for disciplined study. However she did know enough to address the French Ambassador and his wife with snippets such as, *'Enchanté monsieur l'ambassadeur'*, and , *'je te remercie beaucoup; tu es très gentile madame,'* at the reception for the French Foreign Minister at the townhouse of Senor Bersamina. Her accent was impeccable, so that it was a bit of come down for Francophones when the conversation had to proceed in a language other than French. She might of course have been assisted by Bersamina's haughty wife Victorina, who was fluent in French, but Senora Bersamina despised the Florescos as upstarts and would never go out of her way to assist them in any way. However on this occasion the First Lady, whose mind was intermittently distracted by the thought of Manzano's operation, was grateful for the social help of Bersamina himself in the absence of the President, who, she gave out, was afflicted with a mild attack of influenza.

"I'm sorry to hear it, Senora Floresco" Bersamina said with an ingratiating smile. "He was in really top form when we last met—at the opening of your Opera."

"My dear Manuel, the Opera of the Carolines, not my Opera. But anyway that's where he must have picked up the bug. It came on quite suddenly. I noticed several people coughing and sneezing. They should not have come."

Bersamina nearly joked, 'maybe he caught it from Madame Lunacharsky when she was expiring on stage,' but thought better of it. Yet, friendly though their exchanges were, Griselda could not help wondering why Bersamina had stated so roundly, and suspiciously she thought, that her husband had been in top form, whereas Bersamina was in fact wondering over the state of health of the President who, he recalled, had looked washed out when last they met in the cavernous foyer of the Opera. Nevertheless they both moved with aplomb among the guests, admired a small exhibition of three French artists currently working in the Carolines, talked to two armaments manufacturers about their excellent helicopters, the underlying reason for the visit, and above all else were fulsome in their praise of France when they spoke to the French Foreign Minister who, the Canadian ambassador whispered, was said to have presidential ambitions. Ah, like some other people I know, Griselda thought, as she watched Bersamina, with some irritation, telling a story in French to a little group of diplomatic wives who suddenly exploded with shocked laughter. There were cries of, 'Incroyable', 'C'est vraimant bizarre', 'Impossible', and 'Oh Monsieur Bersamina,' from the ladies and a reproving 'Oh do shut up, Manuel' from Victorina, suggesting that Bersamina's tale had been a bit raunchy. Griselda turned away, irritated again by the bigger worry gnawing in her mind: Manzano was surely to be relied on; all must have gone well; yet how had her daughter reacted? No, she could not stop any longer at this damnable reception. Her husband's indisposition would give her the chance to get away.

The Foreign Minister then made a gracious little speech about Franco Caroline friendship dating back to the Napoleonic era, half in French and half in Spanish. It seemed to some a pointed rejection of the role of English where Latin affinity was involved. Bersamina proposed a toast to the President of France and Catalino Guzman, the Caroline Foreign Minister, proposed a toast to the French Foreign Minister. Griselda was annoyed that Bersamina should have reversed the protocol even though the reception was in his house, but she was still joining in the polite applause when a worried ADC, a Cambodian in Bersamina's employ, took hold of her arm. She stared at him amazed at this second lack of protocol. *"Madame, votre fille. Madamoiselle Conchita est ici. Elle est un peu dérangée, je crois."* In fact Conchita was barely a couple of yards behind him and *dérangée* was clearly an understatement about Conchita's state of mind. Her eyes were staring and her face tensed with fury. Some guests, including their hosts Senor and Senora Bersamina, had formed a little circle of onlookers around the mother and daughter. Fortunately the ADC quickly recovered his savoir faire, *"Par ici Madame. Par ici Mademoiselle,"* he said, gesturing at them to move with him towards an adjoining salon, where, joined by Bersamina he left them after shutting the door behind him.

The First Lady was about to address Bersamina but Conchita stopped her saying, "No, let him stay. He is the Minister for Defence, isn't he? He should hear what I have to say." Griselda sat down heavily and asked the others to do the same. Bersamina sat opposite her but Conchita remained on her feet. "Do you know what has happened?" she demanded of her mother. "Do you understand why I am here?"

Whether she knew anything or nothing Griselda was sitting stiffly and not a word passed her lips. Bersamina, sensing danger, stood up and said softly to Conchita, "Senora, whatever it is that is troubling you, please sit quietly and tell us it straight. Neither your mother nor I can say a thing unless you tell us the problem. Is it the President? Is he unwell?"

Conchita remained standing only intent on addressing her mother. Of a sudden she had seemingly become calm and collected. In a dry conversational way she said, "You see mother, I am very like you in many ways. Inside me everything is raging. I really want to scream and shout, but that is over—for now. Look at me then; am I not outwardly calm apart from the tension around my mouth, just like the tension I see your own mouth revealing now? I wonder why?"

The First Lady stood up. She looked statuesque in her national dress, tonight a sombre blue which, below her strong face with its high sweeping black hair, made her every bit as intimidating as she wanted the world to see her. Very proudly she asked tersely, "What is all this, Conchita? Have you gone crazy? Let's all hear what you have to tell us."

"No mother. I have not gone crazy but I think that you have. Why have you had Julio kidnapped? You'd stop at nothing to get your own way; I know that. Now listen to me. I am not telling you anything. I am commanding you. Have him set free at once. If you don't I'll make you regret it for the rest of your life."

"Kidnapped! Kidnapped! What nonsense! I don't believe it." Griselda shook her head in disbelief. "Well darling, if what you say is true I forgive you for breaking in like this. I would understand. But out with your story. I want to hear it. And I'm sure the Minister for Defence wants to hear it too. Don't you Manuel?"

Bersamina was too taken aback to say a word. All sorts of implications seem to be in the offing; a plethora of paths was opening before him and he could not imagine which one he might take. Nevertheless he did nod his head, first slightly and then very decidedly. Conchita's memory of the incident was crystal clear. "It was an old black Chevrolet," she began as though giving evidence in court, "I can remember some of the registration letters—OXT. There were five men in all; no, six because the driver did not get out. The men's faces were covered. Julio and I had just left the Piaf". She turned towards her mother. "You've heard of Piaf, haven't you mother? One of your French cultural icons. A little girl born in poverty, poorer than you ever were. A girl who made it to the top but remained the soul of love, the soul of honesty." Bersamina, though not Griselda, looked chagrined at the sight of tears rolling down Conchita's cheeks as she went on, "They knew we were there. Julio never tells anyone where we are to meet but I am supposed to report my movements to the palace just before I leave. I don't always do so, but tonight I did. So it was only from the DeoGracias that the information could have come. So please investigate your own security men there, Senora Floresco." As she noticed Bersamina's eyes questioning her mother she added, "The Minister for Defence and I should both be given a report on your findings."

Bersamina suspected that Conchita's accusation of her mother was, if unbelievable, probably true. Knowing of her objection to an Abulencia match, Griselda certainly had a motive, but he did not want to alienate her. He began mildly. "Now sit down and relax, Senora." As he spoke he went to a side table on which there was an array of drinks and poured out a large Scotch which, whether she wanted it or not, he set beside the weeping young woman. "Please, Conchita, drink this. Think carefully. Children tend to blame their parents for everything that goes wrong for them these days. But think carefully; what you have told us contains no evidence, not a shred of evidence that Griselda is involved. Personally I don't believe it's possible for a mother to do such a thing. Certainly not our dear First Lady."

170

Griselda had the feelings of a besieged general on the verge of defeat when a relief force heaves in sight. She was still ill at ease but anxious not to show fear. In a resentful way she said, "I know nothing at all about all this. Nothing at all. This is a fantasy, Conchita. Do you think I've nothing better to do than to think about where you and your boyfriend are having a date. Yes, he's a good boy, and I'm sorry for what has happened and we must do our best to get him back safely. Isn't that so Manuel? Now please calm down my dear Connie and consider what we've both told you."

A brief discussion then took place between the First Lady and the Minister on what measures the security forces could take to rescue Julio, though all the ideas came from Bersamina and not from the First Lady, who professed to know nothing about such matters as underground lines of communication. During this exchange Conchita took some copious draughts of the Scotch, which reduced her anxiety but not her conviction that her mother was the cause of Julio's fate. At length, interrupting the conversation she put down her goblet with a smack on a glass topped table—everyone wondered whether it had cracked—and said, "Don't worry about taking action. I'm sure the Police are doing that already. I'm only sure of one fact. My father could never be involved in this outrage. He loves me too much. I shall appeal to him directly. He will hear me. He will help me. I am going to him now." With that Conchita stood up and made for the door.

The First Lady was taken completely by surprise and shouted, "No you can't go. You can't go. He is ill. You can't disturb him with such a matter just now. I forbid you. I forbid you absolutely."

"But you told me that he was comfortable and improving. You said it was all right for me to see Julio. You knew we were to meet." Conchita's voice became withering. "Oh no, mother, I don't believe you had nothing to do with what happened tonight."

"I didn't know where you were meeting or when. It was up to you as well you know it. You said you were going to the Alcazar. I have never heard of a place called the Piaf. So the kidnapping must have been the work of criminal blackmailers or the communists—or both. I had no hand in it, Conchita, no hand in it at all, Manuel."

Bersamina's interest had shifted. His suspicion had not been groundless. The President's illness could even be serious. After all, he was not here, which suggested it was; on the other hand Griselda had come, which suggested it was not. That left him unsure. What was clear was Griselda's failure to keep up her guard when suddenly assailed by her own daughter. He rose and said with the greatest courtesy, "Senora Griselda, Senora Conchita, I think the two of you had really better stay here awhile and talk over your differences—very peacefully I beg you. It seems to me, Conchita, that you have not proved your accusation. So you cannot disturb your father at this juncture—but perhaps when your mother can guarantee that the President is in good health?" His interrogative ended with raised eyebrows in the direction of the First Lady. "But now I must go to my study and tell the Ministry to gather all available information on the kidnapping. Then I must attend to my guests. I can't leave it all to Victorina. The French Foreign Minister is here and pressmen are hanging around like gnats. We don't want speculation about any of us to leak out from here tonight."

Conchita felt that her own significance and the danger Julio was in had been downgraded to low priority. She had, moreover, sensed the underlying mistrust of Bersamina and her mother in each other. Perhaps she, though the President's daughter, would become a mere cipher between these two strong minded creatures in some awful struggle in which Julio's life would just fall between the cracks. She felt like saying as lawyers did on the screen, 'My case rests,' but felt it would be ignored like the words of a witness before a revolutionary tribunal, so she merely nodded politely at Bersamina and said, "Thank you Senor. Please find out everything you can about this matter. You will find my report to the police did not lie."

Bersamina bowed to Griselda and Conchita more like an old fashioned aristocrat than a Carolino and left the room. The door closed behind him and the First Lady thought she heard the click of a key turning, but maybe that was her imagination. Annoyance with Conchita was far stronger in her mind than regret or guilt over her own behavior, which had precipitated the whole fiasco. It had been her intention after the reception to have Manzano issue a statement blaming the communists and saying they were demanding a ransom for Julio. Too late. Now everthing was in the hands of the most ambitious Minister in the régime. She feared that she and Conchita were physically in his power at a time of peril for her family.

After talking briefly to his Ministry, Bersamina returned to the reception, apologising profusely to the French Foreign Minster for his absence and explaining that the First Lady would not be returning because she was looking after her daughter, Senora Conchita, who had experienced a 'mishap' in town. He searched for the word in French and chose, "*Un contretemps,*" at which the Foreign Minister raised an eyebrow, so he said, "*Un mésaventure.*" The Foreign Minister's face became more questioning so Bersamina changed to, "*Un malheur, Excellence,*" The Foreign Minister said he hoped that it was not a serious accident, and Bersamina answered, "*Non, Excellence, pas un hasard,*" leaving everyone in the air over what had actually happened. At this point the Foreign Minister said that perhaps that pretty English gal, "Miss App," was what they were looking for and everyone laughed at his diplomatic wit.

When the house was silent again and Victorina had bid him a frosty good night for leaving her so long to look after the guests, Bersamina sat alone in his study, deep in thought. This was one of the few occasions when the First Lady's actions might rebound on her, adversely and seriously. Of course it must have been her. Conchita's instincts were right. The connections with the Holy Thugs of that disloyal idiot Manzano, who thought he was every rich woman's heart throb, all but proved her case. How disastrous for Griselda if anything fatal were to happen to young Abulencia. For Conchita's sake he did not want that to happen. Action could not be delayed. He had already made up his mind what to do when he heard from the Ministry that the Holy Thugs' movements were known to the military. They had gone back to their hideout in Infanta, changed transport and were now just waiting, probably to leave the capital. "Let them proceed for a while," he ordered, "but keep them under surveillance. See that all roadblocks are on the alert." He put down the phone for a few minutes and then took it up to issue another order, this time to the Commandant of the Infanta garrison; a single word, "Sebastian."

"Yes sir."

No one knew the state of the President's health. But it was wise to ensure that all was ready in case it was a more serious matter than a mild bout of influenza.

Cesar Abulencia was in Hilary Arbuthnot's modest hotel room with Max Bligh when he heard the news of Julio's abduction. The announcement, made on the morning television news, was anodyne blaming no person or group as the likely perpetrator and giving the impression that the matter would soon be resolved without suggesting how. Straightaway no less confidently than Conchita and Bersamina, wily Cesar divined the truth and said, "It's that bloody woman."

Not everyone agreed. Hilary maintained that no mother would be capable of such an act and even Max Bligh, cynical as he was about all human endeavour, concurred only reluctantly when Cesar, with some passion, told him of the Florescos' past hostility towards his family. That being so, Bligh feared, Cesar might do something impetuous like making unsubstantiated allegations to the media, which could delay the completion of their filming just when he was anxious to leave the country. However Cesar was remarkably calm about his nephew's disappearance. When Hilary suggested that Julio might be in real danger, Cesar looked at him benignly and said, "Oh, you haven't been in the Carolines long enough. The criminals, whoever they are, are just doing it for money—from their employer and from the victim's family—two bites of the cherry see. Once a ransom is paid, everything will be back to normal. However, if that woman is behind it all, and I've told you that she is, things may be a bit different. We Abulencias may have to concede something to the régime and I think I know what it is. But we are an old family and know how to play their game."

Max Bligh did not want Cesar to play any game at all. He certainly did not want him to encounter a crowd of reporters outside the Abulencia residence and start blabbing his opinions without evidence. "Let's be cautious. Let's stay here until we hear something substantial," he suggested "And finish our job. You were still recording Cesar."

"Excellent idea, I agree." said Hilary. "And we can turn the rape, no Max, don't shake your head, the word is deliberately emotive, the rape of Julio to our advantage. The boy is already newsworthy; let's make him more so. Cesar could record his opinions of him and about Conchita too. What's more he could get his suspicions off his chest without them becoming public for the time being. This could be our big break. We'll keep Cesar's revelations in reserve." Laughing excitedly at Max and Cesar he said, "Man, I'm thinking world headlines."

Inwardly Max was groaning. With these two everything could go wrong. Already his plans had got out of hand. As a member of a Californian Marxist cell which guessed that the Caroline people were ready to take the path that had led to revolution in Latin America, he had joined Schusters, a left wing firm currently working for Venezuela. Having shown his commitment to the cause he had been offered a directorship and made responsible for the company's contract with the Carolines. His intimate contact with the Floresco régime had already enabled him to assess its political viability, while secretly passing financial support to the Catholic Liberation movement working for social revolution. Yet his second contact with a liberation priest had been blown and he suspected that the police were on to him for his link to Oliveros. Hence his desire to get away quickly. But another problem now beset him; the film that Hilary, with Max's complicity, had all but completed, while providing food for thought about the Carolines, revealed too much about the country's corruption and vice to the disadvantage of the Florescos, whose fury would know no bounds if they saw it. They would certainly cancel the PR contract and even do something unpleasant to him unless the offending footage was deleted. But how to do this when Hilary was proud of every frame of his film? If that wasn't enough, Bligh's disarray had been magnified last night by the abduction of the nephew of his collaborator Cesar, seemingly by the wife of the President, the very man he was working for. The situation was fragile; no wonder he feared a power struggle in Infanta rather than hoping for a peasant revolution in the country. His mission had become untenable. He was a failure.

Cesar, on the other hand, was brimming with enthusiasm. "I'll do exactly that. Get the equipment ready. See; I'll sit in that chair to begin with. I can get up from time to time and move about for the camera. I'll be against the window with the garden behind me." The three of them bustled about in readiness for the shoot but Bligh's gloom was getting deeper. Hilary thought only of creating headlines; Cesar thought of appearing the wise statesmen, the honest leader in waiting. The superficial effect they created was more important to them than the actual results of their actions. To remonstrate would be useless. Cesar had taken his seat. Hilary positioned the camera and said, "Right Cesar, let's go." Max stood and observed. It was like being on a doomed vessel, fascinated but powerless to stop it sinking.

Cesar then spoke but as his words flowed Max found his admiration for this cultured aristocrat growing. He was a man transformed. The tone of his voice had changed; he was the academic at Harvard or Cambridge speaking in carefully modulated phrases with the utmost clarity. And he looked the part; his handsome, no longer young face was calm, his eyes piercing and beyond that were his hand movements, raised or moving purposefully to emphasis a point or to help the process of his thesis. This began in an historical way and contained well-worn Caroline themes: the Malay basis, the Spanish conquest, the imposition of harsh feudalism by the sword and the shackles of Catholicism; then the so-called liberation from Spain by the United States, which had massacred hundreds of thousands of Carolinos who wanted only their freedom; and finally the horrors of war and freedom from Japanese tyranny that only gave birth to an independence mired by corruption, poverty and inane population growth so that thousands of Carolinos were condemned to virtual slavery in foreign countries. His thesis ended with a charge that the Americans, to perpetuate the dependence of the country, had deliberately left behind them a constitution that had petrified the feudal system under a semblance of democracy.

Max knew all this but what followed was new. Cesar had moved from the general to the particular. What actually happened to people who opposed the present régime? He told the story of Nestor, a young writer who had produced a carefully researched article examining the depths of corruption to which the Florescos had descended and how they had so subverted the rule of law that the political life of the country lay in ruins. For his pains he had been arrested and tortured. Cesar did not mince words, giving details of the acts of torture so that any listener, even Max Bligh, could imagine the young man's screams of agony. Nestor had finally been released because of an international protest organised by some French writers and the Abulencias. Happily his talents were now used in writing and editing for Radio Ecclesia, but not all the state's victims were so lucky. Other acts of abuse were in their thousands and they continued. The most recent was, and here Cesar stated it unequivocally, "The rape of Julio." The calm of Cesar's face and of his voice had gone. He had grown passionate and his last words on the crime were a ringing accusation: "And so I accuse President Antonio Floresco and his wife Griselda."

In the ensuing silence Cesar and Hilary scrutinised Max, who knew his judgment was expected. Without hesitation he said. "Cesar. I congratulate you. An excellent thesis. Your presentation was top rate. You were marvellous. The only trouble is…"

"What?" said Hilary anxiously.

"It can't be used."

Expostulations followed until Max shouted, "I mean not in this country. And the President would only want the parts he approves of released overseas."

"Well we'll keep it on ice as we said before. And use the inoffensive parts in the documentary. We did agree to that didn't we?" said Cesar.

"I won't have my work adulterated," complained Hilary. "If you wanted propaganda, why didn't you call in some cheapjack filmmaker; the sort of guys who distort history. There are plenty of them in the States." He seemed prone to a fit of petulant anger. Perhaps some past unpleasant experiences had made him so protective of his work and his equipment. The idea that his creation might not appear as he had made it or that it might be bowdlerised made him extremely tetchy of criticism.

"Yes, yes, yes. We know you are an artist, Hilary. But just be patient. When it's shown abroad you'll be praised to the skies," said Cesar. "Meanwhile, let's just take a couple of hours off. Max why don't you take Hilary for a nice massage? He'll see things differently after that. As for me, I'm going home."

Being somewhat puritanical, like many Marxists and many Americans, massage establishments had never appealed to Max

Bligh, but something else was worrying him. Supposing the good work just done was lost or destroyed. "And what will you do at home?" he asked Cesar. "Talk to reporters?"

"No. I shall just read a book and wait until I'm contacted. Maybe by the goons who seized Julio. Who knows?" Cesar answered airily.

They left the hotel, which was in a less fashionable part of Infanta that contained numerous old mansions one, of which had been turned into the Imelda Hotel named after the first lady of a nearby state. Hilary loved the peace of his large high room, one of half a dozen that opened onto a balcony overlooking a pretty garden that was always cool under the spreading trees, protecting it from the sun. Almost reluctantly he left his haven with Max to get a taxi while Cesar was driven off in his Mercedes.

Max wanted Hilary to be out of the hotel for a couple of hours so he knew what to do. He had heard executives talk about a luxurious massage parlour, not one of those quick time joints where grinning Japanese male tourists queued for a number to link them to a masseuse, but a classy place called the Harmonious Reign. He gave the name to the taxi driver, who, being Chinese, said, "Ah yes, Chong Ho, very best place, very good girls."

"Not too good I hope," said Max turning to Hilary. "The best places often have a menu so you can decide what to order. Freedom of choice—for the client that is. You'd like that wouldn't you, Hilary?" Bligh thought he must sound like a worldly uncle taking an inexperienced schoolboy out for a naughty treat kept secret from his mum and dad.

"Well yes. I suppose so. Just a massage will do," said Hilary modestly. You see I don't want to do anything myself."

"No need you do anything," interrupted the large eared taxi driver. "Good masseuse do everything. Very clever give you good time."

This rather amused Bligh who said, "There you are Hilary. Just say what you want to suit your diet: girl or boy, old or young, fat or thin, like a fat stock market."

"Many massage on menu," said the driver. "Swedish, Japanese, Thai, tantric, sensual, erotic, take your choice. Me, like Swedish. No hanky panky. Preserve vital fluids."

At the Chong Ho the driver, American style, told them, "Have a nice day," and then whispered to Hilary, "You make first time visit. Check price. Very expensive place."

The foyer was notable for its kitch gold-encrusted chairs of the sort favoured by Arab princes and third world prime ministers, but it was comfortable, cool and very clean. A slender middle aged woman in a Chanel 'little black dress' greeted them and said the patroness would receive them shortly. Hardly were they seated when in walked a Chinese lady elegantly dressed but of strong appearance, whom Max Bligh recognised at once as Senora Clarissa Ocampo. Apart from bearing her husband's surname name and sporting a bouffant hairdo like that of the First Lady, she was as Chinese as the Forbidden City and well known about town as a successful businesswoman. The Chong Ho was evidently one of the reasons for her success. Together with the visitors she sat down at a table already provided with drinks and nibbles. Assuming no doubt that they knew of her, she said without ado, "I make it my business to take a personal interest in foreign guests," and Max and Hilary thanked her, respectfully. To Max Bligh she said with the glance of an empress, "And you are?"

"Max Bligh, Senora. I am under contract to the DeoGracias."

"Oh, yes; Schuster, Schuster and Bligh." Clarissa Ocampo smiled graciously but Max felt nervous. How the blazes did she know of him? His thoughts turned to his own safety. A woman in her position could be in cahoots with the very police who might be after him. "And you are?" she asked Hilary.

"Hilary Arbuthnot from Hong Kong. I am a film director."

At the last two words Clarissa looked very interested and then remembered. "Oh yes, of course. One of your works is, *Polynesian Migrations in the Western Pacific*. Is it not? Oh yes, those beautiful natives; bodies so strong and graceful."

"Yes indeed," said Hilary, proud that his fame should have travelled this far at least.

"We sometimes do our own filming here." said Senora Ocampo "But good directors difficult to find."

Max Bligh caught on at once and guessed the nature of the Chong Ho products for the screen. "Perhaps that's a matter you could talk about with Mr Arbuthnot," he suggested. "I'm sure you need a director who is an artist with the human figure, which Mr Arbuthnot certainly is, as you know."

Clarissa frowned at Max as though to tell him to mind his own business, but he was sure that if Hilary didn't behave like a prude he might be approached, which could be a good thing as he was always short of money.

The light chit chat trickled on until Clarissa herself raised the question of the men's requirements. Max said he was not staying, not even for a massage. He had just brought his friend, who was worn out after an exhausting work schedule. He felt that Hilary was in need of relaxation rather than personal vigorous action.

"I quite understand," said Clarissa, addressing Hilary, but now in a quieter, almost an insidious voice. "Perhaps you would like a nice show with your massage." She gave a tinkling little laugh. "We have many shows on the menu. You are an English gentleman so I don't think you want anything kinky like sady masy. What about you watch a lovely girl and a handsome boy making beautiful love?"

"I suppose that would be OK," said Hilary doubtfully. Though tempted he felt a bit alarmed as he remembered the taxi driver's admonition about cost.

"Or a variation." Clarissa continued. "Two girls and one boy. Or two boys and one girl or two boys and three girls. You get my point. You make the choice."

"Every possible permutation or combination is before you," interjected Max, who had been listening carefully.

"Those two words are interesting," said Senora Ocampo whose mood suddenly changed, "I do not know them. My spoken English is good I am told but I am not an academic person."

"You could have fooled me," said Max who then repeated the words new to her and spelt them out while Clarissa wrote them on a note pad, saying that she would look them up in her Oxford English Dictionary. That done she gave a satisfied smile at Max before making off to arrange Hilary's suddenly enthusiastic and very precise request for two handsome boys and a very pretty girl, all young please. Max thought that the order suggested Hilary's real preferences but merely observed, "A very good choice. Provides for a bit of rivalry. My God, Hilary, did you see Clarissa with her notebook. Jesus, the Chinese want to learn everything under the

180

sun. They'll take the West over completely one of these days—but not in my lifetime."

"Don't bet on it," said Hilary as a smiling little maid arrived to lead him to his voyeuristic pleasure. "From what I've seen from my perch in Hong Kong I'd give China much less than fifty years to take over the whole world."

Bligh abruptly took Hilary's arm and said firmly, "This is all on me, or shall I say on Schuster, Schuster and Bligh. So take as long as you want. Ten girls and ten boys if you want, old chap"

"But such expense," protested Hilary not accustomed to this way of conducting affairs.

"Customary everywhere especially among businessmen and bankers. They are the real whores of the world, not the pretty young things you are about to watch. When it's over talk to Senora Ocampo about filming her shows. It's just one of the nicer evils of capitalism, Hilary, and there's money in it. Join up with the Chong Ho and you'll be popular all over the world."

Once outside Max quickly hailed a taxi to take him back to the Imelda. He was sure that he now had all the time he needed. There was no problem in entering Hilary's room. Even without a key you could get into most of the hotel rooms from the balcony. Easy access was one of the charms of the place. Cesar had once joked that the old mansion was designed as a setting for a Feydeau farce. Nevertheless at the main entrance the security presence was as forbidding to strangers as anywhere in Infanta.

Fortunately Max had learned how to operate the expensive equipment Hilary had brought from Hong Kong so he was able to make a copy of Cesar's speech; it was a valuable property and might be more dangerous than a gun in the right circumstances. He also took some diskettes, made a second copy of Cesar's speech as well as two copies of the entire soundtrack. His work might not result in failure after all.

Reporters were out in force at the entrance to the Abulencia town house. It took a few minutes for the guards to open the heavy wooden gates, which gave the opportunity to the more aggressive pressmen to yell questions at Cesar. One particularly formidable snout-nosed American woman kept shouting, "Mr Abulencia, is this just a bum rap?" In the din it was useless to say a word so Cesar sat tight until the car was able to roll forward and the gates closed behind him.

After the news about his nephew, the collaboration with Bligh and Arbuthnot, and the heartfelt speech he had made on camera, he felt exhausted yet not unhappy. He was confident that Julio could be rescued. The Abulencias would pay what was demanded for a loved member of their family. But better than that he believed that he had struck a blow at the dictator. Of course his speech could not be made public for a while, but when it came out the fat would be in the fire. He did not fear his own assassination; the murder of one of the most distinguished families in the Carolines was not an option for the President, whose one course of action would be to prosecute him. The world would then be able to watch the proceedings and listen to the evidence, including all the findings of the unhappy Nestor. If corrupt judges found him guilty it would lead to world protests more violent than those that had led to the release of Nestor. His speech had marked the beginning of the end. The régime's days were numbered.

With these thoughts in mind he relaxed in an armchair by a garden fountain reading here and there in Tacitus' Roman history, his favourite reading when thinking of the lives of tyrants. He was entirely engrossed when the phone rang. He started up thinking that it might be a message from the kidnappers, but his secretary only whispered the words 'Senor Bersamina' when he brought the phone along.

The Minister addressed him courteously in Spanish, in which language they continued to speak. They soon got to the substance of the call when Bersamina said, "My dear friend, I have received the most recent information about your nephew Julio. He was taken out of town last night but we are not sure where the abductors took him. We lost contact with them. They may have a safe camp in the mountains. Maybe your nephew was taken to some such place. I can't say, Senor."

After a pause occasioned by Cesar feeling his heart beating rapidly, he said, "Senor Minister thank you for calling me. I must ask you one question: Is this strange action being done by agents of the State for some valid reason? Please give me a hint as guarded as you may find necessary. If state action is the case I can set my heart at ease, for though I am no supporter of the régime, as well you know, I have confidence that neither you nor the President would want any harm to befall this innocent young man who has in no way offended you. However, I do not believe the communists are responsible because I do not see that they would get any advantage from it. They have much richer sources of funds than those available to my family. It goes without saying that if you are able to give me a reassuring answer, my lips would be sealed, on my honour."

Bersamina replied, "Dear friend, your word alone would be enough for me, but regretfully I cannot give you any such hint. I have no inside information on why this crime was committed or who did it. The only assurance I can give is that the Security forces will do everything in their power to find Julio. I must say however that given the fact that we don't know who we are dealing with you cannot at present live in the certainty of your nephew's early release."

They both concluded with an exchange of felicitations between their families as was usual between people of their rank and standing. Cesar fell into a deep gloom; Bersamina truly regretted that the Abulencias should be made to suffer in a way that he found more appropriate for the lower orders. However, he had no doubt who the culprit was and he was determined that, however things turned out, the maximum embarrassment should be caused to the First Lady.

Within minutes of his call to Cesar, Bersamina was informed that Prime Minister Bienvenido Loyola had arrived to see him; an unusual circumstance, for the Prime Minister summoned Ministers rather than calling on them. It was evident that Loyola knew something was in the wind and his customary aplomb had deserted him. He walked in quickly and began at once with, "What's going on at the DeoGracias? I usually have my weekly session with the President today but a call came telling me that everything was off. No reason given."

"I know, I know," replied Bersamina, eyeing Loyola warily as if assessing his worth in a moment of crisis. "You're not the only one who can't get to him. The fact is that he's ill. How ill God knows—or rather Griselda knows—I suppose there's a difference. Last night when she called on me with her daughter—*l'affaire* Julio you know—I got the impression that she didn't want me to know how serious his illness is."

"So it is serious?"

"I didn't say so. I said she didn't want me to know how serious." Having planted a nagging seed in Loyola's head, Bersamina continued, "If he is really ill surely you're the one who should know and be giving us a lead. Mind you, I'm not saying it is serious but supposing it was. What would we all do? Wait for an announcement from dear Griselda? Or maybe an order?" He emphasised the last word derisively. "Honestly, Loyola, I don't like the way things stand. There should be some sort of contingency plan and it should definitely involve you. Constitutionally it should be you and not someone who is only related to the government by marriage." He rubbed his hands together as if the irritation of the situation had begun to affect him physically. "Quite frankly, you and I have something to worry about. The First Lady resents my control of the Military and, even more so, your control of the purse strings—especially when you upset her pet projects. You certainly know that only three days ago there was a student demonstration against the IMF. Where students are concerned for IMF read 'Loyola and his financial policies'. No, I tell you that if that woman is given authority all the care you've lavished on the economy will go down the drain."

Several courses of action presented themselves simultaneously to Loyola. The first, his favourite, was that he should resign and get back to Harvard. The second was to stay in the knowledge that there was no other member of government who could handle the economy, certainly no one remotely acceptable to the country's international creditors. Even if the First Lady took over she would need him. But need him for how long? Sooner or later their policies would clash and he would be out, with disastrous results for the economy. The truth was that if he wanted to continue his curbs on spending the only man to make it possible would be Bersamina, sitting so suavely before him. He recognised that obliquely an offer was being made to him and that he had to take it. "So what should we do?" he asked, his voice sounding almost plaintive. "Have you been doing anything, Bersamina? What do you want me to do?"

Bersamina's voice fell a little though there was no one but Loyola to hear him. "Well Bienvenido, I have placed the Infanta Garrison on alert. If there isn't an emergency I can always explain it as an exercise. The sort of thing we do regularly. But if the President were to be out of action or," here Bersamina hesitated before stating softly but distinctly, "*muerto*, Griselda would find it difficult to do anything without my consent."

Loyola felt instinctively that danger was imminent, but fortunately the self-confident man before him was prepared to cope with it. He said, "I think she'd try but from what you say, you're prepared for all eventualities—aren't you?"

"No Bienvenido, not exactly. If the worst came to the worst too soon, say tomorrow, we might still be obliged to work out a compromise with her—until elections were held. She's in the DeoGracias; she controls the media. Perhaps in the interim period we might have to let her act as Head of State. After all, she has ministerial status. The Constitution says that should the President be removed from office any Minister of State may act in that role, temporarily of course. But in such an interim period she could use her influence with the People's Action Brigades; her favourite Rich Rarang could mobilise a dangerous mob to back her. Even among our colleagues there are men who'd follow her for the pickings they could get. Griselda might then stand for election or, if she felt secure enough, she might continue the state of emergency and say that elections are not necessary for a while. No, on balance we must be prepared. If and when the President is better we must submit a plan for his approval, stating what must be done if anything happens to him while he and Griselda are in Europe. It mustn't involve me. Remember I shall be with him but you will be here. You would have to act as Head of State."

Loyola did not look at all happy but he assented though with considerable misgiving. "But you would be behind me in any crisis, Senor Bersamina, wouldn't you? I'd have to agree to such a plan but only for the sake of the country. I 'd have to. Economically we are near the brink. Internationally our currency is worthless."

"I give you my word of honour that you would have my full backing and that means the support of all the security forces under my command." At this point Bersamina opened his hands, almost in an attitude of prayer and said solemnly, "Senor Prime Minister, I want you to understand that I, Manuel Bersamina, do not want to be another Antonio Floresco. Whatever we may do together must be the prelude to the restoration of democracy."

Loyola felt reassured by the word democracy but knew he had to take Bersamina's professed lack of high ambition on trust. He nodded his satisfaction; further speculation would be unproductive and so he wondered, as was reasonable, on how the kidnapping of Julio was affecting Conchita, adding, "Poor girl, poor girl," in all sincerity.

"Yes indeed, with such a mother," Bersamina replied darkly. "But Senor, the affair might give us an excuse for paying a visit to the DeoGracias, unannounced of course, to express our sympathy to Conchita. Maybe tomorrow if you are willing." Before Loyola could say yea or nay Bersamina asked, "By the way Bienvenido, do you have much contact with the Cardinal?"

"Rarely. We exchange polite greetings whenever we meet. I make a point of going to the Cathedral from time to time—for appearance sake, but I'm no longer a practising Catholic. Why do you ask me? Another part of your proposed plan perhaps? I guess his approval might be useful."

"I've heard that Peccata speaks well of you. Unlike most of our colleagues you have a reputation for probity and clean living. In a time of crisis his support could be invaluable. Apart from Griselda's People's Action Brigades the Church is the only body that could bring multitudes onto the streets. Oh, and I'm told that Peccata doesn't always express sentiments of Christian charity towards the First Lady. Maybe you could find the time for a little chat with him—fairly soon I'd suggest, Senor."

As Loyola left the office Bersamina observed the worried expression on his face but then remembered that the man always looked harassed, not without reason given the state of the national economy. He wondered which of them had the worse job, Loyola dealing with the economy or himself dealing with security. He decided that he was the luckier because of the excitement involved.

He felt in his bones that political currents in the Carolines were flowing ever more rapidly. Unfortunately, like the water system in an arid landscape, the rivers existed mainly underground. It was difficult to assess their force and direction but one sign had made him think hard: the number of student demonstrations was on the increase—in number if not in size and maybe that was intentional. A big demonstration could always be broken up and the strength of the government made manifest. But small demonstrations, at which the students and workers behaved passively, melting away the moment the police appeared, could not be dealt with decisively. Was this a deliberate way of showing how widely opposition to the régime had spread? He told himself not to let his hunches delude him from the realities but he knew he was not alone in recognising the signs of the times. The First Lady seemed to have grasped the nettle. Why else should she be making such an effort to ingratiate herself with the masses Only today an announcement was to be made of a new housing scheme in Infanta at which titles would be given to several hundred families together with a first deposit on the house. The whole circus was being represented as an initiative of the First Lady herself. A headline in the Times of Infanta, repeated *ad nauseam* on television, ran 'The First Lady's gift of love.' Bersamina knew that the scheme would make hardly a dent in the capital's enormous squatter problem but it made the poor believe that the First Lady was a real beacon of hope as their standard of life got worse. Meanwhile he got all the hatred that erupted when squatters had to be evicted by the police for some laudable commercial project or, and this riled him greatly, when behind the scenes, the First Lady insisted on evictions so that they should not be an eyesore to foreign visitors at one of her splendid celebrations.

Tentatively but somewhat uncertainly, Bersamina then thought about Cardinal Peccata, whose opposition to the régime was growing by the day. In sermons and interviews the chief cleric in the land was constantly bemoaning, with phraseology more appropriate to the Book of Revelations, that the whole fabric of government was immoral and corrupt, for two beasts, a lion with its spoliation of the nation's wealth and a demon with its profligacy, were at the heart of a disease that had spread widely throughout society but especially among the affluent. His words were unnerving everyone, not excluding Bersamina who no longer wanted to defend such a degenerate setup. Yet as Minister for Defence he also felt certain that if the Florescos were gone and he remained in office he could enforce morality and financial discipline on the country as a whole. In this he would require the support of Loyola with his prudent fiscal policies and of the Church with its religious majority.

The temptation that had tortured him for several weeks returned in force. Supposing some opposition group precipitated the event which everyone opposed to the régime was hoping for—the death of the President? His death would certainly be welcomed by another party interested in the equation of power—the United States. If there was one place that the Americans saw as a safe haven for their offensive capability in the western Pacific it was the Carolines, which on that account, they needed to be stable. Their present concern was that the collapse of the Floresco régime might result in a revolutionary government that would want America out. He knew that the Americans thought well of him. Might they not be prepared to support him in a bid, free of risk to himself, aimed at ensuring the country's stability.

A few days ago, when he had been entertaining Jasper Frankfurter, the US Secretary for Defence, at the Caroline Highlands Golf Club, the American anxieties had surfaced. Not surprisingly it was the day after they had visited those allegedly hidden rocket silos deep in the mountains. "We should have exerted tighter control over the money we've been wasting on your régime," Jasper had complained to Bersamina, with no pretence of diplomatic finesse. "Your rich spendthrifts should have been taxed properly and corruption eliminated. That's what's getting your people to the boil. I guess we're on the razor's edge now. Now hear this; America can't afford to lose the Carolines. We need people in charge here who see things in our way." Jasper paused significantly then said, "But my President wants a democratic Carolines; that means a country run according to the Constitutional lines we left behind. Not perfect of course, but it had the outward forms of democracy. But we want it run by people who will not turn themselves into tin-pot dictators. The Floresco régime is a big embarrassment to the US. Do you get me, Mr Bersamina?"

Although Bersamina longed to ask Frankfurter whether he had ever thought that Carolinos might like people in power who saw things their way, he replied cautiously. "I think I do, Mr Frankfurter." Nevertheless he did not comment on the way the American had repeatedly used the word 'your', as though Bersamina was responsible for all the ills of the Carolines. One did not argue with a US Secretary for Defence. Instead he asked politely as they were driven to the next fairway whether the Secretary was going to the opening of the First Lady's fine Opera House. Jasper's weasel face had become narrower at the mention of such nonsense. He told the driver to stop. "Singers," he said in his nasal twang. "And sissy ballet dancers. A lot of goddamn queers. Strutting their stuff in a theatre for queens." He paused and looked around as though imagining that someone was nearby to overhear him, though there was no one apart from the buggy driver and the caddy who were chatting happily to each other in the local dialect. The foreign lingo brought a frown to Frankfurter's face and he shouted, "Drive on, boy," adding just as loudly to make it clear he was informing the menials as well as Bersamina, "I'm telling everyone this: God hates fuckin' queers. The Good Book says what happened to the men of Sodom and it could happen here."

Bersamina could not resist saying, "Well, I wonder why God created them?" The boys both chuckled but the sarcasm went unnoticed by the American, who replied, "God moves in mysterious ways, His wonders to perform—but I don't, Manuel. I'll just inform the First Lady that I'm not going to her shindy. It's just the sort of thing I'm talking about. Money wasted on a lot of lavish ballyhoo: Opera Houses, universities, art galleries, conference centres. It worries me a lot. Yeah, I know the dame has her admirers in the State Department and on Broadway but I'm not one of them. I hate liberals but I understand why they want to remove the Florescos. I've heard say of a few who'd go to any length to get rid of them." He gave a whinnying kind of laugh that made Bersamina think of wild horses. "Funny isn't it, the one topic on which my office and the liberals think alike." But he had not found the exchange funny. He had so worked himself up that he misjudged the wind, and drove his next shot into the rough, losing him his winning position, which secretly delighted his allegedly weaker opponent.

In fact Bersamina was no walk-over, especially where intelligence work was concerned. He too knew of exiles outside the country who had cooked up plans of assassination, but every one of them had failed because of his meticulous system of informers that enabled him to scotch any threat. In these matters his intelligence branch worked closely with the Americans. But at the fifteenth hole Jasper had suddenly said, "Manuel, our agents, yours and mine, waste too much time on all this collaboration crap. Is it necessary when we see eye to eye? Let the guys just get on with the job. For instance if we knew of a dissident who wanted rid of some minister or other, and I mean lay or clerical, so don't get me wrong, but someone say who'd become a dangerous liability, would you want us to spill out all the details or would you leave it up to us to deal with the matter?" Bersamina knew at once what Frankfurter was asking. "No," he replied softly. "We'd leave it up to you, Jasper. Of course we would each bear the responsibility for our separate actions. It would be a question of let not thy left hand know what thy right hand doeth." In that instant Bersamina knew that he had made a compact with Jasper to effect the radical change the USA needed. Which meant that from now on Manuel Bersamina must trim his wings and become a democrat, or at least the man working for the restitution of the old Caroline constitution. The rich had made it work their way before and he reckoned he could make it work his way in the future.

"Right," said Frankfurter, who like many Americans loved to bask in the moral authority of the scriptures. "I reckon we know where we're going, Manuel, so I can sincerely say 'God Bless America and the Carolines'."

Bersamina could not bring himself to bless the USA but sometime in life one had to work with what one despised. But he nodded his acquiescence and later, as they drove down to Infanta, he knew the irony of praising the merits of the President's mountain lair which they could see on a distant mountainside. Jasper reacted with, "Jesus, what a beautiful joint, but so vulnerable. A guerrilla attack would cut him off. Is it well guarded Manuel?"

"Not as much as Berchtesgarden," said Bersamina "But we do our best. Unfortunately the President is rather slapdash over security. He often goes his own way and doesn't always say where he's off to. Actually it's one of his redeeming features. He's always been very easy going."

Frankfurter said, "Wow. Is that so?"

Bersamina did not accept the invitation to informal drinks in the US Embassy. He had had enough of a man he disliked but had to work with. As they shook hands, Jasper said, "It's been a pleasure to talk turkey with you, Manuel. We understand each other. Is that's because I'm learning to think like a Carolino or you know how to think like an American?"

"The latter I guess," said Bersamina for if he did know how, at least he was only thinking of himself.

The First Lady knew that she had made a monumental mistake. She had all but alienated her daughter; she had angered the President, but worst of all, to her mind, she had exposed herself to extreme danger from hostile politicians and parties. As a result she was backtracking furiously, which is not to say that she was not mortified by what she had done. She was resolved not to show her feelings. She was the power behind the President and she intended to keep it that way.

Conchita could not be expected to forgive easily, for day and night her mind was occupied with the danger in which Julio had been placed. The First Lady had reiterated again and again that her objective had only been to prevent an unsatisfactory marriage and that no personal harm had been intended for Julio. "Why then," was Conchita's natural refrain, "did you let the operation pass from Manzano to some other group? He should have kept Julio in his possession."

"Manzano was too enthusiastic in his loyalty to me. You know he has many duties in the DeoGracias. He didn't really grasp my intentions," Griselda protested weakly. "The fool thought he knew best what to do."

"Yes, that was your worst mistake. Call Manzano. I have questions to ask of him." Conchita was firm and Griselda thought it expedient to do as her daughter had asked.

Manzano was now permanently stationed at the DeoGracias as Chief Security Officer, a position he relished for it gave him status and the power to intervene in the personal lives of the palace staff. Some people suspected that his association with the First Lady was based on more than their infantile connection but whatever its strength Manzano's loyalty proved malleable. It was therefore unlike the President's unchangeable love for Griselda, for he worshipped the very ground she walked on. Yet *Il Presidente* was also a man in power, often separated from his beloved wife. He had never admired the virtues of chastity or seen any need for it and so the First Lady had soon learned to turn a blind eye to his occasional fling with chambermaids, film stars, pretty secretaries and the like, some on the spur of the moment. She considered it was his *droit de seigneur*. None of the recipients of his lust lasted more than a day or so, some for less than an hour. He liked to misquote Lenin's dictum that sex, unlike love, was no different from blowing ones nose; do it fiercely and get it over. But some weeks before Conchita had returned from England the President had started a liaison, at first purely sexual, with a Mexican film star who had been hired for a part in a Caroline film. The President's continuing pleasure with the charms of Binkie Lumbera soon drew Griselda's attention and anger. She instructed the ever-loyal Manzano to inform her of the affair's progress, which resulted in him secretly recording the bedtime dalliance of the President. Griselda listened to the tapes angrily to begin with but after a short while the verbal nonsense between the lovers, his in bad Spanish, hers in execrable English, reduced her to tears of laughter. She then thought it might be even funnier to beard the lion in his den with poor little Binkie, but it was her Manzano who blocked her at the bedroom door.

"How dare you stop me from entering," she had stormed at him.

"The President's orders," he had retorted but added, "Senora, I do it for your own good. I must protect you in every way, including stopping you from making a fool of yourself." As his mistress seemed still intent on forcing her way in, he warned her, "Ma'am even a dog will bite if you pull him off when he's fucking."

The truth was that the President, who had far more power to promote or destroy than his wife, had already suborned Manzano. The same powers then enabled him to further seduce Griselda by extending her administrative powers over the whole of the province in which Infanta stood. It was a rich province with a number of important industries in which he encouraged Griselda to take a deep and profitable financial interest.

Most amazing to Griselda was the broad hint he gave her one day about the extent of her freedom. "Griselda darling, you need never worry about the likes of Senorita Lumbera. If she fell into a pool of crocodiles it wouldn't bother me at all though some might find it fun. Such people are ciphers compared with you and me. Do you think I would worry if you were to divert yourself from time to time—without it coming to my or anyone else's attention? No, our fortunes are riveted together. A tsunami couldn't separate us."

Griselda looked at him adoringly and knew he believed what he said. Some time later during another cosy chat he praised Manzano's deep commitment to her service.

"How amazing; I know his fidelity goes back to your nursery days. He's conditioned to you like one of Pavlov's dogs. Do you know, Griselda the other day I saw him swimming naked in our pool. If I were a woman I'm sure I'd find him attractive. He's so well proportioned."

The First Lady hugged her husband and told him she no longer cared about Binkie Lumbera or any other doxy he went with; with the whole of the Infanta province in her care, she had too much to do. But she added, "You really are crude, Antonio, to think I'd fall for a man's body. I'll tell you truthfully: yes I do like Manzano but that's all it will ever be. He's like a pet dog, faithful even if I beat him. Antonio, my dearest, being a woman my family and its future are more important to me than frolics in bed with a man, even one so well-proportioned, as you put it, as Manzano. So now you know his two main attributes, arrogance and a big prick; the male ideal. But as you are not a woman I guess you'll never know what I am talking about."

Griselda decided to give Manzano a thorough dressing down in front of Conchita. When he entered her salon she adopted her favourite posture, body erect, head thrown back and her bouffant hair making her a pitiless tsarina. The shoulders of her national dress were today more pronounced than usual, producing the impression of a rapacious hawk about to soar in flight. She then upbraided Manzano in every possible way. Why had he not kept Julio under his control? Where was the boy now? Why had he done it without consulting her? Why hadn't he done this, that or the other? Her questions uttered in a cutting voice were so rapid that no time was given for an answer. Her voice was like the shriek of a harpy when she demanded how dare he think only of his wife and children when his first loyalty was to the Florescos? The torrent seemed unstoppable. Conchita had never seen a tall, handsome man of military bearing so reduced. He spluttered words of apology only to be interrupted. Then he capitulated utterly, crying that his feelings for his family were as nothing compared with his devotion to Madame, for whom he'd lay down his life if she willed it. Finally the wretched man fell to his knees at the First Lady's feet trembling and trying not to weep.

"Get up, you silly fool," commanded the First Lady. "Stop sniveling, man. You are a man I'm told. What's that bit of paper in your hand?"

"A message from Doctor da Silva. I believe he wants you and Senora Conchita to go to the medical centre ma'am."

"Why didn't you say so before, instead of talking away at me, wasting my time? Get out." The First Lady's voice became normal, indeed amused, "Come along, Conchita dear. We'll see how your father is doing."

Manzano had not fled. Rooted to the floor he cowered at one side to let the women pass, his tearful eyes begging forgiveness of Conchita. She pitied him despite his ghastly mistake and even wanted to say something of comfort to him but her mother gave her a glance, reminding her that she was the First Lady's daughter and must pass Manzano by without throwing him even a condescending glance. Gone was any chance of her questioning him about Julio. It confirmed her view that, however significant might be the financial and military levers controlled by her father, the strongest person in her family was Griselda. Despite her anger and her fearful longing for Julio's safety, she found herself hating yet admiring her mother's strength and wondering whether she could ever match it.

Griselda and Conchita were surprised to find that the President was not in the medical centre. Doctor da Silva, solicitous as the White Rabbit informed them that he had gone unaided to his study. "There was nothing I could do to stop him walking out, ma'am," da

Silva pleaded. Conchita noticed little beads of sweat forming on his face. "I did my best to keep him here, ma'am."

Griselda became all gracious. "Of course you did, doctor. No need for you to come with us. Please go and have a good rest."

The President was sitting at his executive desk, a 'Gift in Comradeship' to him from General Douglas MacArthur, so said a little brass inscription for all to see on the front of the historic piece of junk. Some doubted the veracity of the story, since no one could remember ever seeing the General behind a desk in the Carolines or even him being there, except maybe for a brief airborne stop-down. He rose to greet first Conchita, then Griselda before returning again with a warm embrace to Conchita, saying how angry he was with whoever it was who had masterminded the crime against Julio, who would soon be freed. The perpetrators must be shown no mercy. Conchita found it embarrassing to be with her mother when this was said but she smiled wanly and sat next to her father on the settee. Griselda gave the impression of not listening to his words.

"But daddy, how are you? Doctor da Silva said you had to rest. How did you recover so quickly?" Conchita kissed her father more than dutifully. She knew everything that had been said and written about him but whether he was a dictator, a thief on a monumental scale or a cruel tyrant, nothing could shake her love for him.

"Yes Antonio, tell us how you feel," Griselda said. "You can't imagine how worried I have been."

"Don't you know that a man who has experienced resurrection can imagine anything, anything on earth, in heaven or in blazes. I must have gone to all three when I was lying in that sterile medical centre. Jesus, those sexless nurses buzzing around me, lesbians I'd say. They smelt like shellfish. They made me feel like a specimen. Da Silva has rotten taste in women." The President gave a throaty laugh that ending in a cough, spat noisily like a Chinese labourer into a tissue and asked, "I guess I've come back after the customary three days then?"

Griselda said forcibly, "Two only Antonio. Don't get above yourself."

"Don't worry about it then. It was just a passing indisposition. And don't let it out to the public. You know how the press lies and I want to appear the healthy national leader when I go to Europe."

The President got up and went back to his desk where he picked up some papers. "What the hell is this, Griselda? Why has Bersamina put the Infanta Garrison on a state of emergency? Expecting an invasion from Mars or somewhere?"

Griselda saw no reason to jump to Bersamina's defence but she thought it wise to do so. "Well, it may be my fault. I did say that you weren't feeling well. He might have imagined that you were seriously ill. Really Antonio, you are to blame, falling unconscious and frightening us all. Perhaps Manuel was afraid of repercussions from the liberal left when people heard an Abulencia had been kidnapped."

The President muttered something about Cesar Abulencia and his liberal party being a busted flush, and as useless as a torn condom, but to Conchita sitting next to him it was clear that, though he was affecting to be well, he lacked his usual vigour; his behavior was an act. Nonetheless she was glad that her mother was smoothing out any difficulties that might have arisen. She added, "Yes daddy. You don't realise how much mummy worries about your health. Please don't argue on my account. I'm certain the police are doing all they can to get Julio back."

The President was glad to settle down for a homely talk with his wife and daughter. Conchita saw that the bond between her parents was too close ever to be destroyed by her own opposition, however strong, to their wishes. As they sat happily together it struck her that the kidnapping of Julio and her own distress had even produced a joyful outcome. Her parents had apparently accepted Julio as her lover and future husband. If it were so she would happily be part of their alliance. Just then servants bore in trays of delicious cakes from the Dulcinea cakeshop. Popong and Ricky were soon called from the swimming pool to join the tea party. Both wore thongs and dripped water wherever they went. Everyone began to chat about the President's visit to Europe, especially to Rome and the Vatican.

"I'll have to wear a black veil when I see the Holy Father," said Griselda. "My Spanish lace one will do. The veil Juan Carlos gave me. It's beautifully worked."

"Oh, *vanitas vanitatis*," the President intoned. "All is vanity— even when she's going to see the poor old Pope."

"Only Muslim women wear veils," chirped Popong.

"Nuns too," said Ricky. "Looking at hair makes men sinful—that's what Sister Helena told me. She's really ignorant." Noticing his father looking at him admiringly he rattled on, "An ignorant peasant. If the Pope told her that women must wear veils in Heaven so no one can steal their earrings she'd believe him."

"That would be very sinful," Popong said seriously. "Fancy stealing a nun's ear rings."

"Stupid, nuns don't wear earrings," Ricky said jumping around full of mischief. "I'm joking. They don't wear bras either but they do wear bulletproof knickers—like a police flakjacket—to stay virgins without sin."

"Now both of you be quiet," said Griselda irritated that Ricky had strayed so far from orthodoxy. "You've surely learned that when God created Adam and Eve they didn't know about sin at all so it was OK for them to run around naked."

"If I take my thong off will I be without sin?" asked Popong, starting to fiddle with his only garment.

Ricky was ready for that, "Only when you are in Heaven. There's no sin there so it must be OK for everyone to run around naked. Heaven must be fun. Isn't that what Muslims believe, daddy?" he asked his father, who chuckled but stayed diplomatically silent.

"Like the palace swimming pool," said Popong "I peeped in when Senor Manzano and that nice secretary Miss Wee were swimming there with no clothes on. They were wrestling with each other too. I think they are without sin, at least Miss Wee is. I once saw Manzano smoking a joint." He pulled idly at his thong string and said, "I don't think I know what sin is."

"Perhaps they're training for the Olympics," said the President and everyone began to laugh very loudly, in fact unrestrainedly, including Popong though he did not see the point at all.

The jollity was interrupted by an equerry with a message; the First Lady asked what it was and was quietly told that the Prime Minister, Senor Bienvenido Loyola and the Minister for Defence, Senor Manuel Bersamina wished to speak to Senora Conchita.

She hesitated and then said, "Antonio, Loyola and Bersamina are here. They want to speak to Conchita. Maybe they want to sympathise with her over poor Julio; I can't think of anything else they might want to say."

"I can see them by myself if you wish," interrupted Conchita, who thought that they might well have some news about Julio. "I'll go to the reception room and you can all get on with your party. Daddy loves being just with the boys."

"No, no, no," said the President. "Let them come up here and join us. We'll all pretend we're ordinary people, which is what we are really, having a family tea party. Go and invite them." The equerry left and the President said, "Griselda, order some more cakes. Our little gluttons have devoured more than half of them already. What appetites."

Popong pointed at his father and said, "But you took the best ones. The chocolate torres. I saw you." A heated argument, full of silly recriminations, followed between the President and his two sons about cakes, trifles and chocolate towers and only stopped when the equerry's voice filled the room announcing Loyola and Bersamina, accompanied of course by their titles and positions.

"Ah Bienvenido, Manuel, please join our little party. I know you want to speak to Conchita and you shall. Griselda and I appreciate your kindness. It's a dreadful time for my daughter. However, she knows she has only to wait a little while and the boy will be free. Of course the Abulencias will pay the customary ransom; nevertheless Senor Bersamina, we know your department is already taking action to end all these kidnappings, but our actions must be stronger." He gave time for Bersamina to affirm that he agreed and that he would do as instructed. "In the meantime a difficult conversation for everyone here can be made easier by pleasant company. Ricky, Popong say hello to my two best ministers." The boys, taught to be polite under the First Lady's tutelage, stood and gave charming bows, resting the left arm across the small of the back, to the two guests to whom Popong whispered, "Don't worry about the empty plates; more cakes are on the way."

His prediction was correct but soon after the guests, aided by the little boys, had enjoyed the refreshments, the First Lady took her sons each by the hand and said, "I know you two don't want to sit around while we are talking boring grown up stuff. Would you like to go back to the pool?" There was no problem over that. The boys kissed first Conchita, then their parents, bowed to the ministers and ran off, pursued by the equerry.

"Beautiful boys, very beautiful," said Loyola who then addressed Conchita with, "Senorita please accept the sympathy of myself and all my ministers over this horrid event. I trust all will be resolved quickly. Our wives join us in this sincere expression of our feelings."

Before Conchita could do more than incline her head towards the Prime Minister, Bersamina had taken centre stage, echoing Loyola's sentiment about the beauty of the boys but unexpectedly bringing such aesthetic triviality down to earth by saying in a voice redolent of surprise, "Mr President, the Prime Minister and I really came here to express our sympathy to Senora Conchita," to whom he turned and smiled, receiving a dignified nod in return. "But it seems that we must also congratulate you on your recovery."

"What recovery? I'm perfectly well. Very well indeed. There's nothing wrong with me." said the President. "So I suggest you stand down the garrison as soon as you get back to your office. There's need for a state of emergency."

"I beg to differ, Your Excellency," said Bersamina. "Of course I'm glad to see you in very good health. Senora Floresco told me she thought you might have a touch of influenza. But I see it has passed over. She must have been fearful for your health. Perhaps I reacted to the tone of her voice rather than to her actual words. However the reason for mobilising the Infanta garrison was that I intended to use every man at my command to conduct a search of Infanta, house by house if necessary. I had given my word that I would find Julio Abulencia."

"Oh," said the President, taken aback by this very reasonable, indeed laudable, explanation of Bersamina's conduct.

Bersamina said, with the slightest touch of sarcasm in his voice, "It seems that you got—perhaps that you were given, a wrong impression of my motives." He drew himself up haughtily. "Forgive me if I tell you that I find this slightly embarrassing. Perhaps you would prefer that I should take no action in future should I be worried over some situation." Bersamina paused and then resumed in a concerned way, "But perhaps there are some circumstances about this matter that I've not been told."

The First Lady got to her feet, a sure sign that everyone was in for some sort of address, if not a lecture. "There are indeed, Senor Bersamina and I think I must apologise to you for not keeping you in the picture. The fact is that we have had a sort of domestic crisis. I shall give you the full background." She glanced at the President who gave a little nod, presumably indicating his acquiescence. Bersamina was fascinated; he had never seen the First Lady in such a conciliatory frame of mind. She continued. "We had a disagreement with our daughter about her relationship with Julio, a worthy youth of the Abulencia family. Now you all know that the Abulencias are longtime opponents of our government. In consequence it seemed to us that it was not politically desirable for this relationship to continue. I tell you that the President and I met Julio, we talked to him, we found him delightful, we liked him but we also know that there are subversive forces in this country that want to overthrow our régime, which is devoted to stability, conservative values and economic progress of a Western kind and to replace it with a left wing, even a communist government. Those forces use everything at their disposal to undermine us. That is why, in a moment of stress—I thought Antonio was indeed ill for he lost consciousness for a time—I asked Captain Manzano to take Julio away so that both he and Conchita could decide what to do in the higher interest of the Carolines." She cast a loving glance at Conchita who sat stony faced and clearly disinclined to respond to any blandishment which did not halt Griselda's flow of words. "I believe that both of them are willing to consider their position. Who knows, with time circumstances may arise that will make for their happiness. But I can tell you that Antonio and I agonise with them profoundly for we both understand what is meant by being in love." On these words she looked sweetly at the President only to see a face that was cold and serious, suggesting tenderness to neither man nor beast.

The heaviest of silences fell over the five people in the room, which had been cleared, at the First Lady's behest, of servants, doormen and other staff. The President broke the silence with a deep sigh and said, "Well there it is. You have it all. Griselda might not have acted as she did had I been around to talk things out. But what she did, she did with the best intent. I do not blame her for what has happened." The silence descended again.

There followed a short whispered conversation between Bersamina and Loyola, who nodded his head in apparent affirmation. Bersamina said. "Your Excellency, Madame, the Prime Minister agrees that I should speak for both of us as I am Minister for Defence and my Ministry is directly concerned." He opened his hands towards the First Lady, "As you say Madame this is indeed a domestic matter and neither Bienvenido or I wish to intervene in, or to know the details of a matter so delicate. To you Senorita Conchita, I can only say how sorry I am that you are being made to endure such sorrow. But Mr President, although it is a private matter I can't help thinking that it might have been better if my support had been called for. As a loyal member of Government I could have arranged for Julio to be taken to a place of safety quite easily if you had ordered me to do so. Senorita Conchita, this would not have implied any lack of understanding for you and Julio. I would have done the same if Madame had ordered me to take such action because I have always thought of everyone in this room as a team. Indeed, because we must always act as a team I think that it would be advisable if you, Mr President, were to set up some sort of emergency mechanism in case some other crisis occurs. This might be particularly desirable, to safeguard the régime, whilst you are both in Europe, with me at you side. Perhaps this is where your devoted Prime Minister Senor Loyola should come into the picture."

Without hesitation the President stated that he entirely agreed with Bersamina's proposal and looking at Loyola said, "I want you to draw up a Presidential decree for the establishment of an Emergency Council. Do it quickly. I must sign it before our departure. You, Senor Loyola, will have to accept the chairmanship. Senor Bersamina, have you anything to add?"

Turning towards the First Lady, Bersamina said very gravely, "I have indeed. Madame, by working through your own network in this palace, through Captain Manzano who is an amateur in matters of this kind, you have been put into contact with some very dangerous people. I refer of course to a certain Oscar Diasanta and his Holy Thugs. I confess that my Ministry has sometimes made use of him to do some unpleasant work for reasons of state, actions for which we cannot admit responsibility, but we do not control him. In fact, he is uncontrollable. His people are not only fanatical anti-communists, they are also ruthless criminals. We couldn't rope them all in at present even if we tried. The Holy Thugs work underground in the towns and in the jungle throughout the country, often working through the criminal underworld of which they are part."

"But surely," the President said, "Julio is held here, somewhere in Infanta." He glared at the First Lady whose face had blanched, nor did she utter a word.

Conchita jumped to her feet screaming hysterically at her mother, "What is happening to Julio. Where is he? You promised me that..."

"Of course he must be in Infanta." The First Lady shouted back. "What are you hinting at, Bersamina? Oh, I know; you're out to make trouble for me, aren't you? Antonio, can't you see that this is deliberate ?" The appeal to her husband was met with silence.

Bersamina gestured for calm and proceeded to talk in a soft voice that obliged everyone to give him their entire attention. "I assure you that I am not out to make trouble for anyone. We've all had enough of that already. Please recall that this business is not of my doing. I have told you that I mobilised the entire garrison for action. But a short time ago I was advised that anything I do in Infanta would be useless. The Thugs, with Julio in their power, have left Infanta. They got though all the roadblocks unrecognised. They probably circumvented them guerrilla style. But some peasants in San Felipe have reported seeing Julio being led away by Diasanta's men towards the high mountains, to the Cordillera where our control barely exists. We have no idea where he is hidden or how to find him." Looking coldly at the First Lady he said, "Madame, I wonder if your Captain Manzano will be listened to very attentively up there."

On the day that the announcement of Julio Abulencia's kidnapping was occupying the front pages of the Caroline press, Father Stephens boarded a bus for Infanta. Two days ago he had been summoned to appear before the Cardinal for a discussion of his performance as a parish priest. This did not worry him; he was an honest man and not ashamed of anything he had done. He did nevertheless see that the outcome could be the termination of his present duties. If so he would submit confidently to his Franciscan superiors, whom he had always found men of deep understanding. Rather vaguely he saw the possibility that he might be asked to return to Australia. If that were to happen he might decide to leave the church altogether, but behind whatever course lay ahead lurked regret that a married Salvador would be unable to accompany him.

In some mysterious way, he felt, a chapter of his life was drawing to a close. Forces stronger than he could marshal were dominating the life of the town. Daily he was conscious of rising economic pressure on the people that was making a decent way of life impossible. When the men gathered together the talk was ever on wages, the capacity of their unions to bargain and even, which Stephens found unbelievable, the economy of the country and of the world beyond. A few years ago there was no such perception in their minds, but only of a mysterious expanse of land beyond the confines of San Felipe. He knew that much of their new-found knowledge was the result of communist propaganda and the sort of information disseminated by Father Oliveros and his fellow liberation workers. Interesting too was the involvement of women in such talk where before they had passively accepted their role as child bearers and housewives.

The people came to him as much as ever to be counselled on their moral problems but in other fields he was restricted in what he could say. As part of the bargain he had struck with the authorities for the release of Salvador he had agreed to advise moderation in his sermons, telling the people to be patient and to cooperate with the police and military. Indeed he could not see what else to say unless he was prepared to fuel the fire of dissent that might lead to bloodshed. The people did not condemn him for his role but he was conscious of a slight degree of pity towards him. This had grown stronger, for they knew how much he missed Salvador. In short the traditional relationship between the pastor and his sheep was no longer preserved as it had been in his parish.

The bus was all but empty, with just a couple of peasant women across the aisle clutching baskets of market produce that kept them in deep conversation. He would have liked to talk to someone but as there was no candidate he gazed towards the wooded mountains, where he knew Salvador was living the guerrilla life. He wondered whether the boy ever had time to look down over the plain, maybe to see this very bus snorting along in a cloud of dust. It might look like a toy and perhaps, in the distance, their love too was no more than a thinning trail of dust. No, it could not be. He was sure that the vanished era in which each night he and Salvador were in each other's arms had been not only a revelation of paradise but a thunderclap of freedom, when everything he had taken on trust had been like a log jam disintegrating in a fast flowing river. If he never saw Salvador again what had happened then would remain the keystone that locked them together. The divine love in which he had once believed had never held such glory for him. Earthly love had taught him to accept and to reject all experience in an entirely new way, but not always with ease. He found it difficult to imagine the rest of his life without Salvador yet he feared that his pursuit of the rose might make him indifferent to other flowers. In his loneliness he stared at the blue black range and in that moment of inward burning found himself murmuring his lover's name. One of the women said something to her friend and they both stared at him, first curiously, then with toothy grins; the woman nearest to him offered him a mango. He took it, smiled back and pulled himself together. Why should he, a priest, be carrying on like a lovelorn schoolgirl? What had he gone through, compared with what Salvador had endured and what his other lost friend, Father Oliveros, was going through at the moment?

He intended to visit Oliveros after he had seen the Cardinal. One of the advantages of his relationship with the military had been the development of a friendship in San Felipe with an army officer, Lieutenant Chan, who sympathised with his predicament and the plight of the people. The young officer had given Stephens a letter to a comrade who worked in the Infanta military prison, asking him to facilitate the priest's meeting with political detainee Oliveros.

As the bus got nearer to Infanta it gradually filled up, until it was jam-packed with people standing in the aisle and even between the benches. Stephens tried to give up his place to an old woman but she refused, saying it was not right for a priest to move for the likes of her. But her words made her so happy that she insisted on giving him two of the bananas she was carrying. Useless to try to pay but he did manage to slip a ten peseta note in her bag when she was not looking, just before he got off.

With some time to kill he sauntered along the ancient narrow street that led to the Cathedral and the archiepiscopal palace. The further he went the denser the crowd became. The arcades lining the shop fronts were cluttered by stalls selling everything under the sun that was portable. A huge amount of small trading was carried on here by a vibrant, energetic people whose numbers had willy-nilly risen beyond reason. Day and night the place never closed. It was picturesque but out of control. As a result, once beautiful buildings had become slums divided into cubicles each for a large family. People seemed to be coming out of the woodwork. Whenever he looked down the side alleys he could see behind the shop houses a sea of shanties made of corrugated iron sheets, pieces of wood and cardboard boxes packed together unchecked, making traffic, except for carts and bicycles, a hazard. The open drains in passageways were rivulets of filth; the stench was appalling. He was witness to a ghastly dehumanisation of mankind yet this was not poverty at its worst. He knew that on the banks of the Calayag River people lived amidst refuse, rotten garbage and shit and that they might be drowned when the heavy rain of the annual typhoons swelled the foul water. In the so-called squatter areas existed men, women and children who had to sleep anywhere they could find a space, with no one to turn to for comfort, still less love. Yet most of the people, against all odds, looked neat and as often as not smiling. How did they do it, these Carolinos? And, of course, they went on breeding. Stephens did not ask himself why. An ex-prisoner in Auschwitz had once told him that even in the last stages of degradation there were men who wanted a quick fuck. To survive and procreate were the last instincts in them to die. Yet these people did not face gas chambers; they just struggled to live in a derelict world and they too fucked whenever they could for that brief spasm of joy. No matter that the offspring lived or died, existed like pariah dogs or, healthy or diseased, girl or boy, could be used for a quick fuck by someone as feckless as themselves. All about him he saw children in such numbers that many were already slaves to vice and crime without hope of passing through the years of happiness to which they were entitled.

Suddenly, near the Cathedral, amidst the noise of traffic, loud voices and a plethora of competing pop music he heard a great roar.

He turned a corner into a square crowded with people, mainly young and mostly students. On the plinth of a defaced Spanish monument stood a group of firebrands with banners and placards attacking the government. One read, 'Death to IMF tyranny', another 'Stop Loyola devaluing the peseta', while a large one showed the First Lady unflatteringly drawn against the Opera House, denounced as a Wasteful Whorehouse. A young girl, a teenager he guessed, got up to scream invective against the Florescos, as tyrants, thieves and killers. In fury she shouted, "They won't let their own daughter marry the boy she loves because he's a champion of the people, an Abulencia." She waved a red flag aloft to conduct all the banners around the plinth in a frenzied movement. The sight made Stephens think of the Chinese Red Guards. A boy thrust a microphone into her hands and over the loudspeaker again and again came her shrill words, "Senor Abulencia has accused the President and his wife of kidnapping his nephew Julio". Father Stephens stood still to listen to the fantastic words again: "Senor Abulencia has accused the President and his wife of kidnapping..." It was unbelievable yet around him boys and girls were yelling, "Floresco fascists, Floresco kidnappers." After a break the speaker was switched on again and the young termagant yelled, "Comrades, let us resolutely follow Cesar Abulencia, all his life a fighter for freedom. Join his fight for freedom." Stephens wondered whether the workers and the middle class liberals of Infanta, the bourgeois, had found a leader at last among, of all people, the aristocratic Abulencias? He could not believe it.

The demonstrators were startled by the scream of police sirens and harsh commands from loudhailers coming from the far side of the square, ordering them to disperse.

Instead of obeying, defiant cries arose of, "No, no, no" as the students turned and stood their ground with linked arms against a police wall of locked transparent shields. Anxious to get away Stephens turned only to be confronted by a bigger phalanx of black clad police pouring in from the street with truncheons at the ready. A volley of cobblestones torn up by the students greeted them but were ineffective against leather and riot helmets. The police advanced very deliberately beating their truncheons slowly on their shields in terrifying systole diastole. Abruptly they changed their rhythm and charged; Stephens was trapped. No one cared whether he was a priest or not. Or rather they did. A huge officer, a monster of a man, bore down on him bellowing, "Bloody red priest" and struck him a blow across his face. It knocked him to the ground. Feet stamped on him. He hand was crushed and a few kicks to his body found easy targets. Above his head raged a cacophony of screams and shouts. Then almost as quickly as it had started the battle moved on. He raised his painful head a little and saw demonstrators in full flight. Around him lay groaning boys and girls, some bleeding badly. Policemen were enjoying kicking them hard and mocking their screams and pleas for mercy. Then he saw the monster advancing on him again but suddenly he felt arms around him lifting him, carrying him away and voices complaining, "He's a priest, a priest." He felt guilty. Why should he be treated any differently from the wounded students? Next thing he had been taken into a shop house and the front door was banged on the chaos outside.

He looked up and saw two elderly Chinese men looking down at him. He thought he could hear shots coming from outside. One of the Chinese cocked his head and listened, then shook his head. The other brought a bowl of water and bathed Stephens' face. "Only a bruise, Father," he said. "But a very nasty one, with a cut. And your robe, covered with muck and blood. I've got a long robe you can wear. You'll be comfortable in it. We were watching from upstairs. You got caught by accident. We saw everything. You were unlucky." His companion produced a bottle of brandy and made Stephens take a good swig of it. He lay back and sighed deeply. "My head is aching," he said. "Thank you. What would I have done without you? Thank you so much. Those police. What bullies. Barbarians."

"We've seen far worse," came the reply. "But that won't make your head feel any better."

"Well it does in a way," said Stephens. "I could be wounded. I thought I heard shots. What about those boys and girls outside?"

"Leave them. There's nothing you can do," advised the man who held the bottle of brandy. "Let me put a plaster on your face. The cut is bleeding. Ah Gwong, bring the robe for the Father. Have another drink."

When he was dressed in a long grey robe, looking for all the world like a Chinese scholar, Stephens stared around the room. It was an apothecary's shop. All sorts of herbs and roots were displayed in cupboards of polished black wood and glass with gleaming brass fittings. Near his head a line of dried seahorses made a solemn procession over a field of green baize. At the end of the room was an altar on which stood two tall red candles, various bowls, some of red lacquer, some of porcelain, flanking dignified seated gods. Above them were photos, probably of ancestors but including, Stephens noted, Sun Yat Sen and Deng Xiaoping. The fragrance of incense reminded him of his church.

"You're not Christians?" he asked which might have suggested he thought only that faith could explain their kindness.

"No, we follow traditional Chinese ways," said one of the men and both of them smiled politely.

For something else to say Stephens asked, "Why is Deng Xiaoping above the altar?"

"We are Hakka people so we are very proud of him. His family is Hakka. We are related, distantly. Xiaoping saved China from chaos."

And you saved me," Stephens said with the best smile he could muster. "What can I do to repay you?"

"There is nothing to repay. We are honoured to help you."

Stephens was nonplussed and deeply moved. "I shall return the robe to you as soon as possible."

"No. We shall keep your robe and you will keep ours. It will remind us of each other."

They made him leave by a back entrance from which he soon made his way to the Archbishop's palace, over an hour late for his interview. The Cardinal's secretary, an elderly woman with a vinegary face, did not bother to listen to his explanation but shot into the Cardinal's room where she could be heard saying in a sarcastic voice. "He's finally got here. Shall I send him in or make him wait?" The answer turned out to be yes, and Stephens soon found himself in a large room, sitting on a low chair with a tall hard back before Cardinal Lorenzo Peccata who was at a higher elevation. His bony face looked severe. Steely eyes took in Stephens' elegant silk gown; bushy eyebrows frowned.

"Your Eminence, please forgive my late arrival and my appearance. I was really quite early but I ran into a riot. I was hit by the police. Fortunately I was rescued by…"

"Involved in a riot, eh?" The Cardinal's voice was both querulous and unsympathetic.

"Not exactly. It was a demonstration."

Cardinal Peccata either did not, or affected not to, hear any further explanation. In a world weary voice, he said, "I am all in favour of the Church opposing iniquity on the part of Government. As you know I often speak out about it myself. I encourage good Catholics working in Radio Ecclesia to do the same. But none of us take part in riotous demonstrations."

"I am very sorry for what happened Your Eminence. I assure you that…"

"We need speak no more about it. There are more pressing issues for us to discuss. But before you leave I suggest you arrange with Senora Honteveros, my secretary, to get a more clerical garb. You are not in Chu Chun Chow."

"No, Your Eminence. Sorry, I mean yes Your Eminence."

The Cardinal took a file from a tray on his crowded and rather disorderly desk, opened it and read a page as though to remind himself of its content. After giving a deep sigh, he closed the file and stared hard at Father Stephens. "How different things were in my day—when I was your age. I think we were clearer in our heads about what the vocation of a priest meant. Nowadays all is changing—all has changed." There followed a long pause during which Stephens started to feel a bit superfluous. "But," said the Cardinal suddenly and loudly, "what is eternal does not change. In that we can take comfort. You know that it is the duty of a priest to translate into this world of flux and error, the changelessness of the eternal truth." His eyes roved over Stephens' face. "Father, I ask you in all sincerity whether you have always acted in San Felipe, whether you have always acted up there, in accordance with the verities of eternal righteousness of which, as a priest, you must be aware?"

The language was baffling not because it was incomprehensible but because it sounded antique and therefore irrelevant, like something out of Plotinus whose Enneads Father Stephens had found useful as a soporific when studying theology at College. He therefore replied with simplicity, "I have done my best to be a good priest and to work for the salvation of my people."

"According to your own lights or the lights of the Church?"

"I would like to think that my lights are those of the Church."

"Ah," said the Cardinal warming to the discussion. "'I would like to think'. That is not the same as saying, 'I think', and still less than, 'I believe' or 'I know', is it?"

Alice being quizzed by the Red Queen hovered for an instant in Stephens' mind. It might be best to let the Cardinal have a series of linguistic victories. "Perhaps I ought to have said, 'I should like to think' for my will is to think in accordance with the tenets of the Church, Eminence."

"Will. Will. From what dark regions of the mind, Father Stephens, does will spring? Will does not necessarily partake of the Divine Nature. It can be commingled with, or even entirely composed of, our own selfish desires in which I naturally include our lusts. Will is as nothing unless we are in a state of grace."

"Ah," was all Stephens could reply, wondering the while whether Cardinal Peccata was in such a happy state.

"Father, you are an Australian are you not?" Stephens was happy to assent to a truth that was both untheological and undeniably true. "And though you know a lot about this country, you do not understand perhaps how powerfully evil forces—it may seem out of date to you but let me say it straight out—forces of the Devil, ancient pagan beliefs are still working among the Carolinos."

"The forces of evil are active everywhere, I should think," interrupted Stephens. "If they were not, there would be no need for the Church, no need for our Blessed Lord."

"Let's leave the Lord out of it," said the Cardinal, "and concentrate on you and your Parish." His voice became sharp. "I don't want to discuss theological abstractions. I am interested in how you have been working there."

"Yes Your Eminence."

"I will leave the matter of Father Oliveros until the last. On that issue I suspect you are peripheral. In any case whatever errors Oliveros may have fallen into, much greater issues of Church-State relations have arisen. No, with you only two matters worry me. The first concerns the advice you have been giving to people on the question of family planning." The last two words were uttered with vehemence. "I may say straight off that this is the gravest of the matters I have called you to talk about. I've been told that you are in favour of contraception. Are you not aware of the purpose of Christian marriage?"

"I am indeed," said Stephens making his voice as determined as the Cardinal's. "The family is the most important unit in society, Christian and non-Christian. And within the family the wellbeing and health of the children and of the mother that bears them should be paramount. Yes, I sometimes counsel my people to use contraception precisely because I am concerned that their families should be able to live a decent life."

"So, you admit it?"

"Your Eminence I am concerned that children born of any marriage should have proper food and decent shelter. You know that only a short distance from here there are places where they do not have them. The sheer horror of those slums, the sheer horror of them. You must have seen them. From here you must have smelled them."

"What we see as horrible may not be horrible in the Divine plan. In the eyes of God all life is sacred. To destroy life, to foil the purpose of life is a grave sin."

"Your Eminence, is it not a fact that in the armies of all Catholic States there are Chaplains who confess soldiers going into battle? Do they ever say, drop your guns, life is sacred, thou shall not kill? The Church admits war. In the past it condoned the torture of heretics. In our own time it has supported fascists, real killers, in Spain and South America. It is not a pacifist religion. It does not respect the sanctity of life."

"We live in the real world, Father Stephens. The Lord taught us to render unto Caesar what is Caesar's. Clearly we must serve Caesar when he demands what is his."

"Then the Lord was not talking about the sanctity of life in your way, for Caesar has always been a man of blood," said Father Stephens, whose head was beginning to burn, not from the argument but from the pain in his face which had started to throb. He glared at the Cardinal, who was staring back at him not angrily but with a look of despair. Stephens knew he had not been diplomatic but he no longer cared. How could this man of God reside in a many-roomed palace when outside crowds of his immediate neighbours lived in crowded destitution?

The Cardinal had not surrendered in the least. From his slight elevation he looked down on Father Stephens with sorrow as a man who failed to grasp something quite simple. In a gentle voice he said, "My dear friend, I don't think you understand what I am saying. Have you not read in the Bible that the spilling of seed is sinful? Have you not heard of the sin of Onan?"

The pain in Father Stephens' head had increased. The blow had been more serious than he thought. He felt light-headed but dared not admit it. Yet the sin of Onan was too much. Something seemed to snap in his head. He no longer cared what this Cardinal and his Church said or stood for. He stood up and looked around at the fine chamber with its panelled walls and its heavy Spanish furniture and then up at its coffered ceiling. "The sin of Onan," he repeated incredulously. "Signor Peccata, at this moment your glands and my glands and the glands of every male in the world are secreting millions of sperms which will never get anywhere near an egg. Do you think that all these sperms should be preserved somewhere so that a one day they can be introduced to millions of eggs? Your Eminence, you cannot preserve every living cell. Perhaps you think we should never amputate limbs, never destroy a cancer. They are all composed of living cells and in every cell the pattern of its being is in the DNA. Maybe we should not eat animals—they are composed of living cells. And what about vegetables? Should we devour the living cells of a cabbage if all life is sacred. The sin of Onan. Perhaps such concepts were developed because the Jews were few in number and just wanted to survive. Or maybe some old rabbi who couldn't get it up thought that Onan was too fond of wanking." Having said that Stephens collapsed in his uncomfortable chair clasping his throbbing head.

The Cardinal left his chair and came over to him. "You're not well; I didn't realise. The demonstration; you must have been hurt badly." He rang a bell and Senora Honteveros appeared. "Nina," he said. "bring Father Stephens a coffee and something to eat. And perhaps a

Drambuie or a Cointreau." He drew up a stool and sat beside Father Stephens, took his hand and spoke to him quietly and soothingly. "My dear young man. I understand exactly what you are saying. Do you imagine that I have never thought like you? Or that the Holy Father hasn't faced the same problems himself? I have spoken to His Holiness and I tell you he understands all the arguments. Now listen to me. The problem is that you no longer think in religious terms. You have surrendered entirely to rationalism. Yet the Church no longer opposes the scientific method. You spoke of cells. Who discovered that they possess characteristics and how they are passed on? Mendel, a monk. Father Stephens, you have forgotten that it is possible to use reason without disregarding the ethical dimension. It is the decision to obey or disregard the will of God that matters. There is something like a contract between man and God—that's how I like to think of it—that one cannot break with impunity. The Church teaches us what the clauses of that contract are. And one of them is that marriage should not be foiled of its purpose. On eating roast beef or boiled cabbage the Church has nothing to say."

Father Stephens ate the sandwich brought by Senora Honteveros, drank her coffee and enjoyed a Cointreau. The pain in his face was still there but he felt revived. He almost said to the Cardinal, 'Yes fine, but can we be sure that an ancient book written by bearded old patriarchs two thousand years ago contains the word of God or just their male chauvinist views of life?' Instead, as the Cardinal had become quite genial and Senora Honteveros' thin face had managed a smile, he asked, when he and the Cardinal were alone again. "And the second matter, Your Eminence. You said you had something else to talk about," but he knew what it must be.

"Ah yes," said the Cardinal. "Your relationship with some boy or other. When I was last in San Felipe I was told that the affair was common knowledge and made you happy. Of course it's not important there; rural people still look at things in a pagan way. No, wider publicity is the only problem. These things often happen in the Church. Our enemies are always on the lookout. Just be discreet, that's all I ask. We are not eunuchs. The Vatican always tells us to keep any such lapse under wraps. It doesn't want scandals. At least," he added with a sound that was intermediate between a sigh and a gurgle, "boys don't get pregnant."

Stephens thought, I must remember that: 'keep your lapse under wraps' and remarked facetiously "But is it right to let our seed be wasted on the ground, Your Eminence?"

However the Cardinal's attention was far away. He was on his feet for a turn around the room. When he returned to his chair he said "I like you, Father Stephens. You are intellectually honest and I hope that in time you will return to the bosom of the Church. No, I don't mean that you are not of the Church now but that you are not fully able to accept its truths. I believe that in the end you will do so, for truth seeks out truth even when the way to it lies through dark places. I wrestle with the same problems as you when I see the poverty around us. How easy to say, 'Right let's have a great birth control program; no one to have more than one point three seven children. Let's spend all we have on medicine and housing to achieve a Californian lifestyle—without of course Californian unemployment'. If one sees things only in terms of reason no one could gainsay such an argument. If on the other hand you believe, as I do, that our life on earth is to measure our worth then we have to accept the parameters set by God and work out our salvation with his Grace. It is fundamentally a matter of faith. To me reason without faith will lead to something even worse than the horror, as you rightly call it, of our squatter areas."

Father Stephens listened to the Cardinal's words with emotion tinged with regret. "Your Eminence, I wish I had such faith as yours. But I have come to the point at which I believe that man has only reason to work with." He stood and faced the Cardinal. "In saying this I am conscious of the fact that you and I can afford the luxury of theological speculation in pleasant surroundings. After all we do not live in the slums or have to face hungry children each day."

The Cardinal nodded. "That fact too I have faced. But I still believe there is a purpose, even for the child who is not aware of anything beyond its own sensations." He got up and approached Father Stephens. "Thank you for speaking so frankly. There are some priests who find it hard to be open with me. Perhaps they fear me. Am I so formidable? You don't fear me or anything I'd guess— but you are a cobber as well as a priest. Now Father, I think it might be for the best if we withdraw you from San Felipe—at least for a time. You need an opportunity to think matters over, very deeply. Perhaps a retreat could be arranged for you."

Stephens hoped that a replacement could be sent to his parish as soon as possible. He only needed time to pick up his few possessions and would leave once a new priest arrived. He also asked whether there might be any political objection to him visiting Father Oliveros in prison.

"Of course not," said the Cardinal, "By the way, under the circumstances, there's no need to bother Nina Honteveros about the clerical garb. In fact, if I may say so, that Chinese habit really becomes you. Now when you speak to Father Oliveros tell him that our prayers are with him." He added kindly, "And I shall pray for you, Father Stephens. Go in peace." He blessed Stephens who, rationalist or not, genuflected as it seemed appropriate to do so.

He left the palace in a daze. The interview had been smooth all things considered and he appreciated the Cardinal's understanding. But now, as a result of it his audience, all was going to change. There would be correspondence with his superiors and there were a number of things he would have to wind up in the parish as well as arranging a proper hand-over to whoever replaced him. He did not mind such a delay as it might give him time to see Salvador once, twice, thrice, he could not guess how many times, before he left. Also, scarcely daring to speak its name, was the thought that maybe he could tempt Salvador into at least visiting him in Australia, assuming that was his destination.

He soon found the military prison, which was a squat stone building dating from Spanish times. The thought of the things that must have gone on within it oppressed him. Nor was he particularly anxious at this moment to see Oliveros. He would have preferred to visit him when he could give full attention to his friend's plight, without his own predicament slipping into what he said. He had no difficulty in gaining access; Lieutenant Chan's letter worked like a charm. Even the form filling and the declarations that had to be accomplished were quickly over and he was shown to an unoccupied interviewing booth in a long gloomy room, under the watch of a guard on whose jacket was the name Sgt Lumelay. Seated there already, Oliveros was the first to speak. "Something's happened to you hasn't it?"

"Oh my silk *cheong sam*, the plaster on my face, the bruise; I got caught in a demonstration."

"No, not that. Mere things of the flesh." Oliveros laughed loudly, really at the pleasure of seeing his friend, and Sgt Lumelay further along the room shouted, "No noise there."

"What then?" Stephens asked.

"You look so relaxed. Like you used to look after a night with Salvador. It's coming from inside you. I guess you are happy."

Stephens blinked at Oliveros. "That's hardly the way a man of God should talk, approving sodomy. And what about you? You look well. You've put on weight."

"Let's talk about you first. What's turned you into a new man?" Oliveros insisted Stephens began an account of his day starting backward with his session with the Cardinal. Father Oliveros enjoyed the picture of the head of the Caroline Church and wanted to know everything that was said, but when Stephens suggested that they were using up their time, the Father winked and said that Lumelay was 'one of us' and would not limit the visit while he was on duty. Stephens said that sergeant's capacity to bypass regulations reminded him of the Cardinal's remark that a residual paganism made it easy for his parishioners to accept his love of 'some boy' regardless of the tenets of the Church. Triumphantly Oliveros said, "Peccata said that, did he? Amazing, he actually recognises what we Carolinos are like—even if he can't stand it. Stephens, I tell you, holding hard to those old pagan ways is our hope. They keep the people sane. It's the madness of the Religions of the Book, especially the Roman nonsense imposed on us, that's wrong. Don't look so surprised. I've seen it for years. Almost from the day I became a Priest."

Both of them seemed surprised by Oliveros' bold assertion but after a moment's silence he resumed and said, "Father Stephens, strange that we keep on saying 'Father' when we should say Francis and José but maybe we should just say, 'brother'. We have made the same journey and arrived at the same destination. But you started with love, the love of one of my people; I started with hatred for the system that has enslaved us and still enslaves us. I think that yours has been the happier journey. Life should be grounded in love but I have not yet found it."

Father Stephens' account of his audience had to end with him telling Oliveros that his time at San Felipe must be drawing to a close, which made both of them sad for there had been days in the past when they had both anticipated their work in the town going on and on for another decade or so of their lives. "But I'll never go back there either," said Oliveros. "I'm to be tried as a committed communist and the punishment will be long imprisonment, or worse," he laughed and said, "Perhaps the worst is the best for me."

"They'd never dare," said Stephens. "You are a Priest in a Catholic country."

"That's it precisely," Oliveros replied. "The Government, the President himself and Bersamina want to make it clear that they are adamant in their opposition to communism. The Church, our dear Cardinal in fact, has on several occasions pressed for my release. But nothing doing. In fact I'm told that even if Floresco were to beg for a pardon from the Holy Father his request would be turned down—politely I'm sure. My trial must take place publicly to show that no exceptions, not even on religious grounds, will be made where communism is concerned. We all know that anti-communism is nectar to the USA but where Europe is concerned a demonstration of the President's support for secular values goes down well. Naturally the Florescos want to impress Europe when they are there. He may come from a Catholic country but he's no lackey of the Church. The Pope won't want to embarrass the leader of the only catholic country in Asia save the Philippines. My trial will go ahead. So you see Stephens that your insignificant little Oliveros has become an international figure."

"But how did you learn all this?" Stephens asked. "In prison, where everything is controlled. Why, we might be heard by that guard who is so busy smoking, if we said anything subversive."

"In dictatorships prisons are the last bastions of free speech. Prisoners learn new ways of conversing. The prison staff are often part of the conspiracy." Oliveros' tone changed to the inquisitive. "Tell me Father, do you ever listen to Radio Ecclesia?"

"No, not in San Felipe. It doesn't reach there so we only have our local television station, which is rotten, being Government. Anyway I read a lot. I don't care for TV," said Stephens wondering which way the new subject was leading.

"Maybe you don't remember the Nestor case then, the young man who was arrested for subversion and tortured and then released because of world protests. The First Lady herself was lobbied by French writers and asked for his freedom. She was the one who got most publicity."

"I think I do," said Stephen dubiously "What's he to do with your imprisonment?"

"Well he works in Radio Ecclesia, the only free station left because of the insistence of our dear Cardinal. Nestor is a brilliant journalist. That's why he ran foul of Government. He's visited me twice. He's interested in my case." Oliveros had all the while been speaking quickly and in a low voice, but he looked around as though to make sure the guard was not nearby. "Listen, Nestor told me that he had been approached by a man called Bligh and given a tape to be kept under wraps. He said it contains a speech made by the head of the Abulencia family, Cesar Abulencia. He made copies of it in case his office was raided. It's a sort of potted history of the Carolines working up to the financial depredations of the Florescos and then accusing them of responsibility for the kidnapping of Cesar's nephew, Julio. You're a country bumpkin, but you have heard of poor rich Julio haven't you?" Stephens nodded vigorously as though to prove that he was not as stupid as he looked.

Just then Sergeant Lumelay drifted nearby and said, "Hope you're only talking about holy matters, Father." Oliveros answered back with a grin, "No. I'm telling my friend I'm going to file through the cell bars tonight and make a run—for a girl in town. Come with me. You need a change." Lumelay laughed, said he'd think about it and moved on, still replenishing the murky atmosphere with smoke.

Stephens looked bewildered and Oliveros asked him what was up. "To use an Australian expression, Father, the penny's just dropped. This man Bligh, tall good looking, balding, an intellectual? He came recently to San Felipe making a film about the province. He said it was timed for release when the President is in Europe. He was with a film maker from Hong Kong—a talkative little man, Hilary something or other."

"That's him. That's Max Bligh. He's with a PR firm working to boost Floresco's image in the West," agreed Oliveros who fell silent, drew in his breath and then said, "Stephens, I want to hear it again. What you just said. That Bligh is tall, good looking, going bald, an educated sort of guy." Stephens repeated the description wanted by Oliveros who might have exploded, if outside prison, with the words, "Him! Working for the Florescos? I can't believe it. Jesus, Mary and Joseph. Some months ago he met me here in Infanta in San Anthony of Padua. He gave me a package of money for the people in the jungle. Remember? It ended up in your house."

"Yes, and I passed it on to them," whispered Stephens.

Oliveros' eyes had opened wide. He was very excited. "This Bligh, working for the President must also be working for some group wanting to help us. You know who I mean. But why should he pass a tape to Nestor? Nestor can't be in the Party now."

Stephens said, "Brother, another penny's just dropped. That tape. I think I heard a very fiery girl shouting something from it at the demonstration a few hours ago." He reported rapidly on the demonstration and his rescue by the Chinese gentlemen, concluding with, "Nestor must have broadcast the tape on Radio Ecclesia. So, the accusation of the Florescos by Cesar Abulencia has become top news. José, my brother, people must be hearing it everywhere. No wonder there was a demonstration. I think there'll be a lot more."

Oliveros held up his hand like a policeman stopping the flow of traffic. "You've got one thing wrong. Radio Ecclesia has not broadcast the tape."

"How do you know that?" began Stephens. "I heard it with my own ears."

"You said you heard a girl shouting Abulencia's accusation, not Abulencia himself. Lumelay listens avidly to Radio Ecclesia. He would have told me if Abulencia himself was on the air. No, Nestor would not release the tape; he's been tortured once and he doesn't want to give himself away again. But he's capable of leaking information slyly to the students and that's what he's done. But I guess he's kept the Cardinal in the loop and got his unctuous go ahead. Radio Ecclesia is financed by the church. Like us it wants the information to circulate among the workers to ferment trouble but unlike my party it does not want the revolutionary consciousness of the masses to boil over."

Stephens said weakly "Yes, I suppose so," at the same time marvelling at Oliveros' apparent command of the possibly revolutionary situation even in prison. Surely he would triumph when on trial.

Oliveros said slowly and thoughtfully. "This man Bligh must have released the tape to create trouble on the eve of the President's departure. Who is he working for? He leaked it deliberately. But it won't please the Party. If it causes trouble, I mean real trouble on the streets, maybe a revolt, it will put Abulencia's liberals, the middle class bourgeois, ahead of the Party. Maybe that's what the Cardinal wants because he would know how to control it." Oliveros was now worried. He looked up and saw that Lumelay had gone. "José, brother, I think time's up. Just be careful what you say and do, my friend. No one is to be trusted."

Their hands had met across the table and clasped together. The replacement sergeant bore down on them and said, "No touching. No finger Morse code. Time's up. You should have gone by now, Father. I don't know what that lazy sod Lumelay's playing at."

"We don't have to touch, sergeant," said Father Stephens. "We are both Franciscan Brothers. Nothing can separate us. Live in hope, José. High hope. I'll remember you to all our friends in San Felipe." With that he made his way out into the town and to the nearest bus station where bunches of students were brandishing the sort of placards he had seen at the demonstration proclaiming, 'Abulencia attack on Florescos', 'Liberals and Democrats arise' and so forth. A cyclist arrived with a pile of leaflets. People snapped them up eagerly, read them aloud and soon took to shouting anti-government slogans. A few policemen were watching nervously but kept well away. Unlike the past, police or no police, the people were expressing themselves without fear. Infanta was stirring dangerously, but Stephens found the complexity beyond him.

Julio Abulencia shivered with cold on the floor of the mountain hut where he was held prisoner. Outside loud voiced thugs were shouting, bragging, arguing and drinking. They were not professional soldiers and would never give him sympathy. He had been treated with contempt on the way up, slapped, punched and derided as a rent boy. No food had been given to him, only a chance to drink water when they saw him stumbling. He was weak and on the brink of fever.

He was sure he had not fallen among communists even though some of the men sported five pointed star caps. Their speech and their lack of discipline told him that they were bandits, pure and simple. His existence hung by a thread. In this ultimate danger he could not think of his home and family and hardly of Conchita. She would have to get used to his non-existence, perhaps for the rest of her life. He just wanted to escape and knew that he would promise anything, give anything, do anything to get away.

When he did fleetingly conjure up the image of Conchita it was with remorse. He should have told her sometime during their affair that he had taken good care to see he was next to her on that plane from England. He had deliberately targeted her either out of vanity or with some unformed ambition in mind. She had the right to know that. The fact that their affair had turned out so well did not excuse his falsehood. That initial trickery had led to his present plight—no love, no kidnapping. If he had a belief in the supernatural he might have said this was his karma. But he did not believe in anything except his right as a rich young man to live well and be happy. The very thought of his lost life, which might be gone forever, brought tears to his eyes; he could not stop sobbing. He was not cut out to be a hero, still less a martyr. His only fear was that he might appear to be a coward. No; I am an Abulencia he told himself. If I am tortured I must sustain myself with my family pride because that's all I have left in this foul place.

As the light faded the men became more rowdy. Some of them started to quarrel. Bottles were smashed and there was a sound of glass breaking. Then the anger gave way to roars of laughter as a child, a girl or a boy—the screams were high pitched—was used for the thugs' fun. Julio knew he was next.

The door burst open and a group of men appeared, gloating at him where he lay. He tried to get up but received a kick in the stomach from a youth who demanded, "Who gave you permission to get up, rent boy?" A thin faced man with a Che Guevara beard sneered, "What could any woman see in a boneless rat like that? Let's get him outside and have a lark with him. Make him really yell. Let's see how brave he is."

Was it his weakness, his fear, or his cowardice? Which, he was never to know but Julio broke down abjectly; he got to his knees and bowed his head down to kiss Guevara's jungle boots. He howled piteously. "Please. Let me go. I've done nothing to you. Don't hurt me. I'll give you anything you want. Just let me go."

There was a short silence. Perhaps they expected defiance, outrage, insults but before them grovelled surrender. They called in a grimy faced girl, probably the one they had been playing around with and told her to see how the rich were bigger cowards than a little bitch like her. She spat on him and joined the mocking ring around the slobbering wretch, until the mouth of Che Guevara said in the meanest voice, "Give us anything we want, eh? Bribery, eh? Of course. That's all the rich understand. Bribery. It's how you Abulencias got rich. Well, you can't bribe us, rent boy." With that the lot of them started to dance and stamp on Julio only to stop when he vomited. "Filthy swine dirtying the room," shouted a fat thug. "Lick it up. No, let's roast the muck off over the camp fire." Julio didn't even let himself scream in terror when strong hands made to seize him. He pulled free and pushed his face down to the floor, licking up the vomit with his tongue and sucking it up like an animal.

A raucous shout came from outside. "Oscar's here. Come and greet him. Quick." There was a stunned silence and the thugs and the girl were out in a flash, leaving Julio alone. He wiped the vomit off his face and sat on his haunches resting his head on his knees, willing the pain in his stomach to go. But his fear was rising. He had heard of Oscar Diasanta's cruelty. On the way to the hut from the plain the men had talked about it in grotesque detail. He mumbled to the shade of some ancestor, "I'm sorry I gave in. It wasn't me. I was a terrified pig. Don't tell her, don't tell Conchita. I'll be an Abulencia again."

The noisy racket of the thugs had ceased. Control had been restored. Then came the sound of the loudest voice Julio had ever heard, giving orders about guns, guard duties, food supplies and cursing everyone there. There was a loud thud and a yelp as someone hit the floor. So this was Diasanta. Terrified though he was Julio also felt relief. Soon he would know why he had been kidnapped and what was wanted of him. If they ordered him to beg Cesar to pay for his release he would write to him. Any amount to be free again. But no one came. Outside only a low drone of voices, as though no one wanted him to hear what was said. The pain was subsiding but not his fever. His head nodded forward. He slumped sidewards and fell into a deep sleep.

He was awakened by a hand, male or female, he could not tell but it moved slowly sensually exploring every part of his body from his feet to his head; a hand as soft as Conchita's stroked his face. He opened his eyes. Before him was Oscar Diasanta, a man with the well-proportioned body of a Carolino but on a generous scale. The hand was withdrawn and Diasanta stood up, well over six-foot and broad like a weight lifter, a man who could restore order or create chaos according to his whim.

"You can eat that food when I'm finished with you," the man said pointing at some covered plates on the floor. His voice was low and had a thin silky quality. "They've been giving you a hard time, eh?" He laughed "You've been lucky. You can see what they can do when they get going—but they're not imaginative. Always the same thing, slicing, burning, beating. They're thick. Never anything creative."

Julio found himself saying boldly, "Why do you let them?"

"Because it binds them to me. They are not educated men like you and me, Julio, but sometimes I join in with them. Not to ingratiate myself. I enjoy it. I encourage them to understand themselves by inflicting pain. I like to see how far each man will go. It's like watching a game. Man is a cruel beast. We're not doing anything unnatural when we bare our claws. Of course people like you like to pretend it's shocking. You prefer to accept cruelty without taking part in it."

Julio found the conversation bizarre. The man was something of a thinker but this was neither the time nor the place for philosophy. Or was Diasanta giving him an unpleasant warning that there were no limits to what was possible in this room? He stared back trying to make something of Diasanta's physiognomy. He was handsome in a broad-faced Caroline way but there was something unpleasant about his eyes They were small but fierce as if another person was

223

inside the massive frame looking out on the world with hatred. "You know who I am?" he asked.

"I heard the men calling you Oscar. Then you must be the famous Oscar Diasanta, I suppose."

"You are not to say you were captured by me, Senor Julio."

Julio heart leaped. He must control his excitement. Was he really going to be free to return to his home? He said as nonchalantly as he could, "I promise to say nothing. Senor; will I be leaving soon?"

Diasanta smiled as at a poor joke. "I'd like to say straightaway but it's a bit more complicated than you think."

Julio was glad he had kept calm. This man was a sadist for sure. It would be dangerous to play mouse to his cat. "Well, now you're here, I'm not worried. The mountain air is good. Much better than the pollution of Infanta."

"I'm glad to hear you say so. I've always thought so myself. Come let me give you something to eat." Diasanta brought over a couple of plates to Julio, who had relaxed enough to be squatting on the floor. A waiter at a good hotel could not have put the food down more softly. He lifted the covers one by one. "Fried rice and some chicken I think. And here's one with vegetables. A bit cold but you need the Vitamin C."

Julio began to eat and the act seemed to end the pain he was still feeling in his stomach. Between mouthfuls he asked, "Senor Diasanta, why have you brought me here? What do you want of me? Is it because of the President's daughter? Are you helping the Florescos to get me out of the way?"

Diasanta answered with a question. "Your uncle Cesar is a very rich man. He has no children. Do you know why? It makes you heir to the Abulencia fortune. Doesn't it?" Diasanta paused and shook his head in disbelief, "A rich man but he's a communist."

"He's not a communist," Julio said firmly. "That's the last thing he is. He wouldn't know how to think like a communist."

"But you, Senor Julio, do know how to think like a real Party member, eh? You are a Marxist. I sense it. You studied in Paris, like Pol Pot and those Khmer Rouge lunatics."

Julio gave a quick glance into Diasanta's face. The unblinking eyes glinted curiously, and Julio feared, madly. He had heard a thug boast how their boss, only a week ago, had executed four peasants who supported the communists by slowly boiling them alive each in a steel barrel with their heads sticking through a hole in the cover, while the villagers had to sing until the victims' screams were no more. The man must be obsessional about the Reds. Julio looked at his captor with a disarming expression, "Senor Diasanta, do I look like a communist? I'm just a pampered bourgeois, a bourgeois through and through."

"In fact that's what I'd say about you too," said Diasanta without a trace of humour. "Because you're a sexually depraved atheist."

Julio gasped. What did this change of tack mean? He had only had two affairs in his life. The first with a pretty Parisian waitress whose passion was so consuming that she needed several lovers to dampen it. Back home he had always felt it beneath the dignity of an Abulencia to visit a vice den in Infanta. "My affair with Senorita Floresco," he asked almost in protest, "Is that being depraved?"

"You are not married to her are you?" Diasanta's voice was as harsh as a sex obsessed inquisitor. He had started to breath in and out heavily and the sound of the air, inhaled and exhaled, filled the room so that Julio felt he was imprisoned in a huge lung operated by a machine. He dared not reply; anything he said might be distorted by this perverse monster, who suddenly shouted, "Did you hear me? You're uncle is a very rich man, isn't he? Why don't you reply when I ask you a question?"

Julio nodded rapidly and said he was sorry and, "Yes Senor, he is rich but the Abulencias are not one of the really rich families that run the economy."

Diasanta squatted down and stared thoughtfully at Julio who was wondering what was coming next. It was a quiet confidential question as from one academic to another. "My dear Julio, what would you do in my place? These Florescos. They are so inefficient. The President can't tell his arse from his prick. First I'm asked to seize and hold you. Yes, as you say, to force you never to see your dear Conchita again. Now I'm asked to set you free. What do you make of that?" Diasanta fell silent though still staring intently with his gimlet eyes at Julio, who didn't know what to answer. When Diasanta said 'the Florescos' what was meant? Had the request been put to him by the office of the President or from some interfering Ministry—Bersamina came to mind. "Well?" said Diasanta impatiently, "I'm waiting."

Julio tried to look neither sad nor glad, neither sure nor unsure. In the end he just mumbled, "Perhaps you should obey the last order."

"Order," screamed Diasanta, springing quick as an uncoiling spring from the floor to his full height. "No one gives orders to Oscar Diasanta." He kicked the two dishes and the food scattered all around. Julio sat expressionless as a Red Indian at a pow-wow, waiting to receive the third kick on his body, but Diasanta just said in a steely voice, "If you ever say a thing like that again, I'll have my men boil you for dinner. And when I say boil, I mean boil. I mean it. Look at these." He took some photos from his pocket and held them in front of Julio's eyes, which saw men's heads sticking out of a barrel top. Their expressions were crazed, their eyes had popped out and their tongues stuck out like little snakes from their bawling mouths. "Don't you think they look funny?" asked Diasanta perusing the photos himself. "Those tongues! Really hilarious! See what I mean by boiled?"

In shock all Julio managed to gasp was, "Sir, I am deeply sorry. I did not want to speak with disrespect." Inside his head terror screamed, not me, not me. "Senor Diasanta. Please, please forgive my error."

Diasanta squatted down again amidst the mess of food, vomit and broken plates; a childlike smile had come to his face. Putting his lips to Julio's ear he whispered, "Don't be afraid, my dear boy. Just tell me what your Conchita is like."

Julio was swift to reply, also in a whisper, "She's pretty. She's kind. She's clever."

"No, no. I don't mean like that. All lovers say that sort of stuff. I mean when you are naked together, fucking. Is she really good?" As he spoke his hand slid between Julio's thighs and began to maul him. "Ah, she must be good, even her name makes it stand."

Julio thought it best to respond to Diasanta's 'naughty boys talking about sex' mood and said, "Yes, she's everything a man could want. You'd love her."

"What would she think of me? What would she think of your friend Oscar? Tell me, Julio."

If you want to die now, Julio thought, tell him the truth, but of course after appearing to give the matter deep thought he whispered seductively, "I think she'd admire you. For several reasons— your physique, your strength, your power; yes, your power of leadership." He concluded in a tone suggestive of absolute sincerity, "Oscar, I'm sure she'd think you very handsome. As a matter of fact I think you are attractive too." Longing for a truce, he seized Diasanta's hand and squeezed it, wondering the while whether he knew what he was doing.

The thug führer looked as though he was about to purr. There was indeed something feline about him, the playful cuddling and the sudden vicious claws. "I'm sorry I kicked the food," he said. "I'll order some more." In an instant he was gone but soon back followed by two thugs carrying more dishes and a pail of water with cloths with which Diasanta made them clean up the mess on the floor and on Julio. When they had gone once again he brought the food over to Julio, who decided to eat it even if it choked him. With this lunatic who could say what might come next?

Eating gave Julio ten or so minutes of respite, silence and hope under Diasanta's unremitting gaze. The bandit leader seemed taken with him for when the meal was finished he put his hand under Julio's chin turning his head to the left and to the right to take a good look at his features. "Yes, you're a lovely young man, really lovely," he said. "But a degenerate. I appreciate your invitation just now, but I'm not a sinner. But there can be love without fucking, Julio. For me love has to be chaste; I'm a sincere Catholic. Yet I know the devil has sneaked into the Church, even into the Vatican itself. His Holiness has told us so. Then if the devil's in the Vatican why be surprised that he's in San Felipe. Everyone in the town knows that its priest and his altar boy are buggering each other day and night. But the people do nothing about it. If they were real Catholics they'd boil the two of them, as my men will before long." Julio began to tremble at the word boil expecting another violent shift of mood but Oscar was still conciliatory. "Don't worry Julio. When you try to seduce me I don't blame you. You are a rich degenerate and know no better. But in my book you can be saved."

Julio felt that he was completely brainwashed by now. He had said he would do anything to escape and now he knew that he really would, whatever the price. Like an obedient follower of a prophet he sat at attention and listened to Oscar's sermon, hoping that in it he would find the key to his own salvation.

Cross-legged, Oscar leaned against the wall of the hut; his back was so long that he was still able to look down on his new disciple. "You know, Julio," he began. "I had great faith in Antonio Floresco to begin with, especially when he declared martial law. Carolinos need strict discipline. They're too corrupt to rule themselves. They'll give up corruption only when every one of them is rich; that means never. They have to be corrupt because of the family. Its demands come first. They don't understand what is meant by the state. You may think that you and your uncle are not communists, just liberal democrats. In theory that may be so but in this country now there can be no in-betweens. Anything that is hostile to the régime must be on the side of the communists. You liberals kid yourselves when you talk of restoring democracy. It was never here to restore. Only a corrupt mess run by big families. I kept proclaiming these truths and that's why they threw me out of the Army. I told them that the only way to beat the communists is by using the communist method, complete ruthlessness. When Floresco got rid of the likes of me he was confessing lack of faith in himself."

The disciple decided to ask a question which was much safer than voicing a contrary view. "Senor Diasanta, I entirely agree with what you say but what about the rules of the Church? The Church is critical of the President. It doesn't want Floresco to be all-powerful, does it?"

Oscar was on his feet again lunging several paces this way and that in the small room, like a wasp trapped in a bottle. Julio now had to listen to a diatribe against Rome, which since Vatican II had been betraying Catholicism. "When I was a boy, everything was in Latin. Now real Catholics don't want to go to Church. No Latin, but guitars, electric guitars, the priest facing man instead of God at the altar, human understanding, easy penances, pop music. Vatican II was the hellish gate that opened to let in Satan so he could start his real attack on the Church. How clever he was at corrupting priests and the bishops who knew of the priests' corruption and protected it. They pretend to hate sodomy but the truth is they wallow in it.

Oh yes, I still remember that Latin phrase, *facilis descensus averno*, so easy the slide down to hell, even if the Bishops don't." Diasanta's voice rose to a crescendo. "They've even got a liberal cardinal in this country who does nothing about the priest at San Felipe, but that priest isn't the only one. Julio, Julio, we are together in a raging ocean of sin and we must fight against it. You are a fine young man and you must join me."

Diasanta got down and took Julio's head between his powerful hands. His voice fell again but now to a scarcely audible whisper. "How strange it is, Julio. I can talk to you so easily. No, not strange at all, our souls are in harmony. I feel it. But my thugs outside are reptiles who understand nothing. I'll let you in on the trick I play on them. When they rape anything that moves, their favourite sport, I just watch them and laugh. They think their depravity is pleasing to me and so it is. But my joy is all the greater because I can witness their lust leading them to everlasting damnation where they belong. Yes, I despise my men without exception and that's why I use their depravity to offer them as a sacrifice to Satan." Diasanta took to chuckling at his subtle game and then having deposited two quick pecks on Julio's cheek and grasping his head again, he continued very slowly. "Now Julio Abulencia, I'm going to tell my greatest secret. I shall tell it to no one but you. It will be a mystery binding us together for all time. You must know that the Lord has looked upon me and saved me from sin. Brother Julio, I swear that the Son of God has given me a sign. A month ago in the still of night I went for a walk alone on this very mountain when all my men were sodden with debauchery and drink. My head was suddenly filled with light and Jesus appeared to me saying so sweetly, 'Oscar my son, no longer shall your rod stand up and sin; henceforth it shall hang like a chaste fruit and a proof of righteousness. So my Father will receive you in Heaven on Judgment Day, a pure Christian whose faith is grounded in the sanctity of life.' Those were His words. One day, one timeless day, Julio, I pray that you and I will kneel before the Celestial Throne praising the Holy Trinity, the Blessed Virgin and all the Saints in Heaven." Diasanta then pressed a long moist kiss on Julio's cheek.

Julio felt like a man suddenly rescued from torture and death. A host of feelings fought inside his head: relief naturally, thanks for his own cunning, joy that he would soon be freed but also a sliver of pity for the insane creature who had transformed his impotence into a miracle. He did not try to move from the soft lips kissing him but waited until they had gone. Then he turned his face and said quietly, "Yes Oscar, my friend and teacher. I understand what you have told me. I understand the evil from which you will save me. I thank you from the bottom of my heart." He then returned Oscar's kiss, not for so long, nor with such warm lips, for his body was still cold and trembling, but with the greatest sincerity he had ever felt.

Oscar walked around the room slowly, his head wobbling a little and his lips mouthing unknown words. His serene expression was of the kind that sometimes passes over the faces of lunatics for reasons unknown to the world. Yet Diasanta was as capable of observing his own madness as any psychiatrist. He could put on various habits at the drop of a hat, which did not mean that he was detached from them when they were on his back. Rather he became the music whilst the music played. He was certain that Julio was entirely subdued to his purpose. Taking a neatly folded paper from his pocket he said in as courteous a manner as Stanley Baldwin obliging the feckless King to abdicate, "Senor Julio, please put your signature to this document. It will take care of all our problems. When your uncle has replied to us, satisfactorily, as he will, you can go in freedom. In a few days you will be safely back with the woman you love."

The document, which Julio had signed in desperation without a second glance, ordered Cesar Abulencia quite crisply that he must hand over to the bearer one hundred thousand US Dollars, in default of which his nephew would be painfully and very slowly killed, with evidence of the progress of his execution being provided to his uncle in small parts of Julio's body, on the instalment system as it were. The document was at once carefully concealed in the leather biker's jacket that Diasanta habitually wore, but he had no intention of letting his thugs know a word of its content. This was to be one of his perks quite distinct from the sum that Manzano had already handed over to the gang for the kidnapping. When Diasanta returned to his men they looked at him as expectantly as the Israelites might have looked at Moses when he came down from

Mount Sinai, but they received no commandments. Pulling a chair back to front towards him he sat on it astride resting his muscular arms over the chairback. He sighed deeply, "Listen now. You've all had your share of the money, but that young shit is obstinate. He won't promise not to see the President's daughter."

"We can rough him up," a voice said. "No. Frighten him with a boil up. He'll promise when he thinks we mean it."

Diasanta looked at the speaker with contempt and spat on the floor. The gobbet glistened like a jewel in the candlelight. "Idiot," he said. "What about when he's free?"

"Easy," another thug said. "Kill him now. Quickly or slowly; it doesn't matter which. All the Florescos want is Julio Abulencia dead. It's obvious."

Deep concern appeared on Oscar's face; he rubbed his chin thoughtfully. "Kill, kill, kill; That's all you understand, isn't it Fuentes? No. I'll have to go to Infanta myself. Find out what the head of the Abulencia clan wants his nephew to do. It's all very complicated. But we must get as much as we can out of this. There could be more money in it, more for us all. You know our rules—shared equally. Understand?" He glared at his thugs, who welcomed the chance of increasing their cut. "Good," he said. "I'll be back soon and I want to find that boy in good health—alive." With that he abandoned Julio to the loving care of his thugs and set out for the capital.

Cesar Abulencia decided not to worry, worrying being for the lesser orders. A gentleman should face all problems with equanimity, for a good ship could always ride out a storm. However the phone call from Radio Ecclesia had given him food for thought. It came from the station's news editor, Nestor, whose friendship Cesar had gained on the one occasion when he had actually co-operated with the First Lady in her petition to effect the young man's release from police custody. The call at once revived his suspicions about Max Bligh and that PR firm employed by the President, Schuster, Schuster and Bligh which he had imagined might be connected with the CIA, the Russian Intelligence or even the Chinese. These days one could never tell. Espionage was a dying art with all sorts of riffraff crowding in on the act. Despite which it was obvious that the source that had provided Nestor with a tape of his lecture accusing the Florescos, must be Bligh but with what objective? If Bligh was working, as was not impossible, for more than one control he might be confused over his motives himself. The tape would surely be embarrassing for the Floresco régime, and in consequence it could be dangerous for himself and the Abulencia family. If on the other hand forces within the hierarchy of government were conspiring, as he suspected, to remove the President, whoever emerged as a new leader might welcome the support, now made manifest, of the Abulencias. How then should he act? He was in a quandary.

Though agnostic in disposition Cesar was, like many Carolinos, superstitious. Some, though Christian, resorted to Taoist temples for the predictions of the I Jing, many more still asked village soothsayers to divine their future. Being an intellectual snob, Cesar liked to haruspicate not in the entrails of an offering but in the poems of his Latin favourite Horace, whose works he opened at random. Thereupon the ninth ode, *vides ut alta*, sensibly advised him to avoid all speculation about the future but to count what the days might bring as credit. "So let's relax and see what today brings," he said aloud, as he sat down to a breakfast of strong coffee, croissants and an assortment of Caroline fruits, plus of course the *Infanta Times*, a quick perusal of which on its third page confirmed Nestor's news that his address had not been broadcast, though its content had been printed in various student and left wing rags of no consequence to the political classes that mattered.

Unfortunately the day of Roman stoicism did not last. Cesar had just finished eating when a flustered security guard, one of his family's long time retainers, hurried in and said, "Senor. There's a man who says he wants to see you. He must have cut through the security wire on the walls. He says…" But he got no further. Only a few steps away from the breakfast table was a leather-clad giant who announced himself deferentially as, "Oscar Diasanta at your service, Senor."

Cesar glanced at him briefly but addressing the security guard said, "Heber, I think it might be for the best if you do not call the Police." Then turning to Oscar Diasanta he smiled and said as if their breakfast engagement had been made the day before, "Please, Senor Diasanta. So glad to see you. Do join me. Ah, I'll ring for fresh coffee. The croissants are from the French Bakery. Senor, you'll find them as good as any you have tasted in Paris."

The Abulencia charm or rather flattery that Julio had employed worked again, though Diasanta expected it for his feelings for Julio had engendered in his impressionable mind the idea that he was welcome in this house. He looked around at the elegance of Cesar's patio, part of it indoors but mostly in the open though protected by a pergola over which various flowering creepers had established their sway. "A beautiful place to have breakfast," he said taking a chair opposite Cesar, at which point a maid bore in some fresh coffee and poured out a cup. "Thank you Senorita," Diasanta said to the servant conveying an impression of civility even if the biking clothes did not.

Cesar asked, "Senor, would you like something more substantial? You seem to have been travelling. You must be hungry."

"Thank you no. This is really more than I need," replied Diasanta, who was already enjoying a croissant which he spread liberally with the best English strawberry jam. "Bring some more croissants," Cesar told the maid who was about to leave. "And please tell the family that I am not to be disturbed. They can take breakfast in the dining room." He smiled again at Diasanta and said, somewhat casually, "I have been informed by the DeoGracias that you have been, that you are—looking after my nephew, Julio. A Palace officer, Captain Manzano, has also told me that he requested you to release him and handed over money for this service to one of your men. I assume you have come to tell me how the release can be arranged."

"Exactly so, Senor Abulencia. "You are a man of quick understanding. You have only to say the word and it will be done." Diasanta took the document signed by Julio and handed it across the table to his host. As he did so he said, "Julio is a charming young man and extremely intelligent. We get on very well together, like old friends"

Cesar's eyebrows were raised for a moment as he said, "Really Senor, you do? I'm glad you like him. Well now, you tell me I have only to say the word. I presume it is 'yes' to whatever is written on this document. Cesar put on his glasses and read the message while

Diasanta started on another croissant. "One hundred thousand dollars US," said Cesar quietly. "Of course the answer must be 'yes'. But Senor, don't think me rude if I ask what guarantee can you give me that Julio will be safe."

"I would like my answer to be because I like him, but that would be no surety at all, even though it is true. No, your guarantee rests on the fact that if I broke my word I wouldn't be able to kidnap anyone again. It would be bad for my sort of business. At the same time Senor Abulencia I want a guarantee from you. Nothing is to be said publicly or ever about the sum of money mentioned in my note. This is a secret between you and me." Diasanta hesitated before saying harshly. "I'd have to take action if you let me down. I don't like threatening a gentleman like you, Senor Abulencia. But you must have noticed how easily I got into your presence."

"Of course, of course. On my word, just between you and me." Cesar said affably. "But Senor Diasanta, you have just mentioned a second secret I would love to share with you. How did you get through the razor wire entanglements around the compound wall? I believe some sections are even electrified. You are very talented."

"Very easy if you have one of these," said Diasanta taking from a deep leg pocket a formidable pair of secateurs and explaining like a salesman. "Note the rubber grips in case of high voltage. Made in Germany. It can be used as an assassin's tool—for cutting, stabbing, slashing, bludgeoning. But I didn't have to use it on your guards. The lazy devils were asleep or drunk. Lucky boys. You'd have two staff vacancies if they'd moved a limb."

"I don't doubt it but I'm glad there was no need for you to go to such trouble Senor," said Cesar concealing his anger and putting on a grin as though he was enjoying Diasanta's macabre humour. "Oh by the way, our first secret—about the money. It's because the one hundred thousand is for you alone, isn't it?"

Diasanta nodded and smiled his assent; by now he was thinking of the money as little more than an amicable family arrangement. He almost told Cesar that he might soon witness him with Julio together in this beautiful house but that would require more explanation than Cesar was ready for just yet. The temptation passed and when more croissants were brought in Cesar stood up excusing himself with, "A few minutes, Oscar, a call of nature. Make yourself comfortable."

By now Diasanta felt quite at home in the Abulencia ambience. The thought even crossed his mind as he poured himself more coffee and buttered a fresh croissant that Julio's accession to primacy in the family might easily be accelerated. He then sat right back in his chair and looked up admiringly at the flowers on the pergola and through its interstices far away to a troubled sky beyond. What a shame, it was going to rain heavily and he must be going. His interest returned to his croissant but when he glanced across the table, there, seated opposite him again, he saw Cesar pointing a Browning automatic directly at his chest. "So you are going to kill me, Senor?" he said with equanimity as he pushed the rest of the croissant into his mouth.

"If you try anything, yes." said Cesar who was sitting with both hands holding the gun and his elbows on the table. If he fired there was not much chance of missing.

"And I suppose you are going to tell a servant to call the Police to arrest the kidnapper of your handsome Julio. What good will that do? The President is involved. My thugs and I are protected people. We do special jobs that the military can't do because of liberals like you who can arouse world opinion." Diasanta took a sip of coffee. "In any case if you arrest me my men will make sure that you never see Julio again. Poor boy, the things they can do if they don't like someone."

Cesar continued to point the gun. He said coolly, "I'll never see my nephew again and you know it. That's why I might as well kill you and rid the earth of vermin."

A strange smile passed over Diasanta's face. "I believe what you say, Senor. It will be an honour to die at the hand of an Abulencia. After all I gave you no real guarantee. Why should you trust what I said." The smile returned and became broader; indeed it spread across his sunburnt face revealing two rows of perfect teeth, like a split coconut exposing its internal white lining. Diasanta's gaze then slowly became transformed into something that Cesar found unsettling. The man would really welcome the bullet about to slice through the air into his heart, his head or wherever. He was fascinated as Diasanta slowly pulled down the zip of his jacket to reveal a hairless muscular chest the colour of burnished copper and said, "Go on Senor, I'm ready for your gift."

Unable to pull the trigger, Cesar put the gun down on the table. "Just as I thought Senor Diasanta. You're not brave in the things you do. Not even foolhardy. You are raving mad. You could have killed my guards; asleep or not they are part of my family. Yet you could wipe them out as I might swat a fly. But why should you understand what life means to others when it means nothing to you. You hate life. I believe you hate yourself. Yes, I will pay you. My car will be driven up to the fifth mile on this side of San Felipe in three days time at eight o'clock at night. The money will be in a case with the driver. Check it and release my nephew. Ah, you nod. You agree. I have no guarantee so your nod is all I can rest my hope on." Cesar's tear-filled eyes rested for a moment on Diasanta, then on the table. "I see you have finished all the croissants. I'm glad you enjoyed them. I must now ask you to go. I am sure you can find your way out."

Diasanta was reluctant to leave so quickly. He had enjoyed visiting an aristocratic home which to his mind strengthened the link between himself and his prisoner. Yet the meeting with Cesar had turned sour and there had been no chance to explain that he saw Julio as his future partner in a righteous struggle. Perhaps his young man was too good for the Abulencias under this supercilious family head who had actually called him, what was it? Yes, vermin. And after that, raving mad. Something began to vibrate in Oscar's head. He knew it was the start of a nervous spasm, but he must still make an effort to co-operate with Julio's uncle, to whom he held out his hand to bid a courteous farewell. Unfortunately Cesar did not respond but looked down disdainfully at the proffered gesture, saying coldly, "Good bye, Senor Diasanta. I expect you to keep your word."

With that he turned his back and left his rejected visitor on his own.

Uncontrolled anger raged in Diasanta's head. He made his way out of the house quickly into the compound and then onto the road where his Harley Davidson stood under the gaze of an Abulencia family guard. The man saw the madness in its owner's eyes and backed away, leaving Diasanta to roar off through the suburbs of

Infanta, out to the countryside of endless cultivated plains and on towards the mountains near to San Felipe. At breathtaking speed he passed without ever halting, though fearfully observed by many who knew him, through villages, check points and traffic mix-ups sometimes yelling and sometimes singing into the wind. At length after a long ride he entered San Felipe and went to the Alvarez garage, whose owner, Salvador's father, alarmed by his customer's wild manner, filled the tank and gave the bike a quick servicing. That done Diasanta set off, towards the end on foot along the track that led to his mountain lair. As he toiled upwards for three or more hours ever higher and higher the thought of Julio, the future head of the Abulencia clan as his disciple, raised his mind to joyous ecstasy but, when his camp came in sight, he took to bellowing grief-stricken cries like a man gone berserk. His thugs cowed before him but he saw greed in their eyes. "Nothing more," he shouted. "No more money. We must do with what we've got." Then he turned from them raving, "Cesar, I don't hate life. You didn't take my hand. Vengeance upon you."

Max Bligh sat nervously before Bersamina's desk unsure whether he was to be arrested or deported. Everything he had planned had gone wrong and Bersamina knew it. His bosses, the Schusters, had told him that American Intelligence had expressed disquieting suspicions over his political loyalties and said that their partnership would terminate after the President's visit to Europe. Yesterday the Caroline counter-terrorist police had brought the hapless Nestor in for a painful interview in the lower basement of the Defence Ministry as a result of which Max had been identified as the man who had provided Radio Ecclesia with a tape on which there was a speech by Cesar Abulencia. "Fortunately the speech was not broadcast, but what was your objective in distributing it?" Bersamina asked. "It was surely a strange way, Mr Bligh, of projecting a favourable imagine of the President who is employing your company. But maybe you are waiting the approval of Cesar Abulencia before you show it to the world. Is there some sort of alliance between the two of you? Cesar is a long time opponent of the Government. Is he paying you for your services? Or have you some connection with the Caroline Communist Party?" Bersamina laughed. "Of course it might be that you have no loyalties but several paymasters, in which case you must be doing well. I've heard of double agents but you may be a quadruple agent or more." Bersamina switched on a microphone to record Max Bligh's answers.

Bligh did not answer for the simple reason that he hardly knew the answers himself. He was one of those people who leaned against any available door and when it opened just pushed in regardless of where it led. "I find it difficult to explain myself," he said at length.

"I bet you do," Bersamina replied curtly as he switched off the microphone "So there's no great advantage in recording what you obviously don't know. However Mr Bligh, there's no need to dissemble any further; I know exactly what you have been doing, but unlike you I also know what you are going to do. As a matter of fact I have a memo from Washington explaining what US Intelligence required of you. They planted you in Infanta to report on everyone and everything: Abulencia and his liberals, the First Lady and who she contacts in the diplomatic set, the Cardinal—though you haven't done much in that direction, the communists, the mood of the people at grass roots level—very useful. But they are all passive roles, harmless roles. So why did you release Abulencia's speech to Nestor and Radio Ecclesia? Did you never think what effect it would have?"

Max Bligh shuffled in his seat. "Maybe I got bored," he said. "Maybe I just wanted to precipitate something."

"I could understand that," said Bersamina, "if it were true but it fits in better with your hidden loyalty to a secret revolutionary group within the USA, some amorphous domestic group of financiers and media radicals. Yes, your face tells me you know what I'm talking about. The State Department report to the Schusters suggests that you are already suspect. But don't worry, Max, I won't split on you. As long as you are useful to me." Bersamina leaned forward and smiled. "Max Bligh, getting to know you is like digging down through layer after layer of geological strata. You say you really wanted to precipitate something—like releasing the underlying magma I'd say, but it's obvious you had no idea how things might turn out. That's probably the story of your life. You are a small time player in a theatre that's bigger than you can imagine. However Mr Bligh, Washington, your control and best paymaster, now has something very positive for you to do. When you are in Rome."

"In Rome?" gasped Bligh. "That can't involve me. The Schusters are dealing with the European end of the contract. There's no plan for me to work for them in Europe."

"An economy measure. The Schuster's contract will end once the presidential party reaches Rome. Then you take over; after all only one city is involved. The President's visiting schedule will be handled entirely by you. Don't worry; you will be paid. You will accompany him wherever he goes. He has a habit of making extempore changes so you must watch out and report them to your control when you're in the Holy City. I will be in Europe with the President but you will never, repeat never, contact me there. Do you understand?"

"I quite understand," said Max Bligh though he did not see why nor did he care. He was overjoyed at the idea of getting away from the Carolines with his salary fully paid until he left Rome when, if not detected, he would have the opportunity of finding something else to do in furtherance of that hidden radical agenda concealed within the cocoon of the Stars and Stripes.

"By the way," said Bersamina as he shook hands faring well to the multi-spy, "In case you want to be reminded of our historic past hold on to your copy of the Abulencia tape. It could be useful to you in Europe. It's an interesting record of what you and Mr Hilary Arbuthnot set out to achieve here. Is Hilary still in Infanta?" Max replied that the talented photographer had returned to Hong Kong, thinking as he spoke, 'sly bastard, you know bloody well that he's gone'. Bersamina frightened him; he had a greater mastery of what was going on in the world than anyone Max knew, enveloping all he encountered like a miasma. Beside him most of the country's politicians and public figures were mere amateurs. How depressing the sombre corridors of the Defence Ministry, how good to escape into a street full of human beings and how relieved Max was that he had not ended up for interview in its lower basement floor.

From his office window high up in the centre of the façade of his Ministry, Bersamina watched Max Bligh hailing a taxi on Floresco Boulevard. There went an idealist manqué if ever there was; a man who had lost all sense of reality in a world of intrigue so complex that disorientated agents sometimes switched allegiance after losing all sense of right and wrong. He was certainly fit for purpose in Rome and Bersamina lost no time in sending a message to the State Department, for the eyes of Jasper Frankfurter only, saying that what was required would soon be in place. But the uncertain loyalties of Max Bligh, trivial though they were, had set Bersamina asking where was the loyalty of other players in the government game. For himself he could not reply, 'to the Florescos.' In the early years of the régime none had been more faithful to the President than himself, but as with all traitors Bersamina told himself that it was those he sought to replace who were the enemies of the state. He was the one who had stayed faithful to the aims of the régime. Yet another problem beset him; a coup d'état would require political allies of reputation and substance, not just the generals who were already in his pocket. So it was with kindness and effusion that he greeted Cesar Abulencia, whom he had asked to visit him about a certain pamphlet that the students were hawking around Infanta.

Cesar was dismissive about the pamphlet. "Of course I accused the Florescos over Julio's kidnapping because that woman is responsible. We all know that. You certainly do. The President or the First Lady can bring an action against me if they wish and I shall enjoy defending myself in open court."

"I am not criticising you," Bersamina replied. "Nor as far as I know is the President or the First Lady. Probably neither of them is even aware of your speech, still less of the students' action. They are completely taken up with the plans for their European tour and with the distress of their daughter, as is most natural. I don't think they should be disturbed with lesser matters. However, when I see Antonio later today I am not inclined to raise the matter of your speech. After all it is not yet publicised, just appearing somewhat plagiarised in a student pamphlet which won't be widely read. But I must ask you whether your accusation is deliberately intended to raise the political temperature on the eve of the President's departure. Would you welcome that? I don't see how it would benefit you. Remember the communist insurgency is growing and the economy is faltering. Families like yours and mine would be finished if the reds won."

Cesar shrugged his shoulders but after a little consideration said, "Senor Bersamina, I would welcome anything that led to real political momentum. Anything that could lead to change." Then he added sarcastically. "Wouldn't you welcome that too, Senor?" However as Cesar had more important fish to fry he went on. "Nothing was deliberate. I don't know how my words became public. I could guess but I don't intend to do so." Having dismissed the trivial matter of a mere student pamphlet, Cesar then gave Bersamina a full account of Diasanta's visit and his demand for ransom, ending with a complaint that sounded more like an accusation, "I'm sure you must have known that the madman was here. You know everything. So why didn't you move and put him in your famous lower basement for questioning, or better still elimination?"

"Yes, I did know. We could have got him. It would have given me great pleasure to eliminate him. Sometimes my work has its rewards but it would not have helped Julio and you know it."

"Yes I do know it, only too well," replied Cesar, "and I'm grateful to you for your restraint. Your power is limited but I sometimes wish it were otherwise. But who knows how things may change. However, Senor Minister, you will have to excuse me soon. I have to go to a certain American Bank to collect the ransom money. They have arranged to let me have one hundred thousand US in notes."

Bersamina pricked up his ears at Cesar's speculation on the possibility of change. Did this shrewd aristocrat suspect him of something? But he only commented sympathetically. "A large sum indeed, Senor."

"Not for an Abulencia." Cesar replied haughtily.

"My dear friend. My very dear friend," said Bersamina with unusual warmth allowing his eyes to rove over Cesar's immaculate grey suit and sober tie, "I know the worth of your historic family. I was really thinking that given the involvement of the First Lady in this dreadful business, it might not be unreasonable to suggest to the President that the money should be reimbursed to you from the DeoGracias budget."

"From that source I would never accept anything, anything at all. The DeoGracias as it acts now is a cancer in this country's life." Cesar sat rigidly as he spoke. Gentle, somewhat frail he might look but his deep hatred for the Florescos was palpable.

The moment had to be seized but even so Bersamina's voice was diffident when he next spoke. "Senor Abulencia, Cesar, in the admittedly unlikely event of something happening to the President—I am referring of course to the not unfounded rumours of his declining health—and in the admitted unlikely event of a group of public figures endeavouring to form a Government of national reconciliation—perhaps starting its life with an amnesty to all political opponents; under such circumstances you, Senor, might well be one of those asked to participate—as a Minister of course. You would be heard with rapt attention. It goes without saying that the contents of the students' pamphlet would stand you in good stead. You would certainly be listened to with respect by other opponents of the present government and indeed by some of its current members, such as Senor Loyola."

Cesar already had an intuition that something was in the wind. The fact that Bersamina had not berated him for his accusatory speech tended to confirm his suspicions, and now the suggestion of a Ministry and the name of the Prime Minister? Yes, something was afoot. But caution was necessary. He was aware that history showed, from Roman times onward and probably before, a *coup d'état* nipped in the bud could be accompanied by people receiving sharper cuts. He decided to reply obliquely, "I have always counselled the opposition to refrain from violence against the powers that be which means that I would only be open to offers of co-operation provided they were made democratically—shall we say in accordance with our moribund constitution."

"I appreciate that. I am only speaking hypothetically. But the President is no longer young and like all of us he can't last forever." With that their exchange on a very delicate subject terminated. Bersamina smiled at Cesar, a knowing friendly smile that confirmed that their meeting was but a pourparler. He then said quietly, "I think it might be best if you do not tell Senorita Conchita about the money you are putting up. She is just existing for Julio's release. She feels sure that a ransom will be paid but she doesn't know the problems involved. You know Cesar—there could still be difficulties."

"What sort of difficulties?" Cesar asked ingenuously. He knew what Bersamina meant but wanted to probe him for the experience he must have had with Diasanta.

"Diasanta is unpredictable. His men are a bunch of sadistic killers. They kill for money. They torture if they don't get it. So Conchita's best hope must be that the bait is large enough to satisfy them. Diasanta exercises a hypnotic control over his thugs and he lets them go apeshit if it suits his mood. Senor, anything can happen so it's best if Conchita remains ignorant until a satisfactory solution is reached."

Cesar again asked why the military did not eliminate the gang though he knew it might be beyond the capability of the Army to wipe out a small group of bandits hidden in the jungle. Bersamina's reply was not what he had expected, "Because, Cesar, in that mountainous area we have to counterbalance the communist insurgence. Diasanta is cunning and ruthless and he's also vehemently hostile to the communists. He teaches his thugs to welcome death. They are invincible fighters. You might say that he does work we're not capable of doing."

It struck Cesar that going to a bank to collect the ransom money might be a fool's errand but it was impossible to pull out from the only chance. He said as much to Bersamina and concluded, "Well then it's just as well that Conchita will be in Europe with her parents. It will take her mind off her troubles."

Bersamina said, "Senor Abulencia, let us leave together, you for the Bank and your humble servant for the DeoGracias. We shall meet again after I return from Europe." As they entered the elevator he put his arm around Cesar's shoulder and said, as though to an accomplice, "The Florescos, man and wife, have reconciled themselves to the fact that where marriage is concerned, for their daughter it's your nephew or no one. Senorita Conchita absolutely refuses to accompany them to Europe. The poor creature is on tenterhooks. Cesar my friend, the ball is well and truly in your court. You have to work with Diasanta. Get him the money. I sincerely pray it does the trick. Nothing else will."

The President did not, as had become his habit with Ministers, greet Bersamina formally but with, "Manuel. How good to see you. Do sit down and let's have a drink together. I'm having a Scotch. Neat.

And the same for you? Good." He poured out two measures and they sat at either end of a short settee which immediately produced a feeling of friendship. Bersamina was reminded of those days, so long ago, when they had worked together with such confidence and hope for the future. Now what remained of that hope? Forgotten dreams, failure, and corruption. Was it possible that in the corners of his eyes there was a hint of tears. Antonio must have seen them "Manuel, nothing has changed. It's just that you and I have grown older."

"Yes," replied Bersamina. "Things are just the same at heart, Antonio." And maybe in fact they were, because in his own heart he wanted to say to the President, 'You are to be killed not because of any miserable bit of treachery but because the country which we both love has to be saved from you. So really I am still the most sincere follower you have ever had'.

"Come then, Manuel," said the President, sitting nearer to Bersamina and gazing at him, not as if he were nearby but in a manner that suggested the visionary glimpsing, not the seas and continents over which they were about to travel, but the future itself. "In a week's time we shall be in the Holy City. You know there's not much of the believer left in me but in Rome I always feel truly at home. Do you think that we Carolinos have something in common with the Italians?"

"We seem to eat as much pasta as the Italians nowadays, "replied Bersamina with a smile. "And our music—just as emotional."

"Yes and the way we make love. But I'm not speaking from Italian experience. Just hearsay. Yes, Italy; if I ever had to go into exile that's where I'd want to live and die."

Bersamina put his glass down and walked across to the window fearful that the tears might reappear. He turned, his expression one of concern, and said, "You think that Conchita will be alright on her own, I mean without you and Griselda?"

"Come and sit down Manuel. I can't talk when you're walking about. Good, that's better. There's no need to worry. I have great confidence in Conchita. She has an inner strength, a bit like mine. She'll go her own way and Griselda should have seen that. Unhappily they both have the same drive to win at all costs. It can make Griselda overbearing. That's why I tell her to listen more and not make so many speeches. It gets her into trouble; she stakes out the pitch and expects everyone to play her game. When they refuse she finds it difficult to back down."

Bersamina murmured something about the importance of compromise but he was really astonished. It was rare for the President to make any remarks critical of Griselda nowadays but his surprise increased when the President continued very firmly. "I've told Griselda I'm letting Conchita marry Julio. He's harmless, rather romantic; Conchita will be the dominant one, I'd guess. She'll be back to normal once Julio is free. But she needs something to get on with so I've decided that she should become Governor of Valladolid Province. Old Ramiros has just retired and about time too. She'll be as good as him and probably a lot better. She's capable and will learn quickly."

Bersamina did his best to show no reaction. He knew that Conchita was clever, her academic record, a double first at Oxford, proved that, but he had doubts over her judgment. Surely her choice of a lover from a family that opposed her father raised a question at the least concerning her common sense. He had no doubt that as a governor she would do as well as half a dozen of the incompetents who would be after the post—with its control of a rich province bringing much patronage and plenty of rich pickings. But couldn't the President see that the foreign critics would pick on the appointment at once as a further example of the nepotism soiling the record of the régime, one of the defects that had made Jasper Frankfurter anxious to get rid of the Florescos as the best way of restoring the American style constitution. Why did the Florescos have this terrible weakness of regarding the state as a carcass that they could feed upon at will?

Something seemed to grip Bersamina inside. He could not make out what it was that obliged him to control his breath. Part of him wanted to rush to a phone to invent some excuse to give his Washington contacts, obliging them to abort the plot against their once chosen ally across the Pacific. The word abort brought Cardinal Peccata to his mind. When he was at the helm he would have to trim his unbelief to the principles of the church if he was to hold its support. Would it be worth it or would it not be better here and now to confess his impending treachery to his leader, telling him that he wished to redeem his loyalty. The President would forgive him, of that he had little doubt, but he was equally sure that there was one who would not. The First Lady would use all her powers of persuasion to have the treacherous Minister for Defence removed from his post. Even if she did not succeed the President would surely rule his Defence Minister out of the succession possibly in favour of his wife. Slowly all the reasons that for months had been impelling him to plot the Florescos' downfall reasserted themselves. Their removal was the prerequisite to restoring the Constitution, surely the best option for the country. This moral conviction calmed him down, his breathing became easier and his thoughts began to flow evenly. He decided to say nothing about Conchita's appointment. In a few weeks time there would be no place for Florescos in the government of the Carolines. Conchita could, if she wished, look forward to a pleasant life in Europe with her darling Julio—if he were released. But that was another matter on which Bersamina preferred to say nothing.

There was a matter on which something must be said: the trial of the communist priest Father Oliveros. If Bersamina had got his way the whole matter would have been hushed up and Oliveros would have been posted to some remote place where he could do nothing dangerous, perhaps a parish in one of the mainly Muslim provinces where there would be a good chance of him having an accident. But the President was anxious that the trial should be transparent as a public assertion of the Government's refusal to have no truck with the communists. Since the State must prove that it had a just case, Bersamina briefed the President with a file containing a mass of damning evidence with the necessary depositions. "His Holiness will be bored stiff with such detail," said the President, "But I'll quickly bring a sparkle to this eyes by uttering some unctuous claptrap about the sanctity of life. And after that there'll be an exchange of presents and then photos of Griselda and me receiving the Papal blessing." The President chuckled and said firmly "And I don't want you in the picture for that, Manuel, you son of Satan."

Small talk about the pleasures of Europe ensued and both men expressed confidence that all would be well during their absence under Loyola, who was the subject of a eulogy by the President, declaring that it might be a good idea to build the Prime Minister up as his potential successor. He said, "You and I, Manuel, belong to an older generation who must give way to these young technocrats, men who know everything about economic models and microchips. Do you know I begin to feel like something out of prehistory when people talk of such things. But I'm to see Loyola shortly and I'm pretty good now at pretending that I know what he's talking about."

The meeting had left Bersamina drained. It would be the last time before Europe that he would see the President on his own. Would it be before or after the audience with the Holy Father, and would he then be looking at a colleague or a corpse? He must do nothing to suggest his state of mind and so he left with a casual, "Goodbye Antony. Ill see you at the airport."

The Prime Minister and the Minister for Defence almost bumped into one another in the anteroom outside the President's Office, which DeoGracias aficionados jokingly called the Ellipsoidal Office. They exchanged brief greetings and Loyola asked *sotto voce*, "How's the old man?" To which Bersamina replied likewise, "In good form but stand firm." With some trepidation Loyola entered the President's Office and gave a courteous bow to the Head of State.

"Senor Prime Minister," the President began. "I hope I am not going to take up too much of your valuable time, but as you are to be in charge during my absence there are a number of things for us to talk about." He took a seat at his majestic desk and Loyola sat facing him over an acreage of polished black marble, on which stood a number of ormolu-encrusted ornaments of Spanish provenance. However they gave small protection against the Prime Minister's piercing questions and hard observations, the first of which concerned Senorita Conchita's recent appointment as a provincial governor. The news had only just reached Loyola's office and he had not had time to recover from his shock. Not that he was anything but respectful. He gave his opinion, that the appointment was inappropriate, quietly and succinctly but his words were delivered in a leaden way that filled the President with irritation. If the man's parents and children had just been murdered in some ghastly way, he would no doubt talk about it in the same dreary tone of voice. Where is the man's passion? The President would rather be talking to one of those corrupt, debauched ministers he had been obliged, for political reasons, to have in the Cabinet than to Loyola. At least their excesses suggested some sort of humanity.

"I value your opinion on this matter," the President replied when the first of Loyola's strictures had been concluded. "But sometimes there are family reasons, personal reasons, which make a course of action inevitable."

"Senor President, the weakness of our society is that such reasons always seem to take precedence over the interests of the state."

"Senor Loyola I would hardly be a good Caroline leader if I was not a typical Carolino. The people will understand even if foreigners," the President almost added. 'and people like you,' "do not."

"The people would understand and not care a jot if there weren't other…" Loyola paused, but before he could continue the President burst out angrily, "other scandals. Say it Loyola. Say it. Now we are going to have another of your sermons on the Caroline National Construction Company, aren't we?"

A heavy silence lay between them. The matter of the CNCC was not one of those minor or even medium sized issues on which they disagreed. The failure of the Company, which had grown and grown like a ravenous squid extending its tentacles in undesirable directions could shake the economic foundations of the state. Nor was it one of those matters on which an accusing finger could only be pointed at the First Lady and her sycophants. The President himself was involved up to the hilt; his fallibility was apparent for all to see, yet Loyola had no alternative but to press on. "Senor President, the Company is on the verge of failure. Millions of dollars will be lost: the state's money, taxpayers' money. It might have been better to let the Company go bankrupt years ago instead of wasting public money propping it up. We should seek external sources of finance but who is going to finance a company that is financially so badly managed, that some people are using as a milch cow? Unfortunately I can see no evidence of likely improvement in this regard."

"Loyola, let's come to the point. I am well aware of what people say about Griselda and me. We are arch-thieves salting away wealth just for ourselves. Well yes, some of it is for us but that is not the complete picture. We do not live the sort of life beloved of American bankers and Russian tycoons, whose speculations ruin the lives of millions. We do not live like media stars. We live well but ours is a family life. And we work hard. Griselda attracts a lot of criticism over her clothes. But my dear Loyola, a President's wife is always on stage. Would you expect an actress playing a queen to come on in rags? Griselda is in the public eye and dresses for the people, especially for the little people who love her. The cost is relatively slight. But my expenditure is more important and greater than hers. I need resources to maintain my political power and preserve our régime, which lays down the best path for our country after the post-war chaos which I brought to an end. I also need wealth to be independent of the economic forces that rage about us. Let me tell you, Loyola, how I see economics: first, as regards your economic theories, monetarism, Keynesianism, and whatever else, they all ignore the fact that money, the paper stuff printed by governments and banks, has fallen into the hands of financial speculators and bankers who know, often secretively, when and how to manipulate its varying values in the market to make vast profits. Meanwhile the pillars of real wealth—labour, raw materials, skills, education, inventiveness, are at a discount. Labour, instead of being deployed to its best advantage, is often throttled. Under this imbalanced system the people have become helots with little power to control the economy. Don't you see that economists like you and politicians like me are also helots, buffeted about by financial speculators just like the rest of mankind. Senor, I am no communist but I can see that Marx was right on one matter at least: only when liquidity is provided and regulated by a single international source, devoid of independent banking systems, can the people become prosperous and free. So Loyola, if you understand how I see things maybe we will get on better. For instance every bit as much as you, I know that if the CNCC fails so will its many contracts abroad, from Morocco to Thailand. Then what becomes of the thousands of Caroline workers abroad? Yes, we must keep the Company going."

Loyola leaned forward and spoke now no longer in leaden tones but with a ringing sense of urgency. "Yes we must keep it going but first let me comment on your reference to Marx. Senor President, I agree that he may be right in the long run but we don't live in the long run. We live now in the real world of a complex international banking system. Maybe in time its inefficiencies will force the nations to create the sort of institution Marx postulated but in the meantime what are we to do? We both agree that the Company must be saved but we obviously disagree on the way of saving it. The fact is that your economic activities, if I may grace them by calling them that, frighten off investment both domestic and, which is more important, international. So I return to my approach to the problem. To keep the Company going you must get rid of the people now in charge of it. At the risk of angering you Excellency, I regret to say that Senora Floresco is not trained in corporate management. It is clear that the Company must prune, prune, prune. Sell off useless assets, dismiss people holding sinecures, reduce staff numbers and salaries and, to manifest a clear determination to reform, sell off prestigious buildings and the like; private enterprise will buy them up. If you don't take this advice the Company will collapse." Loyola hesitated, but in criticising the management of the First Lady he had gone too far to retreat, so he said slowly, "And then our régime will collapse and given the strength of the communist movement, something nastier than Marx ever imagined could emerge; another Khmer Rouge maybe."

The President, confronted with the prospect of having to face up to his wife's power, could only prevaricate. He said feebly, "Oh come, Loyola, what evidence have you for saying that? Aren't you panicking, perhaps?"

Something in Loyola's uneasy head snapped. He stood up and looked down on the President. He threw the file he was holding onto the floor. He shouted in a very loud voice, "My God, what evidence? The billion dollar African road from Algiers to Lagos, only five percent completed; the hydro-electric station in Pakistan that doesn't work because the lake leaked away, the Infanta metro system that will be ready on judgment day, the export of good Carolinos to Arab states where they work like slaves and may have their young bodies abused, and of course Griselda Floresco's pet projects—the Opera House, the Conference Centre, the luxury hotels, the mountain golf courses, all finished on time at profligate expense. What other evidence do you want, Antonio Floresco?"

The President remained seated and calm, staring with steely eyes at this man who was so clearly accusing him. "Perhaps," he said, "it would be better, Senor Prime Minister, if you were to resume your academic role in America. Your wife has never given up her post at Harvard. I'm sure she would like you to return. This job is too much for you. It is clear that you are overwrought and so I forgive you."

Loyola declined to sit when the President gestured towards his empty seat. He bent down to pick up his files. In doing so his glasses fell off his nose. He knelt down groping about for them in front of the desk invisible to the President who stood and looked over its wide top at the little man on the floor. The glasses had fallen sidewards and were nowhere near Loyola's hands. The President went round and retrieved them saying, "Here they are, my dear Bienvenido." He carefully put them on Loyola's tear-lined face and in doing so his own eyes, assiduous and kind, swam into Loyola's vision. "My dear friend," he said gently, "Please sit down. Please sit down."

Loyola did as he was told. It was a long time since he had so forgotten himself. "Your Excellency. Senor President. Forgive me. I'll tender my resignation today."

"You will not, Senor Prime Minister. I need you. The Carolines needs you. As to dealing with the CNCC all I can say is that just now I can do nothing. But when I return I promise you that you and I will discuss how to reform the Company and make it viable—whatever others may say." The President looked at his watch. "Now; time is pressing. There are a number of routine matters to discuss. I want you to have complete discretion over the ongoing matters of state during my absence. No need to contact me unless something out of the ordinary occurs."

Together they ran over a number of issues, giving particular attention to security matters. The President said that as Bersamina would be with him, the Defence Staff had been instructed to look to the Prime Minister for leadership. There was also the question of the Oliveros trial which must proceed in such a way as to show the world that justice was administered in the Carolines without fear or favour. Loyola put a number of questions to the President, who gave considered replies. By the time the interview was over both men felt that, somehow or other, they had achieved an unexpected rapport. Just before it was time for leave-taking, the President said thoughtfully, "You know, Bienvenido, I've made many mistakes in my time but making you Prime Minister was not one of them. If anything—anything untoward—were to happen to me while I am away, you will remain at the helm and you will know what to do. I shall put this decision in writing to the Chief Justice to hold in confidence before I leave."

The overt expression of the President's confidence again stirred Loyola to a burst of emotion. He seized the President's hands in his own, his eyes were full of warmth and he said, "Nothing will happen to you. It can't. It mustn't. There's still time left to accomplish the ambition you started off with—to make the Carolines a proud nation. We'll get the economy on an even keel. We'll restore democracy in some form or other. It's your destiny. If I didn't believe that I would never have served under you."

The President stared hard at Loyola, amazed but more than that moved that he had stirred such faith in a cool technocrat. "Yes Bienvenido," he said. "We will do that. We will do it together, my friend."

When Loyola had gone the President returned to his desk and glanced at a few papers without taking much in. He sat back, looking up at the ceiling that some exiled but talented Spanish artist had painted two hundred years ago. It showed Zeus the Thunderer, swirling upward into the bluest sky, surrounded by fleshy nymphs and youths, wafted by the breezes that came from the mouths of wind-god faces at the four corners of the celestial scene. Zeus and his attendants looked terribly unstable, as if they could all come spiralling down at any moment. The thought made the President smile; after all if Zeus fell what would it matter to the world.

He felt very tired, yet at the same time serene. The thought of Loyola's passion pleased him. It had been good to see. Perhaps if Bienvenido let himself go more often he might cease to take himself and his economic theories so seriously. He might even see that neither the economist nor the politician nor even the financier could really change the course of events. They could make ripples on the surface, but the underlying current was greater than them all. History was its own master. In the meantime the money that he and Griselda had appropriated for themselves was chicken-feed compared to what the bankers got. Selfish it might be but, since he was a Carolino, he knew he must protect his own corner against any storm that might arise. Despite which he was sure that whatever cataclysms might occur the Caroline people would survive amidst the vicissitudes of the world. It would do so because the nation was bigger than any good or evil that individuals could do. He did not delude himself that his forecast was profound but it was the only certainty a tired man could predict.

Withdrawing his gaze from the Empyrean he turned to look at a sideboard on which there were photographs of statesmen that he had met. The polished surface held the age upon it. There were giants, some good, some evil; Roosevelt, Churchill, Mao Tse-tung, Stalin, de Gaulle, and either side of them lesser giants; Nehru, Nasser, Sukarno and others. Yet the pantheon they composed was as illusory as Zeus the Thunderer on high. Even the biggest giant had been an ordinary man motivated by the same primitive desires that impel a peasant in the field and he, Antonio Floresco, was no more than the poorest of them. Just behind a photo of Chiang Kai-shek there was a photograph of himself and General Douglas MacArthur, shaking hands on what looked like a battlefield when the Americans had liberated the Carolines. He picked it up, looked at it for a while and then took it out of the frame. The signature of MacArthur was on the right. He added his own on the left. Then he returned the photo to the frame and put it back in its place, not among the giants but not too far away.

Conchita was no longer the carefree girl who had returned from England. Her sleep was constantly disturbed, she had lost weight and her eyes looked deep and tired. Julio and his fate were always on her mind and she lived for his release. No longer could she bank so easily on what was promised to her. She would believe in Julio's freedom only when she saw it.

The imposing large envelope adorned with the Presidential crest that had just arrived on her desk did not interest her. Such documents were two a penny in the DeoGracias. Generally they were packed with verbose contents that concealed nothing but trivia. They were on a par with the ceremonies that often took place in the palace audience chamber when functionaries took oaths to do their work honestly and diligently, though their minds were invariably fixed on the advantages that their new position, whatever it was, would bring to them. Why did her countrymen place such emphasis on outward show and formal appearance when their society was perishing?

Since she thought the place was nothing but a sham she had resolved to leave it as soon as her parents had set off for Europe. Much had to be done; she must start to go through her things, pack the essentials she needed and bag the rest for distribution—clothes for charities, books for libraries, music for youth clubs. It might be that in a few days' time her parents would be surprised to see her in Europe married to Julio, at a civil ceremony of course, and in her mind very happily so. Yet something else ached within her, beside the pain of not being with Julio. How deeply she loved her father and how full of regret she was that from now on her life would be separate from what was left of his. Tonight she and her brothers would take their last meal with their parents before the grand send-off at the airport. It grieved her that the meal might be the last one all of them might take together. Would she be able to control her tears when she was thinking of their past days of happiness together and even of the tenderness which her mother had always shown to her when she was a child?

She tore open the large envelope more to make its content convenient to throw into the waste paper basket than to read it, when her eyes caught a few lines in upright Roman script reading, 'Know by these presents that we Antonio Floresco President and Chief Executive of the Republic of the Carolines do hereby appoint and confirm in office our beloved daughter and faithful servant, Conchita Rafaelita Floresco, as Governor of the Province of Valladolid.' She put the decree down and stared ahead at nothing in particular and then read the words again. At the foot of the document was her father's signature and beside it the bold Presidential seal affixed over a scarlet ribbon. A second page repeated the whole formula again in Spanish. Outward form again, grandeur and the effort to impress. But had her father considered the implications of his act? Aside from whether she wanted such an office had he not seen that it was against his own political interest? If his régime were still popular her appointment would not matter in the least, and under such circumstances, young though she was, she would do her best in the job. But that was not the case. It was her duty to tell him this evening at dinner that, grateful though she was, she could not accept the office. For a moment she thought of writing her rejection below the seal but then a little feeling of vanity overtook her. She would keep the document as a memento of her loving father and maybe, not before too long, she and Julio could look at it and laugh when they were in the kitchen preparing their evening meal, perhaps in a little apartment in the Marais.

Tonight however she must make herself look as attractive as she could. Her father, her mother and her brothers must remember her in this simple mauve Parisian gown, her hair in a lustrous pigtail curving down over her left shoulder, her olive skin a soft resting place for the glinting beauty of an old diamond necklace that had belonged to her grandmother. No earrings, no bracelet but on the first finger of her left hand the gold ring that Julio had given her. He must not be entirely absent from the occasion. Before she left the room she phoned Captain Manzano to ask him, as she had already done twice today, whether he had any information about Julio. He had not but he reassured her by emphasising the time it would take to get a message up to the mountains where Julio was held. It would also take some time, once he was released, to get down the rough track to San Felipe. "Yes, of course, captain. I'm sorry for troubling you so much," she said before putting down the receiver. No, she must not worry so much. All will be well and all manner of things will be well, she repeated to herself like a mantra. On an impulse before she left the room she went to her jewel box and fished out a gold chain she had bought in London. Somehow or other when no one was watching she would hang it around her father's neck and tell him that it would keep him safe for her when they were apart. Now it was time for dinner.

Popong and Ricky were united in demanding their parents' full attention. This often happened when they felt they had been neglected or were going to be left out of something. They were full of questions about their parents' travels and complaints that they were not being taken along. The adults were soon quite occupied in making the boys feel that, taken or not, they were the two people who mattered most in the world. When Popong said crossly that some of his friends were being taken off to Borneo for a holiday with their mother and father, while poor little Popong's parents were setting off by themselves for Europe, Griselda made him sit on her knee and said, "My sweet darling, it won't be long before mummy and daddy will be free to give you plenty of time. Maybe someone else will be president before long." She could never win with that remark because Popong at once replied, "But I want daddy to be president for ever. No one else's daddy can be president."

"I want him to be president for a long time too," said Ricky "But I want him to be with us much much more."

"Well you can't have everything you want in the world," said the First Lady.

"You should be able to if you're the president," said the more worldly-wise Ricky.

In some part of her mind, Conchita thought, she was as infantile as her brothers. She too regretted that her parents' time has been rationed out in small doses so that they had never been a full-time mother and father who only belonged to their children but were parents to forty million other Carolinos. Then the mood of nostalgia for a world that could never be died away and she longed for a future in which she would be just an independent woman. Her relationship with her father might then be better because it would be on the basis of equality. But about her mother she had doubts. Could trust after what had happened to Julio ever be restored between them?

When Popong and Ricky had been sent off and promised kisses as soon as they were settled in bed, Conchita sat with her mother and father in the beautiful circular room that was grand enough to receive important visitors yet small enough to encourage a feeling of intimacy. The President was in a relaxed mood. He looked well and there was no slurring of speech which occurred when he had been subjected to medication. He appeared to be, in every respect, a healthy confident man. In the most matter-of-fact way, he said, "Conchita, darling, your mother and I are deeply sorry for what has happened—aren't we, Griselda?" The First Lady nodded her assent. "And we're going to make it up to you. When we come back we shall announce your engagement and then there will be a grand wedding—that is if you and Julio want it. And by then you will be—

by the way have you received my decree. You haven't mentioned it. The decree making you Governor of Valladolid Province. You and Julio will be so happy in the fine house that goes with it."

Unwilling to account for her silence on the matter, Conchita said, "No daddy. I haven't seen it yet."

"Damn it. The time the messenger service takes to get papers around. Well now you know the news, what do you think of it? A sort of wedding present in advance, eh?"

Conchita kissed her father and said, "But I hope you're not going to announce the appointment publicly until Julio is back. I can't face interviews just now. I know," she added brightly, "The announcement can be your first public act when you get back home. I'd love that."

He agreed and Conchita was relieved, even though she experienced a slight feeling of guilt. Even Griselda seemed to participate in the President's pleasure at the proposed arrangement but soon she went off to kiss goodnight to Popong and Ricky. This gave Conchita the chance to put the gold chain around her father's neck and to say, "And this is my award to you, the most loving man in my life."

"So far," the President said with a laugh. "I wouldn't want to upstage your Julio. But what is this chain for? It's got a little amulet attached to it with a sign. Oh, the ankh. Do you want me to look like a hippie dear?"

"It's the symbol of enduring life, daddy."

"Then I shall treasure it, for life has always been good to me, especially in giving me you, Conchita."

The President left to see the boys as soon as Griselda returned, now in a lachrymose mood, dabbing her eyes with a handkerchief and saying she hoped that frequent separation from their parents would not have an adverse effect on her darlings later in life. Conchita assured her that all would be well because the children knew they were well loved. "If there's love," she asserted, "All sorts of difficulties can be overcome."

Her mother's reply was a non-committal, "Yes, that's very true," but she clearly did not wish to discuss the profundities of love and its effect on humanity in general with Conchita. Indeed her manner was evasive. More chatter about the children was intended to keep her daughter at bay. At the same time it seemed to Conchita that her mother's manner was subdued. Was she smarting under a setback other than the proposed engagement to Julio, perhaps something she had been told by the President? For despite the appearance of absolute concord between her parents Conchita knew that her father sometimes made unilateral decisions that were set in stone by the time Griselda was told of them. Her own appointment as a governor might have been such an instance but maybe there was another matter, something involving her mother directly. Since power was the order of the game Conchita immediately thought of the succession. Griselda's remark to Popong suggested that the same issue was on her mind. Therefore she asked directly, "Mummy did you really mean what you said at dinner—about daddy giving up the presidency, about your wanting to have more time for your children?"

The First Lady sat regally on her chair, her back admirably straight, her head thrown back just slightly, her hands resting together in her lap, a pose ready for a portrait painter. She said with the voice of an expert, "With children you have to say all sorts of things. Their moods come and go. They forget easily."

Conchita wondered whether she fitted into the same category as her little brothers to be so manipulated and deceived, but she only said. "Do they really? Are you sure of that, mother? I seem to remember you telling me about things you didn't like when you were small. The rain on the corrugated iron roof of your mother's home for instance. Hardly forgotten."

Griselda's voice rose a few degrees and she stared angrily when she replied. "I was fifteen then and aware of injustice." She sat back and looked more benignly at her daughter, "But you will learn when you have children of your own, my dear."

"Then I hope it will be soon mummy. Julio and I would like to have two children, two and no more, as an example to our countrymen. And we we'll give them all the attention they need."

"That will give a good example to the country people if you go to your province or wherever it is you intend to live."

The words 'if you go' made Conchita certain that her mother was fishing. It also struck her that a servant might have observed the sorting out of letters and clothes going on in her room and told her mother. But two could fish. Her next question could not have

FREDERICK LEES

been more direct. "You haven't the slightest intention of giving up power, have you, mummy dear, have you?"

The First Lady's eyebrows rose a shade higher, The slightly disdainful look that she had mastered to turn men into stone like the Gorgan passed over her face, as if she was thinking, 'what an idiot question,' but she asked, "What evidence have you for saying that? My power, such as it is, depends on the President. If he goes I go, naturally."

Conchita stood up and walked across to the black marble fireplace which was occupied by a vast bunch of flaming canna lilies—one of her mother's artistic ideas and turned suddenly, "Only partly true, mother. Yes if my father stepped down, he would take you with him. But supposing anything were to happen to him—sickness, assassination. You have given thought to that, I know. You fear that someone like Bersamina would seize power. After all, he is in charge of the forces and I can't see him wanting to restore the old constitution or keeping any of us on in this palace. That's why you have been building up a huge mass following with your patronage in various parts of Infanta. You could wave a wand and a great mob of people would appear in the middle of this city. I didn't realise what you were doing until Julio explained it all to me. Why have you been doing that? It's pretty clear that you've created a weapon that could be used in an emergency."

The First Lady remained seated but stared at her daughter in a way that suggested admiration. She said, "You're cleverer than I thought, and so is Julio it seems. Perhaps you should both be made governors. As for me, I can't win. On the one hand I'm accused of wanting only luxury and power and to hell with the common people. Now I'm accused of getting the masses to love me because of the help I give them. But has it never struck you, Conchita, that maybe we would need my 'mob' as you call it to defend Antonio should he be the victim of a *coup d'état* by the minister whose name you just mentioned or by some military upstart? I would lay down my life to preserve my husband's work and his legacy. I believe in him and I love him deeply. Maybe my attempt to get rid of Julio was ill judged, but my motivation was the preservation of the Floresco régime. Forgive me if I thought of that more than of your happiness."

259

Conchita was disconcerted. Perhaps her mother understood the meaning of loyalty more than she did. Yet wouldn't she do anything in the world to protect Julio? Was her behavior any different from Griselda's? A truce seemed to have been established between mother and daughter, but it could deteriorate if either of them made a wrong move or said the wrong thing. Conchita did not want her father to be a witness of such a situation. Soon after he returned from the children's nursery she professed fatigue and said that her parents must get a good sleep before leaving. She kissed her father and held him close for a little while and then did the same with her mother yet it was then that she felt most near to tears and she whispered into Griselda's ear "I do love you mummy; I do, I do."

The President watched Conchita leave the room with his eyes full of admiration. "She looks so beautiful tonight," he said. "I feel so proud of her."

The First Lady replied, "She is beautiful indeed; not pretty but she has an inner beauty which I should have recognised long ago. I wonder if you realise how much she takes after you, Antonio. If she was ten years older she would be the person to take over from you."

The President looked surprised. "You really think so? You of all people, after your quarrels with her?"

"Yes I do. Conchita and I have crossed swords and we'll go on doing so. But I'm not stupid. I see you in her. Given time she will be the one to be the country's real First Lady, not just a consort like me."

The President embraced his wife. "To me you are no consort. We are as one, Griselda. I don't want to hear you denigrating yourself ever again. Well now, to bed; we must be up early."

"Do you want to sleep in your room, Tony?"

"No I'll have a better night's sleep with you. I want to wake up with you beside me. After all, we won't be together in our love-nest for some time."

When they had made love the President fell asleep almost at once, cradled in Griselda's arms. In the half light she still saw him as a young man, passionate, adoring and ambitious. She loved him as in their early days and was proud to be at his side. Yet she knew that the tide of his life was turning. Gently she kissed his forehead once, twice, three times without disturbing him. She too was tired but was unable to get to sleep. It was true, as Conchita had divined, that she was preparing for an emergency, but could she win if it occurred? And was it right for her to prepare for a power struggle on her own when she still had children to care for? 'Why am I doing this?' she asked herself. 'Why am I preparing for action that might deprive me of the presence and the affection of my children?' Without delay the reply came: 'because once at the top you can't find the will to step down.' "I have to, I have to," she whispered to her sleeping husband. "Whether you are with me or not, because I must fulfill your destiny." At last she fell asleep, but when she awoke Antonio's position in her arms had hardly changed and the first thought that came into her head was again 'I have to, I have to'.

She got up carefully, went to her dressing room and ordered breakfast over the phone. She did not disturb her husband. Let him sleep a bit longer. The days ahead would be heavy, the schedules wearying. Only when there was a knock at the door did she stroke his head, saying, "Wake up Tony, my love. Wake up my dearest. Today we are leaving the Carolines."

It had been decided that they would say goodbye to their three children in the DeoGracias before moving to the airport by helicopter. As was customary, the President inspected a guard of honour on the tarmac before making the usual diplomatic farewells. Then his party walked towards the airliner, the last to take off of three Boeing 747s, of which two were bearing a large entourage of officials and businessmen to Europe.

Since television cameras were there to record the scene, it was arranged that near the boarding steps there should be an apparently informal crowd of adoring supporters cheering the President on his way. There the First Lady, when throwing a dazzling smile at all around for the crowd to reflect back to the cameras, suddenly noticed a face that was not reflecting love at all. Amidst the sycophants, distinct from them by his silvery hair but more so by the fury in his face, was the head of Cesar Abulencia. For an instant the thought of assassination came into her head and she moved briskly to shield her husband, but instead of a bullet came the single word, "Tyrant," though it went almost unheard in the surrounding applause. She looked again. There was no sign of Cesar. Had she imagined it? At the top of the steps both of them turned to wave before the door was closed. She looked again further away. There, near the terminal building, stood Cesar Abulencia, his fist raised in anger. Why had he come to shout like that, to threaten like that? A horrid wave arose in her mind, co-mingling Cesar, Julio, Conchita, the President and herself. The door closed but not on her fears.

As the plane circled over Infanta she looked at the receding city. Down there was a man who hated her and all she stood for. Was his hatred grounded in something deeper than the kidnapping of his nephew? His anger seemed palpable even inside the plane. Yet her husband had felt none of it and was chatting away with a member of the cabin crew who had come to see him. He looked confident and serene while she was just being foolish. Cesar could do her no harm. She would make amends to him over Julio. When the boy was released his anger would abate. Feeling more calm, she retired to her cabin, changed into a dressing gown and put on a video film, one of her favourites, Garbo in *Queen Christina*.

Yet *Queen Christina* left her with the ineluctable conclusion that the destiny of the great is invariably shot through with tragedy. Far from remaining calm, her misgivings had returned several fold; details of things left undone flooded back, not to mention fragments of things she should have noticed more carefully. Why, for instance, only last night had Conchita been sorting out her correspondence, and examining all her clothes? That was what a maid had reported. She pondered uselessly for her questions had grown out of hand and at length she asked the radio operator to put her through to Prime Minister Loyola, who would surely be in his office by now.

"Oh Senora, what a pleasant surprise. I didn't expect to speak with you so soon. Is the flight going well?"

"The fight is excellent, Senor Loyola. Just two things: would you kindly check on the palace to see that Conchita is alright. She was a little upset when we left. Please do that while we are still connected. Your secretary will do it for you. We'll talk while they are checking."

Loyola thought the request a bit odd and considered that Conchita might think it odder, but no one knew what tensions existed in the DeoGracias. He quickly asked his secretary to enquire whether Conchita would like to dine with him that evening. He suggested the French restaurant in the Infanta Hotel. The First Lady heard what he had said and commented, "That was a good way of doing it, Bienvenido; she loves the Infanta. But the main reason I've phoned you is to find out what Cesar Abulencia is up to. He was at the airport, looking daggers at me. I thought he looked rather mad. Can you find out? Just to set my mind at ease. I don't want trouble from the Abulencias while we are away."

"But Senorita, it isn't so surprising in view of what's happened, is it?"

"In view of what's happened?" The First lady's voice was filled with alarm "What has happened, Prime Minister?"

Loyola flinched at her tones. Surely the DeoGracias had been told by Bersamina about the money demand by Diasanta for Julio's release. He gave her the score and quailed mentally when her barrage started up. Eventually her anger was directed not at Cesar but at Bersamina, who had shamefully and deliberately failed to keep her informed. Loyola dared not say that it was just possible that Bersamina had left the matter in the Defence Ministry's hands, as he must have been busy preparing for his own departure, on the second Boeing. Then a secretary put a note on the table. It was signed by Captain Manzano. Loyola swallowed. How could he tell the First Lady this? His voice was thin when he began to speak. "Senorita, I am in contact with the Defence Ministry. I'll do my best to effect Julio's release. But..." his voice trailed away.

"Come Loyola; what are you butting about?"

"Your daughter, Senorita Conchita. She isn't there."

"You mean she's gone out?"

"No, Excellency, she has left altogether. Captain Manzano has checked her rooms. She's left with most of her clothes. Manzano believes Senor Abulencia may have told her about his visit from Diasanta. But he's only speculating."

Loyola held his breath for the volcano to explode, but it remained dormant until a steely voice flowed slowly into his ear, like a sliver of molten lava, "We've not gone an hour and there's a mess already. Find out where my daughter has gone. Do not contact the President directly. Keep in contact with me alone. Do you understand?" Before Loyola could say a word he was cut off.

It was a misfortune that the radio operator on board the President's plane was not as discreet as a clam but a man in the employ of the Defence Ministry, and so it was hardly a few minutes before Bersamina, in the second Boeing, was being given an account of the First Lady's conversation with Loyola. Radio operators not being particularly precise where mere words are concerned, the information reached his ears in a somewhat garbled form, though with certain points standing out; first that orders had been given by Senora Floresco that all communication between the Prime Minister and the plane was to be through her exclusively, with no reference to the President. Second that Loyola was now in charge of the Defence Ministry and third that the First Lady had broken all contacts with Cesar Abulencia, with whom she was apparently furious This put Bersamina in a frenzy, though outwardly he kept his calm. Maybe some leak in Jasper Frankfurter's office in Washington had given a hint to the First Lady that there was a dangerous plot against the President. On that account Bersamina imagined that Griselda was already dispositioning her supporters to foil his ploy for the presidential office. The radio officer was told to keep Bersamina informed of all the First Lady's phone communications but, unfortunately again, her second phone call added to his suspicions. She asked the leader of her People's Action Brigades, Senor Ricardo Rarang, to drill some ten thousand of his followers for a large scale rally which must take place in the centre of Infanta when she returned from Europe. It was in fact to be a sort of triumph for the President but the First Lady did not make that clear. Bersamina again interpreted it as a preparation for a coup if he himself made a bid for power. In a state of panic he cursed the fact that he was isolated on a plane, unable to do a thing. He knew then that the President must have insisted on him going to Europe because he was a suspect. The only light that he could see in a very dark tunnel was that the First Lady had broken with the Abulencias and in consequence with their alliance of liberals and democrats, both of which were potential allies of his constitutional cause. Was there anyone on the plane in whom he could confide? He asked the Chief Steward for a passenger manifest and ran his eyes down it. Incompetent military brass, information personnel, social liaison officers and a host of useless nonentities who would enjoy the bars and night-clubs of the cities to be visited. But one name attracted his eye, Max Bligh, who was to supervise the schedule of visits in Rome, a man he needed to contact. No reason why he should not do so here and now. He asked a stewardess to invite Mr Bligh from the business class seat to the first class bar provided for Ministers. There they chatted of this and that, about the film made by Hilary Arbuthnot, their visit to San Felipe and the sad kidnapping of Julio Abulencia, on the basis of which Cesar had made his accusation against the Florescos. "Have you kept the tape with you, as I suggested?" Bersamina asked, to which Bligh readily replied that indeed he had. "Then hold on to it," was the sharp reply. "Now Max, I think I'll take a nap. I'm very tired and you don't look so fresh yourself. Sleep makes time flow swiftly. By the way, your control in Rome will be a Signor Ghiberti. Don't forget the name and help him when he asks you for information."

The Chief of the Army General Staff and the Head of the National Police Force had been taken aback by the emergence of Prime Minister Loyola as acting Minister for Defence. They had imagined that, with Bersamina gone, they would carry on as if he were present, taking as before most of the decisions themselves in full confidence that in due course they would receive his approval. The Chief of Staff, Mario Untalan, was a handsome, slightly built man remarkable for his velvety skin which gave him a youthful appearance. He had, at the age of forty five, an iron will, was unafraid to act harshly and enjoyed his reputation for ruthlessness, for which reason Bersamina had promoted him rapidly in his service. The Head of the Police Force, Epifanio de la Torre, a large, imposing man with a grand moustache, had similar strong qualities but was reputed to be more cautious, fearing that precipitous police action could sometimes rebound on the force's reputation.

Summoned to the Prime Minister's Office these two distinguished men sat before him like a couple of school prefects called to account for the dereliction of their duties. They had just reported on the way in which the security forces had sometimes used Oscar Diasanta and his Thugs to implement state policies without undue public observation when they heard their new boss expostulate with, "You are actually telling me that this gang is used by officers of your ministry to kidnap private citizens, and that when an officer has paid the gang to release one of their prisoners they are told that he cannot be released unless more money is paid to them. Now isn't that a strange way to run a civilised country?"

The two men glanced at one another uncertainly. They had never encountered the erstwhile Finance Minister before and if asked would have described him as a distant technocrat to be opposed when he tried to impose unwelcome spending constraints on their departments. They saw before them a totally different person, a man of authority acting in deference to no-one.

Nevertheless, Chief of Staff Untalan did say, a little hesitantly, "Well sir, it will seem odd I know but it's the result of using Diasanta in unofficial counter-subversive operations. It always has to appear that his men are in no way our responsibility."

Loyola now looked directly at Epifanio de la Torre, as though he was the one who had spoken. "By unofficial, do you may mean taking illegal, often inhuman measures against peasants who are suspected of helping the communists?"

Epifanio, already flushed, began to splutter out, "But we were always acting under instructions sir, Minister Bersamina…"

"Of course, of course. You acted under instructions. No doubt you would have set up gas chambers if so ordered." Loyola wondered at his own boldness. Was it because he was irritated at being left in the hot seat or had he wanted all the time when in government to put forward his liberal ideas and now had the opportunity to do so? Yet he was not reckless. What he intended was to give an example of how government in the Carolines should be conducted. After all hadn't the President expressed confidence in him and promised to back up whatever he did? He tapped his fingers tips together like a school master resolving a case of indiscipline. "Well now," he said. "Here are my instructions. You are to take action to arrest Oscar Diasanta and his gang forthwith. Of course an opportunity must be given to Cesar Abulencia to hand over the money. But once Julio Abulencia is safe and free, the whole rotten gang must be taken. If they resist, and I believe they will resist, you will know what to do. A word of caution to both of you; Cesar Abulencia must not be told of this. It might frighten him off from his very difficult task."

"Are we to prepare charges against Oscar Diasanta and the gang?" Epifanio thought this would be a wise precaution to give the impression subsequently of legality if none of the gang were to survive.

"I think that would be politic," replied Loyola. "Thank you, gentlemen. You have plenty to do." The two big guys, slightly reduced in stature, but now certain who was the boss, saluted and left. Loyola sat back with a feeling of satisfaction. Had he carried out a *coup d'état* single-handed? Could it be that dominant males sometimes longed for an iron hand? Perhaps things were not going to be so difficult. With a decided feeling of being in charge he ordered a secretary to contact Senor Abulencia. Within a few minutes he was put through. "Cesar," he said gently. "Please tell me. Have you been able to raise the money? Before you answer let me say how deplorable the whole matter is. As Prime Minister I shall do everything to help you."

Cesar replied in an equally courteous way, "Thank you, Prime Minister. I have raised the money. It will be handed over tonight."

Loyola took another step on his own bat. "You will be reimbursed from state funds as soon as possible. You should not have to meet this demand from your own resources. It is the duty of government to protect its people from such depredations."

Cesar gasped, not because of any comfort he derived from Loyola's words but because he sensed that the Prime Minister was no mere lackey. "I'm most grateful to you, Senor Loyola. As you can imagine my main concern is that everything should go smoothly. With a lunatic like Diasanta the unpredictable could happen. I shall do my best to ensure that you are kept fully in the picture."

"Please do so, Senor. Well that's it—no; by the way, I hear that you were at the airport this morning. I spoke to the First Lady a little after take-off. She seems to have been put out by something you said."

"No, not said," replied Cesar, "shouted. Did she tell you what I shouted?"

"Not exactly, Cesar."

"Tyrants! That's what I bellowed. Just like a student."

"But why?"

"To let off steam I guess. Just a gesture. I felt like doing it."

"Be careful in future, Cesar. Gestures can sometimes turn out to be costly."

In a way Cesar regretted his childish actions at the airport. Trouble had made him more reflective but he had not always curbed his emotional behavior. Sometimes he saw himself through the eyes of a future historian, or rather an ancient Roman annalist: 'When the dictator was leaving the capital, Cesar hurled the word 'Tyrant' at him.' Such outbursts were meaningful it seemed in ancient times, now they could just look silly. Yet sometimes he could hold his counsel. He had not uttered a word about Conchita who was sound asleep in Julio's bedroom.

He had smiled at her ingenuity for even he had been taken in by her disguise. Knowing that the Abulencia house was watched, she had cut off her hair, made a little strip of it into a moustache, stuck it on with glue and put on a baggy shirt and worn jeans, so that she looked like a thousand other Infanta street vagabonds when she turned up at the servants' door. He had felt very warm towards her and said that Julio's room was hers as long as she wanted it. She kissed him and said, "Maybe it will be for ever, Uncle Cesar."

Her determination to accompany him when he went to San Felipe with the ransom worried him exceedingly, but she was adamant. She and Julio must leave the Carolines as soon as possible. They had long decided that they wanted to live an ordinary life in a country that made normal living possible. This meant France, where Julio had many friends. All the basics they required were in her case; passports, money and some jewellery. From San Felipe they would easily get to a small coastal town and pay a fisherman to take them to the Philippines or to Borneo, where they could get a plane for Europe. Although Cesar had requested Loyola to ensure that his journey with the money would not suffer interference, he still felt the need for secrecy, so when they left the Abulencia house he sat in the back seat with Conchita lying under a rug near his feet. Both of them were nervous but not as much as Alberto, Cesar's driver, who would be the one to get out of the car with the money for Diasanta.

"Switch on the radio," said Cesar, thinking that a little light music might cheer them all up at such a time. After a few Caroline love songs, the grandeur of organ music, a Bach toccata, flooded into the car and an announcer said in a subdued and reverend voice that the programme was being brought to them by Blenheim Cigarettes. The music at length ended on an awesome resolved chord and coughs and shuffling could be heard until suddenly the incisive voice of Cardinal Peccata boomed from his pulpit in Infanta Cathedral: "For we wrestle not against flesh and blood, but against principalities, against powers, against the rulers of the darkness of this world, against spiritual wickedness in high places." Soon he was inveighing not against spiritual abstractions but quite openly against Antonio and Griselda Floresco with greater vehemence than Cesar had heard from him before. "What a mockery, what an insult to Holy Mother Church, that at the very time when our President is visiting Rome, the See of Saint Peter, when he will have an audience with the Holy Father, that one of our priests is to be tried here in this city for the crime of working on behalf of the people, our poor and afflicted people. Yes my friends, it is true. The day after the President has had an audience with the Holy Father, this blasphemous trial will begin. Wherefore let us take on the whole armour of God that our beloved friend Father Oliveros may be able to withstand in the evil day and having done all, to stand."

There followed a total silence of about ten seconds after which more music started; this time Saint-Saens' *Carnival of the Animals*. "At least," Conchita, now sitting beside Cesar, said, "Someone in the station has a sense of humour."

Cesar was relieved that no reference had been made by the Cardinal to his accusation of kidnapping against the Florescos, nor did he ever want the words 'The rape of Julio' to be aired. What mad ideas might it not suggest to Diasanta's thugs if they heard it? Even though he was sure that Radio Ecclesia had made the tape available to the Cardinal Peccata, he felt equally sure that such a wily man would use it with discretion. He said, "You know, Conchita, I am an atheist. I think the Catholic Church is one of the great misfortunes of this country. What an irony that your father's régime should have driven people like me to support Cardinal Peccata."

"Life is full of ironies," said Conchita coolly. "My father annoying the Church, which helped him in his bid for power. Julio and me falling for one another and bringing a plague on both our houses. Oh, I am fortune's fool, Cesar." She sighed and then, to change the subject, asked Cesar if he knew anything about the priest Oliveros soon to be tried.

"No, not much. He probably has been helping the communists. Many of the Liberation theology priests do that. His mission school for boys is somewhere near San Felipe. By the way I don't want you to enrol there but it's important that you should remain a boy. A lot of people don't like your family around here."

Conchita looked through the window down towards the silver strip of coastline and then over the sea, at the edge of which a remote sun was floating on the horizon like a magic boat. It was a strange sunset; no fire about it. Just a red half disc surrounded by greyness as it drowned in the motionless waves. She shuddered in the coldness of the air-conditioned car. It was as though they were travelling in some land far to the north. The dark trees lining the road must be pines; maybe wolves were following them with their sharp eyes as they sped on. Cesar pressed a button and the window went down with a bored sigh. Friendly warm air flowed in, smelling sweet, and mingled with the odour of burnt charcoal. All at once the land seemed less hostile. Surely all would be well. Julio would be with her soon. "How silly of me," she said turning to Cesar. "I haven't asked you what the plan is. Where do we wait when Alberto takes the ransom up the road?"

"I thought the most neutral place would be the house of the Parish priest. I don't know him but I believe he is an Australian. Some friends of mine came here recently and said he is a sympathetic person."

Conchita wondered what 'sympathetic' might mean—to whom or to what? But she made no comment, merely asking, "Does he know that we are coming?"

"Oh no. We'll just call on him. At this time on a Sunday he'll probably be in his Church. Priest's houses are always open. We'll just wait there."

"Will you explain why we are here?"

"I think I'll have to give him the basic facts. They will be public soon enough. I'm sure he'll respect our confidence." Cesar looked at Conchita. "That moustache is askew. It's most suspicious. Take it off. Just look like a pretty boy. But keep in the background."

It happened that Father Stephens was at home. A new priest, Father Nepomuck was saying mass, after which there was to be what the new man with new ideas was holding—a Clergy-People Interface, which in Father Stephens' old-fashioned English meant a public meeting. He had decided that he and the new priest were not on the same wavelength and that the people must adapt to their new spiritual guide as best they could. However, Stephens was not alone when a grey Bentley drew up on the roadside some distance away from his house. With him on the verandah was Salvador, who had been sent down to San Felipe by his commander on an espionage mission.

Stephens was irritated by the very idea of visitors, whose distinguished car suggested they might be affluent people from Infanta. It had been some time since he had seen Salvador. In fact he thought that they might not meet again. Salvador had been shocked to learn that his lover would soon be leaving the Carolines. He was unable to believe it and kept on insisting, "No. No. It isn't the end. We are meant to be together." He was still insisting when, in the half light, he saw two men walking towards the house.

The car had been turned around and immediately driven off. It was clear that whoever these visitors were they would not be leaving quickly. Salvador whispered, "Frank, I'd better get out of the way. We don't know who they are." He kissed his lover and said he would wait in the kitchen and get something to eat from Lourdes. Stephens called after him, "Stay with Lourdes. She'll want to talk to you. I'll be with you when the coast is clear."

The visitors entered by the verandah door. The elderly, aristocratic gentleman looked familiar—a photo in a newspaper maybe? The boy could be anyone. As soon as Cesar introduced himself there was no need to ask why the distinguished head of the Abulencia family had arrived. Stephens knew he was the uncle of the young man who had been kidnapped, according to the radio news, and who, according to local rumour, had been seen with his captors in the vicinity of San Felipe.

Cesar said, "Father I know I am taking a liberty but I am sure you won't mind it. You may have heard…"

"About your nephew?"

Cesar nodded. "He's being held somewhere in the mountains, not far away."

"Please accept my sympathy," said Stephens wondering in what way he might be able to help. "Do you know who is holding him? The radio claims they are the communists." His eyes sparkled a little when he spoke the last words, which he did not believe in the least.

"Yes, so the radio says," replied Cesar catching the expression on the priest's face. "But neither you nor I believe everything the radio says nowadays, do we?" he glanced towards the end of the verandah where Conchita was sitting and wondered whether the priest might think a boy so young and slim might be his catamite. "Well I've been in contact with the kidnappers. No, they're not communists. No doubt you've heard of a man called Diasanta who has a gang in the mountains."

"Everyone in San Felipe has heard of them. In some cases only too well. So they're the ones." Stephens had grown curious. "It's said that they sometimes operate with the connivance of the Government. Is that so?"

"I think it better if I say nothing other than that I have arranged to pay a large sum of money to Diasanta. That's why my car went off after we arrived."

"Will it bring your nephew back?" Stephens asked dubiously.

"I don't think so. My driver should be given information on where he can be found and when. At least I hope so." He paused and asked politely, "Father, may we wait here until the car returns. I don't want to go into San Felipe. Any publicity could be dangerous."

"Of course. Of course," said Stephens wishing he had the nerve to say, 'Look here, Senor. I'm sorry for you but I'm not a priest any more. My lover is in the kitchen; oh, by the way he's a communist guerrilla and we both want to make love because I am about to be pushed out of the country and it's unlikely that we'll ever meet again. So would you mind taking your problems and your boy elsewhere. There's a little hotel in the town where you could both find a nice room.' Instead, sensing the risks in the situation, he explained that, as he was no longer the incumbent priest, Cesar would have to explain what was afoot to Father Nepomuck who would be back home shortly. In the meantime he would go to the kitchen and try to drum up some refreshments for everyone. This would not please old Lourdes who had all but given up residence in the house, since she strongly disapproved of Father Nepomuck who, she considered, had no idea of how a priest should behave. He treated her as though she was his sister and an equal, which she knew she was not. As to his nasal voice it set her nerves on edge like someone scraping chalk on a blackboard. Cesar, sensing some household difficulty, said that he and the boy would just take a beer and Stephens went off to the kitchen.

He found the room empty. No sign of Lourdes at all. Then he heard Salvador's voice from beyond the open back door. He went out and found his lover smoking a cigarette with the remnants of one of Lourdes' delicious meals beside him but the old lady had gone off. "Who are they?" Salvador asked. "Will they be here long?"

"People from Infanta. They're here about that kidnapped man, Julio Abulencia. He's in the hands of the Diasanta gang. The visitor is ransoming him for a large sum, so he said. He and his boyfriend have to wait for their car to come back." But Stephens had little concern for his visitors when his own lover was right before him. "Look Salvador, do you have to go back? You can sleep here for the night."

"Where?"

"In my room of course."

"What about the new priest?"

"I'll make up some tale. We'll make love quietly. Anyway I don't care."

Salvador stood and clasped Stephens to his body. They stood in silence for a while hugging and kissing and almost unable to stop themselves from going further, but abruptly Salvador burst out, "I want to stay but I can't. Orders. It's dangerous to disobey orders. But I'll come back in two days' time. I think I can make it. No, I promise to make it. Oh Frank, Frank, I don't want to lose you. Take me with you to Australia."

"What about Rosalinda?" Stephens' heart was leaping but he felt he must ask that.

"She's sleeping with my commander. The leaders often take the women they want. Anyway I know she enjoys him more than me. I've heard them at it. Frank, I'm not happy. It's you I love. Take me to Australia."

Stephens' mind was now alight with hope. Yes, it was possible. Of course there were always immigration problems, but Salvador could be enrolled as a student. And if Australia was difficult, they could always try England where he had heard the border controls were ludicrous. He looked into Salvador's eyes and saw only bewilderment and grief. "Yes, Salvador I promise. I'll take you to hell if you want me. With you it would be heaven. I'll make some arrangements. Go back to your unit. We'll meet here in two days' time at nightfall and then get away."

As he made his way through the darkness, Salvador had conflicting feelings. Of triumph that he had accomplished his mission, and of joy that he saw the possibility of escaping with his lover. As his commander had suspected that Julio Abulencia was held in the district, Salvador had been ordered to find out if anyone in San Felipe knew anything on the score. He had only expected to hear rumours but now, quite accidentally, he had learned that not only was the suspicion true but a lot of money was involved. The commander could work out how to get his hands on it. Diasanta's camp must be taken by surprise; the money would probably be there. As to Julio Abulencia, he should be released before the attack was made. Salvador reckoned that when all was said and done he would not find it difficult to get away from the guerrillas. Rosalinda had shown her preference for the commander, whose lust for her was insatiable, whereas once he had made love to her Salvador always found himself regretting his real passion and she knew it. He was sure the lubricious girl would rather stay with her ardent lover than return to her parents. As to the commander, he would be glad to have a risky situation off his hands, for he could not believe that any Carolino could bear his wife being screwed by another man under the eyes of their comrades. Salvador had not revealed these considerations to Stephens for now they seemed trivial to him. He was no longer any Carolino but a man obsessed with a yearning to get far away with the lover with whom he had found happiness.

It took over three hours to return to the guerrilla camp and tell his story. Someone corroborated it because a big grey car had been seen going up and down the track from San Felipe. He was asked several times how much money was being handed over but all he could say was that it must be a large sum. The commander asserted that the money would come in very useful at the present time when supplies were running low. He and two of his officers then consulted on their own but soon came back to tell their nine young guerrillas, two of whom were women, that they must make straight for Diasanta's hideout, the precise location of which was known. Their attack would be sudden and the object was to seize some money, which they could assume would have been brought back to Diasanta's lair by the time they pounced. The comrades were then informed by the commander that they would be able to take the thugs' camp by surprise because up to the present there had been a tacit agreement between their side and Diasanta's that neither should attack the other's camps. Salvador could not see why this was so but a more experienced comrade whispered to him that if each side were to attack the other, with their intimate knowledge of the mountains and forests, they would inflict far more casualties than the government, even with its helicopters, could ever do. Salvador was glad that this agreement was about to be broken for he did not like the way Diasanta's men persecuted the peasants unremittingly. Before they broke camp the commander reminded them that if Abulencia was found he must not be harmed. They must rebut the government accusation that the Party was a kidnapper.

They moved rapidly through the high forest. Salvador could still marvel at the skill of two comrades who seemed to recognise trees, rocks and hidden features known only to them as well as if they were on their own farmland. Sometimes the way led along a stream, other times the course they had taken lacked even the hint of a jungle track. The two experts were quick to whisper whether an animal of some sort had recently passed by. Otherwise no one spoke. Each man moved with the stealth of a cat. Despite his fatigue Salvador was exhilarated. It was like a childhood game of cops and robbers. For sure they would seize the Diasanta camp. Their enemies would flee, leaving the booty, and he hoped poor Julio. When a comrade's life was like this even those dreary sessions on Marxism did not matter.

At length just as a streak of red was in the eastern sky they emerged on to a cliff edge. They moved cautiously along for it was precipitous below. Above them rose trees that burst from among giant boulders invested with unusually tall ferns. They turned again into the forest. There was a smell of smoke, a camp fire maybe. Salvador paused to glance ahead; a few long huts were nestling amidst strange humps of earth, like monsters at rest. There was no sign of a guard but they were cautious. He heard the commander say, "There's something peculiar here. Keep back. Maybe it's a trap. Maybe they got wind of us coming." He beckoned Salvador towards him. Turning to the other men he said, "Spread out on this side of the camp. Salvador and I will go in." He added just loud enough for Salvador to hear, "Let's protect each other for Rosalinda's sake."

Salvador was proud that he had been chosen. He admired the commander for not sending the others in first and followed him with his gun at the ready, rushing quickly from boulder to boulder until they were among the low thatched huts. Between two of them a fire had been kicked out but it still smouldered There was something sinister that he did not like. Perhaps the loud pounding of his heart might awaken the enemy.

They crept towards the first hut and went in stealthily. It was empty except for a few mattresses and empty boxes. They tried another and yet another. Salvador went out of the last hut by a back entrance. He then heard a strange sound, an animal maybe. The sound of whimpering. He hissed to the commander to follow him. There was a small hut in front of them, more solidly built than the others of stout planks, a lock-up perhaps but the door was ajar. The noise came again. It was human whimpering and moaning. The commander went in quickly with Salvador behind him. They could see nothing but heard the sound again from somewhere on the ground. The commander shone a flashlight downwards. Salvador let out a cry. Below them lay a naked young man, his legs spread out, his loins and his thighs spattered with blood. Salvador felt his knees trembling. He sank down beside his commander and had to look. The man's testicles had been neatly severed and lay there between his legs like fallen fruit. Some powerful secateurs lay nearby. Salvador knew at once that it was Julio Abulencia.

"We've got to get out," said the commander not bothering to keep his voice down.

"We can't leave him like this," said Salvador looking around for some cloth to staunch the blood.

The commander was on his feet pulling on Salvador's shoulders.

"Get up. Get up. We can't have anything to do with this, Salvador. Think of Rosalinda. Do you hear?"

Before Salvador could reply there was a burst of gunfire from outside. The commander was on the floor again. "It's a trick. They've trapped us, comrade. Ah, poor Rosalinda."

There was more firing and a female scream. Someone had been hit. Salvador was filled with terror and crouched as low as he could, trying to control his fear. He thought of Stephens and wished that he was back in those protecting arms. Then he took a grip on himself. Picking up a discarded shirt from the floor, he rolled it into a ball and pressed it between Julio's thighs with his left hand. With his right hand he caressed the poor boy's head trying to give some him some comfort if he was still conscious.

The barrage was now intense and the shrill cries were horrible. Their comrades were surely suffering. The commander switched off his torch and took up position with his gun near the door and as he pushed it open a vertical slit of morning light slanted across the inside of the hut. All at once bullets sliced into some of the planks. Again the commander shouted the name of Rosalinda and then fell backwards with not another cry. A neat hole was in the centre of his forehead. In the half-light he looked like a mythical creature with three eyes.

Then the shooting stopped, there was the sound of men running and orders shouted. The door burst open under heavy blows. Soldiers charged in. One of them aimed a kick at Salvador's head, sending him sprawling across the earthen floor. He yelled, "Seize the bastard. Take the little shit. Get him outside. My God look at this. The Abulencia boy. He's had his balls chopped off."

Salvador refused to say who he was or what he was until the lieutenant in charge told his men to make him speak. They twisted and beat him and his screams echoed and re echoed among the rocks and trees, until they were muffled by the angry roar of a descending helicopter that scattered leaves and branches all over the place.

Silence descended when a colonel emerged from the aircraft. He at once required a report from the lieutenant in charge, who took him to see what had been done to Julio Abulencia and then said, "Very strange. Two of Diasanta's thugs were still inside the lock-up. The rest had got away as we ordered. But no sign of money. We've searched. One of the thugs was killed in the firefight. The young one is taken prisoner. We completely surprised the communists. Four of them were killed. The rest, including two women, are wounded."

The colonel replied, "Make sure the report is correct when you write that all of the communists were killed resisting arrest. Rats are best dead."

As the colonel was about to board the helicopter carrying Julio back to Infanta one of the soldiers who had been beating Salvador came up and said, "Sir, the man who was holding Julio's head is not a Diasanta thug. He's just confessed to being a communist and so was the dead man with him."

"So," said the Colonel, "We got it right after all. Julio Abulencia was kidnapped by the communists and one of them castrated him." Just then single shots rang out as the wounded comrades began to be finished off one by one. The Colonel shouted, "Don't kill the one who cut off Julio's balls; we'll need him for evidence—and the secateurs. And Lieutenant, when you're aboard see that the testicles are safe in the medical icebox."

The meeting with the President of Italy had been cordial and brief. Presents had been exchanged and expressions of friendship recorded. Griselda had chatted with the President's wife somewhat longer than the schedule permitted, but apart from that all had gone well. The two First Ladies had then gone off to visit a college for handicapped girls while the Caroline President had been conducted to his apartment in another part of the Quirinale for an exchange of views requested by the Italian Foreign Minister.

The President glanced sideways through the long balcony windows into the great square, where people were sauntering about or sitting around the fountain of the Dioscuri, talking animatedly and taking photographs. He wished he was down among them, wandering anonymously around Rome as he had once done as a small boy in the days when il Duce was at large and Italy seemed more important than it was now.

Count del Boca began a *tour d'horizon* of world affairs. He sounded like one of those superannuated actors who got Italian aristocratic parts in the romantic films the Americans used to make about Italy. He had probably become Italy's Foreign Minster because his English was adequate but the President found the 'e' sounds added to words like *internationale* or the 'a' on *cultura* irritating. Whatever the man said did not matter. This was a ritual that had to be performed.

Count Tarquinio del Boca might well have agreed with him. He often wondered whether his Ministry was necessary at all. Everyone who came to Italy seemed to be interested in things other than the Italian view of world affairs—Italian design, Italian fashion, Italian automobiles, Italian food, not to mention the Holy Father in a part of Italy that independently held the strongest views on the global activities of mankind. However the Count had a certain reputation as an historian and a philosopher, which he himself took very seriously. Most politicians were, in his view, decidedly ignorant and the very least he could do was to inculcate in them his unique sense of history, even if this meant making observations on the leaders of other countries that were far from diplomatic.

"The *problema* of Europa, *Eccellenza,* is that we are an island of profound *cultura* between, how shall I describe them, *due* European *sub cultura*. We are as Attica to Macedonia. Signor, you raise your eyebrows yet *evidentemente* the United States is a European *sub cultura*. Despite its wealth and technology it is only a higher barbarism, *molto barbarico*. And Russia the same: formerly all over that great country there were estates and fine houses, the patrimony of cultivated families who exercised the same civilising influence as the English gentry or the Italian *nobilità*. Now the Russian countryside has relapsed into barbarism. The leaders of all the Russias are sons of peasants, money grabbing peasants with no taste. Just like this American President Souris. Mon dieu, a mouse. The grandson of a Greek peasant. Since the time of Virgil we Italians have always distrusted the Greeks."

"But Greece is the source of..." interrupted the bored Carolino, thinking it time he should say something and in any case he liked the idea of Greece.

Count del Boca threw up his expressive hands. "The modern Greek," he shrilled, "is not a Greek in your sense. Most of them by blood are Slavs, descended from the Vlachs who came into

Europe in the middle ages, and Slav which equals slave, at best a peasant. Ah, you can see the peril of our continent, besieged outside by powerful barbarians and inside threatened by a growing fifth column of its own peasants."

The President found the conversation interesting if unusual. "A fifth column of Slavs?" he asked. "I don't understand. Most Europeans are not Slavonic. Where is this mighty fifth column coming from? Serbia maybe?"

Count del Boca sat back in his magnificently ornamented chair and looked at the President as though he was a simpleton. "*Niente affato*, not in the least. Don't you understand the threat coming from within?" he demanded explosively after which he proceeded to declare in a most undiplomatic way, with his arms gesticulating, "Why from pop music, pop culture, pop art, heavy metal, rap, conceptual art, collages of preserved shit, all sorts of mindless rubbish. We are buffeted by a dangerous rabble of ignorant bawling *ragazzi* who believe that anything they think or do is better than what is sacred in Europe, its traditional culture, its art, its music, its thought. Signor, surely you must see where the fifth column is coming from. I didn't say it is Slavonic by race. We have engendered it ourselves and it is getting stronger with immigrants from all over the world."

The President was no longer bored. He recalled that Count del Boca had once been Italian Ambassador to the Vatican, so he said, "Signor, I suppose the Holy See must agree with your interpretation of these cultural matters."

The Count's expression grew dark and his voice fell very low, as though he believed that some Monsignor with extraordinary powers of hearing might be listening across the Tiber. "This present Bishop of Rome," he said, making a disparaging gesture with his hands, "is a terrible mistake. In the Curia they are absolutely distracted; *si, assolutamente distratto*. He does not understand what is happening in the world out there—where you come from."

The President leaned forward to hear better. "In what ways?" he asked full of curiosity.

Count del Boca was at the ready. "In what ways?" he repeated thoughtfully. "Why now, what is your biggest problem in the Carolines? Too many people. Even if your economic development was three times as fast as it is now, your people are not going to enjoy a better life. I tell you, signor, the position of many countries in the Third World, and I include your country, is already hopeless. In half a century you will all be living like rats. There will no longer be space in which living things can live as they should. And by living things I don't just mean mankind: I mean animals, forests, plants, everything except insects I guess. Yet what does this Pope do? The Church is opposed to abortion; I understand that. But against birth control. Pah—the sanctity of human life, *'basta*. What the Church is doing is to desanctify human life, to degrade humanity. And why? To increase its numbers, for numbers mean political power, especially if the numbers are kept in ignorance because there are no resources to educate them properly. The Holy Father has given up on Europe, though he would like to see a Christian Europe with himself as its spiritual head. No. Too late for that now. He knows that Europeans know too much about science and the universe to be taken in any longer. So the Church concentrates on the poor third world countries like the Carolines, where people still proliferate like animals even though there isn't enough land and soon not enough water. That is the problem of your country, Signor *Presidente* but I've no doubt you will say nothing of this to His Holiness at your audience. You will be impressed by the gravity, the dignity and the kindness of the Holy Father; you'll genuflect and think how marvellous it all is, and like the rest of us in the end you'll succumb to the last echo of the Caesars."

Precisely at that moment a large clock, in the form of a rotating globe with two pensive youths atop, mellifluously chimed eleven o'clock. The interview was over and Count Del Boca took his leave. The President was sorry to see him go; he would never see him again for sure. Such a man could not survive as Foreign Minister for long and his impact while in office would most likely be nothing. The fatuity of so much human effort depressed the President. In one of the gilded mirrors that lined his apartment he saw himself looking distinctly old and very small amidst the gargantuan furniture. It was as though he had strayed into a place that had been designed for people much larger and no doubt cleverer than himself or the Italian President or indeed anyone he had so far encountered in the Quirinale, with the exception maybe of il Conte Tarquinio del

Boca. Yet it was a fact that the men of today were somewhat larger than those of past times. Did they in the past have a requirement for space which people lacked in these later days or were they trying to recapture the immensity of ages further back—the Renaissance or the grandeur of Augustus. He walked about the room examining furniture, pictures, tapestries, but ever and again he caught sight of himself in one of the mirrors, which did not reflect clearly like those of today but imparted a soft yellow light to everything within them, including himself. Whether he was in this room or its strange reflection, what was he but a transitory thing like a wasp that buzzed about for a while only to be brushed up, leaving the stately room to brood on its own again. The antique objects within the room would stay as beautiful as the day on which they were made but he would not be even a memory. The picture of a swarthy shepherd, as brown as a Carolino but more muscular, dallying in a wood with some olive skinned nymphs caught his eye. He could not make out the painter's name but there was a date, MDCLXVI on the frame, not a Renaissance painting but one of a less hopeful, more stylised age. There was something artificial about the poses of the figures but the artist had achieved an effect of languid voluptuousness, which said that nothing had any significance apart from these moments of wanton joy. The shepherd would make love to the nymphs without tiring if no one was looking, but they would all resume their poses whenever someone else entered the room. The mirrors would see, the room would know, but visitors from outside like himself would be excluded forever from the sensual frolics. He and thousands of others, when they looked at the picture, would imagine that they themselves had some deeper purpose in life than what was depicted in this scene of frivolous pleasure, not knowing their own achievements were more illusory. All they would accomplish would be their own decline towards oblivion and the significance of the shepherd's eternal desire would have passed them by.

His dark mood had driven from his mind all thought of doing some preparatory work for the interview he was giving later in the day to a British television personality, the mordant Hereward Knight, whose sarcastic questions and disrespectful manner unsettled most of the eminent people who had the temerity to occupy the hot-seat in his program. The President was not fazed, however. He would play it off the cuff. An old fox had no need to rehearse new tricks. He had cancelled lunch alone with the First Lady so that her sortie with the wife of the Italian President might be open ended. He had observed that Italians were as bad as Carolinos at keeping to schedules. He was quite certain that by now his wife would have persuaded the Italian First Lady to go with her to some fashion house or jeweller down the Corso, where she could spend the State's money, in dollar denominations of course. As he was going to be free for a couple of hours, he called his schedule assistant, Mr Max Bligh, and told him that for the next two to three hours he would be resting or reading on his own. Bligh said sympathetically that the President did indeed look a little tired and hoped he would get a good rest. At midday, when his unknown contact Ghiberti phoned, Max said that the President would not be visible until the interview with Hereward Knight at six in the evening. The President meanwhile was in his bedroom planning how to be free if only for a short time entirely on his own. Just as he was changing into less formal clothes, his temporary ADC, Captain Agapito, knocked at the door and entered with being asked. The tall, surpassingly handsome young officer, whose head, the President had already concluded, was stuffed with straw said clearly and slowly as if each word had to be chiselled from his fine mouth, "These despatches are sent by hand from the Caroline Embassy to your Excellency residing in the Quirinale Palace. They are marked *urgente*." The President, who was only thinking of his escape to freedom, told him to put the despatches on a table and said there would be no reply for the present, after which the Apollo withdrew.

There would be no trouble getting out. The President had observed in his dressing room a door, fortunately not locked, leading out to a wrought iron spiral staircase curving down, he presumed to street level. It must have been constructed to allow easy and discreet access for nocturnal visitors to persons of eminence in need of more than spiritual comfort. He guessed however that the palace security might be more on the lookout for intruders than for anyone wishing to break out, so to deal with the problem of his return he left a note on the coffee table saying, 'I have gone for a walk and will return in the mid afternoon. Please inform the Palace Guards accordingly.' Of course the Palace

Security would be annoyed but he did not care a damn. He went to the dressing room, put on a raincoat and a hat and went down the spiral staircase quietly, though there was no-one about at all. At the bottom of the stairwell was a small ante-room with a bolted door in one wall. It could not have been more considerate. The bolt slid back easily; he opened the door and was in a long narrow street into which the warm Italian sun barely penetrated. He went some way along it until he came across a larger road, which he guessed must lead in the direction of the Via Nazionale, with which he was quite familiar.

To begin with he had walked briskly, but once away from the Palace he started to feel pleasantly anonymous. His pace became slower and soon he was sauntering along, stopping to look into shop windows, examining menus or looking at some monument or carving that caught his attention. As he did so he became aware of a quite unaccustomed feeling of exhilaration. Just for a short while, just once more in his lifetime, no one knew where he was or what he was doing. He took his hat off and stuffed it into his raincoat pocket; then he took off his coat and carried it over his arm, for the street was warming up and full of afternoon light. When the sun's rays fell on his bare arm he felt all at once that he was released from captivity by a touch of infinite power, though of the briefest duration. Yet what was the difference in the life of the universe between this radiant instant and a man's lifetime? Both were mere specks of time and within one of those specks he had suddenly achieved the freedom he now possessed, and its passing beauty was as marvellous as his life's totality. He dismissed the time, a couple of hours ahead, when he must return and resume his normal life, for he wished that this walk in the streets of Rome could go on forever. Yet if his mind was in flight his body was earthbound; a twinge of pain had passed across his back and he leaned against a wall, looking up at the façade of a church nearby. The spasm passed and he went on slowly. The pain had reminded him that it was now too late to give up the presidency and live as an ordinary man with his family. Then he admonished himself sternly. It was no good kidding himself. He had gone on working because he did not really want to stop. Just now he was indulging himself and being as romantic as a schoolboy. The freedom you are enjoying is the freedom of stolen fruit, he told himself. That was the truth but even if that was the cause of his joy, the delight was genuine.

At length he walked up the Via Nazionale towards the Baths of Diocletian. The pain came again and he made for a streetside café, where he sat down and ordered a cognac When the waiter came he wondered whether he had any money to pay and felt in his hip pocket. Yes, the wallet was there. Fortunately it had always been one of his quirks to carry around a few large US Dollar bills just in case, he used to say to his family, though this was the first time since he had been President that the 'case' had actually materialised. The waiter was not averse to changing one of the bills into Lira. As he handed over the money the President was aware that a rather overdressed and over-made up young woman was eyeing him. He gave her a smile and the next minute she came over and sat at his table saying, "You are Japanese, signor?"

"Yes I am," he replied. "How did you know?"

"Ah, I like the Japanese men very much; so gentle, so generous."

"Really," replied the President with some surprise, as he had never found the Japanese particularly gentle and they were generous only when they wanted something. The waiter was hoverin,g so he asked, "Please, signorina, what would you like to drink?"

"Campari," she said and he ordered the drink. "Do you like Campari, signor?"

He raised his cognac to her and took a sip. "I think Campari is a horrible drink, signorina, but all other Italian things I find beautiful."

She gave a little laugh. "You find me beautiful then?"

"Of course."

"And will you come back with me?"

Without hesitation he repeated, "Of course."

She gestured to a yellow Fiat parked near the kerb "Just a few more minutes signor, then we go. Let us finish our drinks slowly."

He watched her taking her time over her Campari. It seemed strange that she wanted to delay, for her gestures were restless. She took a sip and glanced around; she adjusted her broad brimmed white hat that made her look as though she was going to a garden party and she fidgeted in her chair, turning around to look at something in the road so that her full breasts stretched her thin pale blue dress, which was maybe a bit too small, almost to breaking point. The effect of this on the President was to arouse his desire, while making him certain that the experience would probably be disappointing. Their conversation had all but ceased, whether because of her lack of English or because, the arrangement having been made, words were no longer necessary. Well that suits me, he thought harshly. A quick fuck to end my afternoon sortie and then back to the Quirinale.

She finished her drink and gave a sigh. It put the President off a little; it suggested 'ah well, let's get it over'. But almost at once she threw him a warm smile and took hold of his hand. "Forgive me, signor. My name is Anna Ghisloli, from Sardinia. And your name, signor?"

He gave a Japanese half bow, a grin and a slight hiss. "Watanabe, Seiji Watanabe, from Kyoto."

A delighted cry came from her broad and very scarlet lips. "Kyoto! *O-chikazuki ni nareté ureshii désu.* I am glad to have made your acquaintance. But I cannot speak much more Japanese than that. Excuse me. *Sumimasen.* My greatest friend lives in Kyoto. Perhaps you would visit him for me. Come, we'll talk about it as we go." The President thought, oh God. I'm getting into hot water, but he did say *"Arigato,"* in thanks with another little bow. To his surprise she paid the bill, remarking softly that the waiter had underpaid the value of the exchanged dollar. Then, all enthusiasm, she led the President to her car, talking animatedly. "Yes and you can give him a present from me and tell him how much I miss him. Will you do that for me?" The President was about to say 'of course' again, when something made him start. They were passing a newspaper kiosk, beside which a stack of newly delivered papers was on a table. He didn't have to know much Italian to understand the headlines: *"Rivolutione violente in Infanta"*

He opened the door for Anna to get in the car. Then he bought a newspaper, sat beside her and looked at the front page. He could not read much of the text but beside the photograph of himself there were photos naming four people: Cardinal Peccata, Julio Abulencia, Conchita and Father Oliveros. A word in heavy print was adjacent to Julio's picture—*Castrato.* He turned to Anna who was staring at him and the photographs alternately. "Read this," he ordered. "What does it say?"

"So you are not Japanese. You lie to me."

"Translate this sentence. Please," he shouted angrily.

"It say that this young man—he is the friend of the daughter of *il presidente*. Your daughter, eh? She is pretty. It say that this young man, oh *mama mia*, he is castrate. They cut off his testicles, *orribile, tremendo*."

The President cupped his face in his hands. He heard himself moaning Conchita's name. He felt, mingled with his grief, a terrible rage against his wife. "I should have stopped that woman. I should have stopped her long ago," he cried.

He felt Anna's hand pulling gently on his arm. "*Presidente*, there are people watching. I think you are recognised. Where shall I take you?"

There was indeed a crowd on the pavement, growing in size and about to move around the car. He could catch the words, "*Il presidente*. Carolinas," and noticed a policeman talking on his mobile excitedly. "Take me to the Quirinale. Quickly. Please Anna." The next instant she was off, driving as only an Italian in a hurry can drive. He heard a wail of police sirens and a traffic policeman came up abreast signalling and shouting to Anna. She said, "We must follow him. To the Quirinale." Another motorbike joined the first traffic policeman and then a police car and more bikes came up behind them. By the time they all whirled into the great space in front of the Quirinale the impromptu motorcade had brought the President's secret trip into Rome to a very public end.

Before he got out the President pulled out all the dollar bills from his wallet and put them in the car, more than enough for a trip to Kyoto. "Here, signorina. I apologise for not being Japanese." He stared at her. She looked different. Long black hair was flowing down her shoulder. Her eyes were full of tears. She didn't look like a prostitute any more and she was very beautiful. "Your hat," he said, wondering why for a moment a hat should be more important than a revolution in his own country. "Your white hat. Where's is it?"

"It fly away. No matter *il mio presidente*." She took his hand and kissed it. "I pray for your good fortune."

"Everyone is waiting for you in your apartment," said handsome ADC Agapito, who had suddenly materialised. He asked apologetically, "That urgent envelope I left on your desk, Excellency. You didn't read it. I have it here. Perhaps you should look at it before you meet your wife and your officials." The President took the envelope, thankful that Agapito was not as wooden as he looked and said he would join everyone when he came out of the bathroom.

Loyola's despatch made it clear that a revolution had not taken place in Infanta—at least not yet. There had been widespread street demonstrations as a result of Cardinal Peccata's inflammatory revelation that Oliveros was to be put on trial. These had been joined by left wing supporters. Then some Army officers off their own bat had released the news that the kidnapped Julio Abulencia had been castrated by the communists before his liberation by soldiers. This had led to confused riots, in which the President's partisans and the First Lady's People's Action Brigades had come on the streets and started to beat up people suspected of being communist supporters. A number of atrocious killings had taken place in the centre of Infanta. The situation had become extremely confused; chaos rather than revolution reigned. In an effort to restore order Loyola had issued a Presidential pardon for Father Oliveros, who, following his release from gaol, had returned to San Felipe after issuing an appeal for calm. A dusk to dawn curfew had been imposed in the capital and the surrounding countryside and all public assemblies forbidden. It was in the national interest that the President's tour be brought to an end as speedily as possible. Loyola thought he could keep the situation under control until the President's return. Almost as an afterthought Loyola had said that he had not been able to track down Conchita, who had fled the Palace.

The President washed his face and hands, straightened his tie, combed his hair and daubed himself liberally with expensive Italian eau de toilette. Then he breathed deeply a few times in order to appear calm and collected. At what point had Anna lost her white hat? She must have opened the window to hear the traffic policeman and the breeze had taken it away. No matter, she looked much better without it. He looked down to make sure that his shoes were clean. Then he read the despatch over again, folded it neatly and put it in his pocket. Of one thing he was absolutely certain: the communists had not perpetrated the atrocity. They could be cruel but only with a purpose and this act served them in no way. Then he asked himself fiercely yet impartially: could Griselda have been ultimately responsible for the horror. No, she was ambitious, wilful and sometimes spiteful, but incapable of such cruelty. The truth lay elsewhere and must be ascertained quickly. But at this stage of events he would not countenance any offer of Bersamina to precede him to Infanta. Loyola must be unequivocally in charge until he and Griselda were back in the DeoGracias.

An argument was going on in his reception room, the protagonists being Bersamina and Griselda who was stating, "Not my responsibility. Not mine at all." However, like the attendant ministers and officials who had gathered there, they fell silent when they saw the President. He sat down, somewhat apart from them all in an armchair, whence he surveyed them calmly and quizzically like a sergeant facing a platoon after some breach of discipline. "Will you all sit," he said. "I see I did the right thing to go for a walk by myself to think things over in peace." Everyone did as they were told, though it was clear that some were showing their allegiance by sitting near to his wife or to Bersamina. "Well now," he said taking out a cigarette and lighting it with slow deliberation. "I take it that you've done your homework and studied Loyola's excellently clear despatch. Oh, I assume you were given copies." Temporary information officer Max Bligh said that such was not the case, though everyone had heard conflicting reports of the troubles in Infanta. "Oh, then you had better read it to everyone," said the President, putting Loyola's despatch into the hands of Bligh. He at once read it in a loud and clear voice, following which all present exchanged whispered comments while Bligh quietly told the President of his alarm when he had been unable to find him that afternoon. The President chuckled and gave a whispered assurance that it would not happen again.

To give the impression that all was well he went for a few minutes to speak to Griselda, asking how her visit to the school had been and whether she had later gone shopping. She was glad of his attention but her manner showed that she was rattled and suspicious of everyone, perhaps even of him. As soon as he had returned to his seat Bersamina coughed to attract attention and said, "Excellency I think I may have been the cause of the slight altercation which you may have heard when you came in. I was not saying that anyone here was responsible for the terrible thing that has happened to Julio Abulencia. I was saying that I did not believe that the communists were responsible for the deed, despite what the Army has said. I merely observed that the public may find out that Julio was in the hands of a group that had followed the directions of Colonel Manzano in the DeoGracias; a group that my own Ministry has used in the past, as well you know. I was insisting that an act of gross indiscipline must have occurred. The group's leader Diasanta is unpredictable. His hatred of communism had sometimes made him behave very badly but he has been useful to us."

The First Lady stood up and said, "Those indeed were your words, Signor Bersamina, or rather some of them, but I remember you referring to Manzano as my intelligence officer. I am not involved in intelligence activities at all. They are the responsibility of the Defence Ministry. I will not be connected through Manzano with what has happened to Julio Abulencia. That is what you were trying to do, Signor Bersamina."

The President then began to speak slowly and gently, like a psychologist settling with profound understanding the differences and the alarms of people infinitely less intelligent than himself. "You know," he said confidentially, "When you've been at the helm as long as I have you begin to develop certain reflexes; that is to say, you develop them if you have survived. One of the main secrets of being a statesman is to keep on course. Sudden squalls may come but you have to keep on course. Like a yachtsman however I have also learned to trim my sails to the wind. The object of our tour has been to show the world that the Carolines has a responsible government, that we believe in the rule of law, and that in the long run we want our country to develop as a democratic state, part of the free world. I shall remind the world that our Constitution is an American designed one and that we all admire the American way of life. I know that initially the arrest and trial of this Father Oliveros was intended to show that, though a Catholic country, we are also a country in which no one is above the law. The fact that Loyola has issued a Presidential pardon in my name to Oliveros need not be seen as a setback for us. The situation demanded it. Now we shall represent that pardon as an act of mercy and a sincere attempt to effect reconciliation between all the opposing factions in our society. Within the rule of law I shall emphasise that mercy has pride of place. Later I am giving an interview to Hereward Knight, a man renowned for his rudeness and his biting questions. Well, I shall level with him. I will admit to everything that is wrong in our country. I will admit to the criticisms directed at us, warts and all. And I want the lot of you, in all your contacts here in Italy, to follow my lead. Keep your heads high. And after I have seen His Holiness tomorrow we shall return to Infanta where I am sure Loyola will represent what our tour has achieved as a triumph. As to the harm done to Julio Abulencia, we shall deplore it. I incline to agree with Minister Bersamina that it was the result of some gross act of indiscipline. Perhaps however his Ministry should have restricted the use made of Diasanta. Certainly my wife is guiltless in this matter. We shall promise the world that the guilty men will be found out and punished without quarter, because we live under the rule of law."

Confidence had been restored. There had been among the whole crew an obscure feeling that the ship was holed if not sinking, but the captain's manner had reassured everyone sufficiently for them to go about their business, except for one person. The President's last words had convinced Bersamina that when the chips were down his master's entire support would be given to Griselda. Complete reliance had also been expressed in Loyola, even though he had countermanded the President's earlier instructions. And what about those damning words that he, Bersamina, should have restricted the use his Ministry had made of Diasanta? He could not help thinking that everything had been worked out by the Florescos to stand in the path of his ambitions even before they had all left Infanta. His fury might have boiled over into some intemperate act or words had he not taken refuge in the thought that, however admiringly the President might have spoken about the American constitution and the American way of life, Jasper Frankfurter in the State Department would not return the complement in regard to the Florescos. He wanted the embarrassing dictator out of the way. And if that was Jasper's point of view it could not be doubted that President Souris would be of like mind. In fact the die was already cast. Bersamina had sedulously avoided making contact with Max Bligh while they had been in Rome, but having considered the conflicting passions raging in Infanta it suddenly struck him that the accusatory tape of Cesar Abulencia might soon be used to advantage. As they were all walking to their dismal rooms in the lower part of the Quirinale, he tapped Bligh on the shoulder and said, in case anyone was listening, "Oh Bligh, I have that book you wanted to borrow on the Taiping Rebellion." Once the two of them were in his room he asked, "Have you been in contact with Ghiberti each day?"

"Of course Signor Bersamina, but today regretfully I had to tell him that I did not know where the President had got to. He took it calmly enough." At this point Max Bligh noticed that Bersamina was not taking anything calmly at all. His face was flushed, he seemed to be stooping as if under an invisible weight and a nervous tick which was always in his eyes had intensified. The Minister had been frustrated by something which had happened at the meeting. Not the argument with Griselda; he could hold his own with her. Bligh could only think of the President's last words in support of his wife but somewhat critical of the Minister. Strangely enough, despite his varied careers in espionage, it was only then that Bligh suspected that something dangerous was being hatched by Bersamina. Why had he been told by the Minister to keep the mysterious contact Ghiberti informed about the President's movements? He could only think of one reason and it filled him with alarm. He wanted no part in some act that might be traced back to him if it were to misfire.

Bersamina asked, "Have you got that tape with you? The one ending with Cesar Abulencia's attack on the Florescos?"

"Yes, Signor Bersamina."

"When Ghiberti contacts you please give it to him. Tell him it might be useful."

Bligh could only wonder in what way? But he said, "How can I, Signor? I never see him and he made it clear there must be no contact". Then he blurted out, to his immediate regret, "I don't want to see him either."

Bersamina glared at Bligh, who obviously suspected something. Perhaps this informer, who was clearly a self-seeking rogue, was a weak link who posed a risk to the plot. He asked smoothly, "Where is the tape now, Mr Bligh?"

"In my room, Minister."

"Bring it to me straightaway. And say nothing to anyone. Continue to keep Ghiberti aware of the President's timetable. Tell him I have something for him when he phones you." Bersamina hesitated and then said, "Mr Bligh, your service to me is very much appreciated. You will not regret it."

Max Bligh did as he was told but he was worried. The kind words from Bersamina suggested danger. Under the current régime in Infanta, if the stakes were high no one could be sure of his personal safety. Bligh had by now concluded that the stakes were indeed high. He had heard of people having unexplained accidents in the Carolines, so why not here? Having delivered the tape to Bersamina with an obsequious smile he hurried to the Finance Officer accompanying the President's tour party, drew a cheque as an advance on his allowance, saying it was for some expensive jewellery he was buying for his wife and waited in his room for Ghiberti's usual call. It was not delayed, but as soon as he had provided the anonymous voice with the precise time of the President's audience with the Holy Father, and the information that Minister Bersamina had something to give him, he left the Quirinale for the Fiamucino Airport and vanished from a scene which had become too dangerous for a man like him.

Within the hour Ghiberti telephoned Bersamina and said, "Regarding the something you wish to give me, Minister, please give it to the ADC who has been seconded to your President. He is to be depended upon." Bersamina put the tape in his pocket, certain that he would sooner or later encounter the handsome ADC who was on duty with the presidential party.

The First Lady might have been convincing in her rejection of any responsibility for Julio's fate when arguing publicly with Bersamina but in her own mind her conviction was far from sure. To the world she always appeared to be a woman of superb self confidence; she had made it her duty to appear so but her inner reality lay nearer to the nervous young woman who had, at an early age, grasped the fact that in a world of men, beauty, sexual allure and determination could go a long way in the battle for success. The young woman within her was still the same, and in the silence of her own bedroom she looked at herself full in the eyes and saw herself with the masque off. Fundamentally she regarded herself as no more than a simple housewife with a family and she knew that she must protect them, particularly her brood of children, with fierce resolve. She had always been confident that in having the support of Antonio she would be supremely safe. Yet now she was racked with fear. She had learned over the years to minister to the President's needs, emotional, sexual and political. She knew what he wanted and she had made it her duty to give it to him. But the disaster of Julio's kidnapping, which she had initiated without imagining the consequences, had infuriated the President. She had found herself in dire straits with the President before over a variety of matters, some political and some social; in fact there had been several quarrels during their life together. She had invariably yielded to his political judgment but had stood firm on social matters, on which he in turn had generally deferred to her. But this matter was totally different She could not contain it in her normal way because the one person whom the President loved, probably more than his own wife, was Conchita. The First Lady saw the real possibility of a total rift with her husband. What if there was a separation and some other woman came into his life? It was not impossible. Her thoughts turned to Conchita and to her two boys. They were her future and she would be a dragon lady to preserve their rights.

She was sure that Antonio would soon come to see her yet she feared that the support he had voiced for her at the meeting could not be relied on. He often took a way opposite to his real intentions. He had learned to do that in politics and so, for the same reason, his upbraiding of Bersamina did not encourage her. She could not make up her mind how to behave when he arrived. To be distraught over Conchita might be seen as an act. To be apologetic over her role in Julio's kidnapping might look insincere and any overdoing of affection for her husband would look too obvious for words. So she dressed simply, and sat quietly reading a book until he arrived.

He came in quite breezily saying how much he had enjoyed his little sortie out in Rome. He obviously wanted her to behave as if nothing untoward had happened. In fact he was excessively casual. "Do you know I've just had a call from the White House, from President Souris himself. He's very anxious to know whether I will support the continuation of the US Navy base in our country. There are arguments about our intentions in the Senate Foreign Relations

Committee. I told him to have no doubts. 'We are your firmest ally, Mr President'."

"And what else did he say, Tony?" asked Griselda relieved at the inconsequentiality of her husband's behavior.

"Oh nothing much. Sent you much love from himself and poor old Minnie. Said she hates living in the White House. And he ended up as usual with, 'Nice to do business with you, Antonio'. My God Griselda. Souris should just have stayed in Minnesota, in real estate management or whatever it was he was doing. And those speeches of his; he brays so loudly you'd think he was giving the Gettysburg address." The President looked wistful and sighed, "No. It's clear that Minnie isn't a happy woman."

Griselda suddenly changed tack. His 'everything is normal' behavior was too much for her. She asked abruptly, "Are you happy with Bersamina? Do you trust him? Why did he try to shift responsibility for Julio onto me? He was trying to discredit me in your eyes, I know it. I hope that's clear to you too."

The President went over to where Griselda was sitting and pulled her to her feet, embracing her closely and looking up into her face for she was somewhat taller than him. "Little Grissie, I know what's worrying you. Of course I don't trust him. In politics trust no-one—unless you have a wife like I have. How can you doubt me? You and I are partners in everything, in love, in success, in power and our enemies would say in crime. So be it. There is no-one but you. Do you know I was picked up by a woman when I went out and if this crisis had not come up I would probably have gone back to her apartment. But I can tell you this, when I was with her—and she was quite beautiful—and if I had been in bed with her, my heart would have been with you. It's the sort of *hombre* I am. Bersamina is no threat to you. If I die, which I have no intention of doing for a long time, the Carolines will be in the hands of Prime Minister Loyola; Peccata will support him. So for that matter will people like Cesar Abulencia, despite the noises he makes. All of them are bastards really, despite what they profess, for they want to keep the status quo. Their way of life depends on it. That's why they'd put you up as their presidential candidate and you would get in. The Florescos are here to stay, Griselda." The President then laughed loudly and added, "if only because we have Uncle Sam rooting for us. Now, my dear, I'm going to prepare for an interview with this British TV man. I suggest that you call everyone together and have them watch the report on our country which will be shown before I appear. And be very nice to Bersamina. He's a bit neurotic and needs some cuddling, which is more than he gets from that wife of his."

The President went off and Griselda told her aides to call the presidential party to her rooms for drinks and a TV viewing. She was all charm to Bersamina and made him sit next to her, emphasising their need to swing together or, and here she joked, at the end of a rope, the world being what it was nowadays. Bersamina responded as best he could, for even now he kept thinking, shall I confess here and now to the First Lady? Shall I tell her to call her husband and let him know why, for the good of the country, I was persuaded by Jasper Frankfurter to betray you? Then he reflected that he did not know how high Jasper Frankfurter's plot, into which he had been drawn, actually went. Was the White House involved or at least in the know? If he foiled something the USA wanted it would be bad for him. He was racked with uncertainty, but when he looked at Griselda, so welcoming, so generous and kind towards him, he instinctively felt sure of one thing—her insincerity. No. Tell no one a thing. Let the river flow as it would.

The attributions in the film to the participation of Schuster, Schuster and Bligh were still there, even though the firm's contract had all but terminated. But the absence in the room of Max Bligh suggested to Bersamina that there must be things in the film unacceptable to the Florescos. And so indeed it was. It started with a variety of shots of the Carolines, showing the beauty of its landscape, its seascape, its mountains and its Spanish architecture and, most attractive of all, of its people. Attractive boys and girls were seen dancing, playing sports and of course singing, so that the whole place looked an idyllic tourists' paradise. No one could question the skill of Hilary Arbuthnot as a director, but interspersed with the catalogue of beauty some disquieting interludes appeared. For instance there was Cesar Abulencia talking about the Spanish inheritance of old families like his own, then of their part in the revolution against Spain. Soon he became more critical, of the Japanese of course but then too of the United States, which country was portrayed as not much better than Japan, for its massacres after the war of independence and for its economic exploitation after the defeat of Japan. Ambiguous remarks followed about the First Lady herself. During these Bersamina observed that Griselda's face stayed as stiff as that of a Japanese heroine in a Kabuki drama. The Opera House in all its magnificence was shown and short extracts from the Marriage of Figaro sung by Caroline artists but this was followed by a breakdown of the enormous costs of construction in a poor economy. Cesar Abulencia was on next, sitting in his well tended garden beside sprays of orchids and saying regretfully, "The régime is corrupt, bankrupt morally, intellectually and spiritually. It is characterised by nepotism and inefficiency." The little audience jeered at this and a voice said, "Well, to judge by his house he's doing pretty well out of it, isn't he." Cesar Abulencia was thus disparaged quite easily, but such could not be said in regard to an Australian priest, Father Francis Stephens, who showed the viewers around his church and his parish and said many kind words in praise of his parishioners and their hard working lives. But eventually his sad, honest face looking out at the millions of viewers said, "The people of my parish, the people of this country suffer terribly from poverty, disease, and the malpractice of government officials. I know that the President, when he first came to power, tried to effect reform, especially of land tenure, but he ran into a wall of corruption. I truly believe that the steam has run out of the régime." As the documentary came to its rather downbeat end it was indicated that it was being simulcast in many countries in Europe and America.

Bersamina said courageously. "Well it could have been worse. Arbuthnot did a good job artistically. He made the country look beautiful and it remains beautiful. If everyone was so poverty stricken how could so many of them be singing and dancing and looking so fit and strong?"

The First Lady agreed as did all others present but she warned, "Anyway, we are going to listen to the President in a little while. He'll comment on the film. Let's see how well he does it." With that she turned again to Bersamina, this time to talk very seriously about the chances of capturing Diasanta, who everyone acknowledged was responsible for the criminal act, even if the mutilation of Julio had been carried out maliciously by one of his thugs. She knew that Bersamina was in contact with his Ministry and that he might be able to discover where Conchita had gone. Her own hunch was that her daughter had probably made for the hilly area where Julio was being held, near to San Felipe. "The very place," she remarked, "where that Australian Father in the film has his parish. Is the little town so attractive? I should go there." Bersamina found it difficult to reply. San Felipe was where his ancestral estate lay and he could have told the First Lady so much about the place, but how could he act as if nothing was likely to add to her distress over Conchita when he knew that the President might be dead within a few hours. He was completely screwed up mentally and regretted ever getting into such an excruciating position. Controlled though he normally was he had all but lost his grip on his own behavior when the President's ADC came in and presented the First Lady with a little ebony box. This turned out to contain a diamond brooch that she and Antonio had both admired in a shop on the Veneto. Since everyone knew that the President often sent gifts like this to his wife there was only mild amusement among the party, but the First Lady was obviously pleased. Bersamina realised that this had quite fortuitously given him a good chance of handing over the Abulencia tape to ADC Agapito. Indeed he had noticed that when speaking to the First Lady the ADC had stolen the odd glance at him. The moment Griselda turned away to show the brooch to a woman friend Bersamina swiftly took the envelope containing the tape from his pocket and handed it to Agapito, who took it without demur. However, Griselda was one of those people who noted every gesture, not to mention any defect in dress or uniform, about her; in fact she claimed that only the Queen of England was better than her at noting such details, and so the next moment she was teasing Bersamina with, "What are we doing Manuel? Exchanging love letters with the ADC? I can see he is very handsome but I never thought you had such tastes." Captain Agapito, who was more cunning than anyone thought, came to the rescue with the words, "No, Signora, I know I am *veramente bello* but *sfortunatamente* it is just information about your expedited flights to Infanta. It must be passed to the Italian Security service." Just then someone turned up the television sound and said, "The President's interview will start in a minute." Bersamina breathed more freely. He was sure the incident would be forgotten.

The interview started off ordinarily enough. Hereward, whose interviewees were always encouraged to call him by his Christian name, began by recalling the last time he and the President had met. An atmosphere of familiarity was at once created; some important decision was mentioned—a consequence, it was implied, of one of Hereward's own suggestions. The viewer was left with the impression that he was one of the select few on the planet who made history and that it was going to be made again today. Gradually the pace quickened. Almost apologetically Hereward began to probe the President with well-documented questions related to some aspect of the documentary. At no point was the overall picture of an attractive country and its people mentioned; instead the questioning concentrated on the allegations made by Cesar: the graft, the corruption, police brutality and accusations of nepotism. The questions were always cleverly phrased and would have unsettled most politicians facing them. Sitting in the semi-darkness, Bersamina's eyes were glued to the screen. He soon sat upright, rapt by the President's astute replies. It was like a game of badminton in which, Bersamina knew, the President excelled. Hereward's shuttlecock was powerfully served and came over at an impossible angle, but slam, back it went and the President was ready for the next volley. Never did he totally rebut any of Hereward's charges but for each one he had a reasonable reply: yes, there was graft but what about the corrupt officials who had been brought to book? Yes, there was military brutality, indeed more than Hereward seemed aware of, but he, the President, had often been amazed at the way in which his armed forces had kept their cool in the face of cruel provocation by the communist guerrillas. And if there had been torture, yes, this was morally wrong but it had only been used to protect people from further outrages against the civilian population. His expression became contrite when he said that, true, his own family was sometimes tainted by nepotism, though not on the scale that occurred in some Third World countries. Moreover those of his family who had profited from government contracts had always been expected to fulfil their obligations honourably, and with a degree of speed which would not have been achieved had the contracting process been transparent. Yes, the Opera House was expensive but look at the pleasure and the education it was providing to the people. His wife should be praised for her work. Towards the strictures of Cesar Abulencia he was charitable, implying that the Abulencia family naturally deplored the passing of the so-called democratic system, from which wealthy families like theirs had profited. As to the remarks of that Australian priest he regretted that such an obviously praiseworthy young man should have been so badly instructed in Australia that he expected circumstances in a Third World country to be on a par with those in New South Wales. Then the President paused and said familiarly, "You know, Hereward, your problem is pretty much the same as that of the Australian priest," To which Hereward, taken aback, replied querulously, "Problem? Problem? What problem?"

The President sat forward with a benign expression on his face and took out his pipe which he proceeded to light in no great hurry. He knew that the cameramen would delight in taking close-ups of the process and that millions would be thinking, well there can't be much harm in an old guy who loves his pipe like that. He leaned further forward and took Hereward's hand, even applying little strokes in its palm. "Your problem, Hereward? Ignorance," he said. "Lack of grass roots experience in a poor country. Very different from your turf in Islington. My daughter Conchita once told me about the place. You see, I do know your background even if you don't understand mine. Cambridge followed by Islington." From now on it was the President who was running the show. He completely disregarded Hereward's interjections. "You see," he said looking straight into the camera "Everything this good man has been asking and saying is true—in its way. But only partly true. To understand the motives of those who make history you need more than figures, graphs and probing questions; you need to possess their experience, which is always much more complicated than even the best TV documentary can show and much deeper than any interviewer can ever possess. To understand the tragic world of leadership you need the insight and the voices of Shakespeare, Racine, Euripides, a mysterious mixture of poetry, reason and suffering. Yet remember, even when you have listened to their voices you do not fully understand, for being greater than you they have given you not explanations but life itself. And you are back at the beginning of your quest."

His last words spoken as ambiguously as the Oracle of Delphi, the President raised his right hand in a gesture that prevented Hereward Knight from interrupting. "Let me end by giving you the reason for all I have done. When the Americans threw out the Spaniards, they promised my people, who had helped them to victory, all the things the Spaniards had denied them: democracy, education, public health, prosperity and independence. But no independence followed, only draconian laws that kept the people in subjection and obliged them to fight back. Well we all know that the Americans are good at dealing with people who don't fit into the American paradise on earth. After all they all but eliminated the Indians from their own land and they kept the blacks at the bottom of society. You must know that the death toll in my country was every bit as terrible as their slaughter in Vietnam. To hold onto the Carolines the American troops massacred a sixth of our people. And having done that and established their economic grip they kindly gave us a constitution modelled on their own, which we all know is singularly free from corruption. That constitution, as intended, fell into the hands of rich families who manipulated it and twisted it so that the ordinary people were still mired in poverty. If the people sometimes organised themselves and managed to elect someone who really wanted to change things that representative would vanish or be bought off so that nothing changed." At this point the President shook is head as though in woe. "You English people, Hereward, have a tradition like us of fighting back. Why even your own namesake, Hereward the Wake centuries ago, fought for freedom against the Norman tyrants. But you also have a tradition of reform, like the great Reform Act, which began to extend voting rights to the people. You see, while I know your history, you do not know mine. No. You do not. You accept the American myth about the democracy they brought to the Carolines. When I came on the scene as a young man who had fought against the Japanese I had to manage a people who had been shaped by centuries of oppression. They were indifferent to the state. They gave their loyalty only to the family. My task was to create a state in which the Caroline people could stand tall. Unless my people are aware of themselves as a nation, their progress is impossible. I have created that awareness." When he fell silent, there was a remarkable burst of applause from the studio staff in which Hereward was obliged to participate. Little tears like pearls glistened at the corners of the President's eyes. Almost apologetically he thanked Hereward for his attention and was rewarded by the great interviewer, as the fade-out music was heard, saying, "Well, you may not agree with everything the President has said but no-one looking at this programme will doubt his sincerity and his honesty. Mr President, I thank you."

The audience in the Presidential apartments clapped briefly and stood to leave. It was apparent that Griselda wanted them out, for throughout the interview her mind had been dwelling not on what her husband was saying—she had heard it all before and he knew how to route any opponent—only Conchita occupied her mind and the suffering that her daughter must be enduring. She longed to be back home, yet tonight there was a state banquet hosted by the Italian President and tomorrow the audience with the Holy Father. She did however take the time to say goodbye gracefully to Bersamina, knowing that his Ministry might hold the key to her daughter's safety. Bersamina referred to the TV interview with the words, "A triumph, Senora. Antonio is a genius when he's under pressure." He bowed and kissed the First Lady's hand before leaving but his head contained a turmoil. The President's observations on the American role in Caroline history would hardly endear him to President Souris and his fundamentalist all-American wife Minnie and still less to Jasper Frankfurter. And therein lay a danger. If Antonio were to be assassinated soon voices would obviously be raised suggesting that he deserved it for biting the hand that fed him. The conspiracy lobby might even suggest United States involvement in the act and there would be people around to believe it. For that reason he thought that he should contact Ghiberti, who he was sure was must be actively involved in Frankfurter's decision to eliminate an unsatisfactory ally. Unfortunately Bersamina had no means of contacting Ghiberti directly but he suspected that the ADC to whom he had passed the tape might have the key. It was not difficult to find Agapito, who was in an anteroom chatting away to a bevy of Caroline and Italian women, looking for all the world like a beautiful flower enjoying the sun's warm radiance. The ADC saw at once that he was wanted and came across to Bersamina, who asked, quietly, "Signor have you still got the tape?"

"No, Signor Bersamina."

"No? Then I assume you have got it to Signor Ghiberti."

"No Signor."

"Then what have you done with it?

"I did as Signor Ghiberti told me. I gave it at once to *un uomo designato*, a designated man I know in Italian Television." Agapito's anxious eyes swept briefly over Bersamina's no less worried features.

It was no good raging at Agapito even though he would have liked to wipe him off the earth. In despair Bersamina feared that whatever was going to happen would happen. He could neither contact Ghiberti nor stop use being made of the tape. His own attempt to get through from his room to the State Department in Washington having failed, he phoned his Ministry and ordered the duty officer somehow or other to beseech Frankfurter to contact him urgently in Rome. Then he told the Quirinale operators to put through any phone call that came for him to his guestroom, because sickness prevented him from attending the State Banquet.

Within a few minutes there was a call, but not from abroad. The First Lady asked most kindly what was wrong and Bersamina said that he had been feeling light headed, which was true. No, he did not need a doctor. He must rest and would Griselda please forgive his absence to the President. "Or rather both Presidents," he added.

The First Lady put down the phone and got on with her preparations for the evening. She must look as glamorous as possible because the eyes of the world would be on Antonio and herself, especially after that interview. She knew his words would have offended the Americans, but she also knew they would appeal to millions of people around the world, especially in Europe. She had been told by Conchita how strong anti-Americanism was in Europe, how people hated the self satisfied assurance of Americans that their country was the best and protected by God, and were sickened by their capacity to take the moral high ground while forgetting the iniquities they had perpetrated. The President had used the knowledge provided him by his daughter to rebut the insidious pressure of Hereward Knight. The First Lady almost radiated her inner satisfaction as she gazed at herself fully made up in the long mirror, while about her were an admiring group of dressers who believed that they must have created a moving work of art to bewitch the world.

The President joined her, kissed her very gently, not wishing to disturb her face, and congratulated her on her wonderful dress, which was in the Caroline national style and of a brilliant whiteness that was enhanced by a diamond necklace which had once, so it was said, sparkled on the neck of a guillotined Bourbon princess. She told him that his interview had been a marvellous success and her encomium was repeated several fold by all who were presented to them before the State Banquet. There the President of Italy, who was at heart a left wing socialist, was effusive in his praise of the President and especially of the way in which he had, like a modern Garibaldi, strengthened the will of his people, after so many years not only of political subservience but of economic slavery. Everyone knew the USA was in his sights when he added that the Italians and the Carolinos had much in common, both having been occupied economically after struggling for freedom. It was not exactly true but what do a few untruths matter at a State banquet, which was a roaring success for both the President and Griselda. The only adverse criticism the First Lady encountered came from the American Ambassador Wilmer P. Queene (Jnr) whose wife Sadie owned the enormous department store, Queenie's, much patronised by her friend Griselda, on Fifth Avenue. "I don't think your husband really respects the way in which my country threw off the colonial yoke in your country," she whispered to Griselda after congratulating her on her dress. "It isn't going to be appreciated in the White House— and a bloody good thing too." The First Lady held her tongue, though feeling pleased that her husband's words had struck hard. Being at heart a simple Carolina she fully agreed with what he had said, which did not prevent her from kissing Sadie on the cheek and breathing the single word, "Darling."

As soon as they had escaped from the public eye the President said he was exhausted and must sleep, but Griselda felt the need for something different, something unusual before the schedule of the next day. Captain Agapito, loquacious and friendly, was still on hand so she asked him to take her to the ancient Forum for a quiet stroll. It was eerie yet beautiful. No one was around and she marvelled at the mystery of the ruins and the memory of imperial Caesars. The full moon did strange things with the shadows of the monuments and the long nosed Etruscan cypresses. For a while neither she nor the graceful Agapito said a word, for they were conscious of the presence of numinous things. Before they left he suddenly took her in his arms, kissed her and talked to her softly, but she allowed him no more. She was grateful to him. After the unbelievable congratulations and the flattery of the State Banquet her walk with him in the brooding Forum had restored her confidence and banished her unease.

If the State banquet had been a triumph it paled before the praise heaped on the Florescos the next day in the international press. Unlike Hereward Knight, the world's journalists commented on the beauty of the Carolines and its people as shown in the documentary, but all of them took to heart the way in which the President had justified his régime in the aftermath of American colonialism and its ill effects. Even left wing papers like the British Guardian expressed admiration for a Third World statesman tweaking the greedy nose of Uncle Sam. As for the First Lady, she achieved almost an apotheosis on the front pages, the favourite portrait of her being in that marvellous dress glinting with diamonds, her hair swept up so regally and smiled upon by the President of Italy and his popular wife. The newspapers were full of Caroline stories, some of them critical of course but always set against the President's acceptance that not everything in his country was perfect. There were a few remarks about the recent kidnapping of a rich Caroline family member but this was hardly touched upon, it being remarked that kidnappings of the wealthy were small beer in Third World countries. Far more was said about Griselda's Opera House and it was marvelled that she should be the flag bearer of Western art in her region of the world. Press interest in the Florescos had grown so enormous that their motorcade from the Quirinale to the Vatican was almost like a modern Roman triumph.

His Holiness greeted them graciously. The President wore a dark suit and the First Lady a very beautiful dress of black Spanish lace, with a delicate mantilla over her head and shoulders. They both genuflected when they were first addressed. In the Papal audience chamber there were only a few very senior Vatican officials, one of whom was Signor Ottavio Liguti, a Monsignor with close knowledge of the Carolines and a spiritual adviser to the First Lady. Gifts were exchanged, the Florescos receiving some ancient books recording early contacts between the Vatican and the Carolines, whilst the Florescos presented two wooden *santos*, images of saints which had been miraculously saved from a fire in one of the oldest churches in Infanta. His Holiness spoke a few words in Spanish but as the Florescos were not well versed in that language the conversation reverted to English, which his Holiness spoke in a heavily accented yet soft voice. However this did not prevent him from expatiating very fulsomely on how much he was gratified that Father Oliveros, a priest of Christ, had been granted a pardon by the President. It augured well for the future of Church and State relations. He also spoke about the need to adhere to Church doctrines in regard to the Sanctity of Life among the faithful Caroline people at a time when sin was besetting the world. Listening to these words the President stared into the Holy Father's gentle eyes. A silent cynical laugh exploded in his brain, as he thought of an ancient, still used cemetery in Infanta, the shelter of many abandoned boys and girls who had already learned to fuck and who fought in packs to survive on what they could forage. It was an outrage for which the Church's perverse teachings were responsible. Little children merely existing amidst the Sanctity of Death.

To the First Lady, His Holiness expressed his appreciation of her charitable work. He said that it demonstrated the love that was in her heart. She replied, "Father I understand what you are saying very deeply because I have loved. I know that God is love and because of that I am certain of heaven." The successor of Saint Peter responded with a smile and a blessing, uttering the words, "Oh, how wonderful, how childlike." When the audience was over, both Florescos felt that the Holy See had done them proud. The only earthly thought on Griselda's mind as they walked along the corridor from the audience chamber was that she must have some slippers made by the man who had created those beautiful Papal shoes. She might even decide on the same scarlet. Soon they were moving slowly down the Scala Regia, and as they reached the portico the President turned to admire the magnificent stairway they had just descended. Then he remarked how fresh the air was after being indoors. The door of his car was opened and the Swiss Guards saluted him. He loosened his tie and stooped a little to get in. There was a loud crack; something had struck his left shoulder and he fell to the ground. He could see nothing clearly; around him people were moving and shouting but the voices got fainter and fainter. He felt a hand touching his head and Griselda was crying, "Antonio, my love, my love." Now her face was beside his, speaking unknown words. Everything was as peaceful as the Forum, dark with shadows on a moonlit night. He murmured, "That white hat. Where did it get to? Where—white hat?" And then he died.

Cesar Abulencia's driver had taken the ransom money to the ninth milestone east of Infanta to hand it over to Oscar Diasanta. He received it with effusive thanks and promised that Julio would be found the next day at the twelfth milestone along the same road. In their anxiety to bring Conchita's agony to an end quickly Father Stephens and Cesar had agreed that she should accompany them to the rendezvous. But there was no sight of Julio, and the three of them returned dispirited and fearful to the priest's house. Cesar found it difficult to believe that Diasanta intended to trick them. Something must have gone wrong with the arrangement, he insisted. Shortly all would be put right; communications, he averred, were difficult in this area. His reassurance fell on deaf ears and no one ate much of the food that Lourdes had prepared for them. Soon they all went onto the cool verandah to watch the television set that had recently been issued to the priest by the diocese.

They had been out of contact with the capital for just two days, not bothering to listen to the radio for the matter of the ransom was paramount in their minds, but now, abruptly, they were appalled by the chaos that had erupted in the city. On the screen reporters were talking of rioting factions, without making it clear what was at stake in this crisis that had seemingly been precipitated by Julio's kidnapping. However, when the screen showed armed troops patrolling the streets, it was apparent that someone was trying to restore order. Who that person was became all too obvious when an announcer said that Senor Bersamina, Minister for Defence, would shortly be making a statement on public security.

"But that's impossible," Conchita stated. "He's in Rome." But the next moment she burst out, "My god what's happened?" There on the screen was the official face of the President surrounded by a black band. It lasted while the National Anthem was played.

Cesar held Conchita in his arms, for she was sobbing. Stephens beckoned them both to sit down beside him. They all knew they had to watch and listen.

Bersamina appeared, looking grave, tired and sorrowful. He stayed silent for a short time as if unsure of what to say. "People of the Carolines," he began. "By now most of you will have heard of the tragic death of our beloved President Antonio Floresco, who was assassinated by a communist just after he had, in a state of grace we can be sure, had an audience with the Holy Father. He died as he had always lived, in the service of our nation and as a faithful son of our Holy Mother Church. May the Lord have mercy on his soul and receive him into eternal rest. All of us will wish to express to his wife, Senora Griselda Floresco, and to his bereaved family our heartfelt sympathy and our love at this hour of loss in which we all share." There was a brief pause in which, despite her grief, Conchita said, scathingly, "Did you notice that? He didn't call mummy the First Lady." Bersamina continued sonorously, "You will wish to know that as soon as this news reached the head of the executive, the Prime Minister the Honourable Bienvenido Loyola, he summoned me to return rapidly in order that the instructions placed in his hands by our departed President might be put immediately into effect. I can assure you therefore that good government will continue." Here Bersamina placed on a table beside him a large and imposing looking document, which he began to read, "'Interim arrangements for the proper governance of the Republic of the Carolines in the event of the demise of President Antonio Floresco.' It will be published in the press tomorrow and the document itself will be open for inspection in the Ceremonial Hall of the National Archives Building. In brief it provides for myself, unworthy though I am of such an honour, to become acting President and to ask the Prime Minister to form a government of national unity, composed of men of goodwill to conduct the affairs of state until such time as the people may choose, though the elective process provided for in our constitution, a successor to the late President." He now looked directly at his invisible audience. "I know that the steps that I am about to take would have the full approval of our late President. I hope therefore that for the sake of national unity, all Carolinos will obey the instructions that I am obliged to give. Now therefore noting that the assassination of our President has been accompanied by riotous assemblies, deliberately timed to coincide with our great loss, and by vicious acts on the part of the communists, such as the crime against a young man who is a member of one of the most illustrious Caroline families…" Conchita stood up with a cry but she heard the rest of the sentence, "I declare a state of national emergency."

Neither Conchita nor Cesar could accept what Bersamina had said. Their anger was reflected in each other's eyes as they stared at one another in disbelief. "That traitor; I feel sure he played a part in what happened. How could he have been ready to come back so quickly after my father's death?" said Conchita. "Why did he come and not my mother?"

Cesar temporised cautiously. "But surely the First Lady will have to stay in Rome. There will be so many things to arrange."

"To arrange?" Conchita was incredulous. "To arrange, Cesar? Power is involved. People at the top don't care a fig about arrangements when power is at stake, I tell you. I am going nowhere near Infanta until I know what has really happened. I don't trust Bersamina at all. He has always wanted power. And remember he controls the army and the police." She walked nervously up and down the veranda, closely regarded by Cesar Abulencia who was struck by her self-control and determination. Suddenly she stopped before Father Stephens. Looking him straight in the eyes she said, "Father, will you help me to find out what has happened to Julio. What is this crime against him that Bersamina spoke of? It's not just the kidnapping. It's something else. Did you notice that he said a young man who is a member of an illustrious Caroline family? 'Is', not 'was'. Bersamina is always a stickler for accuracy. That's what my father says." She paused, clearly considering the matter carefully. "I think it must mean that Julio has been hurt in some way. I must find out. Father, will you help me."

Father Stephens promised he would do his best but stressed that his capacity was limited. But inwardly he thought that maybe it was not so limited. If Salvador came soon as he had promised surely there would be an information path into the jungle and to many contacts. He agreed with Conchita that the situation in Infanta was suspicious. It was all too pat. He also took on board her words about the control Bersamina had in the Defence Ministry, a government department which he believed to be the source of much misery for the people.

Cesar added to everyone's suspicions when he said, "I don't believe that Loyola is part of this. Surely in the event of the President's death, the Prime Minister should have assumed full power. He might go along with Bersamina for the time being; he might have no other choice, but fundamentally Loyola is a democrat and I don't believe Bersamina has anything in mind but his own dictatorship."

They had all been taken up so much by the TV news that they had not noticed the return of Father Nepomuck, who, from the doorway, had heard Bersamina's announcement and witnessed Conchita's distress. It turned out that he was considerably less rigid than Stephens had supposed. His words, spoken in an unusually soft American accent, were helpful and understanding. "Look, Father Stephens," he said, "I've been here long enough to know that you are not popular with the security people at the moment. Don't go into town. Stay here with your guests. I'll go and see what people are saying." With that he was off with the alacrity of a cat, to which animal, Stephens thought, he bore some resemblance.

Worming out the news about Julio was less difficult than Father Nepomuck had anticipated. A curfew had been imposed in San Felipe in the wake of the declaration of an Emergency but it did not apply to soldiers, so whilst the rest of the population was confined to their houses they were the only customers who could visit the town's three little bars where pretty girls, some of them barely in their teens, were on hand to help lusty young men relax after their martial duties. Among them were soldiers who had attacked the Diasanta camp. Wearing clerical garb, Father Nepomuck was immune from the restrictions, or at least he behaved as though he was and apparently the soldiers and police thought likewise.

He went into the noisiest bar, called Lily Mauler's, which was the owner's name rather than a description of what went on inside and it wasn't long before he was able to strike up a conversation with a couple of privates. They were pleased to tell him they had recently been in a successful action and killed several communists. One boy boasted that he had personally killed the guerrillas taken prisoner, shooting them one by one in the head. They were lucky, he said, to have had no more done to them than that. He and his friends really wanted to have fun with them first but he was under orders. All the prisoners, women included, had been finished off, save for one savage little beast, a local boy called Salvador, the communist who had mutilated Julio. The men's account came out higgledy piggledy with last things first and some things not at all. Nepomuck had to ask, "Mutilated? What do you mean?" to which the happy executioner replied, gleefully rather than grimly, "Cut his balls off, Father. So he won't be able to fuck around any more, will he. One guy less for the confessional."

Nepomuck was deeply disturbed but lest the soldiers were telling soldiers' tales he went into another bar, the Golden Cockerel, and from a half-drunk sergeant got the same account, plus the information that Julio had been taken off to hospital in a helicopter and "his balls with him".

"What to you mean?" Father Nepomuck demanded. "His balls with him?"

"Yes, I saw the lieutenant wrap them up and take them to the chopper. He'd been told to put them in the icebox. For evidence when the trial takes place, I guess." The sergeant then leered at him and asked, "Where are you from? You're too young to be a priest. Priests don't visit bars. Are you a reporter or a homo?"

"I'm the new parish priest here, replacing Father Stephens." Father Nepomuck protested. "I'm from Seattle."

"Stephens! He's the communist priest, isn't he?" said the soldier, but having no interest in a reply he rambled on, "I wish I could go to the USA. There's going to be nothing but bloody murder here." Father Nepomuck bought him another beer and got away.

He decided not to return to his new home straightaway. Conchita and Abulencia would have to wait, for he needed to know more. First he must see Lourdes, who had gone home after serving dinner.

He knew she was not as keen on him as she obviously was on Father Stephens but he could see she was honest and he had to ask her, "This Salvador," he said, "Is he really a San Felipe boy?"

Lourdes looked at him in silence for what seemed to the young American a very long time. She was either thinking deeply or she was stupid. At length she said so softly that he had to crane his neck forward, "Father Nepomuck, Lourdes won't be coming back to work for you when Father Stephens has gone but my niece will go to you. She's a good worker. It isn't that I don't like you, but I can't work in that house when Father Stephens is not there." Tears rolled down her parchment like cheeks and Father Nepomuck was moved by the affection that Stephens had inspired in the old lady. She took his hand and went on, "Father I ought not to tell you this, but perhaps it's best for you to know. And maybe you've been told already. Salvador is a San Felipe boy. He is a very good boy I can swear to it. He was the altar boy and he still would be if he had not gone off to the jungle."

"That means he became a communist, doesn't it? Please, Lourdes, I have to know everything so that I can be of help."

"Didn't they tell you about Father Stephens before they sent you here?"

"Not much. They said he is a friend of Father Oliveros, the priest who is to be tried in Infanta. They told me Father Stephens had some problems with the authorities."

"No, about Father Stephens and Salvador. That they are…" Lourdes fell silent in the presence of the cloth, though otherwise the matter had never given her a moment's worry.

Father Nepomuck caught on. He said, "Thank you, Lourdes. I understand. It doesn't bother me. I know that Father Stephens is a wonderful man. I know it because all the people I have met in San Felipe love him. Lourdes, whenever I hear people judging other men's behavior I like to think of the Lord's words, 'Judge not, that thou be not judged'."

Lourdes looked very relieved. Before he left she said, "Well perhaps I could work for a while in your house. If you want me."

Father Nepomuck had the advantage of being new to San Felipe. Also he was an American, so he could profit from its still lingering vestige of colonial awe of the master, a hangover from the old days when Americans were all-powerful and American troops were always coming and going to their military bases, which nowadays were not supposed to exist. In consequence the police and the military had been going out of their way to co-operate with him. The Police willingly provided him with transport to visit the military prison outside the town where he had been told Salvador was in custody.

He was immediately struck by the prison's good order. Shackled prisoners were attending flowerbeds or painting the marker stones bordering the paths brilliantly white. None of the prisoners spoke or looked up. The guards, muscular toughs, wore in addition to their guns short leather whips to inspire fear. The atmosphere was oppressive. But there was no problem in getting to see the camp Commandant, to whom Father Nepomuck said without more ado, "Sir, I want to see prisoner Salvador Alvaraz. He is one of my parishioners."

The Commandant, who seemed no more than a cherub-faced youth, gave a radiant smile and said, in a cultured voice, "He's a communist, you know, and he's committed a crime."

"That's why I want to see him—as his priest. I take it that you are Catholic, sir? Then you should know that the Cardinal has instructed all his priests to care for people who have been led astray by communism." Father Nepomuck returned the Commandant's grin with a smile of his own, as if they were both enjoying a great joke, "It gives us a lot of work you know. Quite a lot of my flock are communist sympathisers."

The officer's eyebrows shot up. What was this place he had been posted to? But his mind was more on political developments in Infanta just now, so he said resignedly, "Of course, Father, you can see him. In fact we have been expecting a clerical visit. But we thought it might be from your predecessor. Perhaps he can't face up to it. Do you know exactly what the prisoner did to Julio Abulencias? You know he's guilty of a disgusting act, don't you? He must be a horrid pervert to do a thing like that."

"I've been told of the accusation but he hasn't been found guilty by a court, has he?"

The Commandant smiled broadly again as if the Father was an idiot. He said, "In fact a military tribunal has sentenced him. Under martial law the army is empowered to judge by tribunal

313

in the field. The President's Decree on Treason makes that clear. The boy is guilty for sure and he will be executed quite soon." The Commandant saw the priest's eyes blazing at him. Like a tourist guide he continued, "You are new to this country, aren't you Father? An American. So you probably know that US forces sometimes behaved harshly in Vietnam. We have the same communist problem here. After all, our men are human beings and we can't always control them when they get their hands on communist terrorists. In fact it's often best to allow our men to let off steam." The Commandant suddenly changed his manner. He had either recalled that the priest was only talking about justice, not making any accusation about the army's behavior or some other unfortunate occurrence was weighing on his mind. To Father Nepomuck's surprise he took to pleading anxiously. "Please don't be surprised if the boy tells you he has been beaten or abused by the guards or some such nonsense. Prisoners often lie about those holding them."

The cell was spotless; indeed the smell of soap and antiseptic convinced Father Nepomuck that it had just been cleaned. Even the cell walls had been painted. There was no window and a single bulb high up on the ceiling lit the place dimly. On the iron frame bed lay a young man clad in shorts. There were bruises on his face and his body but Father Nepomuck could not help noticing how fine were Salvador's features, which despite their hurt seemed strangely serene. But the boy looked exhausted, possibly in pain of some sort and reluctant to move at all. Father Nepomuck gestured to him to remain where he was and sat on the bed beside him. When the door was closed on them by a guard, the priest said, "I am taking over from Father Stephens."

"I know. I've seen you around. How is Frank? Tell him not to worry about me."

"He's well. He's thinking of you a lot—probably most of the time, Salvador."

Salvador darted a quick glance at the new priest. Then he assumed a poker face and said indifferently. "Give him my best wishes."

"Salvador," said Father Nepomuck gently, "I know all about you and Father Stephens. It is your business and his business, not mine.

But I will with absolute honesty take any message you wish to send him and I will deliver it exactly as you tell it to me."

Salvador closed his eyes and turned his head towards the wall. After a pause. he said, "Then tell him that I'll never forget him. Not until the sea runs dry. Tell him I love him very much. Tell him I'm grateful for all the love he has given to me." Salvador's shoulders shook convulsively. "Ah, Father, if only all this had never happened I would have gone away with him to Australia, to the moon, to anywhere he wanted to take me. Father, you'd better hear this from my lips; I'm not going anywhere. They're going to shoot me and there's nothing anyone can do about it."

Father Nepomuck put his arm around Salvador and made him turn towards him. "Open your eyes. Look at me. Are you still a good Catholic?"

"How can I be, Father? I am a communist."

"But are you a Catholic still? Do you want to confess?"

"I've told them everything already. They don't want to listen to me."

"But God does, Salvador. Do you want to confess to me? To God, Salvador."

Salvador was silent for a while. Then he said, "What I want to tell you, Father isn't a sin and so it isn't a confession. Will you hear me then?"

Father Nepomuck whispered, "I will listen. But just in case anyone puts their head in to see what's going on, please kneel and give the impression that you are making a confession. See, the door is already ajar."

Salvador knelt down before the priest and spoke slowly. "I did not castrate Julio. I found him like that. I tried to comfort him. Diasanta or one of his men did it. They want to blame the communists and so I will have to die, Father. I have to be dead so I can't deny what they say. I believe they are just waiting for the go-ahead from Infanta to carry out the execution. It's just politics." Salvador paused. "But you must tell Frank exactly what I have told you. I don't want him to think that I'd ever do a thing like that." Salvador fell silent and then said in a whisper, "I could not do such a thing, Father, because Frank always taught me that those parts of our body are most sacred and our wonderful love together proved that his words are true."

Father Nepomuck knew that Stephens' view of church teaching was heterodox but he wanted to hear no more than Salvador wished to tell him. All the same he felt obliged to ask, "My son, did they abuse you in any way? I see that this room has been, well, almost sterilised, as if to hide something."

Salvador replied very firmly, "You will say nothing about what you have seen or what you are thinking to Frank. Nothing, do you hear? But Father as I am still down on my knees, let me make you happy. I shall confess." Salvador crossed himself and looked into Father Nepomuck's eyes. "I have not sinned while I have been a prisoner in this place."

"Then I give you full absolution my son. With God's blessing."

The camp Commandant escorted Father Nepomuck to the waiting police car.

"Was the boy in good shape?" he asked anxiously.

"In better shape than you can imagine, for he is innocent." Father Nepomuck replied. "Now remember this; you are responsible."

"To the government, you mean?" asked the Commandant.

"No, to God."

The Commandant had recovered his poise. A smirk was on his face. "Oh, to God. The great dictator who made us in his own image. Well I guess I can go along with that."

When he returned to his house Father Nepomuck was down at heart. The image of the Commandant's smirk weighed on him. It had meant, if we are in God's image what sort of horror is God? He wished he was back in Seattle dealing with the run of the mill sins he knew, like murder, rape and drug induced family violence; he wished he was anywhere but here. Soon he would have to give news to two people whose lives would be shattered by his words. How to say, 'Senora, your lover has been castrated'? How, as one priest to another, both bound by the teachings of the church, could he say, 'Father, your boyfriend is accused of castrating this young woman's lover and he is to be executed any time now even though he is completely innocent'. His houseguests were talking and had not heard him returning. Father Stephens rose and said, "Father, it's you. You've been away quite a time. Did you find anything out? Come let me get you a drink."

"Yes, I will have a drink. A cognac please." Nepomuck sat down heavily in an old armchair that squeaked ominously. His despondency showed in his face. Conchita glanced at him but held her peace. Cesar too saw the expression on the priest's face and decided to get to the truth as quickly as possible. "You've found something out, haven't you? Tell us what it is. Whatever it is."

Father Nepomuck took a sip from the glass that Stephens had put beside him. Then he looked at Conchita and said, "I found out that Julio has been rescued from a jungle camp up in the mountains. It belonged to Diasanta but he and his men have all vanished into the jungle. Julio was taken by helicopter to hospital, in Infanta I would guess." He took a deep breath. It was useless to beat about the bush so he said rapidly, "It seems that a senseless mutilation was performed on Julio. He will not be able to father any children."

A dreadful silence descended on the group. It was as though an icy hand had frozen them. None of the men even looked at Conchita when she let out a little gasp, stood up and walked to the edge of the veranda to gaze across at the darkly silhouetted landscape that fell away from the house.

Instinct told Father Nepomuck that he should blurt out the rest of the story. "They captured a young man who they said had committed the crime—a communist guerrilla. But the accusation is totally without foundation. It was done by Diasanta or one of his gang. I don't think they'll ever be brought to book. They are back in the mountains and the jungle. The truth is that the boy, Salvador, was trying to help Julio Abulencia. He gave me this account, Father Stephens, and he said that you would know that he could never have committed such an act because of what he had learned from your life together."

Stephens' immediate reaction was to ask what he could do to help Salvador but in the middle of talking he broke down and sobbed and could not get his words out. Conchita went to him at once and put her arms around him. "Who is this boy?" she asked softly. "I see that he means a lot to you." She gestured to Cesar and Father Nepomuck as if to say a woman is best at dealing with something like this; the two men caught on and quietly left the veranda.

"A friend," Stephens sighed. "No, not just a friend Senora, much more than that, a lover. Salvador and I are lovers. It must seem monstrous to you, me being a priest. Anyway I can't say I'm a priest any more. I'm not even a Catholic, even a Christian. I can no longer believe in a perverse lie. I've lost my faith and I've lost the one person in my life that I loved and who loved me." He tried to pull himself together. "Just look at me. Talking about myself like this when you are living through such a horror." He stared at Conchita piercingly as though he had only just taken note of her. "There you are, a woman and yet you seem so collected. What are you going to do? Will you go to Infanta?"

"I'm not collected really. I just feel numb. I've imagined everything that might happen to Julio, even this if you want to know. Some men are rational but most are savages. Julio fell among the majority so I was prepared for anything. But even if he was safe and sound with me now I'd still feel numb. And when the numbness goes, who knows how I'll act. I might want to commit a murder. Just now it's as though I don't exist as a person. I'm just an eye looking out at the world." Conchita touched Stephens' face gently. "You are a good man, I can tell. Salvador is very lucky to have you. Why do you think I'd say your love was wrong? Love is love, whatever form it takes. Yes, I shall go to Infanta—sooner or later—to see Julio, but maybe he will be ill or in shock and won't want to see me. There's no point in distressing him needlessly." She turned urgently towards the priest. "More to the point, Father, what are you going to do?"

"I'll go to the prison camp myself. I'll ask Nepomuck to go to Infanta to the Defence Ministry. Or to the Cardinal. Or I'll ask…"

Conchita put her fingers to Stephens' lips. "You'd be wasting your name. Everything in Infanta is in confusion. No one will help you or Nepomuck. As for the Cardinal," she shrugged her shoulders. "Everyone, church included, will be anxious to blame the communists." She said abruptly, "Father, how long have you lived in the Carolines?"

"Nearly five years, Senora."

"Nearly five years, yet you still don't know what to do." A hint of a smile crossed her face but it quickly vanished. "Money, Father. Money. Use you money to free Salvador and get away quickly. In this country money always works." She picked up her handbag from the floor. "Look Father, priests don't have much money but money is the one thing that gives me no problems. See, I have five thousand US dollars. Use them. Go to the camp Commandant and say you know Salvador is innocent. You can even say that a priest broke the vow of the confessional to tell you that the criminal is Diasanta. Tell him the army must not kill an innocent boy and dishonour its colours. But as you speak let him see that you have a lot of money on you, in a bulging pocket or a fat wallet. You will know what to do. Play it by ear. But take care that the Commandant only gets half to begin with, the rest not until Salvador is in your hands." Though Father Stephens' hope was raised he looked dubious; he had never given or accepted a bribe in his life, but Conchita was adamant. "Time is running out, Father." She pressed the money into his hands. "If this doesn't work I'm no Carolina."

Stephens still felt like questioning Conchita's idea, for he wondered whether she fully understood the gravity of the situation. He said, "The Commandant knows that a captured guerrilla will want to go back to the jungle. Salvador is a communist, you know."

"I don't care," said Conchita. "No, I do. He's doing something he believes in to help his people. Maybe his is the only way to purge this country. Perhaps we need a fire before we can start again. I can even imagine going over to their side. Oh, I'm being a romantic. If ever they got power it could be even worse. No it's our nature that's the real enemy, Father. Now go, and go quickly. Make the money work. It's the only chance you have. I'll tell the others where you've gone."

As soon as Father Stephens had made off Conchita joined Cesar in his bedroom, where he was fiddling with a shortwave radio. There was a lot of crackling and intermittent voices, until the Voice of America announced the Secretary of State, Jasper Frankfurter, who spoke in lugubrious tones about the loss of President Floresco, one of America's closest allies who had always supported President Souris in his battle against the twin poles of evil. He even added a few personal reminiscences about his last visit to the Carolines and how he had appreciated the beauty of Antonio's mountain residence, to which in fact no one but a very few private guests were ever invited by the defunct President. Then, changing to a happier mood, he welcomed the accession to power of Manuel Bersamina in whose hands he was confident that the US-Caroline alliance would continue to flourish. After that all that Cesar could pick up was NHK in Tokyo, which was playing the Japanese national anthem very slowly and solemnly like a funeral march. A bit more fiddling and he got the BBC, which gave the latest news very clearly. They listened intently, hoping for news about the Carolines and Conchita pointedly recalled how Gorbachev had relied on the BBC to find out what was happening in Moscow when he was marooned down on the Black Sea. They did not have to wait long. A female announcer whose voice easily pierced the static said that conflicting reports about the situation in Infanta were coming in. According to Government sources the population was grief stricken over the death of the President but many Carolinos were pledging their support for Bersamina, who had declared himself to be Acting President. It was reported that Prime Minister Bienvenido Loyola had agreed to stay in office, that the Cardinal had appealed for calm and offered up prayers for the country and that an opposition leader, Cesar Abulencia, had been asked to join the government of national unity. Cesar laughed and said, "First thing I've heard about it. That alone proves that Bersamina is a liar." The BBC announcer added that unconfirmed reports spoke of demonstrations by students and workers against the state of emergency declared by Bersamina.

Cesar could see that Conchita was inwardly beside herself with worry over Julio, but he also observed that she was determined to act decisively and in her own interests as and when necessary. She struck him as being made of strong stuff, in which she resembled her mother. Father Nepomuck who joined them also remarked, when Conchita went to the kitchen to make some coffee, that it was remarkable how strong the President's daughter was. Cesar opined, after a little consideration, that Conchita has the strength of her mother, the intelligence of her father, but a generosity of spirit possessed by neither of them. "She will come through," he said to Nepomuck, "but I wouldn't like to be anyone who stood in her way."

When Conchita had made the coffee they all returned to the veranda where it was pleasantly cool and they could marvel at the cloud of fireflies sparkling in phosphorescent myriads over the garden pool. They spoke very little, for their minds were also on Father Stephens and what he might be able to achieve for his lover.

Cesar thought he might have a chance with the money Conchita had provided; Conchita hoped he was right and Father Nepomuck wondered quietly at the course that justice took in Third World countries. On reflection however he admitted that justice could sometimes be just as peculiar in the United States. Then on the hour, two o'clock in the morning, Cesar tried the radio again. This time the news from the Carolines was clear and thrilling. The BBC announcer, Trevor Tremaine Philpott, read a statement just issued by the late President's wife, Senora Griselda Floresco, declaring roundly that the death of her husband was the result of a plot hatched by the so-called Acting President, Manuel Bersamina, and a foreign power; that his assumption of power was illegal and that it was the duty of all Carolinos to oppose him. She herself would use every instrument in her power to restore legal government, to which end she would soon return to Infanta. It was then reported that the First Lady had in fact just boarded a chartered Aeroflot jet for Moscow and that she was taking her late husband's body with her.

Conchita for the first time began to show dangerous signs of stress. She started to sob uncontrollably and Cesar did his best to comfort her, though his own mind was beset by worries over his own situation, not to mention that of Julio. Father Nepomuck felt out of place. If he had been in America he might have asked everyone to join him in prayer but it was clear that Conchita and Cesar were not the praying types, so he cleared away the coffee cups and dug out some wine from Stephens' not very well provided cellar. "I wish I'd been in Rome with daddy," Conchita cried. "I wish it had been me, not my father." Cesar said what he felt might help, which was pretty weak, but inwardly even pity could not drive from his mind the enormous dangers that might lie ahead. The right step and he was made; the wrong step and his hopes were doomed. Even the fate of Julio only occupied a small space in his mind at present, in which regard he was utterly different from Conchita, whose brain could not refrain from visualising the physical hurt that her lover had suffered. Was castration final, she asked herself? Could the damage be reversed in any way? She thought not, though she knew little about medical science.

Cesar had started to dream up some unlikely scenario—the emergence of a political impasse wherein he might be able to call the tune. But his dream was halted when he heard Conchita say, "Take me back to Infanta, Cesar. I want to go now. Supposing Julio is ill and wants me and I was not there."

"But Conchita, it could be dangerous," said Cesar. "We don't know what Bersamina's intentions are. And there may be mobs in the streets. We just don't know. You don't want to end up as a hostage to fortune."

"All the more reason to go. What about Popong and Ricky? They may not be safe either." The thought of her brothers in danger confirmed Conchita's resolve.

Cesar pursed his mouth and shook his head in worry. "Of course I'll do what you want. But I have to think what Julio would have me do. You've heard that Bersamina apparently wants me in government. So supposing I say yes, I could get to Infanta and visit places you could not approach. In fact I could get to the DeoGracias and take your brothers back to my own house." Then, as another thought struck Cesar out of the blue, he asked, "Why has your mother gone to Moscow? I thought she never liked it. Antonio certainly didn't."

This set Conchita's mind working. "I really don't know. Perhaps to distance herself from the Western powers at the moment. No. That's not a good reason. The only reason my mother ever went to Moscow was for some state of the art medical skin treatment. No, Cesar, I just think she wants to disappear from view for a while and suddenly turn up. Maybe from Beijing. Yes, Cesar, you must go to Infanta. I shall wait here as you advise. But see that my brothers are safe."

Cesar promised to leave early in the morning and then switched on the television for Caroline news if it was available. It was indeed, courtesy of Euronews. Onto the veranda flooded a cultured if rather pedantic English voice, that of Hilary Arbuthnot, the film director whose documentary on the Carolines had received so much attention. There he sat as dapper as ever under the gaze of veteran interviewer Jeremy Clamp.

In answer to a question Hilary said slowly and manifestly, giving profound attention to the implications of his answer, "You see Jeremy, within the context of the South East Asian situation the image can be as important as the reality. You are aware of the traditional shadow plays of the area?"

"Of course," said Clamp nervously, anxious to dispense with any impression that he was not as au fait with such a fact as someone who merely lived there.

"It's symptomatic of the Caroline way of life that she is pointing the finger at the shadow rather than the reality. The person or persons actually responsible for the President's death are, so she is saying, behind the shadow. By which I mean that in the great powerplay which rages over the western Pacific the communists are not, at the moment, responsible."

Jeremy Clamp was baffled and his anger showed in his narrow-set eyes. "In no way responsible? On what basis do you say so?"

"I repeat, in no way whatsoever." Hilary's voice, though shrill, had an air of authority. "What basis? When you have lived as long as me in the Far East, dear Jeremy, you develop sources of information not open to TV men. What I am going to tell you now is not mere hearsay. I have my sources. The immediate objective of the Caroline Communist Party is to discredit the President but only as part of a long term strategy to overthrow the régime completely. His immediate demise would produce no such result. But there are some powers that are dissatisfied with him as an ally, an undemocratic ally. They feel that to be allied with his régime gives them a bad name. Such a power might want to replace him with a more amenable strongman, capable of destroying communism root and branch but looking less corrupt."

"That man is saying," Conchita interrupted very deliberately, "that the Americans are responsible for the murder of my father, that the Americans are behind Bersamina. They are our only ally. But I can't believe that my mother means the Americans. Can you, Cesar?"

Cesar cupped his head in his hands. Suddenly he felt quite worn out. He looked at Conchita, was impressed by the serenity in her face and yet its intelligence. In time, he thought, she would be every bit as formidable as her mother and, as she grasped the full nastiness of the world, she would become every bit as ruthless. In the face of this awful inevitability he felt revulsion towards public life. He would just like to retire and cultivate his garden. Yet he would take Conchita to Infanta for he must help her, even if it meant letting his personal wishes go hang for the time being. He said, "It figures. Arbuthnot's argument makes sense. The more one thinks about it, a great deal of sense. But where did your mother get information to justify her statement about Bersamina? Coupled with Arbuthnot's suggestion it's explosive. It certainly pits her against the United States."

Conchita was still reluctant to believe such a scenario and said, "It's not possible. My father fought for the Americans. They even decorated him."

Cesar thought it best not to go into the dead President's ambiguous credentials where the end of the war was concerned, so he said, "Dear Conchita, men are capable of anything when it comes to power. Didn't you say that yourself only a little while ago? Come, let's get ready for Infanta. I'll find my driver. I think he's sleeping in the car. We won't go straight to my house. I have friends on the outskirts of town where we can hang out. Then I'll find your brothers and try to see Julio. We must say goodbye to the priests. I'll thank them and pay for their help. Nepomuck is in his study but I don't know whether the Australian is back yet."

Before they left Conchita wrote a letter to Stephens expressing her deep sympathy for him and hoping he would be able to get Salvador released. She also asked him to thank the brave young man most warmly when he was back home for the compassion he had shown towards Julio and she ended by giving both the lovers her own love, even though their acquaintance had been so brief. Then, watched by Father Nepomuck, she walked with Cesar in the morning light down the track to the car.

They were surprised that they were able to get to the capital with little trouble. There were the usual military roadblocks manned by sleepy policemen who looked at Cesar's identity card in a perfunctory way but did not even ask Conchita, who had resumed her boy's disguise, to show one. The police gave the impression of being bemused, as though they were waiting for something to happen with no idea of what it might be. Nor when they got to Infanta did the place look any less than normal. Traffic flowed as chaotically as ever, the streets were full of people shopping and sauntering about aimlessly and radios blared out the usual menu of pop songs, but not a word about politics came from any loudspeaker. Conchita had a feeling that everything that had happened, the death of her father, the tragedy of Julio, the *coup d' état* of Bersamina, was some sort of fiction about which the people of the city knew nothing nor even cared.

Cesar stopped near a bar and went in to make a phone call. When he returned he said he had called his house and learned that no security people were about. "It's safe for us to go there," he said. Then he added cautiously, "Julio has been taken to my house to recuperate. He apparently has some nursing staff to attend him."

The reality of what Julio had become struck Conchita forcibly. "No, Cesar. I don't want to come with you. I'm not ready for this. And perhaps Julio isn't ready either."

"I don't think he will see you. He's sedated and under medical care. It's entirely up to you. But surely there can be no harm in your being near him."

Once in the house Conchita decided that it was best to get her first encounter with Julio over quickly. She saw Cesar talking with some nurses and a man she took to be a doctor but she did not want to join them and ran up the stairs to Julio's room. For awhile she sat in an upstairs salon trying to get a grip on herself before seeing Julio. What she had earlier seen as fiction was after all the truth. Soon she must face up to all the realities she had pushed to the back of her mind when they were speeding though the countryside to and from San Felipe. It was as though she had separated herself from being the President's daughter and was just observing herself quite dispassionately as an outsider from a distance. Now the distance was narrowing and she was becoming that person again. As the process speeded up; she began to feel the fullness of her losses, yet in her sorrow she sensed something stirring—a hint of a new life that she would have to make for herself. She saw a nurse leave Julio's room quietly. Beside the door was another nurse who stood up and said that Julio was not to be disturbed. "Can't I just look in?" Conchita asked and the nurse replied, "Certainly, young man, but do not disturb him at all." She entered the room just a little way and stood looking at Julio, who seemed to be sound asleep. Tears flowed down her face but she uttered not a sound. She could only stand and look and let the sorrow well up from deep inside her until it occupied the entire shape in which she was imprisoned. How handsome, how beautiful he looked; a little thinner, a bit paler but that only made the fineness of his features more acute. Lying there still as marble, he had become one of those figures carved on tombs in ancient churches, so real, so true to life that if one stared and stared, the cold marble told you that death was an illusion. Yet there on that bed the still shape of Julio was telling her that life itself was the illusion. She bowed her head when the nurse came in, thanked her and went down the stairs. Intent on occupying herself somehow or other she decided the best thing to do was to find out about her brothers. Cesar looked as if he wanted to speak to her from among the group of medicos in the hall but she sped out of the house before he could say a word.

Which was unfortunate because he had something most important to tell her. He had been informed by Doctor Agoncillo that Julio was not, after all, an incomplete male, as the doctor had solicitously put it. At the Infanta Medical Centre an operation had been performed which it was anticipated would be a success. Fortunately the severed testicles had been kept in deep cold storage and it had been possible for them to be reattached to Julio's inert body. Cesar was not able to believe what the Doctor told him and asked layman's irrelevant questions to which Agoncillo told him patiently, "You must understand Senor Abulencia, that it was not a testicle transplant. That is not feasible at present. No, that is not quite true. Some years ago there was a case involving identical twins. One had lost his testicles due to cancer but he was able to receive a testicle from his brother. So being identical both would be able to reproduce their own genetic image. In any other case, even were it to be done, a transplanted testicle would produce only the donor's sperm and the recipient would not be able to reproduce his own biological kind. However in this case we had still living tissue which could fuse. The operation took place just after Julio was brought in. So we believe he can probably make a full physical recovery."

Cesar was dumbfounded for a while. Then he asked a servant to call Conchita so he might tell her the amazing news. Unfortunately she had left the house, nor was she in the garden; perhaps she had gone for a quiet walk along the road to think things over. Yet Cesar was still dubious. He said, "If the operation was so successful—you said that it took place very soon after the helicopter brought Julio to hospital—why is he still deeply sedated? Surely after operations nowadays patients are encouraged to move, even to walk if possible."

Dr Agoncillo's face was morose. He asked Cesar to sit beside him. "I have to tell you, Senor Abulencia, that the harm done to Julio's body was not the worst thing that happened to him. He constantly has attacks of terror and when they occur he relives the awful treatment he suffered under the hands of Diasanta. He has relived the horror of it several times in my presence. The trauma is very severe. His words and his cries are fixed in my memory. That's why I have kept him sedated for now."

Cesar felt his body turning cold, yet his limbs were sweating and his mouth had gone dry. He said, "I have to know, Doctor. I have to know it all. Tell me what happened."

Doctor Agoncillo took his time to get it out because it was as painful to speak as to hear. "Diasanta was wearing a red chasuble over his battle dress, with a big wooden cross dangling around his neck. He ordered his thugs to strip Julio—in readiness for a ceremony at which he was the priest. They put him on a table, the altar, Diasanta called it. One of them held Julio's head, others pinioned his arms. Two thugs took his feet and spread his legs wide apart. Diasanta advanced on him between his thighs with those secateurs. But he didn't cut Julio straight away; he began a long, mad sermon, brandishing the secateurs and chanting that he was going to purify Julio by destroying the possibility of his ever sinning again and wasting his sperm like Onan or in condoms. Julio begged him, 'Don't hurt me Diasanta, don't hurt me.' But this only delighted the madman who said that Julio's pleas were the devil speaking and ordered his thugs to rave and bellow aloud to banish evil from the room—some of them were piercing the air with crazy hysterical laughter. It must have sounded like hell. Then he told one of the thugs to pull Julio's penis upward over his stomach before he seized his testicles and cut them off. The poor young man was screaming throughout the whole insane ceremony and he went on screaming until I suppose one of the thugs gave him a blow to the head to put him out—there's a huge bruise where he was hit. Then they must have heard armed men approaching. Diasanta abandoned his victim and fled to the jungle with his crew. First came the communists who

327

were soon ambushed by our forces. Senor Abulencia, I fear that the damage to Julio's mind is likely to be more lasting than the damage to his body." Doctor Agoncillo fell silent and wiped the tears from his eyes.

Cesar was trembling. The sheer horror of what Diasanta had done filled him with loathing for the man. Why hadn't he shot him when he had the chance? He knew that Conchita would have to be told and it would be better if it came from him than from the mouth of Julio, who must be protected from a repetition of his suffering under Diasanta. But when to tell her? He waited for her to return from wherever she had gone, which was to a little bistro a mile or so away. She told him that there she had phoned the DeoGracias, sure that if the line was tapped no one could find her once she had slipped away. The operator at the palace had not asked who she was but merely said, "DeoGracias. Can I help you?" Conchita recognised the operator's voice as belonging to the kindly busybody Maria Tanada.

"I want speak to Captain Manzano," she replied.

"One moment please. Putting you through."

"Manzano. This is Conchita Floresco." She was conscious that her voice made her sound like her mother, especially when she spoke severely. She heard a sharp intake of breath at the other end— the first hint that things were not so normal after all. "I want to know where my brothers are. Do you know?"

Quick as a flash Manzano said, "They are at Senor Loyola's house. He took them off himself—for safety's sake. I escorted them with some of my men. He was afraid that they might be kidnapped. Security round here is not good." Manzano's voice became urgent and he started off with the words, "Ma'am" a title reserved for the First Lady alone. "Can I do anything for you, Senora? You can rely on me, I swear."

"Yes Captain, there is. You will not tell anyone I called you." Conchita then used a bit of cunning and added. "And Maria that goes for you too."

Cesar was glad that she had found out so much but he was not prepared to tell her the news about Julio. Let the poor boy rest. Conchita might wake him up and plunge him into the abyss from which that Doctor Agoncillo was trying to save him. He said, "It sounds to me that some people at the DeoGracias are not supporters of Bersamina. Why spirit the boys away to Loyola's house? I don't think the Prime Minister is with Bersamina one hundred percent."

Conchita replied, "Then you must go to Loyola at once. That's the best place to find out what's going on." She hesitated and then said as though she was entitled to give such an order, "Cesar, say to Loyola that you come in the name of the President Floresco and as my emissary."

Cesar found that Loyola's house was a hive of activity. Reporters clustered in front to the heavy iron gates and a couple of TV crews were competing to take up the best viewing positions and all this despite the fact that there was supposed to be a nighttime curfew. There was no military or police presence nearby except for a few traffic cops who were doing their best to ensure that the stream of cars along the road could continue to flow. The double gates opened and as his car drove in Cesar heard voices calling his name and cameras flashed against the car windows. In the garden a posse of soldiers was on duty. He told his driver to wait under the carport, then strode through the wide open doors and told a secretary that he had to see the Prime Minister immediately and privately on a matter of great urgency. After the shortest delay three cabinet ministers and their civil servants left Loyola's room and Cesar was ushered in.

From the outset it was clear that Loyola was deferring to Cesar. He expressed his disgust over Julio's treatment and said that the criminals would be punished no matter who they were. No expense would be spared over Julio's medical treatment, which he understood was problematical. Cesar nodded his approval but all he said was "I am here, Prime Minister, as the emissary of the President's daughter, Senora Conchita Floresco."

"The President?" Loyola looked puzzled.

"As far as I am concerned, as far I believe all right thinking people in this country are concerned, Antonio Floresco is still President of the Carolines. Unlike some ancient monarchies we can only say, 'The King is dead, but remains King until a new King is chosen constitutionally.' That has not been done."

Loyola glanced nervously around the room as though hidden eyes were prying on him. "Precisely, precisely," he said. "I regard myself as holding President Floresco's mandate. The administration must be kept going. People say I am just a technocrat, but without technocrats states collapse." He coughed and pulled back his shoulders, "You say you are the emissary of the President's daughter—not the President's wife?"

Cesar disregarded the question and replied, "Senora Conchita has not decided what role to play politically at the moment. Just now she is anxious about her brothers. I understand that you have made yourself responsible for their safety." Cesar's words had a slightly threatening sound and clearly implied that Loyola should take the responsibility seriously.

Loyola looked surprised. It had clearly never struck him that a new counter was on the board in the shape of Conchita. Perhaps even Cesar had not realised the implications of his own words until they dropped out of his mouth. Loyola replied reassuringly, "The boys, yes, Popong and Ricky. They are perfectly safe with my own little boy in the games room. Playing on computers I would say. Do you want to see them? Does Conchita want you to take them to your house?"

"Good, good," said Cesar. "Senora Conchita will be very relieved to hear that the boys are well. However I think she would want them to stay in your care, Bienvenido. She has not decided where to stay at present. Also I have an invalid to look after in my house, poor Julio, as I think you must know."

Cesar until then had been sitting opposite Loyola, who was at his desk. He got up and took his place on a comfortable settee where Loyola at once joined him. It gradually became clear to Cesar that he was the one who was conducting the interview. He said in a kindly way, "Now Bienvenido I should like your assessment of the situation." But before Loyola could reply he went on, "You know I'd be less than a friend if I didn't let you know that Conchita is upset by reports that her father's assassination was the result of a plot hatched in this country and involving people known to both of us. These rumours are, I believe, circulating everywhere and Griselda's People's Action Brigades will be lapping them up. Names will be named and disorder is likely to increase. You and I, Bienvenido, must be careful not to align ourselves with anyone who may have been involved in such a crime."

"My dear Cesar, I assure you that I am only doing my best to keep the country running. If trade, industry and farming break down there would be chaos. The interest of the people must come first."

"The people, Bienvenido, is a strange beast. Yes, they will complain if they are not looked after. But they can be ruthless if they think they have been fooled. It won't be enough just to say that you have been doing your duty."

Loyola spoke in a thin, hushed voice. "Cesar, you and I both know that Bersamina controls the military muscle. He has the Defence Ministry and everything that entails, Well he did until…"

"Until what?" Cesar asked harshly.

"The news of the assassination plot, of Bersamina's involvement. I've heard that some of the Defence Ministry men, General Untalan and Police Chief de la Torre are climbing over the fence. Senor Rich Rarang has offered the support of the Peoples Action Brigades. And the Cardinal. He says the Church is reserving its position until the matter of the President's death is cleared up. Meanwhile he exhorts us all to pray. But neither you nor I have time to crawl on our knees, Cesar. Earlier today I called at the Defence Ministry. I saw Bersamina. No longer the old confidence. When I went in to his office he was just standing there staring at Antonio's portrait. He all but begged me to persuade you to join the government."

Cesar saw in a flash that Bersamina's position was being eroded and that Loyola would be in dire straights if he stuck with the Defence Minister. He said, "I'm too much of a politician to think of joining such a man. Unfortunately Floresco destroyed the old political parties, including mine, so I haven't got a power base. My advice to you, Bienvenido, is to go on being a technocrat. I can see struggles developing between mobs of people with different loyalties and a divided army. A recipe for chaos. Try to keep things going, dear Bienvenido, and give your loyalty to whoever wins." Cesar sighed deeply and said, "If only they would all wipe one another out."

Loyola escorted Cesar to his car. A horde of people had invaded the garden while the soldiers were lolling about chatting with each other. The two politicians shook hands under the glare of TV lights and flashing cameras. They both said, "No comment," several times to reporters but Cesar's parting words to Loyola were picked up by the inquisitive microphones thrust in their faces. He had said, "Distance yourself from that man. His days are numbered."

Cesar felt pleased with himself. He had gained the trust of Loyola without committing himself to Bersamina and he must have been seen by millions on their TV screens as a politician who was emerging into the limelight. It also pleased him to see Conchita coming out to greet him, no longer as a boy but as a well-dressed young women radiating common sense and he imagined charm. Her presence belied all that. Close too he could see that her eyes were red with weeping. His mind immediately turned to Julio. She must have seen him. "Come Conchita, please sit with me and let me know everything that is troubling you. Have you been up to see Julio again? It's best to let it all out."

"I have indeed," Conchita said. "One of the nurses told me about the operation and she was full of confidence that it had been a success. She also told me that Julio was conscious and quite calm after being mildly sedated. She said that Doctor Agoncillo had advised that no one but the nursing staff should go in to see him just now but she was sure an exception could be made in my case because Julio had mentioned my name almost as soon as he regained consciousness."

"Well then," said Cesar. "That's sounds good. Did you go to him?"

Conchita replied, "Yes I did. I went to him thinking that all is well, that things will be as they were before, that before long we will be married and find a new life together. But I had not been with Julio, holding him in my arms, for five minutes when he told me that our future was a blank. He did not think we could be married, not now, not for a decade, perhaps never. It was a shock to me. I had been building up so many hopes. I started to cry and my crying upset him. I said, 'Don't hurt me by saying that, Julio, please don't hurt me.' Of a sudden he let out a dreadful scream. He shouted, 'how dare you use my words, how dare you make fun of me'. He thrashed about on the bed and tried to push me away. I didn't know what was happening. A nurse had heard the noise and came in with a hypodermic syringe to give him an injection. And then quite miraculously before she could touch him, Julio grew calm. He actually got off the bed and sat in a chair. He was breathing heavily but he said he had to speak. He asked for some tea and some fruit. The nurse hesitated but went off to get what he wanted."

Conchita stood up, unable to contain her agitation, but at Cesar's bidding she sat by him again and went on, "Julio said then that he should not have spoken to me so abruptly but he wanted me to know his decision. 'I will never be the same', he said. 'Well, not for years. Monstrous memories keep flooding back and I can't cope with them. How could you be married to a man whose brain is damaged.' He looked at me and then he laughed, yes he actually laughed, Cesar. 'It isn't that my balls were cut off, Conchita; it was the way in which Diasanta terrified me. I could find no way of resisting him. I would have done anything he asked just to escape. I was afraid of the mad laughter of his thugs and the sharp pain and what else they might do to me. My cowardice will be with me for the rest of my life. His madness unmanned me.' Then he said, no not said, sort of growled that he had one great desire, even greater than his love for me. He must kill Diasanta. He must destroy his insane ideas. They must be wiped off the face of the earth. He shouted that they came from the church's teaching." Conchita fell silent and Cesar wondered what obscure path Julio's ideas were taking. She continued, "Cesar, I am not a faithful Catholic, hardly a believer any more but I didn't think it right that he should blame the church for what he's gone through. Perhaps it was foolish to contradict him but I wanted to recall him to some sort of reality."

Conchita was anxious that Cesar should hear her out. "You know it's not so easy for me to repeat all this. In a way I feel that I'm betraying Julio for telling you what he said, but it helps me if you know what I heard from him. When I tried to defend the church he told me I had got it all wrong. He was not thinking of his own pain but of the dreadful suffering imposed on millions of people in this country and around the world. Huge families without enough money. Women labouring and having children every year. Children abandoned to pimps and forced to become prostitutes. People living on mountains of trash. People told that they are sinning if they don't procreate like beasts because they must not waste their seed. People told that they must abstain from sex if they don't want children. A perverse madness. To Julio the weird beliefs of Diasanta are not just a perversion, but a perversion of a perversion. The church nurtures the seed that eventually grew into Diasanta's mad tree. He told me that if I was thinking of defending the church's doctrines I should remember the words of Jesus, that by their fruits you shall know them."

"Julio had worn himself out just talking to me but he began to shout at me again. 'Yes we'll marry in fifty years' time,' he cried. 'Can you wait that long for me to become a normal man?' I saw him moaning and crying. I went to him. I kissed him. The nurse injected the drug and soon he lay still on his bed. Ah Cesar, I kissed him again and again and here I am now wanting you to hold me and comfort me."

Cesar held Conchita in his arms until her sobbing died down. He could see nothing but gloom in every situation around him. Diasanta had ruined not only Julio's life but the life of this young woman of whom he had grown so fond. Nor did he see any light in the political situation around them. He anticipated a bloody struggle, something as bad as the Khmer Rouge violating the country, with lunatics like Diasanta emerging from the sewers to torture the Caroline people. Suddenly Conchita drew away from him to give him another piece of unwelcome news. "Oh Cesar, I forgot to tell you. My mother is coming back to Infanta. She's arriving the day after tomorrow. She has called upon all Carolinos to rise against Bersamina. I heard it on the radio while you were away. After what happened to Julio I can't face her. Perhaps I can get out of the country. I could take Julio to some place like Switzerland to cure his malaise."

Cesar sighed. He could see the outcome quite clearly. It would not be himself or Loyola or any reasonable being who would inherit power in the country. The Floresco régime would be restored by the First Lady on the backs of her Peoples Action Brigades and all the dead President's militarist supporters who would rise up to punish Bersamina. Griselda would rule and finally when an exploding population, poverty and corruption had made the country totally ungovernable, the red tide would sweep everything away. He said bitterly, "Don't worry, Conchita, all will be well. Soon you can go back to the DeoGracias with your brothers, forget all the troubles of the people and live like a princess under Queen Griselda, for that's what she will be." He regretted his bitter words as soon as they were uttered, and said, "Forgive me Conchita. I'm tired; you're tired. Let's both sleep on it. Tomorrow will bring what it will."

Conchita said, "Forgive you Cesar? There's nothing to forgive. And things may not turn out as badly as you think tomorrow."

Tomorrow in fact brought the day of the White Hats. When Cesar came down very late to breakfast his house servants were wearing white hats. When he went into the garden two gardeners were working under large white hats made of newspaper. He went out to the road and saw that many passers-by were sporting white hats, even a policeman. When he returned to the house he found Conchita just as amazed by the same phenomenon. She asked Andy the driver, who was waiting to take her to see Popong and Ricky, why he too was wearing a white hat. He said. "You don't know, Senora? Of course that's because you and Senor Cesar have got up late. The First Lady is coming home soon. It was on the TV and the radio. She's asked people to show their rejection of the murderer Bersamina by wearing a white hat. It seems it was the last wish of the dying President. He said, 'Wear a white hat'. Funny isn't it?"

Cesar said, "Some people make the mistake of thinking that your mother is just a stupid woman but she is not. Just think of all the people in this city she has cultivated—Rich Rarang's Brigades of little people, her army of street cleaners, the sports clubs, the shopkeepers, the civil servants and of course everybody's idols, the media stars."

"Oh yes," said Andy who was lounging around waiting for Conchita to go to the car and he began to reel off a list of singers and actors, "Alberto Laminato, Babes Panares. Babes has already written a White Hat song, and there's Ricky Gonzales and Gloria Moreno and…"

"Yes, yes, yes, Andy; we're not at an awards ceremony. But you see, Conchita. She's got support and just think of the thousands of women who follow everything she wears and want to copy her. There may be an avalanche. Everybody is nervous. Bersamina can't rely on the army or the police to obey him. The brass will keep quiet until they see who comes out on top. But if I was Bersamina I'd run for it now."

"I think I'll come with you." Cesar said unexpectedly. "To keep you company and I can have a word with Loyola."

They drove off, calling first at a store to buy toys and books as presents for the two boys but as they drove on, though they were still amused by the rash of white hats, both of them noticed that they were being recognised by people among the crowds that always surged along the Infanta boulevards. Sometimes they were clapped and sometimes cheered and not a few people shouted out, "Conchita, Conchita." This surprised her but added food for the thought that was already being digested in Cesar's shrewd mind. Loyola greeted them and told a servant to lead them upstairs, adding that he would like to have a word with Cesar before he left.

Conchita was not sure whether the tutors had told the boys of their father's death and prepared herself for the sadness of explaining it to them. But children have ways of finding things out, especially when they have access to computers. It turned out that, though Popong was old enough to understand the tragedy of his father's death, little Ricky had found out every detail about it and related them in his shrill voice whether anyone wanted to hear or not. "He was shot in the back, you know. I don't think it was by the Pope. My mum lay down beside him and heard him say something about white hats. I don't know why. Seems funny to me."

Very crossly, Popong said, "Shut up, Ricky. Conchita's as sad as we are. You don't have to remind her that daddy is gone. And she's upset because a lunatic cut off Julio's balls. I've told you that already."

Ricky gave Conchita a big kiss and asked, "Can they sew them on again, Connie?"

Conchita thought 'well, if children can be so matter of fact, why can't I?' So she said, "I think so Ricky, but it isn't like sewing a button on your shirt. The tissue has to fuse with the rest of the body."

"Don't worry," said Ricky. "I'm sure he'll be able to give you babies."

"When I was their age," Cesar whispered to Conchita. "I still believed in storks leaving babies under bushes."

"Times have changed, Cesar. We must accustom ourselves. You

go off now and see Loyola. I'll stay a while with my lovely brothers. They need taking in hand. We have a lot to talk about together."

Loyola was at the bottom of the stairs anxiously waiting for Cesar. "Come in to the study," he said. "You have to talk with me." Cesar followed him but Loyola had never stopped talking. "I've had a call from the Duty Officer at the Defence Ministry. He withdrew the guard on the building because he didn't want to provoke some of the Peoples Action Brigades driving around."

"A useful precaution, I suppose," said Cesar. "No need to involve troops in skirmishes with a mob."

"Yes. But not very useful for Bersamina. Apparently when he saw that the guards had vanished he panicked and left. The Duty Officer thinks he intended to go to his estate at San Felipe. He has men there to protect him."

"A useful precaution, I suppose," Cesar repeated.

"Are you going to say that to everything I tell you," asked Loyola irritably.

"I hope so, because I want you to take every precaution, Senor Prime Minister."

"Very well; then listen to this. I'm accused of being a mere technocrat, a machine without initiative. That only comes with intelligent politicians, I guess. Well, Cesar, technocrats like to work on hard facts. I am now faced with a very hard fact: the economy. The name Griselda spells ruin for the economy. If she succeeds in getting power there'll be no Antonio to restrain her profligacy. I couldn't work with her because I believe that economic ruin would be her first big success. Cesar, she has to be stopped."

Cesar saw the point all right but doubted whether he could stem the incoming tide. He knew Griselda meant not only a death knell for the economy but the same for the possibility of restoring democracy. "I can't see what we could do," he said.

A broad grin spread over Loyola's normally taciturn face. "Can't you now? And I always thought that you were a subtle politician. Cesar, you have the answer in your hands."

Cesar said angrily, "If you think that I should stand for the office of president when the time comes to choose Antonio Floresco's successor, you are mistaken, Bienvenido. I want to live to a ripe old age. No thank you."

"Let's be calm, Cesar. I didn't suggest any such thing. I merely said you have the answer in your hands."

"You mean? No! You mean Conchita? No, she'd never stand against her mother. And she's too young."

"But very intelligent, very well educated, and very determined," insisted Loyola. "Come on, Cesar, don't tell me you have never thought of it."

"Well yes I have," admitted Cesar. "But only as a future possibility, say in five years' time. Before Julio was hurt I even imagined him and Conchita in the DeoGracias together. But your idea is premature."

Loyola's manner changed. His voice fell. Even his body looked conspiratorial. "Have you read the papers today, Cesar, listened to the radio, watched television?"

"No. Yesterday ended up with a very late night, an emotional night. I got up late. So did Conchita," said Cesar.

"Well, my friend," Bienvenido stated. "First, I have a confession to make." He laughed and whispered. "I do not always tell the truth." Then he repeated the words very loudly, "I do not always tell the truth. For instance just now I said that the Duty Officer in the Defence Ministry phoned me to say he had withdrawn the guards on the building. A lie. A complete fabrication. Listen to this." Loyola produced the order left in his hands by the President before departing for Europe and read, "'I, Antonio Floresco, President of the Carolines, do hereby invest Prime Minister Bienvenido Loyola with the powers contained in this document.' In prosecution of one of those powers, Cesar, I ordered the Duty Officer in the Defence Ministry to remove the guards ostensibly to avoid provocation. By the way, the Officer is an old friend of mine and doesn't like Bersamina."

Cesar gasped. "But that could put Bersamina in great danger."

"Precisely," said Loyola. "In very great danger but a useful precaution for us, eh Cesar?"

"I suppose so," said Cesar wondering at the duplicity of the allegedly quiet academic before him.

"And something else," said Loyola, "Had you listened to the news, you would have heard in gruesome detail of the horrible thing done to Conchita's lover Julio, not to mention your own words made some time ago in a documentary, in which you accuse the Florescos of the crime of kidnapping. You would have known this had you bothered to read this rag." Loyola handed Cesar a copy of the *Infanta Times*, on the front page of which was a picture of Conchita and Julio in happier times. "Cesar, I myself ensured that this information has been widespread."

Cesar recalled the shouts of 'Conchita,' as they drove through the streets that morning. He silently cursed Diasanta yet again. A wedding between Conchita and Julio would have sealed a political alliance that, in a presidential race would have been insuperable. "No, she will never agree," he said to Loyola. "You stand, Bienvenido. You have the experience. You are trusted."

Loyola threw up his hands. "I will not stand for the same reason as you. It's Conchita or no-one."

Shortly after that Cesar and Conchita left Loyola's house without anything being said to her about replacing her dead father. Cesar thought it best to let things take their course, but as they drove home it was evident that Conchita's name was on everyone's mind. There were loud cries of 'Conchita' as they drove by and the crowd outside the Abulencia house added to the clamour for her.

Conchita could not help hearing what was being shouted so she said to Cesar. "What rubbish. How could I stand against my mother? She would shout 'Off with her head' like the Queen in *Alice in Wonderland*. But you could stand, Cesar. Many people admire you".

"Once I headed a political party, Conchita, but it was destroyed by your father. And I could not stand on the basis of demanding sympathy for Julio. No, I'm afraid it means Griselda and, as I said last night, you'll soon be back in the DeoGracias."

"A prisoner again," Conchita said. "No, I think I'll take off and visit my old friend Brenda Thatcher in England."

Cesar decided not to mention the matter further. After dinner they watched Infanta television, which was alarming. Various groups, the Action Brigades, disgruntled servicemen, students, trade unionists, and the like were struggling to seize public buildings. Greed for loot was evidently limiting the amount of actual fighting. The TV cameras had boldly found their way into the haunts of all sections of society. Many people were rooting for Griselda, though

Conchita's name was often mentioned by Action Brigade members and many of the women questioned were sympathetic to Conchita on account of Julio. Yet the disciplined behavior of the First lady's Action Brigades convinced Conchita that her mother's return to power was a *fait accompli*. But when it came to the young people, who constituted at least half of Infanta's population, all they wanted to talk about was Conchita and Julio. Interest was before long focused by the TV stations on Julio's operation. Medical people, including Doctor Agoncillo, were asked whether the operation, which was now common knowledge, could succeed. A few comedians tried sympathetic jokes on the matter, often praising the recently discovered paragon Conchita with such phrases as 'Conchita has real balls.' It was clear that the fate of Julio's testicles had begun to obsess the nation and also it seemed the international press. Cesar still said nothing but he could see that matters were stirring in Conchita's mind.

Then something most unpleasant came on the screen. Bersamina was seen in the hands of a mob composed of Peoples Action Brigade members. He had been stripped and tied on a lorry. All sorts of information about the iniquities of the Defence Ministry had been spreading, at the behest no doubt of Loyola, so Cesar suspected. Above the Defence Minister's head was a placard with the words 'Diasanta's friend' scrawled on it in red paint. Worse still, the same paint had been brushed by the sometimes tortured, but now free, writer, Nestor, on his genitals which looked as though they had been hacked off, for red streaks trickled down his legs. The mob of men, women and children, was laughing and jeering. "I cannot watch it," Conchita cried and left the room. "I hope Julio is not watching it! I'm going up to look in on him." She returned shortly afterwards to tell Cesar that in fact he was sleeping. Bersamina was no longer on the lorry for the mob, encouraged by the vengeful Nestor, had thrown him into the foetid River Calayag, where it flowed filthily through Infanta between decrepit squatter houses. He was trying to swim but stones were being hurled at him as the current carried him slowly along. Conchita did not want to look but the sight fascinated her. "Poor man, poor man. He never deserved that."

"How can any man judge what another man deserves?" said Cesar looking at the screen grimly. Depending on which way the wind blows it could be him or me, dear Conchita. Now you see what the people are really like when they are set free. Could you control them if ever you became head of the nation?" Conchita stared again at the screen. No sign of Bersamina; he must be dead, whether battered or drowned. The Calayag River flowed on as stinking and foul as ever but the would-be dictator was never seen again.

The following day Cesar observed that Conchita was very quiet. A telephone call for her came from the DeoGracias. Captain Manzano asked her if she would agree to accompany him to the airport to inspect the arrangements being made for her mother's return. It seemed to be generally accepted that soon the First Lady would not only be back but in control both of the palace and the government. But as she and Manzano drove along the seafront towards the airport, in addition to the white hats now worn by all and sundry there were placards with 'Conchita' written on them, including some that read 'Conchita for President'. At the airport she phoned Cesar and asked him to request Loyola to have such posters removed. Cesar replied blandly that she should not worry. It was just peoples' exuberance, but in fact he was well aware that what was appearing had been orchestrated by Loyola.

Manzano gave her a diagram of the arrangements showing where the First Lady would stand, where would be the guard of honour, the civil servants, and the diplomats, assuming any turned up. Outside the grand terminal, one of the First Lady's architectural triumphs, there would be barriers to hold back the enthusiastic crowds. Conchita asked Manzano "Really, captain. Is my mother so popular?" Manzano replied just audibly, "No ma'am, but you are." The possibility that she might be impelled to power by the mob as easily as Bersamina had been driven into the river made her feel faint. She asked Manzano to leave her whilst she went on her own to the coffee bar for a drink and a rest. There she bought a cappuccino and a croissant and sat in a quiet alcove to look out of one of the long windows. A voice said, "Senora Conchita. How good to see you." She looked up. It was Father Stephens. He was much the same as ever, though clad not in a clerical garb but in a long Chinese gown of grey silk. "Father," she said. "Do join me."

"Just plain Francis Stephens now," he said. "Senora, to judge by the placards it seems that everyone in the Carolines is in love with you. I swear that you will be good for this country."

Conchita was flattered that Stephens accepted it as a fact that one day she would be in power in some way or other. Her instincts told her he was a good man who had been hurt, yet maybe made stronger by suffering. It was probably his honesty that had made him leave the church. She smiled and asked, "Where are you off to, Francis?"

"To Sydney," he replied. "I shall be working in a school there, Latin and Greek."

Conchita laughed. "I wish I had learned Greek. Only Latin, but I once had a dog called Sydney."

"A good name for a dog. He must have made up for the Greek."

They looked at each other smiling, yet knowing that their brief but genuine friendship was having its last outing. Conchita was wondering where Salvador was, but she did not ask. People often said that the loves of gay people sometimes lasted briefly and were soon forgotten. She asked, "The Prison Officer. Did he take the bribe, then?"

Francis hesitated a moment, then smiled back at her and said, "Yes, he took it. If he hadn't I would have sent the money back to you."

Conchita breathed a sigh of relief. "I thought it must be so. So all is well." She glanced around the café. "Salvador is with you then?"

"He has gone ahead of me. I got him into a college where he can train as an athlete. It's his ambition."

"To become even more beautiful, Francis."

"Yes Senora, always to become more beautiful."

The Sydney plane was called. Francis Stephens kissed Conchita on both cheeks and left. She rejoined Captain Manzano, who drove her back to Cesar's house, where she went to see Julio. They embraced but he said again most firmly, no marriage until he was ready and that might be never. She said, "Be still, my love. I can wait. For me there is no one in this world but you."

So that all would be appropriately prepared for the residence of a First Lady she took her brothers to the DeoGracias, where she intended to stay for just one night with her mother. She asked Cesar to talk very gently when she was away with Julio, to whom she would return once Griselda was settled in the palace. The idea of leaving the Abulencia house never entered her mind.

That afternoon the First Lady looked as elegant as ever when she stepped out of the jumbo jet which had brought her from Shanghai. The national anthem was played, the guard of honour was inspected and various ministers made pompous speeches, some of which Griselda actually cut short if she thought them too long. To Conchita her mother seemed the same as ever. She sought in her eyes for a hint of sadness over Antonio's death but it seemed that the pomp and ceremony of the great return were overshadowing everything.

Together the First Lady, her daughter and two sons made a sort of triumphal procession in a motorcade of toadies from the airport along the boulevards to the DeoGracias. Everywhere they saw breaking waves of white hats. "Just as I asked of them," said the First Lady, but Ricky suddenly popped out with, "Mummy, most of the hats have 'Connie' written on them today. I can't see a single 'Griselda'. Oh yes there's one just there."

Popong joined the game. "I can see two Griseldas and lots of Connies. Lets see who can count the most of each, Ricky."

All along the boulevard, thronged with thousands of cheering people as far as the palace gates, the First Lady could not help hearing the tally of the game. Popong and Ricky were counting far more Connies than Griseldas. In fact before long they had virtually given up, as the Connies had become uncountable. They only continued because having started the game they had to do their best to boost the Griseldas. As they approached the DeoGracias the irritated First Lady said, "Oh do shut up Popong; do shut up Ricky. That's enough of the game. The people only write Conchita because they want to show her how sorry they are for poor Julio."

"Then why not write Julio?" asked Ricky. "I didn't see a single placard with his name."

"With or without balls," said Popong, sniggering loudly.

Conchita went with the children to the nursery where they had their supper before early bed, for they were tired out by the ceremony. Ricky said as Conchita kissed him goodnight, "Do you think mummy cried when daddy was shot?"

"I am sure she did, a lot," said Conchita, "but she doesn't like to make others unhappy by seeing her tears."

"When we were out with Manzano last week we saw a Chinese funeral," said Popong. "There were mourners covered with sackcloth, all moaning and groaning at the top of their voices. But everyone was grinning and having a good time, especially when they were paid for crying."

Conchita said, "Well every race does things differently. You must be very good to mummy. I am sure she is sad. We'll all have family breakfast tomorrow."

"It won't be the same without daddy," said Ricky who then fell fast asleep.

The First Lady and Conchita dined together in the circular dining room, which the President had loved. The atmosphere was stiff but Conchita did see tears in her mother's eyes. Neither of them ate much, though the chef had made a real effort for the First Lady's return. Afterwards they sat together and Conchita hardly knew what to say. She was being pushed by politicians to stand for election whenever the election took place and she was sure that her mother had exactly the same plan. She did not know how to raise the issue but started a conversation by asking a straightforward question that had intrigued her very much. "Mummy, how did you find out, no; how did you come to the conclusion, that Bersamina and the Americans were responsible for daddy's death?"

Griselda smiled like a detective novel sleuth about to reveal his secrets. "Intuition, a good memory and an eye for detail, Conchita. That's why I got where I am. For instance I remember everything I'm about to tell you very precisely. You can judge whether my conclusion was right or wrong. There was a man called Max Bligh with us in Rome. Antonio had employed his firm to do a PR job for our visit to Europe. It seems that Bligh brought to Rome some tapes prepared by his firm about the Carolines. I now know that Bligh did not have a single employer. He had several. Well I found out from a very handsome Italian called Agapito—he was your daddy's Italian ADC—that Bersamina had given him a tape to be passed on to someone called Ghiberti. In fact the ADC never met Ghiberti but he was asked by him over the phone to give the tape to a reporter working in Italian TV. Well it contained that accusation made by your friend Cesar that Antonio and I were responsible for the kidnapping of Julio. I can't say that I was not involved. But that tape hit the TV screens the very day after Antonio's murder. I guessed at once that the timing was intentional and intended to discredit Antonio. He was considered an embarrassment by the US State Department, which wanted a stooge they could really control in the Carolines—namely Bersamina, the accomplice and friend of Secretary of State Jasper Frankfurter. Didn't you notice how quickly the State Department recognised Bersamina as acting President? I didn't have absolute proof of all this at the time but my hunches are always good. After Antonio's death I tried to get through to President Souris in the White House. Neither he not Minnie Souris would speak to me. So I came back to the Carolines through Moscow where I still have a good friend who works in intelligence. He provided me with evidence that confirmed my hunch. Easy, because the chameleon Bligh also works for the Russians. By the way, Conchita, if you are going to be in power you have to accept the fact that there are agents everywhere. Anything you whisper can be on the front pages tomorrow."

Conchita had noticed Griselda's words. Now was the time to raise the great problem between them. Inwardly she had already decided that she wanted to stand for the presidency, but if Griselda were to explode with rage she might not be able to stand up to her. With great trepidation she said, "Me in power? What do you mean?"

The First Lady drew close to her daughter and embraced her. "Mummy knows everything my dear. Did you think I didn't get the meaning of the 'Connies' along the boulevards. See, even my clever ruse about the white hats was turned to your advantage."

"But not by me Mummy. Not by me."

"Of course not by you darling, by clever Prime Minister Loyola. Oh, Antonio knew how clever Bienvenido is. And Bienvenido knows that he and I could never work together. He thinks I'm too extravagant, and let's face it dear, I am. I once said that I'm like Robin Hood; I do rob the rich but I do so to make my beautiful projects come alive. And I always rob with a smile. The trouble is, Conchita, I was born ostentatious. It's my nature. But now I must find other fish to fry. My darling boys need a mother. Give me time and I'll see to it that both of them become presidents".

Conchita stared at her mother. "You really think that I could be president? But I'm not experienced enough. Could I work out all that information about agents you've just been telling me?" Then Conchita changed her manner. "Yes, I believe I could. Not just because of Oxford and travel and meeting important people but because I've been able to observe my wonderful parents, with all their many faults, which I hope I shall never repeat. Yet most important because Julio has shown what needs to be done in our country. But are you sure, mummy, that you can step aside for me?"

"I'll tell you the real reason why I will not stand in your way," said Griselda. "Because of your father. I may be a vain, extravagant woman who has done many crazy things, but there's one truth I hold onto, Conchita; the power of love. Love is everything. I said that to His Holiness. I loved Antonio deeply, despite his failings, and mine, which were worse than his. In fact we colluded in one another's wickedness. You know Antonio had tremendous foresight and terrific luck. Being his wife was like being in a world of fiction. I lived for him and he was my life. I cannot go on in the same way without him. So you understand it is not so difficult to stand down. It is almost beautiful. Loyola, Abulencia and a host of clever people will be behind you. Loyola will announce the date of the presidential election tomorrow. It will take place in about a month's time, I believe. You will win hands down. But you will not replace me as First lady. You will be the first woman to be President of the Carolines."

The reconciliation was complete, more or less. Conchita recognised that her mother's outlook had not really changed, nor could it, nor could anyone else's fundamental character. Yet what really mattered to Conchita was her mother's confession that she had been wrong to oppose the love of Julio and her daughter. That alone disqualified her for power, since it was a betrayal of the Griselda gospel of love. Her mother's admission certainly banished the remaining qualms Conchita felt about succeeding her father.

When all had been said and done, Griselda then told Conchita, "You love Julio and despite his terrible experience and his sickness I have a hunch that things will turn out well in the end. Give him time. He loves you and love is the strongest power in the world. Now Conchita, don't stay here with me for the night. Leave me in the DeoGracias with my memories and go to Julio."

Conchita had for long enough learned to distrust her mother's hunches but she did as she was told and drove herself, unaccompanied by outriders, to the Abulencias.

A few months later when on holiday in Alice, Francis Stephens opened a newspaper and saw a picture of the President of the Carolines, Senora Conchita Floresco. She had just given a speech to the newly elected lower chamber of the Congress, gathered for its first session in Infanta. She promised, as victors do, democratic government, human rights and a great effort to spread wealth more evenly. Francis knew the terrific problems of the Carolines, its poverty, its corruption, its overpopulation and could only wish her well. He had known the warmth, the creativity and the beauty of its people. Sooner or later someone had to make the country soar like a phoenix. Perhaps Conchita would be the one.

San Felipe was never far from his mind, nor its people, nor a young man who rested there only a few feet down, silently becoming part of its volcanic soil. Not a day passed without Francis remembering him and the love which each of them had so generously given.

Sometimes, because of his nature, he would find pleasure in the embraces of tough young guys in the town or on the land. Yet however well they made love, for him each new experience of desire was an illusion. The only love that was permanent was the flame that lived in his heart for Salvador. Yet he often recalled a prescient line of poetry that the boy had once written to him:

The fluttering moth burns with desire for the candle flame
But when the candle goes out its heart will burn no more.

About the Author

FREDERICK LEES was born in 1924. He served in the RAF during the war and afterwards studied at Liverpool and London Universities. He then joined the Colonial Service and served in the Federation of Malaya. Subsequently he entered the British Diplomatic Service which took him back to South East Asia. In the 1970s he became involved in the work of British and European non-governmental agencies concerned with Third World development; this for a while took him to the Sudan and Ethiopia. Later he returned to diplomatic work to train the foreign service of Papua New Guinea. The last part of his career in Asia was spent in the Asian Development Bank in Manila. He now lives with his wife in Rye, Sussex, UK, where he has founded a theatre movement to celebrate the works of John Fletcher, the Jacobean Rye dramatist.

www.ingramcontent.com/pod-product-compliance
Lightning Source LLC
Chambersburg PA
CBHW020422030726
47495CB00006B/1627